Calling Mrs Christmas

Carole Matthews

sphere

SPHERE

First published in Great Britain in 2013 by Sphere
This paperback edition published in 2013 by Sphere
Reprinted 2013 (twice)

A CIP catalogue record for this book
is available from the British Library.

ISBN 978-0-7515-4558-6

Typeset in Sabon by M Rules
Printed and bound in Great Britain by
Clays Ltd, St Ives plc

Papers used by Sphere are from well-managed forests
and other responsible sources.

MIX
Paper from
responsible sources
FSC® C104740

Sphere
An imprint of
Little, Brown Book Group
100 Victoria Embankment
London EC4Y 0DY

An Hachette UK Company
www.hachette.co.uk

www.littlebrown.co.uk

To all my lovely readers, particularly those who take the time to brighten my day on Facebook and Twitter. Your support, kindness and humorous comments are very greatly appreciated.

Chapter One

Perfume ads on the telly. First it's Charlize Theron, strutting and stripping her way through some mansion until she's wearing nothing but J'Adore and an alluring smile. Next it's Keira Knightley overacting 'fun' for Coco Mademoiselle. Finally, for Chanel No. 5, it's the stylised Red Riding Hood advert that's been doing the rounds for years with the best-looking wolf you've ever seen. It's only when these luscious advertisements grace our screens that you know the giddy, helter-skelter rundown towards Christmas has finally begun in earnest.

All three advertisements have been screened in a row and it's barely mid-morning. I missed most of the ads last year. At least, the daytime ones. I hear myself sigh. It's a bad habit and I've been doing it a lot lately. This year, as I am an unemployed, redundant couch potato, I am running the entire gamut of Christmas commercialism. It's the first week of October and already Stacey and Jason are extolling the virtues of Iceland's pre-prepared party food.

There is much laughter, much over-indulgence in these adverts, much that is red and gold and glittering. Which is all very lovely. I'd usually buy right into it. Except there'll not be much partying at our house this Christmas. Very little, if any, party food from Iceland – or elsewhere – will be bought. Our table will not be replete with festive delights. Our Christmas tree will not be surrounded by half a ton of presents. It will be a big contrast to last year. I stop the next sigh that threatens to escape.

'Budget' is the watchword of the moment. Closely followed by 'cutbacks'. Last Christmas we had a great time. As is expected, the table groaned with food, the booze flowed, we force-fed ourselves an excess of Quality Street. All the usual things. Wonderful. But last year I had a job. This year I don't. And there's the rub.

This Christmas, any tightening of the belt will be entirely down to our dwindling finances and not, for once, caused by the calorie overload of the festivities. I have now been out of work for a grand total of eight months, four days and, checks watch, three hours. It's fair to say that no one seems to be missing the great contribution that Ms Cassie Smith, age thirty-five, of Hemel Hempstead in the fair county of Hertfordshire has made to the cut-throat world of commerce.

I switch off the television and stare at the walls of the flat. This place has become my prison and my refuge all at once. I hate being trapped in here all day with nowhere to go. Yet now when I get the chance to go out, spread my wings, I'm frightened. My heart pounds, my mouth goes dry and my palms sweat at the thought of stepping out of my comfort zone. Do you think that's how budgies feel? Do they desperately want to fly free, but as soon as that cage door is open, they freeze? If it is, then I feel so sorry for them. I used to be sure of my place in life, but my self-confidence has dwindled just as fast as our meagre savings.

My job, I have to admit, wasn't fantastic. I grumbled about it a lot. To anyone who would listen, really. But, my goodness, how I miss it. I would give anything to be complaining about hauling myself out of bed on a frosty morning, scraping the car windscreen, blowing on my fingers to keep warm, muttering about the crap office coffee. Instead, when Jim gets up for work, I simply turn over and go back to sleep. No need to get up. No need to rush. No need to do anything. No need to be here at all.

I worked as a secretary and general dogsbody for a small engineering company specialising in component design and fabrication. The price I paid for daydreaming in school. But I was good at my job, efficient. People liked me. I was a dedicated and diligent dogsbody. I could turn my hand to anything and frequently did. Sometimes it felt as if I was running the flipping place. Jim and I went to my boss's house for dinner. Three times. He opened champagne. I always went that extra mile, my boss said. He said I was indispensable. In fact he said it the very morning before he called me into his office and told me that, from the end of the week, I would be surplus to requirements. Not enough people, it seemed, needed components designed or fabricated.

I push my misery aside and phone Jim. Just the sound of his voice can pull me out of a downward spiral. His mobile rings and rings. My other half, for his sins, is a prison officer based in the Young Offenders' Unit at Bovingdale Prison. He can't have his phone with him when he's on duty, but I'm hoping that I might catch him on a break when he tries to go out to his locker if he can, snatching a few minutes to listen to his messages and look at his texts. He never used to go out to his locker during his shift when I was at work because I never had time to phone him during the day. We did all our catching up on the evenings when Jim's shifts allowed us to fall exhausted onto the sofa together. Now I spend my entire life on the sofa – primarily alone – and Jim is conscious that he's my lifeline to the world, so he checks his phone as often as he can.

As I think it's about to go to voicemail, Jim picks up. 'Hi, love,' he says, sounding harassed. 'A bit busy right now. Just got a call on the radio. Can I ring you back later?'

'Yeah.'

'Was it anything important?'

'No. I'm just bored.'

'OK. Catch you when I've got a spare mo. Love you.' He hangs up.

'Love you,' I say to the handset.

And that's the trouble when you're not busy. Everyone else is. I switch the television back on. The John Lewis advert. Something sentimental to have you reaching for the tissues as usual. The Argos ad. Then Boots who seem to be trying to guilt mothers into excess present buying. No wonder vulnerable heartstrings are stretched to breaking point. Soon everyone but me will be wrapped up in Christmas. A time when all sensible spending goes out of the window and everyone racks up the debt on their credit cards to pay another day. Well, we can't do that this year.

To be honest, I didn't particularly worry when I was made redundant although, equally, I wasn't exactly overjoyed, as in my view I'd done my best for the company and I believed they were happy with me. But then I thought I'd get a job really easily. I'd waltz straight into another company who'd love me and appreciate me more. Who doesn't need secretaries? What sort of company doesn't have a dogsbody on which to dump all their most depressing and unwanted tasks? Who doesn't want someone to mollycoddle and care for all the staff and their various crises? An office angel. I assumed that the local paper would be filled with opportunities for someone with my skills and experience. It seems that I was wrong.

Chapter Two

I stare at the clock. Nearly ten minutes have passed since I last looked at it. Jim still hasn't called me back. In fairness, he has a very busy job. Unlike me, he works in a growth industry. No shortage of customers in Jim's company. No chance of anyone saying that there isn't enough demand for *his* skill set. The Young Offenders' Unit at Bovingdale is already overflowing and there's a steady stream of thieving, drug-dealing, car-nicking, house-breaking kids that they can't even begin to accommodate.

But no matter how much I hate being unemployed, I couldn't for all the money in the world, for all the tea in China, do a job like that. My Jim is a saint among men.

We've been together for five years now, meeting in a less than salubrious bar in Watford just after my thirtieth birthday and just after I'd decided that true love would never find me. There he was, standing with a pint of Magners in his hand, and for me – for both of us – it was love at first sight.

Sometimes, you just can't put your finger on what causes that strength of attraction, but you know that it's there. It's not that Jim Maddison's an oil painting. I wasn't bowled over because he's a dead ringer for Matthew McConaughey. He doesn't have that kind of movie-star looks. His hair is cropped close, which makes him look a lot scarier than he actually is. From his time in the army, he's got tattoos on his toned biceps. A heart and a rose entwined on one side. A skull with flowers growing through it on the other. Between his shoulder blades there's a colourful phoenix and I love to trace the outline of them on his skin when we're lying in bed. He's stocky, not that tall, has a face that's too pale as he spends his working days locked indoors and we haven't had a holiday in the sun in years. But my Jim has the kindest eyes you'll ever see. They're soft, grey and always have a twinkle in them. He smiles much, much more than he frowns. When it comes down to it, Jim's just an uncommonly nice guy and it radiates from every pore he possesses. Everyone adores him. Me included. Jim is the epitome of the word 'solid' and, since the day I met him, I know what it is to be loved, to be cared for.

By the end of our first week – a week when we saw each other every night – we'd decided to move in together. Just like that. No ifs, no buts. I knew instantly, instinctively, he was The One.

I'd had a few relationships in the past, but no one had ever made me feel the way Jim did. It wasn't that he showered me with flowers or diamonds. Quite the opposite. Present buying isn't Jim's forte. He isn't romantic in a showy way at all, but I watch him sometimes when he's making me some toast or a cup of tea. I see how much care he takes. He's knows that I like my toast well done with loads of butter right up to the edges of the bread. He frowns in concentration as he makes sure that the jam is spread really thinly, exactly the way I do it myself, and that it's cut in tri-angles, not sliced straight across. He puts his feet on my side of the bed to warm it before I get in. He opens doors for me, walks on the traffic side of the pavement and pulls out my chair in restaurants. To me, that's love. It's not roaring down the street in a Ferrari, it's not skydiving out of a plane with an 'I LOVE CASSIE!' banner trailing behind you. I think it's the constant, quiet things that tell you that it's real love. And I feel that I am very loved.

My dad cleared off when I was young. I barely remember him, but something like that leaves its mark and I've always felt wary about getting too involved with men. I always expected them to let me down and, invariably, they did. It got to the point where I hardly dated at all, didn't really trust men. With Jim it was completely different. This might sound mad, but it was like finding the other half of myself. From day one, I knew that I could trust him with my life, that my heart would never be mashed by him. If that sounds corny, then so be it. He is truly my soulmate.

We can spend hours just sitting reading together or walking through the woods. There's never any drama with Jim, I don't have to worry about where he is or who he's with. Jim isn't one for nights out on the lash with the lads; he'd rather be at home with me than anywhere else. And that's all I want too. Just to be with Jim. We're content in each other's company. We don't need the high life, we're happy exactly as we are.

If it wasn't for Jim, I don't know how I would have survived the last year. He's been my only brightness, always there with the right words to cheer me up or knowing when a well-timed bar of chocolate would lift my spirits. When I was made redundant, I thought I'd take a couple of weeks off, have a bit of a rest. A 'career break' I laughingly called it. After all, I'd been in work constantly since I was sixteen and there was no rush to find something else. I'd been given a month's salary as a pay-off. Yeah, thanks for that.

Then, when I'd caught up on the ironing, and the flat was so spick and span that it looked as if Anthea Turner had been through it, and I'd watched all the films I'd been meaning to watch but hadn't got around to, I applied for jobs. There weren't as many of them as I'd expected and some, I felt, just weren't right for me. I was surprised when, having sent off a rash of my splendid CVs, I got only one interview. I was even more surprised when I didn't get the job. I thought the interview had gone so well. Seems I was wrong about that too. After that setback, a little bit of panic set in. I catalogued all our DVDs and old CDs alphabetically and then applied for more jobs. This time I was less choosy. Got one interview. Got no job. And so it went on.

I signed on. Was given Jobseekers' Allowance, went to a workshop that showed me how to present my CV properly and then applied frantically for anything with the word 'vacancy' attached to it. Still no luck.

When the spring morphed into summer and I was still terminally unemployed, I began to lose my nerve. The few interviews I did have went badly. A lot of firms that would normally employ secretaries seemed to have embraced an age where managers did their own donkey work or made use of university graduates who had a degree, thirty grand's worth of debt and were desperate. Instead of 'unpaid slaves', they called them 'interns' and insisted the posts were great and necessary work experience for their CVs. But whatever it was, it meant that people like me – who actually wanted paying – went down to the bottom of the pile.

I don't mean to sound sorry for myself. But I am. Very sorry. I don't want to be like this. I look at the television, at the snowy scenes, at the promises of unfettered festive happiness, at the excessive consumerism, and I want to be part of it. I love Christmas. I want to embrace all of its tacky indulgence. It's my time of year. Perhaps sometimes I let myself get a bit carried away – Jim said the flat looked like a flipping winter wonderland last year – but it's supposed to be like that. I don't want to be thinking of getting a meagre Tesco Value chicken rather than a big, fat Kelly Bronze turkey. We can cut back on presents, that's no hardship. It's the little things that make Christmas special. But I don't want to miss out on the atmosphere.

This is the only difficult part of my relationship with Jim. We never have enough money. We might not aspire to the high life, but we've never actually had the money to try it. Funds are always tight. Even when I was gainfully employed we didn't have a lot left to splash around, and now my not working is a terrible drain on us. Our desires are fairly modest, but I feel as if I've been on a budget since the day I was born. We don't want for much but, sometimes – just sometimes – it would be nice to treat ourselves without having to count every penny. Surely Christmas is one of those times?

I don't catch what the advert is for, but there's a mother on television, dressing the Christmas tree, two mop-haired children and a dog from Central Casting at her feet. Presents are piled around the tree, which sparkles brilliantly. A beautifully set dining room table replete with ravishing food is in the background. Carols soar to a crescendo and Daddy comes through the door to his perfect family and his perfect Christmas. A sigh rises to my throat. Surely there must be someone who needs extra help at Christmas? Doesn't everyone try to run round doing ten times more than they normally do? There *must* be a role for me out there. My ideal job, my *raison d'être*, is organising stuff. What a shame that I can't get paid for celebrating Christmas!

Then something inside me clicks and the most brilliant idea hits me like a bolt out of the blue. A grin spreads over my face. I could be a part of this. I don't have to sit here on the sidelines and let the joy of Christmas pass me by. I can embrace the commercialism and bring in some much needed extra cash. I can do something about it.

My mind is whirring with the kernel of an unfocussed plan when the phone rings. Jim's at the other end. That means it must be his lunchtime and here's me still in my pyjamas. Well, all that's about to change. No more slobbing around the house feeling sorry for myself, I'm going to launch myself back into the world with a vengeance.

'Hey,' he says. 'Sorry I couldn't speak earlier. I was on my break, but something kicked off. It's total madness here today.'

It's total madness where Jim works *every* day. While we're talking about money, they don't pay him nearly enough for the stress he has and what he has to put up with. That's another one of the reasons why we're still renting this tiny flat and both drive clapped-out cars. I want to do my bit. It's not fair on him. I want to get out there again in the big, bad world of paid work. I don't want our life to be like this, constantly living from hand to mouth. I hate having to accept benefits from the government just to get by. We're young, we're resourceful. We shouldn't be in this situation. I know I can do more. And I might just have a plan as to how.

'Are you OK, Cassie? Still bored?'

'No,' I say.

I can feel myself beaming widely. It's as if a terrible fog has suddenly cleared from my head. A light bulb has gone ping-diddy-ping in my brain and it's burning brightly. I let out a bubbly laugh, a sound that I'd forgotten I could make.

'You'll never believe this,' I tell him. 'But I have just come up with *the* most brilliant idea.'

Chapter Three

By the time Jim comes home in the evening, I'm buzzing. I pounce on him the minute he swings through the door of the flat, twine my arms around him and give him a big kiss.

'Hey,' he says. 'I like a welcome home like this.' Even though he looks weary, he takes me in his arms and returns my kisses. 'What have I done to deserve it?'

'You've just been you,' I say. 'All these months I've been a terrible moody cow and you've stood by me.'

'You've lost your confidence, Cassie,' he says softly. 'That's all. You'll get it back.'

'I have,' I babble. 'I'm just so excited about this idea.'

'Tell me about it again. I couldn't concentrate properly at work,' he admits.

When I talked to Jim on the phone I rushed through my explanation of my plan, babbling like a loon. To be honest, it was all just forming in my brain as I was speaking and I must have sounded like a mad thing. As always, when he's at work, I could tell that Jim had only one ear to the conversation. Now that I've had time to mull it over properly and put some thoughts down on paper, I still think it's a great idea.

Jim drops his bag to the floor and I help him take off his jacket.

'I was watching television this morning.' As I always do. 'It was nothing but Christmas ads.'

'Already?' Jim looks as if he has a heart-sink moment.

'It'll be upon us before we know it,' I remind him. 'That's why I have to act fast.'

'It seems to come round more quickly every year.' He puffs out a tired breath. 'So what's the master plan, Dr Evil?'

'I want to offer a complete Christmas planning service,' I remind him.

Jim untangles himself and we go through to our titchy kitchen where I've got dinner on the go. It's Wednesday and we've got tuna risotto, which, if humanly possible, is even less glamorous than it sounds. Just think, if I could get this business off the ground, we could upgrade to prawns! We could eat meat more than once a week.

'What on earth does that involve?'

'Everything,' I say, excitedly. 'Putting up trees, writing cards, baking mince pies. I could buy presents and gift wrap them. I could put Christmas lights up outside houses. Well, maybe you could do that bit.'

He raises his eyebrows at that.

'A lot of people are into that whole over-the-top decoration now and it's a total pain, putting lights up and taking them down every year. That would be a great service. I could do their food shopping, organise parties. That's just for starters. I'm sure there's a lot of things that I could do that I haven't even thought about yet.'

'Hmm . . .' He rubs at the shadow of stubble on his chin.

'You know what it's like,' I rush on. 'Everyone has eight million things to do before Christmas. If you're not careful, then it just becomes a lot of hassle rather than being the most wonderful time of the year.' I remember to pause for breath. 'If I could take the pressure off people, for a small fee, then it's a win-win situation. Some people will pay anything for the perfect Christmas.'

Jim looks thoughtful. 'You love doing all that stuff anyway.'

'I do.' I used to adore getting ready for Christmas. My favourite job in the world is wrapping presents. And I think I'm good at it. Good enough, with a bit of polishing, to provide a professional service. 'I'd try to offer everything to take the stress out of Christmas. So all the client has to do is pay up and have fun.'

'It sounds like an awful lot to take on, Cassie.' There's a concerned frown on his brow.

'I know. But I have to act fast. People lose all sense when it comes to money at Christmas. If I'd ever had the cash to spare I'd have bought in help myself. I've just never seen anyone offer it. Certainly not round here.'

Jim purses his lips. 'That's true enough.'

'It's a niche market that I think I can explore.'

'Are you sure you wouldn't just be better off looking for another office job?'

'I've tried that, Jim. There's nothing out there.' I stir the risotto and add some more herbs to try to inject some excitement into it. 'I've got my name down for seasonal work at a dozen different shops, but I've heard nothing yet. Even retail outlets are cutting back. Where there are vacancies they're filling them from a list of regulars. No one even wants me as a shelf-stacker.' He knows how hard it's been. 'At least I could try this. If it doesn't work out, I've not lost anything but my time.'

'Starting your own business is always tricky. You know what it's like out there at the moment. The current climate is hard for everyone.'

'This will be for a short period only. It's purely a seasonal thing. Everyone goes raving mad at Christmas. We all like a bit of festive escapism. Buy now, pay later. Batter the credit card. We've done it ourselves. That's what it's all about.'

Not to put too fine a point on it, I'd like a bit of that action too. I can't sit here on my bottom all through the winter, eking out our measly income and feeling miserable. If I can work hard for the next couple of months, cash in on Christmas, then we'll at least have a little bit more money behind us to start the new year. If it goes well, I could maybe think of another business idea or, at worst, go back to the Job Centre with my head held high.

'You could look at commuting into London,' Jim suggests. 'There must be jobs up in town.'

'I'd have to leave at some ungodly hour in the morning, get home late at night. The cost of the rail ticket is extortionate now. With your shifts, we'd never see each other.' Plus, from what I've heard, I think that the city of London is probably suffering from intern overload too. 'I'm also frightened of rejection again,' I admit to Jim. 'At least with this, I sink or swim on my own merits.'

'That's what I'm worried about. You've had a tough time, Cassie. I don't want you to take on too much.'

I chew my fingernail. My first doubt creeps in. 'You don't think I can do it?'

He wraps his arms around me and hugs me tightly. 'Of course you can do it. It's simply a question of whether there's the business out there.'

'I'd like to try.'

'Let me go and have a quick shower, then we can talk some more about it.'

Jim is always conscious that he smells of the Young Offenders' Unit, which is a pungent mix of teenage boys, institutional food and despair. I think he also likes to wash work out of his hair the minute he comes home. I don't care what he smells like, I just feel safe in his arms.

14

While he hits the bathroom, I fiddle about, pulling the table out from the corner of our living room that doubles as a dining room, and then set it. One thing about my being at home is that we do now eat together at the table rather than slum it with a tray on our laps, watching the telly in a stupor. The only downside is that by the time Jim comes home I'm usually pacing the floor with anxiety. Waiting for someone seems so much worse when you haven't been anywhere yourself.

Catching sight of myself in the full-length mirror in the hall as I bustle about, I realise that the last few months haven't been kind to my appearance either. I've let myself go, no doubt. I've never been slim, but now I'm definitely curvier than I should be. Too many hours spent on the sofa. No visits to the gym. To economise I gave up my membership months ago. To save money I've also not had my hair cut since January and it now graces my shoulders. Jim says he likes it longer, but I can see that it's out of condition and, at the very least, the ends need trimming. Thankfully, there's no grey showing in my brunette hair – not like my dear sister who's been dyeing hers for years – so I don't feel the need to have it coloured yet. My complexion is usually good – very peaches and cream – but now my skin looks dull, tired. My green eyes have lost their sparkle. I felt pretty once, but not any more. I huff sadly at my own reflection.

Jim's standing behind me. 'You still look beautiful to me.'

'I feel old and fat and forgotten.'

'You're none of those things,' he insists. 'You're my gorgeous girl.' He hugs me and I rest my head against his shoulder. What would I do without him?

'You must be starving.' Jim gets a free meal at lunchtime and he tries to fill up then, but I know the food is not all that it might be. 'Sit yourself down. I'll get dinner.'

I shoot into the kitchen to sort out the risotto. When I had my brainwave, I was actually motivated to go to the supermarket and buy the tiniest piece of Parmesan cheese I could find as a treat to liven it up. I grate some on top and make the dish look as respectable as possible with a sprinkling of parsley.

'Hmm. Looks lovely,' Jim says as I put it down in front of him.

It doesn't, not really. It looks exactly like what it is – a dish knocked up quickly and on the cheap. But he's always so incredibly kind and encouraging.

'It won't always be like this,' I say and tears spring to my eyes.

Jim takes my hand. 'Do you think I'll love you any more if we have steak for dinner every night?'

'Yes.'

'Mmm. Maybe you're right.'

I kick him under the table and he laughs. After he's said, 'Ouch.'

The flat's OK really. The block's a bit tired. Built with all the style the 1970s could muster, it looks like the sort of square, grey lump that you'd imagine more akin to Stalingrad or somewhere Communist and depressing. The windows need replacing as a howling gale comes in around the edges and our communal stairwell could best be described as functional. I'm sure we could make a bit on the side by renting it out as a set for slasher movies. It would be perfect.

We've lived here for two years now. The landlord's a bit of a twat too and, as is the way, we have to make two dozen phone calls before he'll deign to come out and fix anything. Usually, Jim just ends up doing it. We try to make the best of it and have the place as nice as we can. But it's not home, is it? Not when you're renting. It's still always like living somewhere you don't really belong. I didn't think this was where I'd be at this stage in my life. I thought I'd be happily married, have my own home, maybe even a couple of kids. I didn't think that I'd still be scratching an existence in rented accommodation with a baby about as distant a prospect as a trip to the moon. I want to marry Jim. I want to marry him on a tropical beach with colourful flowers in my hair and white sand and waving palm trees. That's my dream. I don't want a massive church bash with three hundred guests and a disco. I just want me and Jim and the sand beneath our feet. But how am I ever going to achieve that if I can't even get a job as a secretary? Which turns me back to the plan in hand.

'So, do you think I should give this business a go?' I desperately need Jim's approval, otherwise it's dead in the water. I don't have the nerve to do this without his backing.

He plays with his fork in the risotto. Today he seems more wound up than normal when he comes home from work, as if he could do with a good glass of red. But, for reasons that you're now well aware of, there won't be one. 'We've nothing put away now, Cassie. It's all gone and the credit cards are maxed out.'

'I'm well aware of that, Jim,' I say more crisply than I mean to. 'Surely that makes it even more critical that I do something? I'd try to keep the outgoings to a bare minimum. A lot of the services I'm going to offer won't need any outlay at all.'

He doesn't look convinced. 'Even if it takes off, it would more than likely stop dead in January.'

'I know. But if it goes *really* well, then maybe I could carry on doing a similar sort of thing for the rest of the year. Event planning or something. There's always Valentine's Day and Easter. Mother's Day too. It's just that Christmas is The Big One.' I touch his hand. 'I feel that I have to try. It would get me out of the house. Get me involved in life again. I'm going mad being at home all the time. I feel worse than useless.'

'I can tell that it's got you all fired up again.' He smiles at me. 'That's good to see.'

'Can I go for it? Will you support me?'

'Of course I will. You know that I'll do all I can. Whatever you do, you'll be brilliant at it.'

'I love you.' I reach across the table and squeeze his hand. 'Thank you for your faith in me.'

'So,' he says, 'have you got a name for your brilliant new venture?'

'Yes, I have,' I say proudly. 'Calling Mrs Christmas!'

Chapter Four

The next morning, I get up when Jim's alarm goes off. While he shaves and potters about, I make him coffee and toast. He's very surprised by all this. But I hate to disappoint him: it's not just my desire to make breakfast for my dearly beloved that's motivated me out of bed today. The truth is that I can't wait to get to the computer and start doing some work on my business plan. I could hardly sleep last night for thinking about it.

I kiss Jim goodbye and wave through the window to him as he drives away. Then I take my coffee through to the spare bedroom, which, apart from the desk in the corner, is our general dumping ground, ironing room, gym (unused exercise bike in the corner, which doubles as extra wardrobe space) and computer room.

Ignoring the mounting pile of ironing, I hit the desk, put down my mug and settle myself in front of the screen. I'm so keen to get started that I haven't even bothered to get showered or dressed yet. I start to search the internet to see what I can find – decorations, invitations, cards, Christmas cake, mince pies – and I'm not disappointed. Five minutes later, I'm on YouTube and a whole world of previously unexplored festive delights opens up before me. I click, click, click on a multitude of clips and gorge myself on an array of Christmas goodies.

It's eleven o'clock when I come up for breath, in which time I have learned how to wrap a present in luxurious style, make a bow for it, dress a tree/table/mantelpiece, create a spectacular centrepiece, do Christmas calligraphy, decorate cupcakes, make and ice snowflake biscuits and knock out my own mince pies. I'm positively brimming over with inspiration and I haven't even left the flat. I always thought that I was pretty good at doing these things, anyway, but now I've taken my Christmas skill set to a whole new level.

Surfing some more, I then make a list of all the things I think I can offer. It makes me smile when I realise that the list is quite extensive. I have talents that I've hidden even from myself. Surely *someone* will need my services?

The next time I glance at my watch it's nearly lunchtime. It's my sister's half-day today. Gaby works as a receptionist at a dental practice not far from her home in Leverstock Green. If I get a wriggle on, I can be round at her house just after she gets in and we can have a sandwich together. I can't wait to tell her my plans as she's been very worried about me over the last few months and she'll be delighted that, at last, I've found something that I can really get my teeth into.

I print off my list, run round the shower, throw on some clothes and sprint out of the door. It is a long time since I've done sprinting and my smile widens to a grin. Outside, the day is cold, damp and the sky hangs down to the trees, but I have never felt better. My feet fly over the pavement. My heart hammers with happiness. I feel as if I could walk all the way to Gaby's house on the clouds but sense prevails and I jump into my clapped-out car and drive down instead.

Five minutes later, I pull up outside her door. 'Hiya, sis,' she says as she lets me in. 'Didn't expect to see you today. Everything OK?'

'More than OK,' I tell her as I follow her into the kitchen. 'I've come up with a *brilliant* plan.'

'I like the sound of that,' she says. 'Want something to eat?'

'I wouldn't mind.' I love my sis. She never fails to deliver on the food front. Anyone who walks through her front door is instantly fed.

'Cheese on toast?'

'Perfect.'

She and I have always had a close relationship and, in many ways, she's more like a mum to me than my sister. Gaby's the one I've always turned to when I've been in need. My own mother – my *real* mother – has always been somewhat neglectful of her maternal duties. All the time we were growing up, she was fairly hands off in her nurturing. She kept a roof over our heads, just about, and paid the bills, sporadically, but other than that, she did little more for us than she absolutely had to.

Dad left us years ago – I was five and Gaby was eight – and we haven't seen hide nor hair of him since. We woke up one day to find him gone and Mum never spoke of him again. We were a single-parent family when they weren't all that fashionable. The sad thing is that I really don't remember my dad all that much. We don't talk about him often now, Gaby and I. The truth is that we don't even know if he's dead or alive. When we were younger, Gaby used to tell me things about him. He liked cars and country music. He had yellow fingers because he smoked a lot. And he danced very badly, Gaby said, but that could apply to any dad. She doesn't talk about him now. Hasn't referred to him for years and neither have I.

When he pushed off, my mum went a bit mental. She didn't get out of her dressing gown for weeks on end, despite Gaby doing her best to coax her. When she finally did, she put on her lipstick and high heels and then we didn't see her for dust. Sometimes she didn't come home until the middle of the night. Sometimes not at all. It was Gaby who, red-eyed through lack of

21

sleep, would get us up and dressed for school. It was Gaby who scoured the cupboards, looking for something for us to eat. I shake the image away. It's just too painful to dwell on.

So, as she makes our lunch, I sit on one of her kitchen stools and fill her in on my new business idea.

'Wow,' she says as she takes it all in. 'I'm impressed. This sounds like your perfect job. Why did we not think of it before? Since we were kids, you've always been the one who loved Christmas.'

Did I love it? I remember it being just Gaby, me and Mum. It was the one time of the year that we had a lavish meal on the table as Gaby used to put money away from her Saturday job into a Christmas Hamper Club run by one of our neighbours. That was the highlight of the year, that hamper arriving, laden with its luscious Christmas pudding, a tin of ham, cranberry sauce, fancy biscuits and jams and always a tin of Walkers shortbread. Gaby and I used to get all the contents out on our bedroom floor and admire them in awe. Mum would buy us presents – a doll, a book, one year roller skates. We used to meticulously cut out paper shapes to make Mum a card. Quite often on Christmas Day, Mum would get drunk and teary. She would hug us to her and weep into our hair when we just wanted to watch television and gorge ourselves on the contents of the hamper. But it was the one day of the year we could guarantee her being around and, perhaps, I loved it for that reason alone.

'You'll be brilliant at it. You've always put me to shame with your decorations. And you pick the best presents. I don't know how you do it. You always manage to find the right thing.'

'Hours spent surfing the internet,' I confess. 'You think I could do it?'

'No one better,' she confirms.

'I'm going to get on to it right away,' I say. 'No time to lose.'

'Only sixty shopping days to Christmas.'

'Really?'

Gaby laughs. 'Give or take a few. I don't know. Thankfully, I haven't *actually* started counting yet.'

'I'm panicking slightly about the timescale,' I tell her. 'But I'm trying to see it as a challenge.'

'I'm just glad to see you've got your spark back. I've missed it.'

'Me too.'

'You know that I'll do anything that I can to help.'

'I might hold you to that. You could come in very handy for my mince pie and Christmas cake baking service.' Gaby is an excellent cook. Her cakes are held in high esteem in this family and she produces them with unfailing regularity. 'Fancy giving cupcakes a go? They're still all the rage.'

She shrugs in acquiescence. 'Sure.'

I'm certain she could easily turn her hand to them. Or, at the very least, help me to improve mine. She's a stickler for perfection. I'm more the slap-it-about merchant. However, I realise that if I'm offering a professional service, that is going to have to change.

'I've faffed about with them a bit already. I've got plenty of icing nozzles and stuff that you can borrow.'

'You have?'

'I'll dig them out after we've eaten.'

'That's great.'

'If you do get this going, you'll be absolutely knackered by Christmas,' Gaby observes. 'You are both coming to me for lunch again?'

It's a habit that we've got into over the years since she's had her own family. I guess that on Christmas Day it's easier for Gaby to be at home with the kids where they've got all their new toys, rather than for us all to be squashed in our flat. This year, though,

I feel we'll need it more than ever. 'Don't think that you always have to invite us. Your husband might want you all to himself for once.'

She guffaws at that. 'As if!'

'You know what I mean. I don't like to presume.'

Jim and I love being with Gaby and Ryan on Christmas Day and we normally try to get here in time to see the kids open their presents. Even though it does mean a ridiculously early start. Last year we actually slept over on Christmas Eve so that we were already here when they woke up. At four o'clock. Maybe we'll stay in our own bed this year and try to catch the tail end of the paper tearing at about seven.

'It's a time for family,' Gaby insists. 'All of us. Besides, I know that money's tight this year. Come to us. If this business does take off, you could well be a gibbering wreck by then.'

I look over at my sister as she's checking on our cheese under the grill.

The question has to be asked and I dread it. 'Is Mum coming?'

'I'll ask her. But you know what she's like, Cassie.' My sister smiles ruefully. 'She'll wait to see if she gets a better offer.'

Mum had us both when she was still a teenager and maybe that was part of the problem. Being a mother when you're still a child yourself is never going to be easy, is it? I think her family must have ostracised her as there never seemed to be any aunties around and I've never met my own grandma. It's another subject that's taboo.

Mum's only seventeen years older than Gaby and is, therefore, not your typical granny. She's in her mid-fifties now and wears her clothes too tight, still drinks too much, smokes and has inappropriate boyfriends. Lots of them. If one of her men offers to take her to Spain for the holiday, she's on a plane quicker than you can say easyJet. If, on the other hand, all of her boyfriends are with their wives, then she'll be here complaining loudly about her lot and how little she sees of us. I wish she'd take up knitting and sip sherry instead of knocking back vodka shots, and realise, late in life, that she should have been there for us more. But she does none of these things. I know that she's my mother but, most of the time, I could joyfully choke her. My sister has a lot more patience with her than I do.

Gaby is still the first person I'd turn to for advice. We're a lot alike and neither of us is remotely like our mum, so I'm assuming that we took our genes from our dad. My sister is also curvy. Her hair is long and dark, currently dyed borderline black as she started going grey in her late teens. I'm not surprised with all that rested on her shoulders. Thankfully, she struck gold when it came to men and she's married to a lovely guy, Ryan Healy. He's cut from the same cloth as Jim and is as steady as the day is long. Ryan works as a train driver for Virgin Trains on the main line into Euston and his family is his life. He's got a sunny, affable nature and makes my sister laugh a lot. They've got two lovely children, George who's seven and Molly, five. The same sort of age that Gaby and I were when Dad left. I can no more imagine Ryan walking out on his kids than I can see him on stage with Lady Gaga.

My sister, in spite of our flaky upbringing – or because of it – could write a handbook on perfect parenting. She does everything for her children. I love my niece and nephew more than life itself. They are the children I've never had and I see them nearly every day. When I don't, I miss them dearly. My sister's house is a small, terraced place just off the green in Leverstock Green. She's terribly house-proud and has done it out fashionably with that big-flowered wallpaper that's so popular now in shades of brown and duck-egg blue. They both work hard to keep it nice. Their lawn might be the size of a postage stamp, but Ryan mows it every weekend and the garden's always full of colourful flowers.

The dentist that Gaby works for is just round the corner at the parade of shops. It's a job that she enjoys but which doesn't take her away too much from her family, who are her total priority. She has all that I want for myself.

Gaby puts my cheese on toast down in front of me. 'You're a star,' I say. 'Thanks.' She takes the stool next to me and I root in my handbag to find my printout. I push it across to her. 'Calling Mrs Christmas!'

'Wow,' she says between mouthfuls. 'Like the name.' She scans my list of services. 'Can you really do all this?'

'Not yet,' I confess. 'But I'm a fast learner.'

'It looks like great fun. I know a few people who'd book you to do stuff. I bet you're going to be busy.'

'I hope so.' Then I turn to her. Suddenly, my euphoria deserts me. 'I'm frightened, Gaby. This is the first time I've ever had a business idea. What if it doesn't work?'

'Nothing lost,' Gaby assures me. 'The only loss would be if you didn't bother to try it. This is a great idea and, for most things, you can ask for payment in advance. For a lot of the services you're offering there'll be only a small layout and if you ask for a deposit, that would secure most things.'

'Excellent idea.' I find a pen in my bag and write 'Deposit!' at the bottom of my list.

'What does Jim think?'

'You know what Jim's like. He thinks that anything I want to do is just fine. He's Mr Supportive.'

'You've got a good one there.'

'I know it.' Then I feel a pinch of melancholy nip at me. 'I hope that I do make some money at this. I'd love for us to get married next year.'

'You could just pop down to the register office and get married next week.'

'Jim keeps saying that.'

'Maybe he's right.'

'I've nothing against Hemel Register Office, but I've always dreamed of having a lovely wedding, Gaby. You know that.' We used to lie in our bunk beds at night, talking about it often enough. 'I don't want a big marquee and a meringue dress, but I do want it to be something that I'll remember for ever.' Cue video of white sand, sunset, sparkling sea, Jim and me hand in hand. 'Before I have children I want to be married and have our own home.'

Unlike Mum, is the unspoken tag. I didn't find out until I was in my twenties that Mum and Dad were never married. Gaby and I had Mum's surname – Smith. I can't even remember my own father's surname. That's not unusual these days, I guess, but there's part of me that doesn't want that for my own family. He went and left us with nothing. As Mum was regularly late with the rent, there was the constant threat that we might lose our home. Even at the age of ten I understood that it was a bad thing. Gaby was the one who was pushed forward to explain to the landlord why we couldn't pay while Mum ran down the back alley to hide in a neighbour's house until he'd gone. It makes me go cold to remember it.

'I need to be secure.'

'You are secure, Cassie. You have a man who would do anything for you.'

'But we're always struggling for money. We have nothing behind us.' Jim does a fantastic job. A worthy job. The problem is that worthy is never going to make us rich. 'I don't want to be like that.'

'I have to work,' Gaby points out. 'We weren't born with a silver spoon in our mouths, sweetheart. We have to get out there and earn it. It's not the end of the world. At times it feels as if

27

Ryan and I are trying to keep a dozen different balls in the air, but somehow we manage. You should stop over-analysing it. Just get on and do it.'

'I know.' My eyes fill with tears. 'I'm thirty-five, Gabs. My ovaries are on a slippery slope. I do want children. A matching pair, preferably. I'm running out of time.'

'It'll happen. You'll see.'

I don't like to remind my sister that I've had numerous 'accidents' in the contraception department and times when we've briefly thrown caution to the wind despite our rickety finances – none of which has led to the patter of baby feet. It took Gaby an age to get pregnant the first time. What if I'm the same? I never wanted to be a teen mum. Even the thought of it utterly terrified me, so I kept my legs firmly crossed for years. Now, ironically, my worry is that I don't want to be an old mum.

'What if I can't afford to give my kids the little luxuries in life? What if I do have a baby now and then can't get back into the world of work? I don't want to be the sort of mum who gives her kids cereal for dinner.'

'You wouldn't do that,' Gaby says softly. Again the unspoken sentence is that our mum did. Sometimes, when her pleas for Mum to replenish our empty cupboards fell on deaf ears, Gaby used to steal money from her purse so that we could sneak to the local Co-op and buy food. We never mention that now either. 'You've got to move on, Cassie. You and Mum are totally different people. Besides, do you think I'd ever let that happen to you?'

'No.' I shake my head. Even though I've just eaten, my stomach growls as I think of the nights that Gaby and I went to bed hungry.

My sister puts her arm around my shoulders. 'Let's hope you make a flipping fortune, then, and can have that Caribbean island wedding that you so want. I'd better start saving up for a hat.'

'I'm at the point where I probably would be happy just to go to the local register office. Should I do that?' I sound despondent even saying it.

She hugs me. 'Don't give up too easily. If this idea flies, that dream could come true sooner than you think.'

I push my plate aside and get up from the table. 'I'd better get a move on with my grand plan then.'

'When you print those brochures, do a leaflet too and I'll stick it up in the reception at work.'

'Thanks. I'm going to go straight home and crack on this afternoon.'

My sister pinches my cheek affectionately. 'Stick at it, kid. I have every faith in you. You're the most organised person on the planet. If you put your mind to it, you'll get there.'

I can only hope that she's right.

Chapter Five

When Jim comes home the flat is a complete disaster zone. I've been baking. My first ever batch of Christmas cupcakes is sitting proudly on the work surface. They look fantastic – even though I say so myself. All those hours of sitting watching daytime television while I've been unemployed haven't been entirely wasted. Without realising, I've obviously been unconsciously improving my baking skills by absorbing a surfeit of cooking programmes through the ether. *The Hairy Bikers*, *Baking Made Easy* and *The Great British Bake-off* have clearly left their mark on me. I wonder whether I have also now subconsciously become a whizz with antiques or could renovate a dilapidated property with my eyes closed.

My solo bake-off hasn't been entirely without incident, though. There was much swearing as I tried to wrestle Gaby's Wilton Mr Whippy nozzle into submission for the buttercream icing. These cakes haven't so much been made by love as born of frustration and grim determination. Plus I had to run backwards and forwards to and from the computer, watching clips of tuition on YouTube. Thank the Lord and all that is holy for the internet! How did people ever manage without it?

Jim stands there looking dazed. 'Oh my goodness me.'

I did drop a bag of icing sugar too and it's still liberally scattered over the floor. I'd forgotten the finer points of cake making and also lifted the electric beaters out of the batter before I'd turned the mixer off. There is cake mix up the walls and tiles. Buttery fingerprints make a trail across my cupboards. It feels as if there's a festive snowstorm of flour in my hair.

In the bag of goodies that my sister rustled up for me, there was also sugar paste and several different shades of food colouring. I'd forgotten that Gaby is the kind of mum who knocks together some sort of novelty birthday cake for each of her children and, therefore, has a lot more wherewithal and equipment than I do.

Following Connie Rosenblatt from Boise, Idaho, I've learned how to make a fondant sugar paste figure of Santa and a snowman. My reindeer was a bit of a disaster, so I ate him. And my Santa looks more than a little tipsy. His head is so heavy that it's slowly sinking into his neck. But I will know better next time. I've also made little cone-shaped Christmas trees studded with silver dragées to decorate my cakes and I'm quite pleased with how they've turned out. Not bad at all for my initial efforts. I'll need to acquaint myself with the local cookshop and stock up on sprinkles and the like. Though I have actually no idea what 'the like' might be.

The red colour from my Santa, however, is daubed liberally throughout the flat and has dyed my hands a lovely shade of scarlet. Very festive. It does look, ever so slightly, as if there's been a murder in here.

Jim is quite clearly horrified. Due to my having a lot of time on my hands, the flat is normally as shiny as a new pin. 'You've been very, er ... enthusiastic.'

'Thought I'd better get started. Gaby gave me a load of baking stuff.' Despite the mess, the flat smells all homely, filled with the scents of baking. I'm glad I've done it. I feel as if I'm on my way.

'Good.' He sounds as if he's not sure if it is good.

'Cupcake?' I offer him my wares.

'Later,' he says. 'Although they do look delicious. And very tempting. Don't want to spoil my appetite. What's for dinner?'

'Ah.' In my flour frenzy I have singularly failed to remember to make anything for us to eat tonight.

'No dinner?'

'I didn't realise the time.'

Jim just grins at me. 'I'm glad to see that you were so absorbed.' He comes and winds his arms round my waist.

'You'll get covered in flour.'

'See if I care. What say we go a little crazy and get a takeaway? We could see what old films we've got on DVD and snuggle down on the sofa.'

'I love the sound of the takeaway and the snuggling, but I'm going to learn calligraphy tonight.'

'You are?' He looks a bit wide-eyed at that.

'No time to lose. Gaby also gave me a bag of calligraphy pens that she had lying in the back of her wardrobe. She said they were Mum's.'

'I can't imagine your mother having the patience to sit and do ornate writing.'

'Me neither,' I agree. 'Maybe the tutor was her fancy man.' It is the only possible reason why my mother would buy calligraphy pens and attend classes. But buy them she did and now they're in my hot little hands. 'Phone up for a takeaway and then have your shower while I clear up this little lot. After we've eaten, we could try to do calligraphy together.'

'Really?' Jim doesn't look enthralled by this. 'The couple who write together, stay together?'

'It could be fun.'

He looks as if he thinks that slumping on the sofa in a post-Chinese coma might be more fun.

'If the business takes off, then I might need you to lend a hand.'

'You've really thought this through, haven't you?'

'I've been working on it all day.' Then I chew my lip anxiously. 'This is a big risk, Jim. I've never had the courage to do anything like this before. I think I always stayed in a job that was well within my comfort zone because I've liked the security. This is all down to me.'

'Not such a risk,' he counters. 'You gave everything to your last company only to have the rug pulled from under you. How can this be worse? At least this *will* be down to you. Until you try, you won't know what you'll be able to achieve. And you couldn't have come up with anything better. This business will use all your fabulous organisational skills and Christmas is right up your street.'

'I know. One minute I have a really good feeling about it and the next I'm full of jitters.'

'That's only natural.' He pulls me in close and I rest my head on his chest. 'I'm proud of you.'

'I haven't done anything yet.'

'You will. The fact is you've got your mojo back. That's all that matters to me. You rock my world, Cassie Smith.'

'And you keep mine steady.'

He rubs his hands together. 'Now, what are we going to have from the Kam Tong? Shall we have exactly the same thing we have every single time we order or shall we go off piste?'

'Same as usual.'

If I'm having such a radical change in my career direction, I'm not sure I could handle a change in our choice of Chinese food too. My stomach flutters at the thought of what I'm embarking on. Baby steps, I think. Baby steps.

Chapter Six

And so it goes on. I print out a basic brochure and make it as inviting and as pretty as possible. It's all reds and golds and very seasonal. If this doesn't strike Christmas into the heart of everyone who sees it, then I don't know what will. There's also a small but perfectly formed poster, which Gaby puts up in her dental practice. I go round all the local shops and ask them nicely to put posters up for me too, which they seem quite happy to do.

I would like to say that all I have to do now is sit back and wait, but that's as far from the truth as is humanly possible. My days are spent learning new skills from the internet. I tell you, what I can now do with a Poundland piece of tinsel is nothing short of a miracle.

Two weeks go by and I still have absolutely no bookings. I've called round all the companies, big and small, on the business park to tell them of my services. They were all very polite and said that they would get back to me. As yet, they haven't. Every business that would take one of my posters has been given one, but still my phone stays silent. I have chewed my fingernails down to the quick. What if no one does need the expertise of Calling Mrs Christmas! after all? What if I've read this wrong? I've sent a press release to the local paper, which, thankfully, they're including next week so I'm hoping that might kick-start things. What else can I do?

Then, later, when my mind is on freeflow and I'm baking gingerbread biscuits in the shape of snowflakes, I get my first phone call.

'Is that Mrs Christmas?' a voice asks.

I am beside myself with excitement. It's all I can do not to run round the kitchen. 'Yes. Yes.'

The woman introduces herself as representing the flyer for local businesses. 'We're doing a special offer on Christmas advertising,' she says.

Maybe this is what it will take, but I simply don't have the cash. 'I'll think about it,' I promise and hang up, despondent.

Ten minutes later and the phone rings again. I sigh. It had better not be someone else trying to sell me advertising.

'Hello, dear,' says the lady at the other end. 'Have I reached Mrs Christmas?'

'Yes, that's me.' I try to sound hopeful and bright and get my answers ready to repel salesmen.

'You're just the woman I need,' she says and my heart lifts.

Mrs Ledbury goes on to tell me that she lives in a cottage in Boxmoor. 'My poor old fingers are crippled with arthritis, dear,' she explains. 'My handwriting is so terrible now that no one can read it. I thought it would be nice if you could do my cards for me this year. It takes me so long to write them. Is that the kind of service you offer?'

Is it ever! Christmas-card writing, in my new swanky hand, is at the very top of my list. I agree that I'll be there in half an hour. Instantly, I phone Jim.

'I've got my first job,' I tell him.

'That's great.' I can hear that he's distracted.

'Everything OK?'

'Bit busy. There's a bit of a fight going on in the unit.'

A daily occurrence.

'A lot of shouting and swearing,' he says. 'A few chairs flying.'

'I'll leave you to it.'

'Yeah. It's been going on all morning. I came out for a quick breather. I'm about to head back in again,' he says. 'Can I call you later?'

'Don't worry. I'll tell you all about it when you get home. Be careful.'

'Always am,' he assures me.

'Love you.'

He hangs up without saying anything else. Sometimes I worry about him at work though. I've mostly got used to it by now and, to be honest, Jim very rarely talks to me about the boys in his care. He says the odd thing, but he's not the type of man to come home and download all his woes every night. He deals with the many and varied difficulties of his career in a quiet, contained way, as he does everything else. I do know, however, that sometimes it can be dangerous and he's constantly under the threat of assault.

I leave my biscuits cooling, grab my mother's resurrected calligraphy pens and hotfoot it – or hot-drive it – down to Boxmoor.

Mrs Ledbury's cottage is very pretty. It's in a lovely part of the town, right alongside a wide-open space called Blackbirds' Moor, and I park up under the trees. Estate agents now bill this as the 'village' of Boxmoor and have pushed up prices accordingly, but it's still only a short walk from the High Street.

Not everyone likes Hemel Hempstead, but I love it here. I've grown up in the area and wouldn't really want to live anywhere else. Over the years, I've seen the High Street develop into a lively shopping centre. The scrappy old tower block, which used to be home to Kodak headquarters, is now swanky 'high-living' apartments with price tags that would make your eyes water. At the other end of the High Street, the Old Town with its ragtag of Victorian, Georgian and Tudor houses, its antique shops and nice restaurants, has still retained its charm.

Where we live is a bit of a sprawling seventies estate on the outskirts of Hemel town. Not exactly the prettiest place, but it suits us. I'd like to live down here in Boxmoor, given the chance, but I think the houses will always be way beyond our reach. But then where isn't expensive? Where we live *now* is out of our price range. Unless I make my fortune as Mrs Christmas, then we may well be in rented property for ever. It's a vicious circle. Even for our modest place, we pay a really high rent and that makes it even harder for us to save for a deposit. What little we had managed to save has pretty much all gone now on supplementing our income while I've been unemployed. And that's without having had a holiday or any luxuries this year. I live in constant dread of an unexpected bill coming in. It's been grim. Not as bad as some people have it, of course. I don't ever go up to Jim's workplace so I really don't know what it's like and he doesn't talk about it much. Jim keeps everything pretty close to his chest, but when he does tell me about his job, I wonder how some of those boys will ever make it through life. They've often had such terrible starts.

Goodness only knows why my mum had two children – I am sure both Gaby and I were unplanned. She was never deliberately neglectful, but we did spend many of our formative years eating crisps for breakfast and, for dinner, frozen ready meals followed by Angel Delight. I've probably got chemical-based arteries filled with pure lard. Gaby, at the age of twelve, stepped in and took over the cooking, the cleaning and the laundry. I helped as best I could. And that suited my mother. It left her free to pursue unsuitable men who could pay our bills.

I think that's why my sister is as she is now. Her children are blanketed in love, get fed the finest of organic foods and take part in every conceivable after-school activity known to man. Gaby and Ryan will go without themselves rather than let a shadow fall on their children's lives. And, though they could have turned into spoiled brats, they are polite, balanced and very entertaining children. I want two just like them. I want to be the kind of mother Gaby is too.

I cross the road to Mrs Ledbury's cottage. It's white, half-timbered and set back from the road, beautiful, but slightly fraying round the edges. The small garden at the front is a little overgrown. When I ring the doorbell, it doesn't work, so I rap the knocker. After a few long minutes, Mrs Ledbury answers the door. She's a tiny, frail old lady, smartly dressed in a tweed skirt and pearls.

I hold out my hand. 'Cassie Smith,' I say. 'I'm here from Calling Mrs Christmas!'

'Oh, hello, dearie,' she says. 'That was jolly quick.'

'No time like the present.'

'I know it's perhaps a bit early, but I do like to be organised for Christmas and I've got cards that have to go overseas. Come on in.'

I slip into step behind her and follow her shuffling gait through to the small dining room, crammed with dark wood furniture.

'I've set them out already.'

Sure enough, there's a pile of cards all ready and waiting for me. I get out my cache of writing equipment.

'Shall I make you a cup of tea while you work?' she asks.

'Maybe afterwards,' I say. 'I'd be worried about spilling it on the cards. They're beautiful.'

'I don't send many out these days – all my friends are dying off.' Her laughter sounds tired. 'So I can afford to buy some nicer ones. The trouble is my handwriting is so awful these days.' She holds out her gnarled and twisted fingers. 'Arthritis,' she tuts at herself. 'I can hardly grip a pen now. It took me so long to write my cards last year that my hands would throb. Even then half of the people I sent them to couldn't read who they were from.' She smiles sadly at that. 'I was delighted to pick up one of your leaflets in the card shop. Now the writing can be smart too.'

As I settle down to write the cards with a flutter of nerves, I'm glad that I've been practising my calligraphy faithfully every evening. I don't want to mess up even one of these as I can tell that Mrs Ledbury has spent quite a bit on them.

'Can you read my address book?'

The handwriting is spidery, but I think I can make out most things. 'Can you sit with me and I'll read them out to double-check before I commit pen to paper?'

'What a splendid idea. You're very organised, young lady.'

Mrs Ledbury moves the lace runner and the bowl of fruit to the sideboard and we take our seats at the table. I check the pen is filled with black ink and then write the cards, making my hand-writing meticulously clear, adding a few of the flourishes that I've honed over the last fortnight. I address all the envelopes neatly, checking the details of the recipients with my client. I concentrate so hard that I feel a bead of sweat on my forehead. When I've finished, Mrs Ledbury admires my handiwork. 'That's really very lovely,' she says.

'I can get stamps and post them for you too,' I say. 'I'll check the posting dates for overseas and then could put the rest of them to one side until the beginning of December.'

'You won't forget?'

'No. Definitely not.'

'You're a darling girl. That would be something else I don't have to think about.'

'Call it done.'

'Would you like that cup of tea now?'

'Yes, please. Shall I make it for us?'

'Why not? I'll show you where everything is.'

So I make us both a cuppa in delicate china cups. While we drink it, I ask, 'Do you decorate your cottage for Christmas?'

'Not any more,' Mrs Ledbury says ruefully. 'Again, it's too much trouble with these hands of mine and I daren't venture into my loft. If I fell, who would know? My son used to come and do it, but he's so busy himself now.' She sighs. 'It is a crying shame as this cottage looks so pretty in its festive finery.'

'I could help you with that as well,' I offer.

'I used to so love having all my decorations up,' she says, wistfully. Her eyes mist over. 'I used to buy one wherever I went. The whole of my life in Christmas decorations is in my loft.'

'It wouldn't cost very much if you wanted me to come back and do it.' I've made sure that I've priced my services keenly.

'Really?' Her eyes light up. 'That would be wonderful. I'm at home by myself this Christmas. My daughter's in Australia. My son and his wife are going to Thailand for the season. I've been dreading it. How miserable would it be without a tree up or even a little bit of tinsel?'

'Shall we make an appointment then?'

'Yes, let's.' Mrs Ledbury claps her hands excitedly. 'This is getting me quite in the mood for Christmas, Cassie.'

I can't wait for it either. The fun, the laughter, the excesses of food, maybe some presents if I can keep busy. If we're lucky, we might even get a sprinkling of festive snow.

I smile back at her. 'Me too,' I say.

Chapter Seven

Jim Maddison pulled up in the car park outside Bovingdale Young Offenders' Unit. He'd had to go to the bank today before his shift and now he was running late. It would take so long to get through the barrage of security gates until he was on his wing, but it was a routine that he was well used to.

Unfortunately, he'd had no choice but to pay the branch a visit today. Their overdraft was mounting steadily and he'd needed to go in to ask the bank to extend it. He didn't want to risk that chat with some faceless call-centre person based in Mumbai or somewhere. He wanted to speak to a real human being who knew him and had known him for years. But they were becoming more rare now. Of course, after making him beg a bit, the bank had agreed to extend their overdraft. It was now running much higher than Jim was happy with and it meant that the bank charges they paid were horrendous. Only a lottery win would clear this little lot. Jim sighed to himself. The money he earned as a prison officer would never run to holidays in the Bahamas and this debt had been racked up just by keeping their heads above water. The sooner that Cassie could start earning again, the better. Jim glanced at his watch. Mission accomplished, but it would have to be a quick change into his uniform as soon as he was inside.

He stared ahead at the unit. The steel-mesh walls were high and topped by rolled razor wire. Sniffer dogs patrolled the inner boundary, trying to catch the scent of the drugs parcels that kindly relatives or friends attempted to throw over the wall to their loved ones. It was on a depressingly regular basis that they had to call in the security team to do a sweep of the place to clean it up.

The unit housed lads from the age of fifteen to eighteen – juvenile offenders to give them their proper title – but, to all intents and purposes, it was a prison. Bovingdale was a mixed Young Offenders' and Category C adult facility that was home to five hundred inmates. In the Young Offenders' Unit alone, there were some of the most dangerous and disturbed kids in the country. Jim gave one last glance at the clear blue winter sky and headed inside. It was time to go to work.

He nodded at one of the other officers as he went through the main gates, 'Afternoon, Bill.'

The man nodded back. At every stage as he got closer to his wing, a set of hefty security gates shut firmly behind him. The dead clang of impenetrable metal, the rattle and thunk of the heavy keys, all noises that provide the soundtrack to prison life. The sound of freedom fading. It was something that, even after all this time, he'd never got used to. But at least he would get to leave again at the end of his working day.

Jim had been in the army for ten years. He'd joined up when he left school only because he hadn't really known what else to do and, back then, university hadn't really been an option. He was from a working-class background and no one in his family had ever gone on to higher education. His family saw no reason for anyone to start now. Then he'd done enough tours of duty in Afghanistan and Iraq to realise that war was a mug's game. After a decade of dodging bullets, he'd come back onto civvy street, still with no idea of what he might want to do with the rest of his life.

Someone suggested the prison service and he'd signed on the dotted line. The thinking was that it was steady employment to buy him some time while he thought of a suitable career. He'd considered training as a sports instructor or a PE teacher, but never had. He'd been at the same unit now for the last ten years. Despite the fact that an increasingly large part of his career involved being loathed, spat at and disrespected by the motley crew of youngsters who passed through these gates, Jim felt he had found his niche in life. He was a good prison officer and, God willing, that's probably what he'd remain until he picked up his pension.

His own wing, Starling, which housed thirty lads, stank of stale chip fat, sweaty teenagers and too much testosterone. The cells, their solid doors fitted with small inspection windows, ran on two tiers. They were joyless places, all painted the same dirty-cream colour and usually stained with unspeakable brown patches from what were known as dirty protests. The lads were allowed to put up posters – most of which were naked women with the occasional Ferrari thrown in – but they weren't allowed glue. So they stuck them to the walls with chewing gum, tooth-paste and, sometimes, when desperate, their own body fluids. One of the worst jobs that Jim ever had to do was kitting up in his white suit and scrubbing down a cell. He did it quite a lot.

Each cell, not even three metres square, was home to two lads. If they both kept their noses clean and earned privileges, they could share a telly. The bunks were hard, the sheets dark brown, which hid a multitude of sins. The open metal toilet stood in an alcove with no door. If anyone thought Bovingdale was some kind of holiday camp, they should try paying it a visit sometime.

Ready to start his day, Jim strode out into the association area, a space between the cells where the lads could socialise – or fight. It contained a pool table, its faded green baize almost worn through. Lads were huddled in groups, probably all scheming against the others. Gang warfare was one of the unit's biggest problems – and there were many gangs to choose from.

Sometimes Bovingdale got Home Office directives that dictated that officers should call the lads by other names. 'Clients' had been one. Currently it was 'children'. But it was hard to see what was childlike about some of the kids who'd passed through. Quite a few were over six feet tall and built like brick outhouses. In among the burglars, the brawlers and the persistently bad drivers were rapists, murderers and drug dealers. Their faces were aged, lined by a thousand years of experience already fitted into their short and brutal lives. They were hardened against society before they'd even begun to know what it was. Some had tragic upbringings that had left them in the wrong place at the wrong time, making the wrong choices. Others were just evil buggers who'd graduate from the unit to spend their remaining years in and out of prison until, for one reason or another, they became lifers and would never see the light of day again. Only a politician sitting in London behind a mahogany desk could think of this bunch as 'children'. So, whatever the directive, at the unit their charges were always known as 'lads'.

If you had to be banged up at all, then Bovingdale was a relatively good place to be. It had one or two institutionalised, borderline sadistic officers – you got them everywhere – but the majority were right enough. Most of the officers went for the softly-softly approach, happier to be father figures rather than wielding the baton. Jim always treated the lads as he'd want his own son to be treated – if he was lucky enough to have one in the future – if the boy ever had the misfortune to get into trouble.

Everyone makes mistakes. Here the inmates got a chance to learn from them.

The governor David Hornshaw, a youngish bloke, was sound with progressive views. He placed good store on education and, as a result, the reoffending rate – usually eight in ten nation-wide – was much lower. Bovingdale had won awards for its education programme. Most of the lads couldn't even read or write when they came in, so what chance was there for them to escape a life of crime when they were on the outside again? Out of sixty thousand prisoners currently on remand, it was reckoned that forty thousand were unemployable, mostly because they were illiterate.

Two lads played pool, one leaning insolently on his cue while the other was bent over the table, deep in concentration. Each wore the standard-issue uniform of a grey tracksuit and trainers.

'All right, lads?' Jim said, affably. 'Who's winning?'

They both grinned at him. 'Rozzer as usual,' the younger lad said.

Rozzer. The seventeen-year-old son of a policeman who'd got caught way too many times buying and selling weed to his mates and was now on his second stint.

Jim watched the lads pot a few more holes.

'Give us a game?' they asked.

Jim laughed. 'You know that I'd thrash you both,' he said good-naturedly.

Sometimes there were lads in here who simply shouldn't be. You could see it in their eyes that they were essentially good kids. By now, Jim thought himself a pretty good judge of character. You could tell instantly who were the ones beyond hope. Similarly, you could tell who were the ones who, with a bit of help and a following wind, could turn their lives around.

Rozzer, otherwise known as Andrew Walton, had learned his

lesson this time. He wouldn't be back inside again, Jim was sure. It was a tough lesson for one so young.

Since his incarceration, his family had disowned him, which was going to be hard for him to get over. When he'd come to Bovingdale the first time, he used to smarten himself up every week ready for his family to visit. His hair would be combed, his face scrubbed until it shone. They never came. Not one of them. No man wanted to see his son locked up and, for a policeman, it must be doubly difficult. Jim could understand, at a push, why a father wouldn't want to visit the prison that held his boy. But what mother could stay away? There were some bad lads in here who'd done terrible things, but their mams still came to visit them. It had been heartbreaking to witness his disappointment every week. In those first few months, Rozzer had been on suicide watch more times than Jim cared to remember. Being the son of a policeman was never going to make for an easy life inside. He was frequently beaten black and blue, as Jim had to record in his reports time and again. Jim wondered if it could have turned out differently if his parents had supported him more – or at all. But then you never knew what went on in someone's home. Now Rozzer never even mentioned his family.

The second lad at the pool table was Kieran Holman. He had just turned sixteen and was slight, from years of under-nourishment, probably. His blond hair and boyish good looks made him a favourite of the gay inmates, which he hated. He was terrified of their attention – a legacy from the streets, perhaps, where he'd been forced to turn tricks to survive. The mental-health nurses were on to it, anyway, and kept a close eye on him.

Kieran had been living rough in a wheelie bin with nothing to his name but a sleeping bag that he'd stolen from Millets. He'd been light-fingered once too often – mainly stealing food and booze from Tesco – and had eventually ended up in Bovingdale on a six-month stretch. He was known as Smudge because the grey griminess of the street remained embedded in his skin. The soap that could get rid of that hadn't yet been invented. The minute Kieran had got out last time, he'd smashed all the windows of the cars in the staff car park and had found himself straight back inside. The second time he'd come into the unit, there was only relief in his eyes. He shared a cell with Rozzer who was then serving a year. It had been a lucky move for both of them as they'd bonded instantly and had become more like brothers than close friends. Even so, Smudge was still scared of his own shadow and had screaming nightmares on a nightly basis. He was a lad who had no visitors either.

'What was lunch like?' The servery was at the end of the hall.

'Shit,' Rozzer said.

The education programme might be decent, but the food was never going to win any Michelin stars.

'Here.' Jim palmed a bar of Dairy Milk that he had in his pocket and passed it discreetly to Smudge. He'd bought it for the lads when he'd filled up with petrol at the garage on his way into work. It was against the rules, of course. But then this whole place was born of broken rules. 'Share it.'

Smudge's eyes lit up. 'Thanks, Jim.'

Jim remembered those wide blue eyes when Smudge had first come to Bovingdale. They showed his terror at being banged up alongside relief that someone had rescued him from the streets. It was drummed into officers that they should at all times keep a professional barrier between themselves and the lads. A psychological process went on in any prison known as 'conditioning', where prison officers were sucked into personal relationships with the inmates. Sometimes it could be deliberate, sometimes it was subconscious, but it invariably ended in boundaries being crossed.

For the last ten years Jim had managed to avoid being drawn to any of the prisoners, but it was hard to keep your distance when you got to know them the way he knew Rozzer and Smudge.

At times the unit was so under-staffed that it was impossible to find time to get to know individuals. Sometimes they were inside for only six-week stints and it was hard enough to remember their names then. These two were different, though. They'd been in Bovingdale a while and they were both good lads. They toed the line and tried to keep out of trouble. That was a big ask. Encouraged by Jim, both had been signed up to the Listener Scheme, which was a peer-support programme run by the Samaritans to give prisoners someone to talk to if they were in need. Even with Bovingdale's good record, the level of attempted suicide was shockingly high. Someone was always trying to hang himself. With Christmas coming, it always got worse.

Rozzer had been trained as a listener for some time now. He was a bright boy, cocky, but level-headed beneath his bravado. He was solid, having learned how to stay out of the way of trouble. If all the prisoners were like that, it would make Jim's life a lot easier. Rozzer and Smudge had become even closer since the younger lad had spent so much time availing himself of the Listener Scheme. Despite his repeated warnings to himself, Jim had warmed to them and in a way had taken both of them under his wing. They were both due out soon and he hoped that he wouldn't see them back at Bovingdale again. At the same time, he'd actually miss them.

Then the siren sounded and a bunch of officers charged along the corridors. Jim felt himself sigh inside. Someone had kicked off again. The whole place was a tinderbox and it often took only a very minor or perceived slight to ignite it. A fellow officer, Dan, stuck his head out of the Control Room. 'Dirty protest on the top.' He cast his eyes heavenward. 'Shit up the walls.'

Rozzer and Smudge gave Jim a sympathetic glance. Soon they'd be on lock-down while it was cleared up.

Sometimes Cassie complained that he didn't talk to her about his job but on days like this Jim wondered what on earth he could say.

Chapter Eight

I'm hardly back from Mrs Ledbury's cottage when my phone rings again. 'Calling Mrs Christmas!' I answer, trying to sound like a chirpy little Christmas elf.

On the other end of the line is a small company from the local industrial estate. They want me to buy and wrap gifts for all of their thirty staff. They've had a good year and want to give them a surprise Christmas treat. I like the sound of a company that does that rather than dishing out redundancy notices at Christmas as so many of them tend to do now.

We sort out a budget and talk about the kind of gifts that they want and they agree to email me a list of their employees' names so that I can individually address the gift cards. I thank them for their business and then dash to my trusty computer to see what I can source. For the ladies, I decide on some gorgeous hand-made chocolates from a little shop in the Old Town. For the men, I find a limited-edition bottle of wine and manage to source it from an independent retailer also in the Old Town. Back in the car.

I race to Paper Roses, a shop that I've always loved, to buy my first industrial-quantity batch of luxury wrapping paper, tags and bows, and double-sided tape. All the things that my internet tutorial told me were essential to make it look high-end. I load everything into my boot. While I'm out, I grab some salmon to grill for dinner and a pack of pre-prepared veg. Such decadence!

When Jim comes home, I'm sitting on the living-room floor with gift wrapping and presents spread out all around me. I've got bright red and green paper with silver ribbons and bows. I'm trying to do all my corners neatly as I learned on YouTube, 'fingerpress' all my folds so that they lie flat and I'm doing invisible sticking with my double-sided tape. Who knew there was so much to it? I always thought my present wrapping was pretty hot. Now I realise I was a mere amateur. But not any more.

'Wow,' he says. 'You've been busy.'

'Second job of the day,' I tell him, my excitement bubbling over. 'I went to write some Christmas cards this morning for an elderly lady. I'm going back to dress her tree in a couple of weeks when it's nearer to Christmas. And now this.' I gesture at the mess. 'Thirty prezzies for the staff down at Aveco on the industrial estate.'

'Lucky staff. They look very impressive.'

'You think so?' I glow a little with pride. I'm quite pleased with them myself, I have to admit.

'More importantly, you look as if you're enjoying yourself.'

'If I can make any money at this, then it's quite possibly my dream job. It doesn't even feel like work.'

'Organising the pants off stuff *and* all things Christmas. Sounds like you've struck gold,' Jim agrees. 'How many weeks are there to the big day?'

'Not enough.'

'Is it going to be like this all the time from now on?' He throws a despairing look at the flat.

'I hope so,' I admit. 'I'm going to try to get these all wrapped up tonight, so that I can drop them off tomorrow. I want to stun them with my über-efficiency.'

'So my intentions of ravishing you on the rug in front of the gas fire will have to wait?'

I laugh. 'Maybe later. Come and give me a kiss.'

'I'm a bit stinky,' Jim says. 'You might want to wait until I've had my shower.'

'Bad day?'

He shrugs. 'No more so than usual.'

I pause in trying to wrestle the wrapping paper into submission and look up at him. 'You seem quiet.'

A sigh. 'Two of the lads that I've grown fond of are due to leave shortly. I'm worried about them.'

'You old softie.'

'Yeah,' he agrees. 'That's me.'

'Rozzer and Smudge?' Jim doesn't talk much about his work but these names have cropped up more regularly over the past months.

He nods. 'They're just kids, Cassie, and they'll be turfed out onto the streets right before Christmas with very little support. They'll have to sink or swim on their own merits. I hope for their sakes that they don't end up back in the unit.'

'They're repeat offenders?'

'They've both been in already. Sometimes, even with all the downsides, it can be easier on the inside. At least someone keeps you warm, feeds you and gives you medicine when you're ill. Out in the big bad world, you're on your own.'

'No family?'

'I suspect it's because of their families that they're in there. At least in one of the cases.'

'Nothing you can do to help?'

'You know me,' Jim says, his voice weary. 'I'd bring half of them home if I could. Some are lost causes who'll never be any bloody use to society, but others just need a chance to change their lives.'

'It's a hard time to be out on your own, just before Christmas.'

'I know,' Jim says. 'It's hard any time, but it does seem worse then somehow.'

'Need a drink tonight?'

'It wouldn't go amiss. Have we got anything?'

We always used to keep a few beers on hand, maybe have a wine box on the go, but we've stopped all that.

'I got a great deal on this wine,' I tell him, holding up a bottle. 'So I got one for us too.'

A long and grateful breath leaves his lips. 'You're a star.'

'I think my first day back at work being gainfully employed is a cause for celebration. We deserve a bit of a treat.'

'You're my clever girl,' he says.

'I love you,' I say, suddenly teary. 'I know I've only done two little things, but already I feel better about myself. I've got a reason to get up every morning.'

'*You're* my reason to get up every morning,' he tells me and I know in my heart that he means it sincerely. 'And as soon as I've had my shower, I'm going to show you my everlasting gratitude.'

'What does that involve?'

He wiggles his eyebrows. 'You'll have to wait and see.'

'I'm not sure that I can.'

'I won't be long.' Jim disappears towards the bedroom, stripping off his sweatshirt as he goes.

Before I turn back to my wrapping, I notice that there's a weary slump to his shoulders. He's got a lot on his mind, I can tell, and he's been such a brilliant support to me in my hour of need. I promise myself that this year I'll do all that I can to make Christmas truly wonderful.

Chapter Nine

Then I have a week or so when nothing much happens. I get a couple of calls about organising catering for Christmas events and I do my quote speedily and efficiently, but never hear back from either of them. I begin to wonder if I've made a terrible mistake. Is money so tight for everyone that people are cutting back this year rather than splashing out on the luxury of a Christmas concierge? I try to hold the faith, but faced with a silent phone and an empty diary, it's tough. I start to scour the job ads in the local paper once more.

Jim is nothing but encouraging. 'It'll kick in,' he assures me. 'You wait and see.'

And he's right. Just as my knees are getting really shaky and I'm checking the bank statement online every day, October clicks over into November and my telephone goes mad. It never stops ringing from morning until night. I've got trees to dress, presents to buy and wrap, cards to write, cakes to bake. All the things that you'd do for your own Christmas, just multiplied by a million. I had no idea when I started that the business could be so busy, but I'm really delighted that it is.

I've taught Jim how to do calligraphy too and we both spend most of our nights writing out cards. Most of them are for small businesses that want their Christmas greetings to look more personalised than sending out printed ones with mass-produced labels. Nice touch.

I glance up at Jim. He's sitting with the coffee table in front of him, cards spread out. I've bribed him with a glass of whisky and he pauses to take a sip. He can feel my eyes on him and stops dead, looking guilty. 'What?'

'Nothing,' I laugh. 'I just really appreciate you helping me so much.'

'No worries. I quite enjoy it. Doing this fancy writing is surprisingly relaxing. My twiddles are coming along a treat.' He takes a moment to admire said 'twiddles'. 'Who would have thought that Calling Mrs Christmas! would take off so quickly? What will it be like when we hit December and people realise how close we are to Christmas?'

'I had a heartsink moment when I thought it wouldn't work,' I admit.

'I knew you could do it.'

'I wouldn't be able to manage without you.'

The intercom goes and I abandon my cards to go over and see who it is. 'Only me,' a voice says when I press the button.

'Come in!' Seconds later, I open the door to the flat and Gaby breezes in.

'Mince pies,' she says. 'Loads of them.'

'Ten dozen, I hope.'

They've been freshly baked for an event run by Hemel Hempstead Means Business trade organisation. They're having a Christmas launch party tomorrow evening for local businesses and retailers. Yours truly is going to decorate the room I've hired for them at the Old Town Hall and provide champagne, mulled wine and mince pies. It's my first proper event and I have to say that I'm quite nervous about it. When I was a secretary, I organised a lot of drinks-and-nibbles affairs so I shouldn't be too worried. But now they all seem very low-key compared to this. Tomorrow's event is for over a hundred of the town bigwigs and I want it to be fabulous. My own business will be very much on show and, if it goes well, it could generate a lot more leads for me.

'All present and correct,' Gaby says, holding up a box. 'My poor oven doesn't know what's happening. These are just a sample.' She proffers her mince pies. 'The rest are in the car. I thought we could switch them over to your car rather than lug them up here. I've got the two Christmas cakes you wanted too. They've turned out nice.'

I kiss her cheek and then peek into the box she's brought. 'The mince pies look gorgeous.'

They're golden brown and dusted with icing sugar. I know from past experience that Gaby's pastry is always light and crisp. She says the secret is adding ground almonds to the mix and who am I to argue with that? 'Good enough to eat?'

'I did put in an extra three for us so we could have them with a cup of tea. We have to road-test them, don't we?'

'That is why I love you and am happy to call you sister.'

'Wait till you see my invoice.'

'Make sure you've covered all your costs,' I insist. 'This is a business and they've been quite generous with their budget. I don't want any of us to be out of pocket. It might be the season of goodwill but we're in this for the cold, hard cash.' We both have a giggle at my newfound, ruthlessly commercial streak.

'Listen to you,' Gaby chuckles. 'You sound like flipping Lord Sugar.'

It's true that I have to keep reminding myself that it's a business as I'd happily do all this for nothing. I love it! Being Mrs Christmas has definitely released my inner Christmas elf, I think. 'You're still all right to come along and help me tomorrow night?'

'Wouldn't miss it for the world.'

'Go in and see Jim while I put the kettle on. He's busy addressing Christmas cards.'

'He's such a saint.'

'Tell me about it. I couldn't have done any of this without him. His calligraphy is coming on a treat and he's had a couple of lessons on cupcake decorating.'

'Have you sold lots?'

'More than I ever thought and I don't think that the busy period has even kicked in yet.'

The shops this year seem to have been later starting than normal. Most of them are only just getting into gear with their displays and special offers. The supermarkets are setting up their arrays of Christmas goodies. Which is nice. There's nothing worse than when Christmas starts in July. I think a good, brisk sprint to the finish line is the way to go. Plus I'm thinking of all those lovely people who are totally disorganised and will be picking up the phone to me during the last week before the twenty-fifth.

'It's amazing how this has taken off this week,' Gaby says.

'I know. I wish I'd thought of it years ago.'

All that wasted time when I was frightened to take a risk. Bizarre that I had to wait to be made redundant before I had the courage to try out my wings.

'Do you need a hand getting ready tomorrow? I finish work at one,' Gaby says.

'I should be OK. I'm going to get everything organised in the morning and I can start setting up the room at two. The reception doesn't start until six, so that should leave plenty of time.'

'You know where I am if you need me. Both of the kids are going to play with Sylvia's two down the road straight from school, so I'm a child-free zone for a couple of hours. Ryan can always pick them up when he comes home.'

'I might take you up on your offer then.'

I wish you could see our spare bedroom. It's an avalanche of paper. There are spreadsheets for just about everything. The last thing I want to do is drop a ball when it's my job to be organised. This has taken over our entire lives and I know that it will be all hands to the pump for the next two months. Perhaps when we're done Jim and I could take a little holiday somewhere. Even if it's just a weekend break in this country, that would do. This flat has felt like a prison over the last nine months. There are times when I think that I could have gone mad just sitting staring at these four walls. Well, all that's changed now. Thank goodness for Christmas!

Chapter Ten

The next morning when Jim has gone to work, my phone rings. I should be up already, but I'm enjoying five minutes of luxuriating with a cup of tea brought to me by my dearest and delivered with a kiss. I want to be nice and relaxed for the event tonight and well prepared, so I've got nothing else booked in. I was just going to make another batch of cupcakes to put in the chest freezer that we have out in the garage.

I answer the phone with 'Calling Mrs Christmas!' I don't even bother giving my own name any more as the calls are never for me unless it's Jim or my sis. A lot of my friends mysteriously faded away when I was unemployed. I'm hurt by it, but I can't say that I blame them. It's hard to go out on a girls' night when you haven't got any money. My closest friends would always offer to pay my share for the first few months but I felt terrible about accepting their charity when I couldn't reciprocate. After that, to be honest, it just became easier not to go along. There's nothing worse than not being able to pay your share of the bill or buy a drink without worrying where you're going to find the money. Plus when they were all chatting away about their work and their kids, what did I have to talk about? Nothing. I couldn't bring myself to read or even shower half the time. All I could do was watch rubbish telly. Now I could kick myself. I could have spent those wasted hours learning a new skill. When I think of all the things I've forced myself to do in the last few weeks, I'm just adoring the new, creative me!

'Hello,' the voice at the other end says. 'It's Janet from Hemel Hempstead Means Business.'

'Hi, Janet.' I get a momentary flutter of panic. Hope everything is OK for the event this evening.

'It's about tonight,' Janet continues. 'We've got some Hemel Hempstead Means Business pens and USB sticks that we can give away, plus some other bits and pieces.'

'Do you need them gift wrapped?' There are over a hundred people expected tonight. I think I'm having palpitations.

'No, no.' Janet laughs at the very thought. 'There are far too many for that.'

A woman after my own heart.

'Thought it might be nice if we could have Santa pop along and give them out, though. Could you organise that for us?'

'Er … I … Yes, of course.'

Santa! My mind is racing, wondering where I'm going to find a Santa costume at short notice and, more importantly, a man to fill it. Then I hit on the perfect solution. Jim. It's going to have to be Jim. Who else?

'He could come along about seven, if that's all right,' Janet suggests. 'When everyone's settled in.'

'Yes,' I say. 'That's fine. Everything else is organised. I'll see you later.'

The minute Janet hangs up, I'm on the phone again, ringing round party shops to see if any of them have a Santa suit that I can hire. Jim was going to come along anyway tonight to help serve the drinks. All he'll have to do is pop out for five minutes and slip on the Santa suit. Sorted.

I'm on to the third fancy-dress hire place and starting to

perspire a little before I'm successful. But this shop, thankfully, has one in stock. It's a size that fits all, they assure me. So I book it over the phone, jump out of bed and run round the shower.

It's only just gone ten o'clock by the time I'm parking up outside the shop. Still well ahead of myself. I dash inside to collect my Santa suit.

The girl behind the counter hands it over. 'He'll just need black boots to go with it,' she says. 'Wellies or something.'

Jim wears big, black boots every day with his uniform, so I'm sure they'll do. I give it a cursory glance, pay up and dash out.

I'm on my way home when the phone rings again. Thank goodness I've also invested in a hands-free, Bluetooth thingy as I've never taken so many calls in my car.

'Oh hello, dearie.' It's Mrs Ledbury. 'I know that you're not due until next week but my family have decided to pop along this weekend and I'd so love to have my decorations up by then. I might not see them again before Christmas. Is there any chance that you could come and put them up today?'

I glance anxiously at my watch. Theoretically, there's plenty of time to do it, although that means putting pressure on myself. But I really don't want to let her down. She was my very first client and, as such, will always have a special place in my heart.

'It would mean a lot to me,' she adds.

That settles it. I'm such a sucker for a sob story. If Mrs Ledbury wants her Christmas tree up today, then Mrs Ledbury shall have it. If I go straight round there, I can do the tree from eleven until one, dash back for a bite of lunch, collect all my gear and head up to the Old Town Hall for two. No worries. Easy-peasy, lemon squeezy.

'Of course. Can I come straight round? I'll be there in about ten minutes.'

'Perfect,' my client says. 'I think I would like a real tree, if that's possible.'

Real tree. Unplanned-for diversion to garden centre.

'No problem. I'll pick one up before I come to you.'

I hang up and, instinctively, my foot presses that little bit more firmly on the accelerator as I speed out towards Water End garden centre to buy a real tree.

I'm astonished at how many people want their Christmas tree up in November. I thought it was just me. Jim's the opposite. He likes it thrown up as near to Christmas Eve as possible and down again the day after New Year. He doesn't mind Christmas, but he's not one for keeping it hanging around. This year especially, I feel I should have the tree up *really* early and get the flat in the Christmas mood. But, at this rate, I'm going to be lucky if I find time to put my own tree up at all.

Chapter Eleven

I squeeze through Mrs Ledbury's loft hatch. There's no proper ladder, so I'm balanced precariously on the top of some wonky steps. There's no light either so I'm holding a torch even more precariously between my teeth. These are things that I didn't really consider when drawing up my business plan.

'Stand well clear,' I instruct while trying to keep a firm grip on the torch.

Mrs Ledbury is standing on the landing beneath me and the last thing I want to do is fall out of the loft and crush her. That would be *bad* for business. She's as excited as a child and my heart goes out to her.

I rummage around in the darkness and the cobwebs until I find the boxes marked 'Christmas Decorations'. Thank goodness. I'm sure that my hair's full of spiders.

'Coming down,' I shout and start the dangerous business of getting back down the steps carrying bulky boxes. This is definitely a job for Jim. He'd make it look easy work. Which reminds me – I haven't yet called him to let him know that he's required to perform Santa-style duties tonight. Not that he'll object. He never objects to anything.

I take one box down to the living room, Mrs Ledbury hot on my heels. The tree and stand that I've just purchased are already set up in the corner, perched on a little table that's done the job for the forty years that Mrs Ledbury has lived here. I picked a Nordman Fir as the tree has to last for a long time and, according to my research on the internet, this is the best one for the job.

'It's a lovely tree,' Mrs Ledbury says. 'That was my husband's favourite job of the year, picking the Christmas tree.' Her eyes fill with tears. 'I've been on my own for too long. Doing everything alone is no fun. Even Christmas loses its magic.'

'Well, this year, we'll dress it together.'

'We'll have a glass of sweet sherry and a mince pie while we do,' Mrs Ledbury declares.

I don't like to turn her down as her papery cheeks are pink with joy, but as I'm driving I'm a bit concerned about drinking. When Mrs Ledbury reappears with two glasses on a tray that are the size of thimbles – particularly small thimbles – I realise that I needn't have worried. I'd probably need about twenty of them to feel even remotely squiffy.

While she fetches the mince pies, I go and get the other box of baubles. I spent last night on the internet researching the very latest in Christmas-tree-decoration styles, but I feel that Mrs Ledbury's taste will be very traditional.

Together we sit on the sofa and open the boxes.

'Oh, my word,' she says. 'How you forget from one year to the next. All of these are so dear to me.'

I'm worried that I don't really have adequate time to go on a trip down Memory Lane for each and every bauble but, similarly, I want this to be special for her. I don't just want to throw up the tree and run. So I force myself to relax while keeping focussed.

The baubles are beautiful, all fashioned from delicate glass. 'These are gorgeous.'

'Some of them are actually from Murano,' she tells me. 'I

bought them when I was there with my husband. We went three times in all. Venice was one of our favourite places.'

I turn them carefully in my hands so that they catch the light. I bet some of these are worth a fortune.

Mrs Ledbury picks one up too. 'We were so happy then,' she sighs.

I drape the tree with strands of tiny white lights that look like little fairy wings and persuade Mrs Ledbury that thick, gaudy tinsel is a bit old hat and that her decorations will be better shown off without it. Instead, I dash out to my car and scrabble around in the boot for some strings of minute silver beads that will set off the pretty fragility of the baubles so much better. I've also got a few pretty artificial branches that I bought the other day, laden with frosted berries. Back in the warmth of the living room, I strip the branches down into individual bits and wire them to the tree. It's so hot in here that I do wonder how long the tree will last.

'Keep an eye on the water in this container,' I tell Mrs Ledbury. 'That will keep the tree perkier.'

'It's looking lovely,' she says.

'Do you want to hand me the baubles now?'

She passes one to me. 'This one was for the birth of my daughter,' she says. It's in the shape of a teardrop. 'It's quite appropriate. She has certainly caused me some tears over the years.'

'She's the one who lives in Australia now?' I remember writing her card.

'Yes. I haven't seen her for many years. Six, I should think. I'm too old to travel out there and they never seem to have the money to come back. There are five of them now. One grandchild I've never seen.'

'That's sad.'

'I have a bauble for each of them.' She hands them to me, reciting each of their names as she does. 'This one is my son's.' A large round ball with delicate frosting on it. 'He doesn't live too far away, but he's busy. Has a very good job.'

I'm beginning not to like Mrs Ledbury's family. She's such a lovely lady. It's plain to see that she's lonely and would love to see more of them.

'He's the one who's coming this weekend,' she adds. 'They have a lot of corporate events to go to before Christmas, that kind of thing. They like to spend the actual holiday on the beach. Thailand this year.'

'Yes. You said.' Selfish buggers.

A lot of the baubles need new wires at the top, so I do that and thread them over the branches until the tree is fully laden. 'Is that just about everything?'

'The angel for the top,' Mrs Ledbury says. 'We mustn't forget her. You'd better unwrap her. I'm frightened that I'll drop her with my old hands. This little one is very special.'

At the bottom of this cardboard box in a wad of yellowing tissue paper, I find the most exquisite glass angel. 'Oh, my goodness. This is beautiful.'

'Yes.' Mrs Ledbury sniffs surreptitiously. 'I had a daughter who died. She was only two months old. She was too tiny to survive. She was, indeed, an angel. I bought this for her.'

I see the yearning in her eyes. 'You should hold her.'

'Yes,' she says.

So I hand her the angel and she cuddles it to her, gently. After tenderly kissing the fragile glass face, she gives her back to me.

Carefully, I lift the angel into place. Then I switch on the lights. The tree sparkles in the corner of the room, dispelling any hint of winter gloom, shining brightly.

Mrs Ledbury's face lights up. 'Doesn't she look just lovely?'

I realise that this isn't about wanting her Christmas tree up early, it's about having her children around her. All of them. Then I give her a hug and we both cry together.

Chapter Twelve

They were doing a cell 'grab'. This usually happened when a prisoner had kicked off, set fire to his bed, tried to top himself – something like that. Jim was sure, in this case, that it wasn't necessary. If only the officer who'd pressed the green emergency button had come to see him first.

It was Smudge who was refusing to come out of his cell. A dozen officers crowded round the door, all tooled up in visors, stab jackets, slash-proof gloves, batons. There was no need for it. Kieran was a danger to no one but himself. Everyone was shouting and Jim knew that he'd react badly to that.

With a weary sigh, Jim joined in. 'Stand back. Stand back,' he yelled at his colleagues. He hated to raise his voice. But sometimes it was the only way to make yourself heard above the din. The other officers could often be just as noisy as the lads and he knew that he'd lose the battle with the softly-softly approach on this one.

Everyone else had been put on lock-down and Smudge's cellmate, Rozzer, was nowhere to be seen. They must have banged him in with someone else for the time being until the situation calmed down. Jim pushed his way to the front of the scrum so that he could see what was happening. Smudge cowered in the corner of his cell, half hidden by his bed. There was blood pouring down his face and smeared down the wall behind him.

'Head banging?' Jim asked.

Someone to one side nodded. It was clear that the lad had been nutting the wall in frustration. From the state of his face, he might have broken his nose.

It was a pitiful sight. Why they'd felt the need to wear slash gloves for this, he had no idea. Jim held his colleagues back with his arm and lifted his visor. 'Smudge,' he said. 'What's the deal?'

The young lad just shook his head. Jim could see, amid the blood, tears rolling down his cheeks. The other officers finally fell silent. 'If I get rid of this lot, will you talk to me?'

'Will they put me in Seg, Jim?'

'Seg' or the Segregation Unit was something that all prisoners dreaded. It was the isolation block where they kept all the loony tune offenders. The ones who rocked in corners, the ones who talked to God, the ones you couldn't turn your back on for a second. The ones who, in reality, should have been in maximum-security mental institutions, not Bovingdale. They were on suicide watch, observed night and day by the specialist mental-health nurses.

'I don't think so, lad.'

Smudge cried some more. 'I don't want to go.'

'If you've hurt yourself, they'll more likely take you to Healthcare.'

Smudge looked relieved at that.

'Let's talk about it,' Jim said. 'You don't need this lot, do you? Let me know that you'll be nice and quiet. I'll get them to find Rozzer for you, if you want.'

Smudge nodded.

'That means you'll be a good lad? No hurting anyone? No hurting yourself?'

Smudge nodded again. Self-harming was commonplace in here. The lads were allowed to buy plastic safety razors, ostensibly to shave, but most of them were used to cut themselves. Smudge was a past master at it. He had a line of silver scars along the length of his inner arms. The Healthcare nurse had told Jim that his thighs were cut to ribbons too. They'd had a lad in here once who'd inserted a piece of broken plastic spoon into his own arm through a cut. By the time they'd realised it, the lad's arm had been severely infected and eventually he'd had to lose it. Tragic. It was the last thing that he wanted for Smudge.

'You've not got a razor?'

A pause and then Smudge tossed the sliver of blade to the concrete cell floor. An audible sigh came from the team behind him. Perhaps they had been right to kit up. Sometimes you thought you knew prisoners so well that you could let your guard down. It wasn't always the right thing to do.

'We're good now?'

Again Smudge nodded.

'Promise me.'

The lad looked up at him. He was a pitiful sight. 'Yeah,' he whispered.

Jim turned to his colleagues. 'All right, lads. I'll take it from here.' He loosened his helmet. 'Will one of you go and find Rozzer and bring him here?'

He took off the helmet, put his baton back into its holster and stepped inside. He left the cell door open, knowing that one of his colleagues, at least, would be waiting just outside on the landing as back-up in case anything kicked off again.

Jim sat down on the bed opposite Smudge. 'Are you going to get up now? No one's coming in.'

Smudge wiped his sleeve across his face, covering it with blood.

'You've probably done your nose, lad,' Jim observed.

The boy touched it gingerly and winced.

70

'I'll have to take you down to Healthcare. They'll want to clean you up properly.'

After a few moments' consideration, Smudge slowly inched himself up onto his own bed and sat with his back against the wall, knees hugged into his scrawny chest. He looked about twelve years old.

Jim took his time. 'Want to tell me what it's all about?'

Smudge shook his head.

'Easier to tell me,' Jim said. 'Otherwise you *will* be going straight to Seg to get one of the psychiatrists to prise it out of you. You know what a pain that is.' Smudge had been taken to see the psychs often enough to know that he didn't want to go down that route. 'Let's see if we can't sort it out without all that, eh?'

He waited but there was no answer. There was no rush. He was on shift all afternoon. All he had to do was get to Cassie's event for six o'clock, make nice and give drinks out. Hopefully, this could all be done and dusted by then.

'It was all going so well, lad,' Jim tried again. 'You've been making good progress. You and Rozzer get on great. You haven't had a fall-out, have you?'

'No,' Smudge said.

'Then why the long mush? You're ugly enough without trying to bust up your own conk.'

A glimmer of a smile touched the lad's lips.

'You're getting out in a few weeks,' Jim reminded him. 'You don't want to do anything stupid to set that back.'

The lad's head hung lower. Blood dripped onto his trackie bottoms. Then it dawned on Jim. That was probably what was troubling him. Jim remembered what had happened the last time Smudge had been released.

He softened his voice. 'You are OK about getting out this time?'

71

At that the lad burst into tears. Deep racking sobs shook his body. Jim wanted to go and put his arm round him, comfort him, but that wasn't possible. If the professional barrier didn't remain in place, then he'd be answering to the governor. Instead he waited for the lad's tears to subside.

'I'm frightened.' Smudge's voice was small. 'At first I thought it was scary in here, but this is a walk in the park compared to out there.' He flicked a thumb towards the one tiny window high up in the wall.

'There's help,' Jim said. 'The probation service will be keeping an eye on you and there's a charity that we can put you in touch with. They're good at sorting out somewhere for you to live.'

'I was living in a wheelie bin, Jim. Nicking food. No one helped me then. I can't go back to that.'

'There's no need to.'

'I want a job,' Smudge said. 'My own place. A key to let myself in and out. I'm sixteen and I've already been banged up twice. What mad fucker will give me a chance?'

Jim sighed. It was the age-old problem. He'd been at Bovingdale for ten years, seen governments come and go, and no one had managed to sort it. Once cons were on the merry-go-round of crime, it was hard for them to get off even if they wanted to. The easier option was to keep offending, to keep getting banged up until you learned how to be better at it and not get caught. A lot of the regulars were keen to help with that kind of education.

Kieran here was barely literate. It was only because of the lessons he'd had while he was in the unit that he was able to read and write at all. What he'd done at school, God only knows. There were very few jobs that he was going to be able to walk into and, so often, it was easier to get back into thieving.

'Have you talked to Rozzer about this? He's your listener.'

Smudge shook his head. 'He'd think I was a wuss.'

'He gets out about the same time as you. Rozzer might be feeling the same way. You should talk to him.'

'I'm worried that he won't want to see me when we're out of here.' The tears started again. 'He's the only proper mate I've ever had. What if we go and live in different parts of the country? What if he goes back to his family and forgets me? What if we get banged up again and get put in different units? Then what?'

Rozzer stood in the doorway, flanked by an officer who asked, 'All right, Jim?'

Jim nodded. 'Yeah.'

The officer turned and left Rozzer behind. 'What have you been doing, you stupid cu—?'

'Language,' Jim said.

'Sod,' Rozzer corrected himself. He came into the cell and sat down next to Smudge. 'You look a mess.'

'Want to tell Rozzer what's wrong?' Jim prompted.

Smudge shrugged.

The lad was right to be frightened. It was going to take every ounce of his strength to keep on the straight and narrow. Jim just hoped that he would make it on the outside. He looked at the two awkward and lost teenagers in front of him and his heart squeezed. He hoped they would both make it.

Chapter Thirteen

I arrive at the Old Town Hall only a little bit later than I planned. And I am only a little bit stressed about it. When I get there, however, the venue is looking good. The large Christmas tree that I ordered is standing proud in the corner, ready for my titivation, and it's a smasher. Big, glossy and green. The fresh pine scent that it's giving off is heavenly.

I found an enormous Christmas warehouse online that's not far from Hemel where they sell decorations for domestic settings as well as for commercial use. So I shot over there a couple of days ago and stocked up on giant baubles and garlands. They also have those fantastic illuminated figures for gardens and I was itching to buy loads, but no one has asked me to use them yet.

As I'm bringing in all my boxes from the car, the champagne and glasses are delivered, along with a case of red wine for me to mull. Recipe obtained from the internet, of course.

I call Jim again but, as it has done all day, his phone goes to voicemail. He didn't even ring me at lunchtime today and I'm worried that he's forgotten about tonight, even though I reminded him a dozen times. He seems to have a lot on his mind at the moment.

There's not a moment to waste. So I sign for the delivery and then set it all up in the kitchen. I bring in from the boot of the car the oranges and spices that I'll need and, with the red wine, leave them to one side to heat up later.

I collect the rest of my decorations and then move my car to the car park in the square so I'm not blocking anyone in. As soon as I'm back, I get cracking on dressing the tree and making the room ready for the party. I set up my stepladder so that I can reach the top of the tree. This time a glittering golden star will grace the pinnacle, not a beautiful angel. I've put a Christmas playlist on my iPod, which I connect to their sound system and let the songs fill the space to get me in the mood. Since I started this business, I think that I've grown even keener on Christmas than I was before. I just love it all. I've never felt happier than when I'm dressing a Christmas tree and I can only hope that this is something that I can make a living doing.

For this tree, I go for a very traditional look. Swathes of red and gold tinsel, large baubles in the same colours. The lights are shaped like candles and give out a soft, mellow glow, not harsh like the new bright and twinkly LED ones. After an hour, I'm finished and I stand back to admire my handiwork. It looks lovely. But no time to go all dreamy, I've just got a few minutes to grab a quick coffee before I start on inflating balloons. No rest for Mrs Christmas!

I make a table ready for the mince pies with a gold cloth and displays of pretty scarlet poinsettia plants in gold pots that I bought from the garden centre. Next step is to learn a little more internet floristry so that I'm comfortable with doing my own table decorations, maybe even a swag for a mantelpiece in case I'm asked.

Glancing up from my helium canister, I see Gaby arrive. I've already got a hundred balloons blown up, beribboned and arranged artistically around the room.

'Wow,' my sister says as she takes in the room. 'Looking good.' She kisses my cheek. 'Really Christmassy.'

'That's the idea.' I risk a look at my watch. It's already five o'clock. 'Flip, is that the time?'

'It is indeed. What do you want me to do?'

'You could start to put out the mince pies and the nibbles, if that's OK. You look lovely,' I tell her.

My sister really does look nice in a black pencil skirt and fitted white shirt. She's put on some make-up and her hair is swept up. It's the first time in years I've seen her wearing heels. I look at her and my heart fills with love. Sometimes I feel that Gaby is older than her years. She didn't have much of a childhood as she was always having to look after me. And here she is again, helping me out when I need it.

'It's the only chance I've had to dress up in ages.' She smoothes down her skirt. 'That's quite sad when you think about it.'

'We'll make sure to have a couple of celebratory glasses at the end of the night,' I assure her. 'Assuming all goes well! I'm done here now. I'll pop into the kitchen to get the mulled wine going. Better keep the drink flowing.'

'Not so much that they don't appreciate your lovely decorations.'

In the kitchen, I slice the oranges and mix the spices. I find a couple of enormous pans in the cupboards and pour in the wine. When it's simmering nicely, I slip into the ladies' loo to change out of my jeans and sweatshirt and into my waitressing clothes. I'm also wearing a black skirt and white shirt. I've brought the same along for Jim – white shirt, black trousers – but they're now accompanied by the Santa outfit, which I've yet to tell him about.

Too soon, it's a quarter to six and – after looking at my watch every three seconds – I am just beginning to panic when Jim arrives. His face is drawn and he looks as if he could do with a few beers and a night in front of the telly, rather than doing a waiter's shift at the end of his long day.

'Everything OK?' I ask.

'Yeah.' He shrugs.

'Tough day?'

'Yeah. I had a shower before I left work, I've just got to get into my clean shirt. You did bring one?'

'Yes. It's all here.' I chew my lip. 'There's one other thing. I've been trying to call you all day—'

'I know,' Jim says. 'I only just got your messages. We've had something on today. Haven't had the chance to ring back.'

'They sort of wanted a Santa. At the last minute.' I whip the Santa suit from the top of the nearest cardboard box and wiggle it at him.

His face falls.

'I was sure that you wouldn't mind.'

Jim sighs. 'Not today, Cassie. Any other day, I could probably gear myself up to be Santa. But a ho-ho-ho is totally beyond me now.'

'Have a drink,' I suggest. 'Or two. Loosen up. I know it's tough, but I've said that I could do it. I've got the suit and everything.'

Now his shoulders sag.

'Is it such a big deal?' Normally Jim will do anything for me. I can't see that this is a massive ask. 'You might enjoy it. All you've got to do is be jolly and hand out some USB sticks.'

'It's the being jolly part that I'm struggling with.'

'What else can I do, Jim? I can't let them down.'

'Someone might recognise me.'

'With this big white beard on?'

He eyes the suit with contempt and a certain amount of resignation. 'You want me to put it on now?'

77

'In half an hour or so,' I say, my heart lifting. 'Let's get everyone welcomed and settled with drinks, then you can slip away to get ready for about seven. You'll look fantastic. You'll *be* fantastic.' I give him a grateful kiss.

'You owe me for this, Cassie,' he says. And he doesn't smile or laugh as he normally would.

Chapter Fourteen

When the guests begin to arrive I turn up the Christmas music to get the party started. Gaby, Jim and I drift around serving the champagne and the mulled wine. The atmosphere is lovely. Very jovial. The room is full to bursting point now and there's a friendly hubbub of chatter. Ideally, it would have been nice to have had real musicians, but the budget didn't go quite that far. Maybe next year, if they have me back.

We circulate with the nibbles and mince pies, making sure that the food and wine are flowing. The business cards that I've scattered discreetly around the room are disappearing with satisfying regularity and I'm making sure that I replenish them as I top up the glasses.

Janet from Hemel Hempstead Means Business comes to congratulate me for doing such a lovely job. 'Wonderful, Cassie,' she gushes. 'Simply wonderful. So many people have commented on the beautiful Christmas tree. It's the prettiest party we've ever had. I'm quite looking forward to Christmas now.' Her cheeks are flushed, probably from the glass of mulled wine that she's knocking back.

I'm pleased that it's going so well, but there's a knot of anxiety in my stomach that probably won't disappear until it's all over and I've packed away my boxes.

'The mince pies are divine, dear,' someone says to me as she helps herself to another one. I think we could have done with twice as many tonight and I make a mental note.

'Thank you. I'll pass the compliment on to my baker.' I wink at Gaby and give her a sly thumbs-up sign.

It's nearly a quarter to seven, so I sidle over to Jim and say, 'It's probably time that you put on the Santa suit.'

He gives me a dark look again, but it's a shade less black than the previous one, so I take that as a good sign. 'I'll come with you to help.'

Leaving Gaby to man the fort, I slip away with Jim, grab the Santa costume and steer him towards the walk-in pantry.

'In here?' He baulks when he sees the small space in between the stacks of tins and crockery.

'We can't risk the loos. Someone might see you.'

'And realise I'm not the real Santa?'

'Indulge me,' I plead.

So, in the storeroom amid the tins of tomatoes and bottles of cooking oil, Jim strips off his shirt and trousers and hauls on the Santa costume. 'It's massive,' he says. 'I need to be about two stone heavier to fill this.'

'I have a solution.' I disappear to delve into one of my cardboard boxes. Minutes later, I'm back in the pantry, clutching a pillow from our bed. 'Stick this up your front and I'll buckle you in.'

'You've thought of everything.'

I meet his eyes. 'I hope so.'

'It's going really well, Cassie,' he assures me. 'Nothing to worry about.'

'Thanks.'

Then we both huff and puff, stuffing the pillow into his outfit, and I tighten the thick black belt. I fix on Jim's beard and then his hat. He puts his big work boots on and there are black gloves too.

'I'm roasting alive in here,' he complains.

'You look fantastic,' I tell him. 'Just like the real Santa.'

'Ho-naffing-ho,' he chimes.

I put my arms round him. 'Day that bad?'

'Yes,' he sighs. 'Bloody awful.'

'Want to tell me about it?'

'No. This is your night to sparkle. I'll get over myself and go and wow the boys and girls.'

'Catch them quick before they're all pissed.'

'Got my sack of swag?'

I show him the festively striped sack that I filled with the corporate branded goodies that Janet left out for me. 'I think there's enough for a couple of presents for everyone.'

Jim heaves the sack onto his shoulder. 'It's certainly heavy enough.'

I kiss him tenderly. 'Thanks for doing this for me.'

He raises his eyebrows. 'Wish me luck.'

Following him to the kitchen door, I stand and watch as Jim emerges into the fray and bellows out a hearty, 'HO-HO-HO! MERRY CHRISTMAS!'

He's really very good. Then I realise I should top up my tray again and make sure that everyone's drinks are replenished. Having done that I hurry back out. In my haste, I bump straight into a man who's just turning to walk in my direction. I try to pull up to a sharp halt but it's too late. My tray collides with his chest and, of course, it's a glass that's bearing mulled wine and not champagne that topples over and tips onto his crisp, white shirt.

'Oh God!' I say. 'I'm really, really sorry.' The dark-red stain is spreading across his stomach, making him look as if he's been stabbed somewhere vital.

'No harm done,' he says magnanimously. 'Well, just to my shirt.'

We both look down at the mess. 'Come into the kitchen, quickly,' I beg. 'If I don't sponge that off now, it will stain. You'll never get it out once it dries.'

'It really doesn't matter,' he says. 'I was just leaving.' Perhaps he can see the tears forming in my eyes, as he touches my arm and adds kindly, 'Really. It's not a problem. It's just an old thing that I threw on.'

I know that he's trying to make light of it, but the very last thing you want is to tip a drink over an important guest. 'Two seconds,' I beg. 'It will take me two seconds to sponge it off. It would make me feel much better.'

He laughs and concedes, 'Let's do it, then.'

Together we turn towards the kitchen. I ditch my tray at the first opportunity and, grabbing a clean J-cloth, I run it under the cold tap and get to work, dabbing at the stain while my victim stands patiently and lets me.

After a few seconds, I step back and appraise my efforts. 'It's not gone completely,' I confess, 'but it's a lot better. Please let me pay for your shirt to be cleaned.'

'There's really no need,' he says. 'You've been kind enough. Thank you.'

At that, operation clean-up finished, I look up at him properly for the first time. This poor, unfortunate man with wine spilled all down his front is, as it turns out, very handsome. I should think he's a bit older than me – in his early forties perhaps – but he looks as if he's had a life of ease. He's tall, very slim, with an elegant bearing. His hair is brown, glossy, his eyes the same rich shade of brown. Curls that could easily be wayward are groomed within an inch of their lives. His tanned skin suggests a surfeit of sunny holidays. Dashing would be the word I'd use to sum him up. Teamed with the white shirt – albeit now stained – he wears a black linen jacket and jeans. An outfit that looks beautifully tailored and expensive. Now I feel even worse about my clumsiness.

'Janet said that your company has set up this event,' he says.

'Yes. It's a new venture for me. I'll organise anything festive. Can I give you a card?'

'I'm afraid that I'm not much looking forward to Christmas this year,' he confesses.

'Perhaps I can change that?' I suggest, then realise it sounds far too much like flirting and flush.

He laughs. 'Perhaps you could.'

I fumble for a card and hand it to him. He glances over it. 'Calling Mrs Christmas!' A chuckle. 'Great idea.'

'That's me.' I hold out my hand. 'Cassie Smith.'

He takes it in fingers that are strong, confident. He's clearly a man who shakes hands on a regular basis. 'Pleased to meet you. I'm Carter Randall.' I seem to know that name but can't for the life of me think why. 'Business good?' he asks as I'm busy racking my brains.

'I'm off to a promising start.'

'You should come along to our Hemel Hempstead Means Business get-togethers. It's only once a month and it's very useful networking. They'd be great for contacts.'

'I might just do that.'

'What sort of Christmas would you put together for me?' There's a smile sparkling in those dark-brown eyes.

'I can do anything from writing a few Christmas cards to choosing a gift for someone special.'

'Ah,' he says, sadly. 'Probably won't be needing that particular service this year.'

'I can also organise your whole Christmas – top to bottom – if that's what you'd like.'

'That definitely sounds more appealing.'

'Call me if you need any advice.'

He smiles at me and then looks at my card again. 'I might just do that.'

'If you'd excuse me, I'd better get back to the guests.'

'Ah, yes.' He checks his watch. 'I must go too.'

'It's been nice meeting you, Mr Randall. Thank you very much for being so understanding.'

'Carter, please,' he says. 'I hope we meet again.' Then he looks at me steadily and I go all funny. Hot, cold, shivery and weird. 'I'll definitely ring you, Cassie Christmas,' he says. 'You can count on it.'

And with that he pockets my card and leaves.

Chapter Fifteen

All the guests have gone. The lights from the Christmas tree are still on and although the room is empty, it still looks very festive. Turning the music down so that it's soft background noise, I sweep the last of the debris from the floor and lean on my broom. I'm exhausted.

'Glass of fizz for us all,' Gaby says and holds up three flutes. 'I think we've earned it.'

'You're telling me,' Jim says and collapses into the nearest chair. Gaby gives him a glass.

I put aside my broom and go to sit on his lap. 'Thanks,' I say. I'm handed a glass too and we all clink them together. 'Couldn't have done it without either of you.'

'It was a great success, Cassie,' my sis says. 'You should be proud of yourself.'

'I am,' I admit.

There's nothing quite so strengthening for the self-confidence as doing a hard day's graft and I'm grateful to be back in the world of work again. Even though I've been on the go since first thing this morning and my feet are *killing* me! It's all for the greater good.

Gaby knocks back her fizz. 'Better get a wriggle on. Ryan will be wondering where I've got to.'

'You go home,' I say.

'Are you sure there's nothing else I can do?'

'We'll finish up here. Don't you worry. I'm going to have one of your mince pies before I do anything else. They were a big hit. I hid two in the kitchen before they all went.'

'I took a few decent-sized orders for office parties.' Gaby glows. 'I'll give you the details tomorrow.'

'Well done, you.'

I'm so glad that this is working out for Gaby too and that we're able to do something as sisters. It feels nice.

'Love you,' Gaby says as she kisses me and then Jim.

'Love you too,' I say. And off she goes.

When we're alone and all is quiet, Jim lets out a sigh and pulls me close to him. Because we were so busy serving drinks, he didn't even have time to change back into his waiter's outfit and he's still dressed up as Santa. I prod him playfully in his pillowy stomach. He runs his hand up my thigh, under my skirt. His fingers are hot, familiar, and I get a sudden urge to make love to him.

'Hmm,' I say. 'This feels slightly sexy in a pervy way. I've never shagged Santa.'

'Hmm,' Jim echoes. 'I've never shagged one of my little helpers.'

Buoyed by the gulped champagne, I giggle. 'Shall I lock the door?'

'Oh yeah,' Jim says.

So I jump off his lap and run to the door, making sure it's securely locked. The last thing I want is Janet from Hemel Hempstead Means Business turning up here again at an inopportune moment. Not after everything has gone so well.

'Let me take this off.' Jim tugs at his beard when I get back to him.

'I think you should leave it on,' I say.

'Really? And the pillow?'

'Come to mama, big boy.'

Jim laughs and it's the first time that I've seen his face relax all evening. This is a good idea. I take his beard in my hand and lead him towards the Christmas tree. We lie down together on the carpet beneath it and I wriggle out of my skirt. I tug at Santa's big belt and put my hand down his trousers, feeling very slutty.

Jim laughs. 'I can't take this seriously.'

I giggle as I straddle him and bounce heartily on his pillow, making him double up with laughter. Then I pull off his beard and hat, fumbling with the buttons on his costume as he pulls at the ones on my blouse. We're not laughing now and are both filled with lust. I don't know if being unemployed is a passion killer but I haven't really felt like sex in months. Not properly. I've gone through the motions for Jim's sake, but my heart, my body hasn't really been in it. But now I'm mad for him. It seems that hard work and the adrenaline buzz of success have got all my juices flowing again.

Soon, our clothing is in total disarray and we're naked in each other's arms. With a relieved sigh, Jim eases into my body and we hold each other, not moving. The Christmas lights twinkle.

'I love you,' Jim says, above me.

'I love you too.'

Then we make love, silently, softly with the sounds of Slade and 'Here it is, Merry Christmas' filling the room.

Chapter Sixteen

Jim climbed over the pile of presents that occupied most of the living room. You could hardly move for them. Even the sofas were stacked high. Somewhere underneath them were his trainers. But where? Cassie caught his look. 'It's not a problem,' he said, holding up his hands.

'They'll be gone by the time you're home tonight,' she promised. 'I have to get them out today.'

'Really, don't worry. It's a minor inconvenience that our home has been turned into Santa's distribution depot. You're loving it and it's certainly bringing in the dosh.'

Since the night at the Hemel Hempstead Means Business party, the phone hadn't stopped ringing. Cassie had been booked to organise three more Christmas events for small companies and one home party. Plus there were a dozen bookings for tree dressing, present buying and wrapping, and goodness knows what else. Her sister's oven was probably busier than Mr Kipling's, given the rate at which she was churning out mince pies.

'If it carries on like this, we could probably do with an extra pair of hands – or even two. I might have to see if the Job Centre can send me a couple of casual workers to do some gift wrapping.'

She could be right. Even with all hands to the pump, they were struggling to keep up. From the minute he came home from work to the minute he fell into bed, Jim was doing nothing but writing Christmas cards, wrapping presents and scouring the internet for stuff that Cassie needed. Still it was only for a short period of time. Come January, their lives would be back to normal again. Except that they'd have a few very welcome extra pounds in the bank.

Cassie wound her arms round his neck, then got distracted and straightened his collar. 'You're going to work early.'

He wasn't on shift until two o'clock and it wasn't yet noon. 'I've got something to do.'

'Anything I should know about?'

'Two of the lads at the unit are due to leave soon. I'm going to have a word with a charity I know that helps offenders to rehabilitate.'

'It's not like you to get so involved.'

'I know.' Jim shrugged. 'I've got a bit of a soft spot for these two. They're not bad lads. Not really. They've just been unfortunate.'

'I'm sure someone must have said that about the Kray twins.'

Jim laughed. 'You're probably right. But I feel that if I can do something to smooth their way on release, then I should do it. Some kids you know you're going to see back in the unit whatever you do or whatever anyone else does for them. I think it might be different with these two. They just need a bit of luck.'

'Smudge and Rozzer again?'

'They're a cut above your average young criminal,' Jim said with a smile. 'Smudge's real name is Kieran Holman – he's the most vulnerable. He's actually more scared of getting out than he is of being in the unit. I'm worried about him. When he was first arrested he was living rough in a wheelie bin.'

'That's awful.'

'Yeah,' Jim agreed. 'How the other half live. The other's called Andrew Walton. He's got it rough in a different way. He's a copper's son who's been disowned by his family.'

'Tough love?'

'Something like that. I don't know the details. But it's going to be even tougher for him out there alone. He's from a fairly middle-class background and just got in with the wrong crowd. He won't know what's hit him when he gets out.'

'You don't think his parents will relent?'

'Who knows?' Jim said with a shrug. 'It's not looking likely at the moment. They haven't been to see him once all the time he's been in the unit.'

'You don't normally talk much about your prisoners.'

Cassie was right. It was his policy to keep everything that happened at work to himself. Sometimes it was better that what happened in Bovingdale stayed in Bovingdale. Leaving his day behind those imposing walls made it easier to feel cleaner when he got home. Literally, if he'd spent a day scrubbing down after a dirty protest. '*I scrubbed some little oik's shit off the walls today, love.*' What wife or girlfriend wanted to hear about that kind of thing over the dinner table? There weren't many aspects of his job that made great social chit-chat at parties.

'They'll be gone soon,' Jim said. 'And the next lot of scallies will be in their place.'

'What can this charity do for them?'

'I hope that they'll be able to find some way of keeping them together. They've become quite close and, to be honest, they could do with leaning on each other for support.'

'The prisoners get help when they come out, don't they?'

'Yes, but it's of variable quality and frequency. The government cuts are hitting hard. Their main priority won't be the lads' relationship. With the best will in the world, social services just want to tick some boxes. I know these lads and I'm worried that either one of them could go to pieces without the other. If they can stay together, I really believe that they've got a good chance of turning their lives around.'

'Good luck with that then.'

'Thanks.' Jim eyed the pile of presents and nodded towards them. 'Good luck with *that*.'

'I've been thinking, Jim,' she said. 'With all that's going on, shall we not bother with Christmas presents for each other this year?'

'It's up to you, love. Wouldn't you like something special after all this hard work?'

'Maybe we could treat ourselves in the new year when it's all died down. Just something small. We've got a lot of debts racked up. We'll have a better picture of where we are when I know what I've actually earned from all this, see if we've got any cash to spare.'

He shrugged. 'Sounds sensible.'

'We could just have a romantic dinner at home one night and exchange cards. That would be nice, don't you think?'

'Yeah. If you're sure that's what you want.'

'I don't want to put either of us under any more pressure than we have to.'

'At least I'll be able to write my card prettily now,' he teased.

'I think your calligraphy is better than mine,' she conceded. 'Marginally.'

'I'll see you later,' Jim said and he kissed her before he picked a careful path to the door.

The charity Starting Over was housed in one of the less salubrious parts of Hemel Hempstead. Though, in truth, none of it was really awful – not compared to some of the sink estates in London where some of the lads came from.

Starting Over ran six flats. Most of them were single units with just two for a pair sharing. If Jim could get Smudge and Rozzer into one of the shared places, he'd consider that a result. The building was less than inspiring to look at. It was a two-storey, flat-topped box covered in grey pebble-dash, but Jim knew from past experience that the flats were well maintained. They might not be up there alongside the Ritz, but neither were they damp, rat-infested holes run by sleazy landlords who charged rip-off rents for those who couldn't provide good references or credit checks.

Jim rang the bell. The manager of the block, Vincent Benlow, was a big, black guy the size of a small block of flats himself. He and Jim had been at school together, in the same class. Once upon a time, before life got in the way, they had played five-a-side footy together. They occasionally bumped into each other in the pub in Leverstock Green, which they still called the White Horse although it was now called something else.

Vincent, Jim knew, stood for no messing from his residents. Either they toed the line at Halfway House or they were out on their ear. Jim thought that living there with someone like Vincent to watch over them would be a good thing for Smudge and Rozzer. He could only hope that there was room for them as places were always in demand and he knew he should have thought of it much, much sooner.

Vincent, who had a shaved head, a soul patch and a ready smile, answered the door and clapped Jim on the back with one of his big, bear-sized hands. 'Man,' he cried. 'Ain't seen you in so long!'

'Busy, mate,' Jim said.

'Ain't we all. What brings you to my door now, man?'

'Favour to ask,' Jim said as he followed Vincent through to the kitchen. Without asking if Jim wanted a drink, Vincent automatically flicked on the kettle. A lot of Vincent's counselling was done with a strong mug of tea in hand.

In addition to the flats, the residents had the use of a laundry room, this tiny kitchen and a light, bright communal living room that looked out onto the scrubby garden where they could all get together and talk or just hang out rather than sitting in their rooms by themselves. Vincent was on site full time and had been for years. A couple of other social workers gave him back-up and a handful of volunteers took up the slack on other duties. Jim dropped in every now and then to lend a hand, particularly if some DIY needed doing. Then he'd get alongside one of the lads and show him some basic skills.

'How's life up at Bovingdale?'

'Not so bad,' Jim said.

'Ever thought about moving on?'

'Not really. Probably in for the long haul.'

Vincent made them instant coffee, a cheap supermarket brand. It tasted vile, but Jim was grateful for it and hugged the chipped mug. Vincent waited for him to speak.

'I've got two lads,' Jim said. 'Coming out soon. I'm worried about them. They've become great mates while they've been inside and they'll be completely lost without each other.'

'Harsh.'

'Wondered if you'd got any room coming up here for them?'

Vincent shook his head ruefully. 'Not on the cards, mate. Totally rammed. As usual.'

'Thought as much. It was worth an ask.' Jim shrugged, but was disappointed nevertheless.

'It's important to you?'

'Yeah,' Jim admitted. It suddenly mattered a lot that Andrew and Kieran would be all right after they left the tender loving care of HM Young Offenders' Unit, Bovingdale. 'Keep me in mind if anything does come up.'

'You never know, Jim. People come. People go.'

'You've got my mobile number?'

Vincent waved his phone at him to indicate that he had. Jim downed his coffee.

'Could do with a hand with some painting, man, if you've got a couple of hours to spare?'

'It's madness before Christmas,' Jim said. 'Cassie's started this new business. Calling Mrs Christmas! It's gone crazy. I've been roped in to do things I never thought I'd do in my lifetime. But, after Christmas, I'm all yours.'

'I'll hold you to it.'

'Don't forget to call me if you can take in two lads.'

As he walked back to his car, Jim wondered what else he could do to help Smudge and Rozzer as he couldn't bear to think of them out in the big, bad world on their own. Not so close to Christmas.

Chapter Seventeen

It's just after one and I'm making magnificent progress with the living-room Christmas-present mountain. Soon I'll be able to see carpet! Never have I needed so much double-sided tape. I'm running low on my second roll when my phone rings.

'Calling Mrs Christmas!' I trill happily.

'This is Carter Randall's office,' a posh voice says.

'Oh.'

The man I met/threw wine down at the Hemel Hempstead Means Business event.

'Mr Randall would like you to come up to the house at three o'clock this afternoon.'

'The house?'

'Randall Court in Little Gaddesden.'

'Oh.'

I know where Little Gaddesden is, but have no idea where Randall Court is. Sounds like an office block.

'He wants to talk to you about Christmas.'

Then I'm his woman.

'Yes,' I say. 'Yes, I can do three o'clock.' Good job. Sounds as if Mr Randall has already decided that I'll be there then. 'What is it that I can help with?'

'Mr Randall will discuss that with you.'

'OK. What's the address?'

'Just come to Little Gaddesden. If you're driving from Hemel, go to the far end of the village. Randall Court is clearly sign-posted. I'm sure you'll find us easily enough. We'll see you at three.' And she hangs up.

Huh. OK. We'll see what Mr Randall has to say about Christmas. I seem to remember that he said he wasn't much looking forward to it. Wonder why? No doubt I'll find out later.

Then, I don't know what grips me, but I get a sudden urge to wash my hair and get out of my jeans and, generally, not look so much like a tramp. So I run round the shower, wash and dry my hair, and put on smarter trousers and a fluffy red jumper that looks quite festive.

At two-thirty, I'm in my car and heading out to Little Gaddesden. It's a bright sunny day. The crisp frost that covered everything this morning is now lingering only in shady patches where the weak winter sun has failed to reach. It's stunning up here when the autumn leaves are in full colour, but even the dark bleakness of the winter trees holds me transfixed. This is a really beautiful area. Jim and I love to come up here and walk in Ashridge Park at the weekends. There's a magnificent bluebell wood in the springtime that we come to see as often as we can when the flowers are in bloom.

The car parks are always overflowing and the park is filled with families whose kids sport flowery wellies and have those robust 4x4 prams that are all the rage now. When I see them, it never fails to make me want a toddler of my own to swing between our arms and hoist, laughingly, onto Jim's shoulders. I picture a little girl with a rosebud mouth and blonde curls even though both of her would-be parents have dark hair. It also makes me want to own a dog. A small, yapping one with attitude that will love us unconditionally. I hope that one day, now that

96

I'm back in the world of work, both of these things will be achievable rather than seeming like a distant dream.

I climb steadily upwards, crunching my sticky gears merrily, a festive song in my heart.

The village of Little Gaddesden sits up on a hill surrounded by miles and miles of the spectacular Ashridge Forest. This place is posh. Seriously posh. I think it is compulsory for all adults to wear Hunter wellies – even in bed. We've been so busy that, unusually, we haven't been up here for weeks now and suddenly, as I swing into the village, the very prettiness of it all takes my breath away.

The trainline into London, with a quick service into town, is a stone's throw away so the area is home to all kinds of minor celebrities who like to escape 'the smoke' at the weekends. Hang out in the one and only pub and you'll catch a glimpse of people off the telly. Jim and I have seen newsreaders, the woman – I think – who does *Antiques Roadshow* and a couple of well-known footballers whose names escape me. There's a rumour that Formula One racing driver Mark Webber lives here. But then it seems that everywhere I go there's a rumour that Formula One racing driver Mark Webber lives there. Perhaps he just has a lot of houses.

The benefit of all the trees being bare at this time of year is that you can catch a glimpse of the properties normally secreted inside thick copses and tucked away down long winding drives. I slow down as I pass house after house, all of which are unfeasibly large. As instructed, I head to the other end of the village and then I see a prominent sign for Randall Court. Perhaps I shouldn't be surprised that Randall Court is one of the large houses. What does surprise me, though, is that it seems to be the very biggest one of all. By a long way.

It's so imposing that I actually pull over to the grass verge and hesitate before driving in. I take a moment to check the aluminium name plaque on the stone gateposts against the note I've scribbled on a pink Post-It just in case there's another, somewhat smaller and less scary Randall Court and I'm in entirely the wrong place. Of course, I should have checked it out on Google Earth before I got here, but it didn't occur to me. I might not have been quite so shocked then.

'Bloody hell,' I gasp to no one but myself.

This looks like the kind of place that should have an entryphone system with someone bossy at the other end trying very hard to keep me out. But it doesn't. The tall gates are thrown open and, despite wishing my car was a posh Audi or anything other than a crappy ten-year-old Clio, I decide to go for it. Too late to wimp out now. So I take a deep breath and thank the heavens above and all that is good that I had a shower and changed into something quite smart. Then I crunch my elderly gears and, tentatively, make my way down the sweeping, tree-lined drive towards the awesome country pile in front of me.

I go slowly, absorbing my surroundings, which are truly spectacular. The route is lined with specimen trees and, even in the depths of winter, a lawn that looks as if it enjoys the tender loving care of Green Thumb on a regular basis. The house, when I approach, is no disappointment from close quarters either. It sits grandly in the midst of its land. It's symmetrical, three storeys tall, I'd say, and the same wide. There's a door in the centre flanked by banks of large, airy Georgian-style windows. It's relatively modern, but built in a mellow brick that ensures it blends well into the landscape. I can't begin to imagine how much this place cost.

I drive up and park in front of the bank of five garages next to a flashy silver Bentley. Surely I won't be blocking anyone in here. I get out of the Clio and lock the door. Then I laugh to myself.

Like anyone's going to steal my Clio and leave that Bentley behind.

Before I walk up to the door, I straighten my trousers and jumper. I ring the bell and, as I wait – for an absolute age – for someone to come, all I can hear is the sound of my own heart thumping.

Chapter Eighteen

Eventually, a pretty girl comes to let me in. She's probably in her twenties, slim, dark, and wearing tight-fitting jeans and a pale-blue sweater. They look expensive. I wonder if it's the woman I spoke to on the phone, but she sounds younger, chirpier.

'Hello, I'm Cassie Smith. From Calling Mrs Christmas!'

'Oh, hi. I'm Georgina, Mr Randall's assistant. Do come in.'

I step into the vast hall. It's probably bigger than our entire flat. I didn't even know that they made homes so big. I went to my previous boss's house a few times and that was pretty flash, but this is opulence on a whole new scale. It's all decorated in white with chrome flourishes. Mirrors abound. I think the floor might be white marble. Ahead of me the staircase, which I'd guess is solid oak, ascends to a galleried landing. It looks more like a five-star hotel than someone's home and I try not to gape. I think I fail.

'Mr Randall is with his wife at the moment,' Georgina says. 'Do you mind awfully waiting? He shouldn't be too long.'

'No.' I think of all the presents I could be wrapping.

'Take a seat in here,' she says, showing me into a small living room off the hall with two large cream sofas and expensive-looking artworks. 'Can I offer you tea or coffee?'

'Tea would be nice.'

She smiles at me. 'I'll let him know that you're here.'

When she leaves, I walk to the window and look out. The grounds sweep away from the house as far as the eye can see until they merge seamlessly into Ashridge Forest. There's a small formal area by the house, with a pretty terrace and a fountain, but most of what I can see is a vast expanse of immaculate lawn. I don't know how Carter Randall has made his money but, clearly, he has lots of it.

I look around me. There's a white coat draped over the arm of one sofa and a Burberry handbag abandoned next to it. So I take the other sofa and sit patiently, trying to look relaxed. As there's no background music or noise of any kind, I can – if I listen carefully – hear raised voices. A man and a woman are having a right old ding-dong somewhere in the house. The woman's voice in particular seems to be getting louder and louder.

My tea arrives, brought by another older lady who looks as if she might be a long-standing housekeeper as she's comfortable here in a way that I'm not. 'A nice cuppa for you, dearie,' she says cheerfully. 'Shouldn't be long now.'

There's a loud slam from somewhere above me and she raises her eyebrows at me in a knowing way, forgetting that I have no idea about what is so obvious to her. She leaves me to my tea and I anxiously nibble one of the chocolate digestive biscuits she's also brought.

The shouting seems to be reaching a crescendo now and I feel as if I'm intruding on something that I shouldn't. I can't make out what the argument is about, but it's apparent that someone isn't at all happy. Perhaps I should just finish up my tea and biscuits as quickly as I can and tiptoe away. I could simply ring Carter Randall's office and make another appointment. It doesn't really sound like the right time to be talking about Christmas arrangements.

But before I even have time to fully consider my options, the door bursts open and a beautiful and impossibly slender woman crashes into the room, followed, hot on her heels, by Carter Randall.

She pulls up short when she sees me and Carter, still in full flow, careers into the back of her.

'Who on earth are you?' the woman says.

I stand up hastily and overturn my cup as I do. 'Sorry, sorry.' I scrabble around on the tray, trying to right it.

She folds her arms, regarding me coolly.

'Ah,' Carter Randall exclaims. 'It's Mrs Christmas!'

'If this is a bad time—' I start.

'No, no,' he insists. 'In fact, this is the perfect time. My wife, soon to be ex-wife, and I were just discussing our Christmas arrangements.'

'I am *having* the children, Carter,' she spits. 'End of discussion.'

'I think you'll find, Tamara, that I have access to the children this Christmas. It's what we agreed.'

'I didn't agree.'

'Read your solicitor's letter,' Carter insists. 'I am, my love, the one with access rights.'

I want to be somewhere else. Anywhere else.

'You said you were going off to Verbier, skiing with the Olivers,' he continues.

'The children can come too.'

'Two kids in a house of hard-drinking adults? Why put them through that when they can stay here with me and you can have your fun? As soon as you come back you can have them right through New Year.'

'But I want them for Christmas.'

It sounds as if they're squabbling over two packages.

'We should draw lots,' his wife says scathingly. 'Short straw gets Christmas without the kids.'

I look from one to the other. 'I should go.'

'Stay,' Carter implores. Perhaps he sees me as a diversion. He turns to his wife. 'If we did that, would you stick to it?'

'What?' She and I both look appalled.

'We can't seem to sort this out any other way, Tamara. Let's draw lots.'

'You are joking, Carter?'

'It was your suggestion,' he reminds her.

Tamara purses her lips. 'Will Mrs Christmas be our witness?'

'Yes,' he says before I can reply. 'You'd do that, wouldn't you?'

'Well . . .' I say. Then I think, I seem to be in for a penny, so I might as well make it a pound. 'If you don't mind my offering an opinion, this doesn't seem quite the right way to go about deciding how your children spend Christmas.'

Tamara takes one long disdainful look at me and then turns to Carter. 'We'll do it.'

'Right. I'll be back in two ticks.'

Carter rushes out of the room, which, unfortunately, leaves me alone with the pinched-faced and somewhat enraged wife. She glares at me, making it patent that she's unhappy at having me around, and I can't say that I blame her. Whenever Jim and I row, which is fairly rare, I wouldn't want a third party standing in.

'Sorry,' I say when clearly none of this is my fault.

If she wasn't scowling quite so much, it would be fair to say that Tamara Randall is a stunning woman. She is tall, unusually so, and I wouldn't be at all surprised to learn that she was, or had been, a model. Her wispy blonde hair is piled high on her head, showing off her long neck to good effect. Her skin is flawless and, bucking the usual trend, is as white as the driven snow. It only serves to make her soft grey eyes and full pink lips more striking. She's wearing a baby-pink, cashmere-wrap ballet cardigan over a white T-shirt and white jeans. If I wore white jeans they would

103

be, instantly, covered in mud, grass, tea. Tamara's, needless to say, are pristine.

'How do you know Randall?' she asks grudgingly, otherwise we'd be standing here in hostile silence.

'I don't really know him,' I offer when I find my voice. 'I met him at a Hemel Hempstead Means Business event a few weeks ago. I organise Christmas.'

She forces a laugh at that. '*All* of it?'

I shrug. 'Pretty much.'

'How very dreadful for you.'

Then, thankfully, Carter reappears and our fledgling conversation stalls in mid-flight. In his hand he clutches two lime-green drinking straws and a pair of scissors.

'You're not really serious about this?' Tamara asks.

'Darling,' he says with a sigh, 'we have tried all other ways to sort this out, including extortionate solicitors. Let's give this a go. Promise to abide by the decision?'

'You could just ask the children where they want to go?' I try a last-minute intervention. This is no way to decide how to divide up your children's access rights.

They both look at me as if I'm mad.

'The straws,' they say simultaneously.

So Carter cuts them across diagonally with a rather theatrical flourish and holds them up to show Tamara. 'Happy?'

She nods, reluctantly.

He hands them to me. 'Mix them up behind your back and then we'll draw.'

I do as I'm asked, even though I think this is way beyond my job remit and it's a total bloody cheek of them to drag me into their tawdry domestic. When they're as mixed up as I can make them, I hold out the straws, keeping the tops level whilst hiding their length in my palms.

'You choose first,' Carter says to his wife.

'This is ridiculous,' she says.

I couldn't agree more. They're adults, a grown woman and a grown man, clearly both successful and they're resorting to this – lottery . . . to sort out their childcare arrangements.

Nevertheless, Tamara snatches a straw from my fingers and huffs at it. The straw looks quite short to me but, then, what do I know?

I open my palm and hold out the remaining straw. Even from here, I can tell that it's considerably longer.

'They're mine,' he says when he looks at it. In fairness to him, there's no triumphant note in his voice. I'm not sure, if the boot had been on the other foot, that it would have been the same for her.

Tamara's face is stony. 'That's settled then.' She grabs her coat and handbag from the sofa. I can see tears welling in her eyes, but it's clear that she's not planning on crying while she's still here.

I feel a lump in my own throat. Now Carter looks abashed too. 'I'll call you, Tamara,' he says. 'Tomorrow.'

His ex-wife flounces out without speaking. A few seconds later the front door bangs, echoing through the empty entrance hall.

Carter sinks onto the nearest sofa, head in hands. 'That wasn't very edifying, was it?'

'No,' I agree, and sit down opposite him.

'I may have won this skirmish,' he says. 'But we're in a war that hurts everyone.'

'Especially the children.'

He nods and weariness mars his handsome face. 'Especially the children.'

Chapter Nineteen

Carter orders more tea for us both. While we wait for it, he stares out of the window, surveying the amazing grounds, and I sit quietly, giving him the space he needs to compose himself.

When it arrives, he says to his housekeeper, 'Sorry about all that, Hettie. I do apologise.'

'Has Mrs Randall gone now, sir?'

'Yes, yes. She's picking up the children tonight. They'll be back here at the weekend. It's just me for supper.'

The housekeeper leaves and we're alone. Carter pours the tea and hands me a cup, then settles back into the sofa with a sigh. Today he's wearing a fitted black shirt and jeans. He looks more like an off-duty pop star than a businessman. It makes me catch my breath when I look at him. He really is very handsome and I'm not the sort of person whose head is turned by other men. For all the years we've been together, I've only had eyes for Jim. I don't see the point in window shopping. I'm a one-man woman and that's the way it's going to stay, but Carter is an exception. His chiselled cheeks set my impressionable heart a-flutter and I can imagine that he and Tamara once made a beautiful couple.

At the moment, he simply looks jaded. 'I don't suppose that you feel like discussing your Christmas arrangements now?' I say.

Carter shakes his head. 'Tamara won't stick by it,' he says. 'Whatever she's said in this room. Straw or no straw.'

'I'm sorry to hear it.'

'She ignores every single solicitor's letter. I don't know why he keeps on sending them. I had hoped that we'd be able to have an amicable divorce,' he admits. 'Perhaps I should have realised that, with Tamara, it was never going to happen. But even if the situation is volatile between us, we shouldn't be using our children as weapons.'

'It's an easy thing to do.'

'They're wonderful kids.' He reaches into the back pocket of his jeans and pulls out his wallet, takes out a photo of his children and hands it to me. 'That's Eve, she's nine.' The child has clearly inherited her mother's beauty, though, hopefully, not her temperament. 'Max is seven.' He looks exactly like a miniature version of Carter, who glows with pride. 'Do you have children?'

'No.' This is always a slightly painful question, which gives me a pang of longing. 'Not yet.' Not ever at this rate. I hand back the photographs. 'They both look lovely.'

'They're *lively*, there's no doubt of that. This past year has been terrible for them,' he says sadly. 'Tamara and I finally called it a day after *last* Christmas.' There's an ironic note to his hollow laugh. 'We've been fighting over the detail ever since and it's dragging on interminably. It's not good for the children. They need to know where they stand.' Carter looks at me over the rim of his teacup. 'I want to give them both a big treat for Christmas. No expense spared. That's where you come in.'

My eyes widen.

'I'm terrible at Christmas,' Carter confesses. 'Tamara has always handled everything like that. I've never had to do it. I haven't bought one single Christmas present for them. Ever. That's a terrible admission, isn't it?'

107

I nod in acknowledgement.

'It's not that they've gone short,' he adds. 'It's just that someone else has always sorted it out. I confess that I need help, Cassie Christmas. I'm useless at this kind of thing. Whether I eventually have the children here or not on the day, they'll be here at some point over the holiday and I want to make it magical for them. Absolutely magical.'

'That sounds good to me.'

He smiles and it lights up his face. I can't help but smile back at him.

'It does, doesn't it?'

It seems like a good time to flick open my pad and pull my pen from my handbag. 'Have you any ideas?'

'No,' he says. 'I'll leave it all to you. I want them to have everything that there is to have.' He fixes his eyes on me. 'I want to take them on a holiday. Just a few days or maybe a long weekend so that the school – and Tamara – don't create too much of a fuss. Let's make it something to do with Christmas. Something out of the ordinary. Can you organise it for the first half of December? Let's kick off the festive season in a big way.' He pulls out a BlackBerry.

I hesitate. This sounds like a dream contract, one that I would die for. But it's also much bigger than anything I envisaged handling. I'm worried that it's way beyond my expertise. What do I know about the world that Carter moves in? I organised a few holidays for my previous boss, some lavish presents too, but I think that what Carter wants is several steps beyond that.

'I feel that I should point out that I've only just started this business, Mr Randall. I wouldn't want my lack of experience to let you down.'

'I like you, Cassie Christmas, and I think that I'm a good judge of people. You'll do your best for me and you won't rip me off.'

'Both of those things are true.'

'Keep in touch with Georgina. She's been my assistant for years. She knows what I like and what I don't. I'm a fairly laid-back chap. I don't think I'm difficult to please.'

I wonder how true that is. Do people who are laid-back and easygoing get to the sort of position that Carter Randall is in?

'Are you happy to go ahead?'

I nod, still in a state of shock. 'If you are.'

'Let's put a tentative date in now.'

'I'll need to know your budget too,' I say.

Carter throws up his hands. 'No budget,' he tells me. 'Spend what you need to. Just make sure that it's utterly fabulous. I want the holiday to be the trip of a lifetime. Something they'll never forget.'

I feel myself gulp. 'Right.'

'Let's go to town on the house too.' Carter is clearly on a roll now. 'I want it to look amazing. Like a winter wonderland.'

Carter's budget may have no limits but, unfortunately, my imagination does. What can I possibly organise for them that they haven't done before? This is going to take some serious research. While he's flicking through his BlackBerry, my mind is bouncing all over the place.

He gives me a possible date for the holiday trip, which I jot down. It isn't far away. I'm going to have my work cut out setting up anything at this short notice, let alone anything totally exceptional. Yikes.

'Just draw up some ideas for me to look at and we'll meet again when you're ready. Perhaps we could have lunch.'

'I'd like that,' I say. Though I actually feel completely intimidated by his presence, this house, such ostentatious wealth. 'It will have to be in the next couple of days.'

'That'll be fine. The sooner we get it sorted out the better.' He looks at me apologetically. 'I'm sorry again that you had to witness that scene between Tamara and me but, in some ways, I'm glad that you were here. There could have been blood on the carpet otherwise. Mine.'

As I start to pack away my pad, he continues, 'The more we get embroiled with solicitors the harder it is to do this civilly.' He gives me a rueful glance. 'We always had a volatile relationship. Tamara and I both run demanding businesses. I'd be in one half of the world and she'd be in the other. We'd got to the point where we rarely saw one another and, when we did, we found that we no longer liked each other very much. Eventually, she found someone who could give her more attention.'

'Oh.'

'But you don't need to know all this. I'm sorry to burden you with my troubles.'

'That's OK,' I say, honestly. 'I don't mind.'

'You could stay for a sandwich now, if you like,' he suggests. 'Hettie will whip us up something. I'm feeling quite peckish. Strangely, my appetite always comes back when Tamara leaves.'

While he chuckles at his own joke, I make a pretence of checking my watch. 'I have to go.'

'Christmas is coming,' he teases.

'I have a lot of presents to wrap, cards to write.'

'Then I'll let you go.' He stands up and shakes my hand. His skin is warm, smooth. He closes his other hand over the top of my fingers and holds it there as he smiles into my eyes. A heat passes between us that makes me hot all over. 'Have a lovely evening, Cassie Christmas. I'll look forward to hearing from you soon.'

'Very soon,' I agree.

I retrieve my scalded hand and race out of Randall Court as fast as I can, my mind whirring.

Chapter Twenty

Jim was sitting in a meeting that had been called by Dave Hornshaw, the governor of the unit. 'It's a new initiative,' he intoned.

No one actually groaned out loud, but Jim could sense the team's reaction in the air. There were a lot of 'new initiatives' foisted on them by the government. Each lasted a few weeks before being quietly abandoned, only to be replaced by even more 'new initiatives'. Most of the officers would tune out at this point, but Jim forced himself to listen.

'This, potentially, is a good one,' Dave assured them. 'If we can make it work. It's being put in place to help rehabilitate lads who are about to be released. Three months before they're due to leave us, if there's a job for them, they can start to go out on unsupervised placements.'

It sounded like pie in the sky. It was hard enough for ex-offenders to get work, let alone those who were still on the inside. Who in their right mind would want to offer them jobs?

'We're working hard with social services,' the governor continued. 'I'll keep you posted over the next few weeks and let you know when it's fully in place.'

A few stifled yawns and then everyone shuffled off back to their wings. Jim headed to Starling. It was quiet today. It was past lunchtime and no one had yet kicked off. A miracle. Perhaps it was because chicken curry was on the menu, always a favourite. A bunch of lads played pool, nicely, with no argy-bargy for once. Clearly no one's honour had been disrespected over some imagined slight. Jim was thankful for that. He wasn't in the mood for a full-on brawl. Sometimes he wondered if he got paid enough to intervene in a fist fight virtually every day.

Other lads hung around in huddles along the corridors, probably plotting their future life in crime, exchanging tips in burglary or dealing. In front of the communal television, Smudge and Rozzer sat together, both with their hands down the front of their trousers in standard prison style while staring blankly at the screen. One of the mental-health nurses had told him that hugging their gentleman's tackle was something to do with the lads feeling vulnerable, a basic instinct. Jim wondered if it was simply a bad habit that they picked up because everyone else in here did it. All he knew was that it made them look stupid and he wished they'd stop.

Some unedifying creature with black roots was screeching on *The Jeremy Kyle Show*. If he was governor at Bovingdale, he'd make sure that the inmates were able to watch only stuff like *Frozen Planet* and *Stargazing Live*. Programmes that would educate them rather than wind them up. It was hoped that a diet of cartoons and reality shows would keep the lads placated, though it rarely worked.

Jim pulled up a chair next to them and sat astride it. 'All right, lads?'

Smudge and Rozzer nodded at him.

'Everything cool?' He was still worried about Smudge after the events of last week even though the lad was back in counselling. The lad still had faint bruises round his eyes from nutting the wall, but thankfully his nose hadn't broken. 'Anything happened about your release yet?'

'No.'

'Haven't you spoken to the Fresh Start team yet? Or social services or any of the charities?'

They both shook their heads. Time was marching on. By now something should be in place for them. But as so often happened in these straitened times, services were stretched to breaking point. Which meant, invariably, that on their release date the gate would be opened and they'd be turfed out into the cold with nothing but a few pounds from their discharge grant, a travel warrant to get them home, what clothes they were standing up in and all on their bloody tod. Was that any way to help prisoners avoid reoffending?

'They *will* speak to you,' Jim assured them. 'You'll be entitled to benefits as soon as you get out. There are organisations that can help you to get work and a roof over your head. I went into a place today that might suit. They have two-bedroom flats in Hemel Hempstead for ex-offenders. I've asked them to put you on their list.'

'You did that? For us?' Both of the lads brightened up at that.

Jim shrugged, slightly embarrassed. 'You are going to be staying in this area?' he asked. Neither of them had mentioned plans to move away, but it was a conversation they hadn't had.

Smudge and Rozzer looked at each other. 'We just want to stay together,' Smudge said. 'It doesn't matter where.'

'That makes us sound gay, you cu—'

'Language,' Jim said.

'We're friends,' Smudge reiterated. 'Friends stay together.'

'It can be a shock being back on the outside. Even if you've been here only a relatively short time. You both need to start thinking about it,' Jim said.

Smudge raised his eyes from the screen and looked at Jim. There was real fear in the depths of them. 'I think about nothing else,' he admitted.

Jim had to concede to himself, he felt pretty much the same.

Chapter Twenty-One

The minute I get home I google Carter Randall. Should have done it before. Obvs. Perhaps if I had, then I wouldn't feel such a nolly-noddle now. Carter Randall is the owner of the Pure Pleasure beverage company. A self-made man who broke onto the global scene big-time about ten years ago with his range of alcoholic smoothies and ice lollies. To say that they have proved popular with the general public is something of an understatement. They're in every bar you can think of. *Everyone* drinks Pure Pleasure smoothies. Me included. They are totally lush. But I enjoy them – or used to do – only when I was working full time because, believe me, they're not flipping cheap. How was I to know that Carter Randall was the brains behind it all? No wonder his Christmas budget has no discernible limit.

Then I google Tamara Randall and find out that she is, indeed, an ex-model. Of course she is. Now she also runs a global lingerie chain specialising in rather racy undies. I should have known that too. The exclusive stores Lacy Lady, distinctive for their cream and gold livery, are the favoured haunt of the A-list celebrity. The likes of Victoria Beckham and Madonna shop with Tamara. Even though she's a mother of two, there are far too many pictures on the internet of the nearly ex Mrs Randall in nothing but her fancy knickers. I don't even want to consider the shortcomings of my underwear in comparison.

When I've finished snooping on Carter and his wife, I move on to thinking about the trip he wants to book. This needs to be special, lavish on a scale that's beyond what I have ever experienced or am ever likely to. I set up a Pinterest board, then search and search, trawling for ideas through the websites of high-end holiday companies and interior designers, pinning up bits and pieces, jotting down notes when I come across something that catches my eye. I look at fantastically expensive Christmas sites for gift ideas. I look at hotels that have eye-watering numbers of noughts on their room rates. I'm still searching when I hear Jim's key in the door and realise that I've lost hours doing this and that the outstanding Christmas-present wrapping that's piled high in the living room is still waiting patiently for my attention.

'Hey,' I say when Jim comes into our tiny spare bedroom, filling the space.

'Busy?'

I abandon my computer searches to wind my arms round his neck. 'I've had the most *amazing* day. I spent half of the afternoon in the biggest mansion I've ever seen in Little Gaddesden.'

Jim's eyes widen, as well they might.

'I witnessed a massive domestic punch-up between two of Britain's richest entrepreneurs *and* bagged myself a stonking great contract.'

He laughs. 'Really?'

'Oh, yes. This takes Calling Mrs Christmas! to a whole new level.'

'Wow.'

'There is, however, no dinner ready,' I confess. 'I've been on the internet since I got home.'

115

'I'll knock up some pasta,' Jim says. 'Won't take a minute. What's this fantastic contract then?'

'It's not entirely signed and sealed yet,' I admit, 'but it's for Carter Randall!'

Jim looks at me blankly.

'We met him at the Hemel Hempstead Means Business event. He's only the owner of Pure Pleasure drinks.'

I get another 'Wow.'

'The bloke I threw a drink over.'

'Not so wow.'

I shrug. 'Looks as if he's forgiven me. He's only asked me to plan his *whole* Christmas and a special holiday of a lifetime for his kids.'

'And how are you going to do that? You're already stretched.'

'I have absolutely no idea,' I admit. 'But I have to, Jim. Somehow I've *got* to do this. I know that work's piling up, but I couldn't ever have hoped for something as fabulous as this. It could take me to a whole new level. We'll have to bring in the cavalry.'

'Gaby's being brilliant in helping out.'

'As are you.'

'I love you,' he says. 'I can tell that this is the first thing you've been really excited about in months. I don't want to stand by and see you struggle.'

'I could just do with an extra pair of hands – or two – on a casual basis.'

Jim frowns. 'Hmm,' he says. 'Let me think about that.'

'You go and shower. *I'll* put something on for dinner.' I log off the computer.

'You didn't tell me what the bust-up was all about at the mansion. I hope you didn't cause it.'

In response, I punch him playfully. 'O ye of little faith. The

116

Randalls are getting divorced. Acrimoniously, it seems. I happened to walk in when they were in full flow.'

Jim grimaces.

'It wasn't pretty.'

Jim circles his arms around my waist and kisses me. 'I'm glad that we don't argue,' he says. 'Some couples thrive on it.'

'Well, you learned very early in our relationship that I'm always right. Saves a lot of conflict.'

He smacks me on the bottom. 'Cheeky woman,' he throws over his shoulder as he heads towards the bathroom.

So while Jim has a shower, I go and open a packet of bacon, flash-fry some onions and mushrooms, and whang it all together in a tin of tomatoes. Serve with pasta and salad with the wilted bits picked out of it. Yeah, Jamie Oliver, who needs your *15-Minute Meals*?

I'm ladling it into bowls when Jim comes in, still rubbing his damp hair with a towel.

'Did you have a good day?'

'Quiet,' he says. 'For once.'

'Good.'

We both sit down at our cramped table amid the towering parcels and I get a flashback to the opulence of Carter Randall's home. Perhaps I should be dreaming up a new style of alcoholic drink rather than trying to create the perfect Christmas if I want to make my fortune. As Jim adjusts his chair, he knocks into one of the towers and the presents topple. Quick as a flash, he catches them and we restack them in a less wobbling manner.

'Sorry,' he says.

'No harm done. It's not the ideal space really, but needs must.'

Jim picks at his dinner, one eye still uneasily on the gifts. 'There's a new initiative at work,' he says. 'If the lads can get some work experience, they can get out on licence for a few hours or a day. Why don't I ask Kieran and Andrew to come round tomorrow night and we can, hopefully, make a dent in this present mountain? We can pay them the minimum wage and still make a pound or two on top. They wouldn't normally allow lads to come to the home of an officer, but I could put my case. If the governor agrees, we could have this lot done in a few hours.'

'You want to bring two of the prisoners here?'

'Yeah.'

Now it's my turn to reel. 'Seriously?'

'They're good lads,' Jim insists. 'Just kids. I think these two do have a chance of going straight. If only someone would give them an opportunity.'

'And *you* want to be that person?'

'I do. If you agree.'

'Won't they steal all the presents? Or nick our credit cards and run up massive bills?'

'They might come back when they get out and murder us in our beds,' Jim adds, teasing. 'But I don't think so.' Then he hesitates. 'If I've read them right.'

'And if you haven't read them right?'

'Then I will completely lose my faith in humankind.'

'Oh,' I say. 'Can't really have that happening, can we?' I sigh at him. 'All right. Ask the governor if we can have them. If he says yes, then we'll make it work somehow.'

Chapter Twenty-Two

The next day I work like a fiend in the morning and deliver two lots of presents to small companies on the industrial estate. Job done. One of them also asks me to organise their office party for forty staff and, gladly, I put it in the diary. I hope that Gaby can help me with that. Back at home, while I'm grabbing a sandwich two people call to ask me to source and dress their Christmas trees. Then a social club rings and asks me if I can supply Santa and two elves on Saturday afternoon for their pensioners' Christmas party as their usual Santa is suffering from depression and can't face going ho-ho-ho even for an hour. Quickly checking Jim's shift rota, I say that I can. Santa sorted. Quite where I'm going to find two willing elves is another matter.

I put my plan together for Carter Randall, remembering that expense isn't an issue. When I think I've finished it and have done the best I possibly can, I call Carter's office.

'Hi, Georgina. It's Cassie here.'

I've spoken to Georgina on virtually an hourly basis while I've been working on it. As Carter suggested, she is the fount of all knowledge when it comes to the likes and dislikes of Carter and his family. I don't know how I'd have done this without her.

'Can I make an appointment to see Carter, please?'

'He has lunchtime free today, Cassie,' Georgina says. 'That's about it. He's in Belgium for a few days, and, after that, New York.'

'I better had come at lunchtime then,' I say.

This plan will need finalising if I'm to have a hope of getting everything into place in time. Not much point in having a fabulous Christmas set-up if you can't actually fit it in until January, eh? I need the go-ahead and I need it now.

'Last time I spoke to Carter, he did suggest that we have lunch together.'

'I'll book it at the house, if that's all right,' she says. I wasn't envisaging a swanky restaurant, anyway. 'He doesn't have a great deal of time available.'

'That's fine. Thanks.'

Now I feel cheeky, but it *is* what he said. No wonder he's struggling to fit Christmas into his busy schedule. Perhaps he was simply being polite when he asked me to have lunch with him. Hopefully, it will be just a sandwich and then I can eat it and run.

So, at exactly twelve o'clock, I find myself swinging into the drive of Randall Court once more. A neat buff folder containing my master plan is on the seat next to me. I can only hope that this is suitably lavish for a multimillionaire. As I make my way up to the house, I'm no less intimidated the second time around.

I pull up, ring the doorbell, wait an aeon and, again, am eventually let into the mansion by Georgina. We're friends enough now that she kisses my cheek warmly. This time Carter is quick to greet me and there's no background shouting from Tamara. Hopefully, the absence of the fancy Bentley indicates that she's not visiting today.

'So glad you could come,' Carter says. 'You've been very quick in organising this.'

'Speed is of the essence,' I tell him. 'It's not long until

Christmas.' I have a degree in stating the bleeding obvious. Never before have I marked off the days on my calendar so fastidiously. 'If you're happy with my suggestions, I need to get all this in place.'

'I've asked Hettie to serve lunch in the garden room,' Carter says. 'I hope you're not vegetarian.'

'No.'

'Thank heavens for that! Let's go straight through.'

He tucks his hand under my elbow, steering me out of the hall into a light and spacious room that overlooks the grounds.

'This is lovely.'

The large table is all ready for just the two of us and Carter pulls out my seat for me. On the table is a platter of antipasti – salami, Parma ham, artichokes, olives, cherry tomatoes, roasted red peppers – and a basket of ciabatta.

'A glass of something sparkling?' Carter asks.

'Just a small one. I'm driving.'

He splashes some pink champagne into a glass for me, lifts his own and toasts me. 'To Christmas,' he says.

'To Christmas,' I echo. 'Shall I go through my plan as we eat?'

'Please do.'

He offers me the servers and I transfer some of the meats to my plate in as delicate a manner as I can manage. While Carter tucks in, I jump straight into my plan.

'For your trip with the children, I thought Lapland. Home of Father Christmas.'

'Fabulous,' he says. 'Why didn't I think of it? I'm sure the kids would love that.'

'Georgina told me that they've never been before.' Good old Georgina. I make a mental note to buy her a gift for her help. 'I've found a great wilderness lodge in the middle of nowhere, surrounded by forests. Nothing too basic though. It looks beautiful and has all mod cons. Centrally heated, own chef, hot tub. I can organise a variety of activities from there. Dog-sledding, snow-mobiling, whatever you and the children would like.'

'Oh, sounds wonderful,' Carter enthuses, making me feel as if I'm the most clever Christmas planner ever.

'I've tentatively reserved it, subject to your approval. The only thing I'm struggling with is flights.'

'Book a private jet,' Carter says without hesitation. 'I'll ask Georgina to give you the name of the company we normally use.'

Right. OK. Private jet. Why didn't I think of that? Carter Randall is hardly going to travel Ryanair, is he?

'I thought a night in the Icehotel would be fun too.'

'Great idea. I've always wanted to go there, see the northern lights.'

Not sure that I can book those to order, but I'm thinking that I'd better give it a go.

'These are the rough costings.'

I push the piece of paper across the table and try to dip some ciabatta in olive oil in a nonchalant manner while simultaneously concentrating on judging his reaction. It really is an extraordinary amount of money by anyone's standards.

Carter doesn't bat an eyelid. 'That's fine.'

Thank goodness for that. 'Now the plans for the house and Christmas at home?'

'Really, do whatever you want to,' Carter says. 'I'm clueless.'

'I thought a bright and fun colour scheme for the children.'

'Perfect.' It's clear that he doesn't want to be troubled by the detail. He wants it to be fabulous and is happy to foot the bill. End of.

'There'll need to be a party in the run-up to Christmas. A big one. Georgina will give you the names of the usual guests.'

'Right.' Hadn't bargained on that one.

'And we'll need a chef for Christmas Day and Boxing Day. Hettie doesn't work then.'

A chef. Of course. I'll give Nigella a ring, see if she's busy. I jot it down in my notepad. 'There'll just be the three of you?'

'Yes,' Carter says with a sigh. 'That'll be pretty glum, won't it?'

I could probably rent them some friends if he wants that too.

'When she's not here, they miss their mother,' Carter says. 'We try to pretend that the children are adaptable, joke that they're just like the rest of their friends now with divorcing parents. But it's hurting them.'

'Kids do cope,' I say.

I think of my own absent father – gone at such an early age that I can't even remember him – and how Gaby had to step into my mum's place because my own mother was terminally incapable of parenting us. Carter's kids might be shuffled between two mansions but, from what I've seen, they don't seem to be having it too rough.

'Yes,' he agrees. 'I'm sure they do. They're away at school all week and they love Tamara's new home in London. It's just that I see them only every other weekend. That's not right, is it?'

I choose not to comment.

'I wanted them to have a stable background, as I did. My parents have been married for fifty years and are still going strong. They still hold hands and live for each other. Tamara and I barely managed a decade.'

'That could be considered long term by many standards.'

'How sad is that?' Carter picks at the food on his plate. 'Sometimes I wonder how we made it as far as we did, how we managed to produce two such great kids. The truth is that we should never have got married. Tamara and I are totally unsuited. We should have had a brief, passionate affair and then gone our

123

separate ways. We might be great lovers but we've never been very good friends.'

I bet the make-up sex is great with her in her fancy little pants. I push the image away.

Carter continues, 'But when you've got two young children, you need to be more than good bedfellows, right?'

'I think it helps.'

'The children are the best thing that's ever happened to me,' he says wistfully. 'I'd have more – another two, four even. I've always wanted a big family. Tamara didn't really want children at all. I was the one who drove that. Then she most definitely wanted to stop at two. She didn't want to lose her figure or her business.'

I can imagine that all too well.

'Strange,' he carries on, 'but I'd give all this up for them in a heartbeat.' He waves an arm towards the garden. 'All I want is for them to be happy.'

'That's all anyone wants for their kids.'

He reaches across the table and puts his hand on top of mine. 'You *must* have children,' Carter says. 'Lots of them. I think you'd make a lovely mum, Cassie Christmas.'

If it wasn't for the lump in my throat, I'd have to agree with him.

Chapter Twenty-Three

When I got back from my meeting with Carter, I immediately booked the wilderness lodge and the Icehotel. Georgina gave me the name of the company that supplies the Randalls with private jets and I have booked that too. The family can now fly straight from our local airport at Luton into the tiny town of Kiruna, which is two hundred miles inside the Arctic Circle, and be there in just a few short hours. No messing about with three-hour check-ins, luggage restrictions and buying your own tea and tub of Pringles on the plane. How the other half live.

I also sourced a chef – a very minor celebrity – to cater for them over the Christmas period and I organised a company to provide the food for the Christmas party that Carter had requested. The guest list, when I received it from Georgina, was two hundred strong. It was never going to be a casual affair for a few mates, was it? The scale at which he spends money is quite staggering.

I'm cross-legged on the living-room floor, sorting out ribbons and bows, when I hear Jim's key in the lock and realise that it's already six o'clock.

'Hi, honey, I'm home,' he calls.

'Hi,' I shout out in response. 'I'm naked and waiting for you, big boy!'

A moment later he comes into the room. 'Um,' he says, looking rather relieved that I'm not naked. 'We have visitors.' He's followed closely by two very pasty-looking boys.

'I'm sorry,' I say, flushing. 'So sorry.'

The boys study their feet, faces red. These are the child criminals who are coming to help out with tackling the ever-increasing present mountain that's threatening to consume the flat. This work is clearly becoming the bread and butter of my business and I'm not complaining as it's lovely and relaxing to do. It's just that we could do with bigger premises. Or helpers. Which is where the boys come in.

'Hi,' I say to them.

They shuffle shyly behind Jim and grunt in reply. They're both unbelievably white – lack of sunlight, I should imagine – and look terribly undernourished. They wear what I assume is their prison garb of slightly grubby grey tracksuits and smell of stale food and unwashed teenager. They're hunched into themselves, defensive. It's the first time I've ever met any of Jim's charges and it suddenly gives me a tiny insight into what he has to deal with on a daily basis. They both look so lost and pathetic that it makes me want to cry. No wonder Jim wants to do something to help these young lads. I think I'd want to take them all home with me too.

'This is Kieran.' Jim nods to the youngest, most frail-looking boy. He's pretty with blond hair and huge blue eyes that seem too big for his face. 'And Andrew.' More sullen-looking, he's as dark as the other one is fair. He might once have been stocky.

'I'm Cassie,' I say and they look surprised when I stand up and shake them by the hand.

'They're out on licence for four hours,' Jim informs me. 'I have to have them back by ten, so we'd better get cracking.'

'OK,' I say. 'What do you say I show you the basics of professional-quality present wrapping and then I can order in some pizzas for eight o'clock?'

They both look at each other cagily.

'Come and sit down on the rug. Make yourselves comfortable.'

Another mutual exchanged glance before they step forward to sit on the floor.

'Can I have a quick word, Cassie?' Jim nods towards the kitchen and I follow him. When we reach it he lowers his voice. 'You are OK with this?'

'Yes.'

'I'm sorry I didn't have time to call you and let you know they were coming. The governor only gave me his approval at the last minute. It was touch and go.'

'I'd have thought he would have been pleased.'

'It's a real no-no bringing prisoners into your own home. I managed to convince him that these were special circumstances.' He nods back towards the living room. 'I'll kill these buggers if they let me down. Are you OK if I leave you with them for five minutes while I go and shower?'

'Yes, of course.'

Despite my misgivings, I don't think that either one might murder me in my bed. As Jim said, they look like disadvantaged boys who deserve a break.

'I love you,' Jim says, kissing me. 'Thanks for this.'

'We can only give them a chance. Let's see how they do.'

So Jim goes off for his shower while I return to the boys and crouch down beside them. 'Right. Let's get started.'

They move in closer. I think I'm going to have to Febreze the living room when they're gone as they're both a bit ripe.

I nod towards the pile on my left and pull one of the presents closer. 'These are for the same family, so I've got a selection of co-ordinating wrapping paper. One of you can tackle them.'

Kieran raises his eyebrows and says quietly, 'All these for one family?'

127

'Yes.' And I sourced and bought them all.

He looks as if he can't believe his eyes. It makes me realise how little he might have had in the way of material goods in his life.

'We always use double-sided tape and fold the paper so that no untidy edges show. Let me show you the standard I expect.'

As best I can, I demonstrate all the techniques I taught myself from the internet and am quite surprised to see how far I've come as I whip out a beautifully wrapped gift in two minutes flat.

'I'll make the bows for the top until you're used to doing the presents and Jim will write the cards with a calligraphy pen. If you can just put a Post-It note on top to say what's in the box, I have a list of which present is going to who.'

They both look perplexed.

'It might take you a while to get going, but take your time, do it properly. I'm not expecting miracles. Start with the square or rectangular boxes. If there are any tricky shapes, just ask me for help. Kieran, you start with this pile.'

I shift and bring another heap forward. Boxes of chocolates from a small artisan shop in the Old Town. Unfortunately, I didn't get a free sample, but I live in hope.

I put a Christmas playlist on the iPod to get us in the mood and we start a production line going. It's slow at first and I keep having to stop and help the lads. But soon they forget that they have sausages for fingers and begin to get into the rhythm of wrapping.

Jim comes back, freshly washed and shaved, to join us. The boys look at him slightly agog and I realise that it's quite possibly the first time they've seen him out of his uniform and in his civvies. It may well be the first time that they've viewed him as an actual human being.

Two hours later, we've made a reasonable dent on the pile. When the pizzas arrive the boys are more relaxed, chatting away.

I make them wash their hands and we take a quick break while we eat. For a moment, I forget that they're young offenders and see them just as teenage boys keen to earn a few pounds even though we're paying them minimum wage plus pizza bonus. It's nice to see Jim joking with them. He has a natural, easy manner and I can see why he makes a great officer in a young offenders' unit. He has a good rapport with the boys and it only strengthens my view that, one day, he'll make a great dad.

They wash their hands again before we carry on, as the last thing I want is tomatoey fingerprints on my expensive gifts. By nine-forty-five, half of my present mountain has been wrapped, bedecked with a bow, labelled and moved to the other side of the room ready for delivery in the morning.

'We could do this again tomorrow night,' I say as we finish up. 'Do you think the governor would allow it?'

'I can ask,' Jim says. 'If the lads want to.'

'Yes,' they both say eagerly.

They've dealt with all of the presents quickly, with very few mistakes and to a high standard. I'm pleased with what they've done. More than pleased. I feel that all they need is some attention, some encouragement.

'It's been nice,' Kieran says politely, cheeks reddening. 'Thank you for having us.'

'I didn't think I'd like it,' Andrew admits. 'But I have.'

'You've been very helpful,' I tell them both. Then, before I think better of it, 'I have a vacancy for two elves on Saturday afternoon. Just for two hours at a pensioners' party. If you're interested?'

The boys look at each other, alarmed. But then Andrew, clearly the bolder of the two, says, 'Yes. We'll do it.'

'Good.'

'I'll make sure you get permission from the governor,' Jim adds.

'Thanks, Jim.' Now all I have to do is find them suitable costumes.

'Come on, lads,' Jim says. 'I'd better get you back on time, otherwise the governor won't let you out again at all.'

'Thanks for the pizza, Mrs Maddison.'

I don't point out that I'm still very much Ms Smith as Jim and I aren't yet married. Or that I'm hoping, at some point, this business might make enough to fund a wedding. 'You're welcome. I hope I'll see you tomorrow.'

Jim ushers the boys out of the door in front of him. 'Won't be long, love,' he says. 'See you in a short while.' Then he winks at me and lowers his voice. 'You did very well.'

'They're great boys.'

But, to my own shame, it doesn't stop me checking that my purse is still in my handbag where I left it.

130

Chapter Twenty-Four

It's the first weekend in December. The calls for Christmas-tree dressing begin in earnest and I rope in Gaby to help out. I'm taking several boxes of baubles round to her so that she can decorate a tree in the reception area of one of the big corporations in the town. As I haven't seen her to talk to in days, I stop by for a quick cup of coffee. As it's a Saturday, my scrumptious niece and nephew are at home and they clamber all over me the minute I walk through the door. I'm sure they see me and Jim as part auntie and uncle, part climbing frame. But we both love a rough-and-tumble with them and inventing games to play, so I suppose we bring it on ourselves.

'Hey,' I say, hauling Molly onto my knee as I sit at the breakfast bar. 'What have you two imps been up to?'

'Karate,' George says. At seven he's too cool to be cuddled for long and so leans against my leg instead in a way that says he's not bothered whether he does or not.

'Nothing,' my niece says.

Molly twists her hair around her thumb and tucks it in her mouth. I remember that Gaby used to do the same thing when we were little, lying in our beds at night, waiting for Mum to come home from wherever she'd been. It was then that I knew she was frightened, just like me. I wonder what Molly has to make her anxious or are habits like that inherited, tucked deep in the DNA?

'Mummy says that you know Santa now,' Molly continues. 'Does that mean we get more Christmas presents?'

I take the opportunity for a good tickle. 'Only if you're extra specially good and make your own bed every day.'

'Hmm,' Gaby says. 'That's not going to happen is it, Mols?'

'No,' Molly agrees sagely.

'Where's Uncle Jim today?' George asks.

'He's a bit busy this morning.'

Getting ready for his Santa gig with his two criminally inclined elves. But I can't tell that to George, who still believes implicitly in Santa.

The governor at the unit is being really good about allowing the boys out to do work for me and they seem to be enjoying it. They've done three consecutive nights of present wrapping at the flat and are now demons at it. With only a modicum of reluctance, they've even moved on to making their own bows.

I've asked Jim to bring Kieran and Andrew up to the flat first for a good scrub in the shower before they go to the social club. I can't be sending out smelly elves.

'How many days is it now to Christmas?' George wants to know.

'Not enough,' I say. It would actually be very helpful if Christmas could be moved to 25 January, then I might have a hope of doing all my work in time. To think, at one point, I was worried that this wasn't going to take off.

'Look on your advent calendar, George,' Gaby suggests. 'You didn't have your chocolate this morning yet.'

And, of course, that makes my nephew shoot to the other side of the kitchen in a blur of speed.

'I'm so busy with everyone else's Christmases that I haven't even thought about my own yet,' I admit as I lower my niece to the floor and wolf down one of Gaby's mince pies.

'That's not like you!'

'I know. I must do something to the flat and start my Christmas shopping.'

'You have your mind on other things this year. Don't worry about it.'

Gaby's kitchen has become quite the cupcake and mince pie factory, which is keeping the money rolling in nicely. Which is great because I can trust Gaby. She just gets on with the orders without fuss and they're always ready and waiting to be delivered when they should be. I know the extra cash is helping her out with the inevitable slew of Christmas bills too.

'Mum *is* coming here,' Gaby informs me with a wry smile. '*All* day.'

I harrumph. 'That'll be a miracle.'

'She can't help being like she is, Cassie,' Gaby says in her 'reasonable' voice. I'll remind her about this the next time Mum lets her down at the last minute for some random bloke when she's supposed to be babysitting. 'Mum's always liked lots of attention.'

'Shame she couldn't find time to give us any.'

'I feel sad that, at her age, she still hasn't been able to find happiness.'

'She's not much older than us,' I remind her. 'Happiness is never going to be found chasing married men. She should be growing old gracefully and enjoying her family.' To my mind, she's lucky that we still have anything to do with her at all.

'She loves the kids,' Gaby counters. 'She may not be a conventional grandma, but she does love them. In her own way.'

Mum doesn't even let the kids call her grandma. She insists on them calling her by her first name, Angela. And that's because

Gaby draws the line at Angie. It's as if grandma is a swear word. 'In the same casual way that she loved us,' I retort.

Gaby tuts. 'Cut her some slack, Cassie. Whatever her short-comings, she's the only mum we've got. You should pop round and see her more often.'

The last part is probably true. Mum lives only a five-minute drive away and yet I hardly see her. I can give you all kinds of the-dog-ate-my-homework-style excuses, but the truth is that I do avoid seeing my mum. I still feel so angry with her. I look at kids like Kieran and Andrew and, but for the grace of God and Gaby's good sense, we could have ended up like them. It's in spite of Mum, not because of her, that we've turned into fine, upstanding citizens.

'You're more like a mum to me.' I feel myself welling up. This is always a tricky subject for me. I've always been desperate to be a mum myself and yet am terrified of turning out like my own mum. It's a head-fuck that I've never quite come to terms with.

'I didn't mean to upset you.' Gaby puts her arm round my shoulders. 'Angela might never be the mum that you want her to be, but she could be a friend to you. She can be fun and she does miss you.'

'She could call to tell me that herself.'

'I can't make you want to see her, Cassie. It's up to you.'

'OK.' I relent. 'I'll try to get to see her in the next week or so. I promise.' Gaby still looks doubtful. Then I check my watch, something I do now a dozen times an hour. 'I'll have to go. I'm meeting the man from the Fir Play Christmas-tree nursery up at Carter Randall's house. He's delivering the trees.'

'How is the millionaire's Christmas coming along?'

'Very well. Spending money like water.'

'It's all right for some.'

'The funny thing is that he seems really down-to-earth. Although money is no object, he's not really flash with it.'

'Apart from the mansion, the ten Mercs and the private jet.'

I laugh at that. 'You'd know what I mean if you spent time with him.'

'Ooh.' Gaby's eyes widen. 'Sounds as if you like him, sis. Does Jim need to be worried?'

'No.' I dismiss the thought with a girly giggle. 'It's not like that. But, for a man of his status and power, he's surprisingly nice to be around.'

'You'd better get up there then. You might see the dark side of him if his Christmas trees aren't up to scratch.'

'I might see the dark side of the Fir Play man if I'm not there to give him the cash for those humongous trees.' I grab my bag and kiss Molly and George goodbye.

'Take these mince pies to the millionaire. Tell him that your big sister baked them. I'm inclined to run away with him myself.'

'I saw him before you,' I tease her. 'I have first dibs on him.'

Gaby gives me a big hug. 'See Mum.'

'I will,' I say and, before I make myself late, I shoot out of the door.

Chapter Twenty-Five

The size of the lorry actually frightens me, let alone the size of the trees it's carrying. Did I really order ones so big? Yikes. I took advice from Tim, the Fir Play man, who assured me that they'd be just perfect. I hope he's right. To me, they look as if they ought to be in shopping malls or something.

Tim's lorry comes to a halt in front of Randall Court. 'Hi, Cassie,' he says, as he and his burly colleague jump out. 'Where do you want these buggers?'

Couldn't have put it better myself.

'The biggest is staying out here. It goes there in front of the house.' I point at the prime spot on the lawn where it's to be fixed. 'The smaller one,' and it's a relative term, 'is to go in the entrance hall.'

'Right.' Tim nods to his co-worker. 'Let's do it.'

'You're sure they're not too big?' I ask, worried.

'They'll look great,' he assures me. 'Don't fret yourself, lass.'

But fret myself I do.

It's a bright, winter day but there's a nip in the air and I've taken the precaution of wrapping up against the cold. Which is just as well as I could be here for quite a while.

I can hardly bring myself to watch as they lift the trees from the lorry with a hoist and swing it towards the chosen spot. As

I'm standing there, cringing, racked with anxiety, the front door of the house swings open and two children race out into the drive. They can only be Max and Eve.

They barrel over towards me. 'Careful,' I say to them. 'Don't go too close. Come over here and watch it with me.' I wave them to my side and they run the last few metres.

I look up to see Carter following them. He's also wrapped up against the cold in a thick sheepskin jacket over black jeans and a sweater. He's looking very sharp.

'Hey,' he says as he approaches. 'This is looking great.'

The tree swings giddily in the air until Tim's mate guides it into position. If all goes to plan, a company that designs 'conceptual festive lighting' will be coming along shortly too. They'll be wiring up the Christmas tree and covering the front of the house in an American-style light show. They told me they are masters at doing this and usually decorate stores or provide the lighting for concerts. Their managing director helped me to trawl through their online catalogue until we found something suitable. Understated is not the look I've gone for, but I'm hoping that it will be classy in an over-the-top way too.

'Say hello to Cassie Christmas, kids,' Carter says to Eve and Max.

'Hello, Mrs Christmas,' Eve says.

'Cassie is fine,' I tell her.

'Daddy says that you're making Christmas for us,' she lisps shyly.

'I am.'

'This tree is enormous!' Max says, wide-eyed. He runs round behind me, arms out like a plane.

'Lovely children,' I say to Carter.

'Thank you.'

They're both bright-eyed, polite and articulate. When Eve follows her brother, I lean towards Carter and say, 'I have everything organised for your trip. We just need to go through a few details.'

'As soon as they put this tree up we can go indoors and have a hot drink,' Carter says. 'We'll go through them while we get warm again. I bet Lapland's going to be chilly.'

Minus fifteen, if the forecast is to be believed. 'Yes,' I agree. 'I've organised for you all to have Arctic gear when you're out there.'

'We've got some ski stuff too,' Carter says. 'We have a place in Gstaad.'

Of course. Why wouldn't you?

'Then I'd plan on taking it with you.'

'Perhaps you can help the children to pack. Maybe me too. I normally travel light, but I may need more this time.'

I make a mental note to add 'packing' to my list of to-dos in my pad.

Eventually, the tree is in its intended place, secured and held upright by retaining wires. It looks truly fantastic. Lying on the truck bed, it might have seemed gigantic, but it blends in perfectly here.

'Kids,' Carter says, 'what do you think?'

They both come to admire the splendid fir. 'It's lovely,' Eve says, in awe.

'Will it have lights?'

'Lots of them,' I assure Max. But the lighting company is in charge of that, thankfully. Some jobs, I've quickly realised, are far too big for me to handle by myself and I have to let the experts take control.

As the Fir Play men struggle to take the smaller tree into the entrance hall of the house, with perfect timing the people who are doing the lights turn up. Carter and I run through the plan with them and I'm pleased that they definitely seem to be Men Who

Know What They're Doing. This is the first time that Carter has seen my vision for his house and garden, but he seems enthralled.

The front of the house is to be strung with a cascade of white lights that will go through a range of settings. The back garden is getting a similar treatment. I've organised for the existing trees to be strung with white lights, as well as a temporary pergola to be installed and also covered with lights. Ashridge Forest is famous for its deer and, as a slightly tongue-in-cheek homage to them, I've arranged for a group of deer-shaped sculptures to be sited as if they are just emerging from the woods. Tacky? Possibly. I think I've lost all reason on this brief. If Carter hates it when it's done, then we'll just whip it all out again.

'Shall we say hello to the tree?' I suggest. It seems only right to make a little ceremony of it. My sister's always doing this kind of thing for Molly and George, so I guess it's rubbed off on me over the years. 'Let's all hold hands.'

Eve and Max join hands and then, not quite as I'd imagined, Carter takes mine in his. The electricity that shoots through me is as sudden as it is unexpected.

He laughs uncomfortably. Perhaps he felt it too.

'Static,' I say pathetically. 'It's the cold air.'

'Oh,' he says, a smile on his lips. 'Is that what it is?'

'Come on,' I say. 'Let's make the tree happy it's here.'

So I lead them in a dance round the tree, skipping and running. It's also helping to warm us up. Then I start to sing 'O, Christmas Tree' and they all join in.

When we're done and the tree is thoroughly welcomed, we're laughing and breathless.

'Let's go inside,' Carter says. 'I don't know about you, but I think we need a treat.'

'Yay!' the children chorus.

I glance back at the beautiful tree as we head towards the

house and wonder if I'll be allowed to bring George and Molly up here for a glimpse of the lights when they're finished. They'd love it too.

We go in through the kitchen door and it's another *Homes & Gardens*-magazine-style room, all white cupboards and grey-granite surfaces. You could eat your dinner off the floor, it's so sparkly clean. Hettie is at the large, stainless-steel range cooker. 'Oh my,' she says. 'Look at those rosy cheeks. I've never seen the like.'

'Hettie, put some hot chocolate on for us all,' Carter says. 'Lots of whipped cream and extra marshmallows.'

'Hurrah!' the children shout.

Despite me having the slight feeling that I'm in a Famous Five story, they're great kids and I'm not surprised that Tamara and Carter are having a hard time being away from them. Surreptitiously, I glance at my watch. Wow. Is it so late? I should be packing up and getting down to the social club to see how Jim and the boys are getting on, not sitting here being indulged with hot chocolate.

This would be a good time to make my excuses and leave. But, to be honest, I don't want to. I very badly want hot chocolate and whipped cream and extra marshmallows. So, instead, I join Carter and the children, and we sit round the kitchen table while Hettie whips up our drinks.

'Guess what, guys,' Carter says. 'Cassie Christmas has organised a holiday for us.'

Max gasps. In unison, the children swivel their eyes to me. 'Really?'

I nod.

'It's going to be fantastic,' Carter continues. 'I'm not telling you where we're going. It's a surprise, but it will be brilliant fun.'

Max claps his hands in excitement.

140

'Will Mummy come too?' Eve asks softly.

Carter's face falls slightly and I notice the bleakness in his expression. 'No,' he says. 'Mummy's a little bit busy, sweetheart. This is a special trip for just you two and Daddy.' Then he turns to me. 'And Cassie will be coming with us.'

I rock back in my seat. 'Me?'

He frowns. 'You're coming too. Aren't you?'

'I ... er ... well ... er ... I hadn't planned to.'

'Oh, but you must,' Carter insists. 'Otherwise you'd have to organise a nanny for us and it would be someone we don't know. That would be tedious. I know that I can trust you.' He turns to Eve and Max. 'You'd like Cassie to come with us, wouldn't you?'

'Yes!' they both cry out.

'Oh, do come, Cassie,' Eve pleads. 'I want you to.'

'Well ...' Now what do I say?

'There's plenty of space on the jet,' Carter slips in. 'What else would you need?'

'I don't have any cold-weather gear.'

'Get yourself some,' Carter instructs. 'Go down to the Snow + Rock shop at the Snow Centre in Hemel Hempstead. We have an account there. Put whatever you need on it.' I'll get Georgina to tell them you're coming.'

As simple as that.

Oh, my goodness. I never dreamed in a million years that I'd be going along on this trip too. As far as I was concerned, that wasn't even in the brief. But what can I do? If he wants me there, can I turn him down? I'm up to my eyeballs in wrapping and tree dressing and events and card writing and baking and flower arranging. How will I find time to swan off with Carter and the children, even if it's only for a few days? What will Jim say? Could he possibly hold the fort for me with Gaby's help?

I bite my lip, mind churning. I know that I should say no. Of

141

course I should. I must fix Carter up with some nubile Nordic nanny – who would no doubt be six foot tall, naturally blonde and have tits like nuclear warheads. I should make all the arrangements and happily wave the family goodbye at the airport. But this is the trip of a lifetime. I should know because I've booked every single element of it. It will be fantastic beyond belief. Lavish beyond my wildest dreams. Luxury a-go-go. I'll never get the chance to do this ever again and, here it is, being handed to me on a plate. What on earth should I do?

Hettie delivers a tray of mugs brimming over with whipped cream, topped with a mountain of marshmallows and chocolate shavings. There's a plate of freshly made cookies too. Everything in Carter's life is excessive, it seems.

'Well,' Carter says as he takes a biscuit from the plate. 'Are you coming with us, Cassie Christmas? I'd really like you to.'

My heart is pounding just thinking about it. I should talk to Jim first to see how he feels about it. That's what I should do. But then I know in my heart that I couldn't miss it for the world. And, though everything in my brain is saying that I should think this through more carefully, my mouths opens and out pops 'Yes.'

The children shout out happily.

Carter lifts his mug of hot chocolate and clinks it against mine. 'You won't regret this,' he says. 'We'll have a great time.'

With a wide grin, I lift my hot chocolate to my lips. I'll drink to that. Ohmigod. I'm going to Lapland. On a private jet. It's going to be flipping fantastic!

Now all I have to do is tell Jim.

Chapter Twenty-Six

The Boxley Social Club was more than a little shabby round the edges. The window frames were mostly rotten and the front doors could have done with a fresh coat of paint.

Jim sat outside it in the car, with Smudge and Rozzer in the back. As Cassie had instructed, they'd both been washed and scrubbed at the flat before coming down here. He had to admit, they did both smell a lot fresher. There was an aroma of Original Source Tea Tree and Mint shower gel around them, rather than stale chip fat and despair. Both had washed their hair and it was combed down flat more in the style of elves rather than spiky in the modern style of One Direction.

The lads, it was fair to say, looked glum. Jim didn't think they quite realised what they had signed up for when they'd agreed to be elves.

Mind you, he wasn't that enthralled at being Santa – particularly not for a load of pissed pensioners. He knew from experience of previous volunteer work what these oldies could be like when there was a whiff of gin about. Jim turned round in his seat.

'Right,' he said. 'Little elven pep talk, if you don't mind, lads. The only C-word that elves use is Christmas. Neither do they use any words beginning with F – unless it's festive. Got me?'

The lads nodded, the bells on their green felt hats jingling.

They both looked glummer than ever, but they said in unison, 'Yes, Jim.'

'Elves don't put their hands down the front of their pants and hold onto their crotches.'

Sheepishly, they both took their hands out of their bright-red, baggy trousers.

'You're not in the unit now.'

'No, Jim.'

'And remember to refer to me as Santa at all times.'

'Yes, Jim.'

Beneath the uncertainty, he could tell that there was now an underlying level of terror.

'It'll be fine,' he assured them.

Jim could understand their being scared. He wasn't keen to be seen in his Santa outfit and he was damn sure two cool teenage dudes wouldn't want to be seen dead in those green-and-red polyester elf suits, which were pretty diabolical. To be honest, it was weird enough for him to see them out of their prison-issue tracksuits, let alone dressed as elves.

'We've got to hand out some presents to the old folk. Give out some cups of tea and mince pies. Job done. What can go wrong?' Jim put on his beard. 'Can you give me a hand with the pillow for my tummy when we get out of the car?'

They both nodded.

'Ready?'

'Yes, Jim . . . Santa,' they both said.

All three of them got out and stood in the chilly car park. The tarmac was badly pot-holed and the whole thing needed re-surfacing. Smudge and Rozzer pushed and shoved until the pillow was firmly in place.

'How do I look?' Jim said.

'Like a tosser,' Rozzer volunteered. 'How do we look?'

'Like *total* tossers,' Jim countered. They all burst into fits of giggles. 'Come on, lads. Smiles on. Let's get this over with as quickly as possible.'

They strode towards the social club. Well, Jim strode. Smudge and Rozzer trailed behind him, exuding reluctance.

Jim had thought that Cassie would have been here by now. Perhaps she was waiting for them inside, but he couldn't see her car in the car park. She'd told him that the presents – all sourced and wrapped by her – were in sacks stashed in the kitchen ready for them to distribute.

Once they were inside, the hall looked considerably more Christmassy. It was clear that it had been decorated on a tight budget, but Cassie had done her best with limited money. The day after they'd asked her to book a Santa for them, they'd rung back and asked her to deck out the hall too. As with normal hall-decking, there were no boughs of holly, but there were dozens of helium balloons and streamers. She'd done the tree nicely, with big cardboard boxes beneath the bottom branches that the lads had wrapped to look like oversized presents. The party was in full swing and the pensioners were already waltzing round the floor to something that might have been sung by Des O'Connor or Val Doonican. They seemed to be having a great old time.

Jim felt a warm glow of pride at how much Cassie had achieved in the last few weeks, even though it had made their life feel as if a whirlwind had gone through it. He couldn't remember the last time they'd just sat together and watched telly without having to wrap presents or write Christmas cards. In truth, he'd be glad when it was all over and they could have the flat to themselves again. But as it had been so successful, there was no doubt that Cassie would do it all again next year. The only thing he wasn't that keen on was the amount of time she was spending with that Carter Randall. He seemed to be really demanding and

Cassie seemed only too happy to drop everything and put him at the top of her list. The guy was obviously used to getting his own way and it was certainly true that money talked. Oh, well. Christmas would soon be here and, hopefully, Carter Randall would be out of their lives.

Jim introduced himself to the woman in charge, who showed them to the kitchen where Cassie had stowed the presents. He hoisted one of the sacks onto his back and Smudge and Rozzer flanked him, also carrying their own.

'Let's do it,' Jim said. 'Ho-ho-ho!'

'Ho-ho-ho,' the lads echoed.

Smudge and Rozzer grinned and fell into step behind him.

There was a big cheer when Jim entered the hall and shouted out 'Merry Christmas!' They spent the next hour going from table to table, handing out gifts to the elderly people. Cassie had wrapped gloves and scarves, cosy, functional presents that seemed to please everyone.

'Come over here, boys,' the old dears shouted at the lads. 'Sit on our laps!'

The elves put up with the teasing stoically, though after half an hour of it, both were starting to look mildly traumatised – even after time served on Starling wing.

Now that all the presents had been given out, they were serving tea and mince pies. All credit to the lads, they'd done a good job. They'd shadowed him perfectly and had been polite to all the party-goers. Jim couldn't help but look at them with pride. A few weeks ago they'd been stuck in the unit with very little hope for the future, and now look at them. OK, so being one of Santa's little elves wasn't exactly a brilliant career move, but it had given them something to look forward to, a reason to get out of their bunks as well as put some money in their pockets for when they got out.

A short while later, while Jim was taking a two-minute breather, Smudge and Rozzer sidled over to him.

'The old pensioner ladies keep pinching our bums, Santa,' Rozzer told him.

Jim hid a smile in his beard. He could sympathise, as he'd had his cheeks pinched between gnarled fingers more than a dozen times too – his facial cheeks, though. No one had gone for his bottom yet. Perhaps he was too old for them and the ladies liked the younger blood. They'd certainly got more raucous as the afternoon wore on and he knew that they were definitely putting nips of something strong in their tea.

'Man up, Rozzer,' Jim said. 'This is excellent life training.' Checking his watch, he noticed that the party would be over soon and their part would be done. 'We've not got much longer to go. Just be glad it's not the men pinching your bum.'

'True, dat,' Rozzer muttered.

Jim wondered where Cassie had got to. It wasn't like her not to turn up to one of her own events. He knew she'd been up at that posh place again this morning with a lot to do, so perhaps things had overrun there. Jim slipped into the kitchen to ring her. Pulling off his beard, he searched for his mobile phone.

The lads followed him in. 'All the mince pies have gone, Santa,' Rozzer said. 'Is that us done?'

'Yeah,' he replied. 'I think so. I'm just going to ring Cassie to check.' He grinned at Rozzer. 'I think it's safe for you to call me Jim again now.'

As he located his phone beneath his big red costume, the door opened and Vincent Benlow, his mate who ran Halfway House, came in.

'Hiya, man,' he said, gripping Jim's hand. 'What brings you here?'

Jim indicated his suit. 'Delivering presents for the boys and girls who've been good. What are you doing here?'

'My mum's over there.' Vincent pointed through the serving hatch to a tiny lady with white hair.

'Didn't even recognise her, Vince,' Jim said. 'I'll go and say hello properly.'

'I expect she didn't know you with the beard either. She'd like to see you, Jim. You were always one of her favourites.'

'These are the lads I talked to you about,' Jim said. 'Andrew and Kieran.'

Vincent shook their hands. 'Nice to see you out and about, lads.' They both looked self-conscious.

'Vincent runs the Halfway House that I mentioned,' Jim explained. 'I've put your names down for places. Vince here would be looking after you.'

'I've some news on that,' Vincent said. 'One of the lads has done a runner.' He shook his head sadly. 'It was on the cards. He was on a warning as he was back into the drugs. We don't allow any of that.' He threw the lads a stern glance. 'If he hadn't absconded, then he probably would have been out on his ear. So I've got one room in a two-bed flat. It'll be available from next week.'

'I was looking for someone to take them both together,' Jim reminded him. 'There's no way that you can do a shuffle round? Squeeze in an extra body?'

Vincent sucked in his breath and tutted. 'Don't think so. If it were me, I'd take the available room. That's all I can offer at the moment, but you never know what might come up.'

'Thanks, mate,' Jim said. 'When do I need to let you know?'

'As soon as you can. Come tomorrow, I might have to take someone else. By Monday, I'll have a dozen people knocking my door down.'

'OK.'

'I'll go and see Mum,' Vincent said. 'Come over. Say hello.'

'Will do,' Jim said. 'I just need to make a call.'

He watched Vincent walk across the hall and then turned to the lads. 'What do you think? Rozzer, you're going to be out before Smudge. Is it best for one of you to take the place on offer and then we'll try to get the other in as soon as possible?'

'He didn't sound very hopeful,' Smudge said anxiously.

'It's a nice place,' Jim said. 'It would give you a good, solid base to start out again. Vincent would look after you.'

Smudge looked alarmed. 'I don't want to be without Rozzer.'

'It might only be for a short time. We could sort something out.'

The lad was starting to look panicked now.

'It's just an idea, Smudge,' Jim assured him. 'Nothing to worry about. We can talk it through.'

'But that bloke said he needs to know now.'

'It would be a shame to miss out on a place there,' Jim conceded.

'I'd like to go,' Rozzer chipped in.

Smudge blanched. 'What about me?'

'Jim said he'd sort something out. He's never let us down, has he?'

'What if he can't get me in anywhere?' Smudge's voice was rising. 'What if I come out and I'm back on the streets? What if you're all settled in this flat and just forget about me?'

'Don't be a twat.'

'Language. You're still one of Santa's little elves.'

'Sorry, Jim.'

'I think Rozzer should take the place,' Jim advised. 'If I've got one of you in there already, I'm hoping that getting the other in too might be easier.'

Smudge's eyes were filling with tears. 'What if it's not?'

'Whatever happens,' Jim said, 'I won't see you on the streets again.' He took Smudge by the shoulders and looked into his eyes. 'I promise you that.' Then he turned to Rozzer. 'Do you want to see if I can organise for you to go and view the flat?'

'If you think it's a good place to be, then I'm happy with that.'

Smudge's face twisted with anguish, but Jim couldn't worry about that now. If he could get one of them sorted, that was a good start. 'Shall we grab hold of Vincent now and tell him that on your release you'll move in?'

'Yeah.' Rozzer nodded earnestly.

'Then let's do it.'

Rozzer caught hold of his arm. In his eyes there was relief, gratitude and perhaps even a glimmer of affection. 'Thanks, Jim. You're a top bloke.'

'Thank me when you're both in there and settled,' Jim said. Then he hot-footed it after Vincent before he missed him.

Chapter Twenty-Seven

'I'm really sorry that I didn't make it to the party,' I say.

By the time I get to Boxley Social Club, Jim is already in the car park packing up and he's out of his Santa outfit. Which is a shame as I rather like him in it.

'Did it go off all right?'

'Fine,' Jim answers. 'The lads made great elves.' He flicks a thumb to where they're sitting in the back of his car. 'They didn't tell one single person to "go fuck themselves".'

'Excellent. Always a bonus.' We grin at each other.

'The pensioners loved their presents and the hall looked great.'

'Thanks, Jim,' I say. I really have no idea what I'd do without him.

'So what kept you?'

'This contract with Carter Randall is much bigger than I ever imagined, Jim,' I admit. Though I think it wise not to mention the bit about the lingering over hot chocolate and home-made biscuits. 'You should have seen the size of the trees that arrived. They're enormous. Then I had to stay and co-ordinate with the lighting company. It's very exciting but quite daunting.'

'It's going well, though?'

'Fabulous. Carter's really pleased. He just keeps asking me to do more and more.' I'm not quite sure when I'm going to raise the subject of my going to Lapland with Carter and the family for four days. It's just four days, I tell myself, surely I won't be missed for that lickle-ickle, teeny-tiny amount of time. Surely?

'Carter?' Jim laughs. 'On first-name terms now, eh?'

'He's nice,' I say lamely. 'I met his kids today. They're nice too.'

'We'll talk about it tonight,' Jim says. 'I have to get the lads back before four. Why don't we get a takeaway and a bottle of plonk?'

'Sounds good.'

I can't face cooking tonight, although it's a habit I don't want to slip into, otherwise all my profits will go to the Hong Kong Chinese Takeaway and the Australian vineyards instead of being saved for a wedding and a baby. I don't want to lose sight of that goal.

'I'll just say thanks to the boys. Can you take them to McDonald's as a treat on the way back?'

'Not really got enough time,' Jim says. 'Besides, they've got a choice of their prison gear or red-and-green elf costumes. Don't think they'd want to be seen out in either.'

'Oh.' Now that we seem to be absorbing them into our lives and my business, it is, occasionally, easy to forget they they're not just ordinary boys. 'I was just trying to be nice.'

'I'm sure they'd appreciate it. Unfortunately, it's not practical.'

'It's not long now before they get out, is it?'

'Rozzer's out soon. If we're lucky they might let him go before his due date. I've managed to fix him up with a place at Vincent's Halfway House.'

'Is that supposed to be down to you?'

'No. There should be loads of help for the lads in place, but it's not much in evidence at the moment. Cutbacks. Everyone left has massive caseloads. They do their best, but it's not always enough. I'm just doing what I can to lend a hand.'

'That is *so* you.' I stand on tiptoe and kiss his cheek.

'Well,' he says, shyly, 'you do what you can, don't you?'

I go over and tap on the window. The boys lower it. 'Thanks so much. Jim says you've worked really hard today.'

They both mumble that it's OK, or some such.

'Good news about Andrew's flat too.'

He beams back at me, but I see Kieran's face fall. Jim has told me that they want to stay together after release, that they've become family to each other while they've been inside.

'It won't be long before you're out too,' I reassure him. But he says nothing. 'Hopefully, I'll have some more stuff for you to do this week – if you're up for it.'

More nodding and mumbling in a teenage style. I'm growing fond of these boys already. They're damaged and vulnerable, but underneath their tough exterior and their couldn't-care-less attitude, I think that they're just crying out to be something better. I can tell. And so can Jim. That's why he's taking so much time with them. That's why I'm trusting them with my business.

'Better let you go,' I say. 'Catch you in the week.'

'Are you going straight back to the flat?' Jim asks.

'Er . . .' I'm planning to go into Snow + Rock as instructed and kit myself out with Arctic-strength ski gear. I've looked at the weather forecast in Lapland and it's truly freezing up there. The temperature is falling rapidly and I feel that things may get a little frosty round here too. But I can't explain all that to Jim while we're standing in the car park and he's in a rush to get the boys back. Instead, I settle on, 'I've just got a few errands to run first. You might be home before me.'

'OK.' He kisses me quickly, embarrassed by our surroundings and our audience. 'Love you.'

'Love you too.' I watch him jump into the car and drive away. I wave and the boys wave back.

153

When they've gone, I head to the Snow Centre and park up. Carter has told me what to buy for myself, so I'm armed with an extensive shopping list. I can't believe that I'll need all this clothing for four days but Carter seems to think that I will. As I'm going to be in charge of co-ordinating the itinerary while we're out there, I don't want to be shivering in the corner.

This place is amazing. I've never really had cause to come up here before as skiing really isn't my thing and, if the mercury falls too much, then I just don't go out. The Snow + Rock shop is filled with fabulous multicoloured offerings and I'm happy to spend time browsing and trying on gear. A lovely assistant, Ben, helps me with my purchases and soon I'm toddling out with carrier bags overflowing with good stuff.

Back at the flat, Jim is already home when I push through the front door. He's taking the opportunity to write some Christmas cards for me in front of the football on telly.

'Hey,' he says when he sees me. Then his expression darkens when his eyes light on all the carrier bags. 'Wow. Please tell me all that is for someone else.'

I sigh. Moment of truth. 'No,' I say. 'It's for me, but someone else is paying for it all.'

He waits patiently until I dump the bags on the floor and peel off my coat.

There's no easy way of putting this, so I might as well just spit it out. Jim is the most understanding and placid person on the planet, but I can see that even he might have an issue with me going away on holiday with a millionaire and leaving him on his jack at home. Which makes me wonder why I've agreed. My mouth goes dry and I know that I'm giving out guilty signals.

'Carter has asked me to go with him and the children on the trip that I've organised for them.'

'I take it that you've agreed.'

154

I sit on the sofa next to Jim. He turns off the football.

'How could I not?' is my argument. 'He is my best client, Jim. I didn't feel that I could refuse.'

'This is your busiest time, Cassie. There's a million things in the diary. How are you going to deal with all that?' He huffs at me. 'Are you simply going to let your other clients down?'

'I don't know. It's only four days.'

'Have you even looked at the stuff that's backing up?'

I admit that I haven't. That was going to be my very next job. 'I thought that you and the boys could still help out. And Gaby.'

'Oh, that's nice. You swan off to Lapland with a handsome millionaire and leave me here to pick up the pieces.'

I start to formulate an argument, but I simply can't come up with a valid one.

'You're right,' I say. All the fight goes out of me. 'It was a really crap idea. I'll call Carter and tell him that I can't possibly go. It was madness to think that I could. All this stuff can go straight back to Snow + Rock.'

I shake my head to clear it. What was I thinking? Of course I knew that Jim would be pissed off. Even a saint has his limits.

'It was stupid of me to agree to go. I just got caught up in the moment and Carter's paying me an extraordinary amount of money to accompany them. It would have been very lucrative.'

'Plus you're going on a private jet.'

'Yes.' I grimace. 'Am I really that shallow?'

He risks a smile. 'Yes.'

'I can't help it.' I tut at myself. 'This trip will be fantastic. I know because I've booked it all. It literally will be the trip of a lifetime. I might never have another chance like this. But I'll ring Carter now. I'll have to find him a nanny for the kids.'

'Is that why you're going?'

'Yes. I met them today and they're so sweet. They're really

missing their mum and wanted me to go with them. You're right though, it's idiotic. I need to be here.' I find my mobile in my pocket and pull it out. My eyes fill with tears.

'Wait,' Jim says. 'Let's go through the diary. See if we can work round it.'

'We can't,' I insist. 'It's not possible.'

'Don't be hasty,' Jim says. 'I'm sure we can cope. You should go. Of course you should.'

'Do you mean that?'

'We'll look at the bookings. If the lads and I can manage, then we will. You're right, Cassie, from what little I know of it, the whole trip sounds fantastic. You've had such a terrible year that you deserve a treat.'

'Really?' I search his face. 'Are you sure this is *really* how you feel?'

'I'd rather be coming with you,' Jim admits. 'But you've been so good with helping the lads out too that I can't deny you an opportunity like this.'

'Oh, you are brilliant.' I throw my arms round him and let my tears roll down my cheeks.

'It would help if Carter Randall wasn't such a handsome millionaire,' Jim confesses. 'But I can live with that if you promise me that you'll come home safely.'

'I will. Of course I will. And I'll work twice as hard the minute I get back.'

'I'll hold you to that.'

'Let's have our romantic dinner before I go,' I suggest.

'I've got a heavy week of shifts.'

'We'll have it when you get home one night. I'll do everything. I'll cook something special and we can exchange our Christmas cards. No presents, though,' I reiterate. 'If we're going to be really busy, then we might not have another chance. It will be my thank-you to you for being so wonderful.' I snuggle in next to him.

'OK,' Jim says with a contented shrug. 'Romantic dinner it is.'

'I'm just so lucky,' I say, resting my head on his shoulder. 'I'll never forget that.'

Chapter Twenty-Eight

So another week goes by in a blur with Jim and me both working like mad things. As a bit of a breather before I head off to Lapland, our romantic dinner is scheduled for tonight. I'd like to take the day off to relax, pamper myself and spend a ridiculously leisurely time preparing the meal as I feel as if I haven't stopped for a minute recently. But I can't. There's too much to do and Christmas is getting ever closer.

I can feel the excitement rising inside me and it's not just because of my impending trip. More than ever, I've really got the whole Christmas bug this year – which is just as well, as our entire lives are revolving around it.

Instead, I have a quick soak in the bath, run the razor over my legs and, when I'm dry, splot some nail varnish on my toes. You never know, good food might put Jim in the mood for good love. It's not yet ten o'clock in the morning but I'm marinating chicken to make a Spanish dish that I found on the internet. I'm going to have to shoot out to get the rest of the ingredients and I want to make a nice dessert too as Jim has a sweet tooth. I've some cupcakes to make and decorate for an upcoming event and I want to check that Gaby's on the case when it comes to the mince pies.

Carter and the children have been away all week. Carter's

jetting round the world being an entrepreneur and the children are with their mother in London. Which means that Randall Court is empty. I'm hoping that Jim and I can go up there and get started on their Christmas decorations. The Randalls are meeting me at Luton International Airport tomorrow evening. Carter is sending a car to whisk me straight to our waiting private jet. I cannot believe just how fabulous that sounds. I would like to say it out loud to a lot of people but, as there's only me here, I am thwarted in my attempts to show off. The joys of exclusive travel mean that, with good luck and a following wind, we should be in the small town of Kiruna, deep inside the Arctic Circle, a few hours later.

I've ordered some fabulous decorations for Carter, and I need to collect those today too. Which all adds up to no slacking for me. I get dressed and am out of the door, grabbing a cereal bar as a breakfast substitute on the way.

The weather here has taken a turn for the worse and, after the mild autumn we've enjoyed, the sharp slap of frost is a shock to the system. I scrape my car windscreen, hoping that, one day, we'll have enough money behind us to move out of the flat and into a house with a garden and a garage so I can put my car away at night.

First stop is the Christmas warehouse where I load up the back of the car with my purchases. For the outside of the Randall mansion I've gone for a very classy look – in a completely over-the-top way – but for the interior, I've decided to be more playful. After all, Carter wanted the house to look nice for the children, so I've taken that into account.

Next I stop off at the supermarket and buy the rest of the ingredients for my romantic dinner with Jim. I'm going to do a sticky toffee pudding for dessert as that's his favourite and it's just the sort of weather for a big, fat comfort pudding. When I've got all the food, including a gorgeous box of chocolates, I browse the greetings-card aisle.

I want something lovely to reinforce to Jim just how special he is to me. When you've been together as long as we have, it's sometimes easy to let the romance slide and I never want that to happen to us. I choose a suitably soppy card and pop it in my basket. It would be great to be able to treat Jim to something nice and perhaps I will for Christmas. We'll have to see how the money goes, but it certainly looks as if the business is set to turn a decent profit and I'm so relieved that my crazy idea wasn't just pie in the sky.

With the car stuffed to the gills, I head home, singing along to the Christmas tunes on the radio. Then, as I pass through Boxmoor, on the way back to the flat, I get the urge to call in on Mrs Ledbury, to see how she's doing.

I don't text in advance, I just roll up outside. If she's got something else on, then I'll go home. Minutes later, I'm ringing her doorbell and, as I do, I wonder why it never occurs to me to pop in and see my own mum like this. Gaby does and she's always nagging me that I should too. But when I don't even really have five minutes to spare, I'd still prefer to call in on a stranger. Perhaps it's because I've always felt as if I got in the way of my mother's life rather than being an integral part of it. I know that Mrs Ledbury will be delighted to see me, whereas with my own mum I'm never quite sure.

As I'm beating myself up, Mrs Ledbury answers the door and, of course, her eyes light up. 'Come in, my dear,' she cries as I knew she would. 'How lovely to see you.'

'I've only dropped by on the off chance that the kettle is on. If you have time.'

'I have all the time in the world,' she tells me. 'Do come in.'

I follow her through to her living room.

'The tree is looking wonderful.' She indicates my handiwork. 'If only there were more people here to appreciate it.'

The delicate angel is still there in pride of place. 'Did your son's family like it?'

'Oh, they didn't make it in the end and they haven't had time to come yet,' she says, a catch in her voice. 'They're so busy. So very busy.'

I feel my guilt towards my own mother ratchet up. But at least my mother isn't old and frail and doesn't sit at home waiting for me to call. My mother's young and vibrant and is, generally, too busy out having a good time to think of me or Gaby or her wonderful grandchildren at all. In fact, Mrs Ledbury looks much more like a grandmother should. She wears A-line skirts and cardigans, not low-cut T-shirts emblazoned with the word 'SEXY' picked out in hot pink sequins, teamed with five-inch heels. Mrs Ledbury has white hair in tight curls whereas my mother's long red hair is plumped up with extensions. She dresses as if she doesn't want to acknowledge that she is a mother and a grandmother to boot. But then Mrs Ledbury is old enough to be a mother to my mum. Perhaps, one day, my mum will grow into her role.

I daren't stay long at Mrs Ledbury's as I'm already running behind myself. So I down my tea, have a few more minutes of chit-chat and then I'm on my way with a cheery wave. Mind you, I still find a few extra minutes to go back to the flat the long way round so that I don't have to pass my own mother's house.

At home, I finish off the chicken recipe, put that in the oven on low to slow cook and then whip up the sticky toffee pudding for later.

While I'm watching a video on YouTube, instructing me in the art of creating Christmas garlands for banisters and mantelpieces, I get a text from Carter. Without me wanting it to, my heart skips a beat.

'*Did u get all ur ski gear?*'

'*Yes. So excited,*' I text back.

'*Me 2.*'

'*Will be up @ house decorating tree, etc.*'

'*Shame I'm not there. CU tomorrow. T says kids r totally hyper.*'

I'll bet they are. The furthest I ever went as a kid was to Brighton for a day trip. Holidays weren't high on my mother's agenda. It's only since she discovered the delights of married men with villas in Spain that she likes to travel. I snap my messages off, then sit and wonder how Tamara feels about someone else taking her kids on holiday. I know that Carter and I aren't romantically involved but it must be weird for her nevertheless. If they were my kids, I'd want to be with them.

I finish watching my YouTube clips, write Jim's card, set the table including posh candle and check on dinner. When I'm sure it's not going to burn, I slip through to the bedroom and change into something more slinky. Well, more slinky than trackie bottoms and a sweatshirt. I check myself in the mirror and am glad to see that I don't scrub up too badly. There were times this year when I couldn't face getting out of bed or showering or washing my hair. I feel that this is the start of me getting my life back on track again.

Jim and I have certainly got something to celebrate this Christmas. Now, everything's ready. All I have to do is wait for my loved one to come home.

Chapter Twenty-Nine

There had been tension on the unit all morning. A dozen different punch-ups had broken out, most of them gang related. All Jim had done was fight fires since he'd started his shift. To try to quell it, all the lads were on lock-down in their cells. Now it was fast approaching lunchtime and they were all going to have to come out peaceably or go hungry. And, of course, that was against Home Office rules and probably infringed their human rights too.

Thankfully, there were very few days when this job made him weary down to his bones, but this was one of them. Perhaps if Cassie made a go of her business, he could give up the prison service and, instead, have a career that involved writing Christmas cards and dressing up as Santa to entertain giggly pensioners. There were a lot worse ways to spend your days.

He only hoped that Smudge and Rozzer had stayed clear of the trouble. They shouldn't be doing anything to jeopardise their release. Not now that they were so close. But he hadn't seen them in the middle of any of the brawls and he was grateful for that, at least.

The siren sounded so he knew they were going to do a roll-call, just to make sure that all of the lads were present and correct. All the officers went round checking the cells. This was one of the more tiresome rituals of prison life. Everything stopped until the final call-out came of 'Roll correct!' and the day could start up again. Jim was instructed to take the top level and made his way up there. He worked his way along the landing with his big bunch of keys, unlocking the cells and recording the presence of the occupants. They were all pissed off this morning and even Jim, who was normally considered one of the more respected screws, was subjected to regular torrents of abuse.

He opened one of the cells and found Rozzer in there. 'What are you doing here? Why aren't you in your own cell?'

'Smudge is having a total mare today,' he said. 'He just needed to be on his own.'

'Not a luxury you can have in here, lad,' Jim pointed out. 'It's not a bed and breakfast establishment. Come on, back to your own place.'

Rozzer pulled a face. 'Not for much longer.'

The lad stood up wearily and Jim escorted him along the landing. 'Remember this,' he said. 'Remember all that you hate about this and you won't be visiting us again any time soon.'

'I'm not coming back. No way. Not this time.' Rozzer fell into step beside Jim. 'But I'm worried about Smudge,' he confided. 'He's finding it hard that I'm going without him.'

'If there was another place at Vincent's Halfway House, I might be able to make a special case for him. He's kept his nose clean in here. You both have. Model prisoners. I'm sure the governor would look on it favourably. But, as it is, there's nowhere for him to go. I'd rather that he stayed here where I can keep an eye on him until we can get him into Vincent's place with you.'

'I hope it won't be long,' Rozzer admitted.

'Vincent will come through. I'm sure of it.'

He wanted to tell the lad how much they had both come to mean to him, but it wouldn't do to let his professional barrier down totally. With all the things they'd been doing together for Cassie's Christmas business, it was hard to maintain the necessary distance that the prison service quite rightly advised. Still, there was only a short time to go and then he could, hopefully, be the mentor to them that he wanted to be.

They walked the remaining few yards to the cell in silence and Jim unlocked the door. As it swung open, Rozzer gasped out loud.

'Oh, sweet Jesus,' Jim breathed.

Smudge was slumped on the floor of the cell, his arms held out in front of him, blood dripping down his hands. It was instantly clear to Jim that he had slashed his wrists. This wasn't the first time he'd seen it happen and, God help him, it wouldn't be the last. The regular cell searches that stripped out everything usually found sharpened sticks or bits of razor blades, anything that could be made into weapons, but there was always the chance that they'd miss something.

Rozzer slumped to the floor next to him. 'You stupid fucker!' he sobbed. 'Why did you do this? We could have sorted it out. You didn't need to do this.'

Jim was already on his radio, calling for medical assistance from Healthcare. Having done that, he too dropped to his knees next to Smudge and went into autopilot, checking his airways, breathing and circulation.

The lad opened eyes dull with pain. He was slowly slipping into unconsciousness.

'Hang on,' Jim said. 'Help's on its way.' He knew that, in minutes, he'd hear the medics' feet pounding down the corridor as they ran to respond.

'What can we do?' Rozzer said.

'Get the loo roll. Quickly.'

Rozzer dashed to bring it over to Jim.

'Make a pad and press it on the wounds.'

With fumbling fingers, Rozzer unfurled a wodge of toilet paper from the roll and pressed it onto his friend's slashes. From what Jim could see, Smudge had cut his wrists across the vein – thankfully, the most ineffectual way to try to kill yourself. If he'd cut down the length of the vein, they'd be in a lot more trouble. Despite the amount of blood, it didn't look as if the cuts went deep.

'I'm sorry,' Smudge whispered. 'I didn't want to be on my own.'

'You're not on your own, idiot,' Rozzer said. 'You've got me.'

'You're leaving me,' Smudge wept. 'I don't think I can manage in here without you.'

'Jim will look after you,' Rozzer assured him softly. He dabbed at the blood and stroked his friend's hair. 'He'll get you a place with me and everything will be great.'

It made Jim's heart break to listen to him. What had he done? They had such faith in him. He'd made himself out to be some sort of saviour who could fix their lives and now they'd come to depend on him. What if he let them down? What if he couldn't get them a place together? What if Smudge was tipped out of here and onto the streets as he feared? Suppose Rozzer got on so well at Vincent's that he suddenly felt he didn't need his old cellmate? It happened. Prison was a funny place where unlikely relationships were formed.

Two of the medical staff arrived seconds later, breathless and with a heavy medical bag and gurney in tow. Jim eased Rozzer out of the way, 'Come on, lad. We need to get him down to Healthcare as fast as we can before he loses any more blood.'

After some basic checks, the men in white coats lifted Smudge onto the trolley.

'Will he be OK?' Jim asked.

'This time,' one of the medics said and they rolled him away.

Rozzer was crying now and Jim's heart went out to him, but there was little he could do to comfort the lad.

'I've got to lock you in,' he said to Rozzer. 'I need to follow them down to Healthcare, fill in a report. But I'll come back and tell you how he is as soon as I can.'

'Look after him, Jim,' Rozzer said.

The sad thing was that that was exactly what he was trying to do and it looked as if he had failed spectacularly.

Chapter Thirty

By the end of Jim's shift, Smudge was settled in an in-patient bed in Healthcare and his wounds had been bandaged. Thankfully, despite losing some blood, he hadn't needed a blood transfusion – otherwise that would have meant a trip to the local hospital hand-cuffed to an officer, which was always a humiliating experience.

Now Smudge was enjoying a long, drug-induced sleep. He looked pale, paler than normal, and terrible. His hair was matted to his head with sweat, and blood was smeared on his face. Whoever had cleaned him up hadn't done the best of jobs, but at least the lad was alive. The psychiatrist who'd looked at him had concluded that it hadn't been a serious suicide attempt but a cry for help. Jim could probably have told her that. A suicide attempt wouldn't delay Smudge's release, but it made Jim even more fear-ful for the lad when the moment came. He just had to sort something out for him.

The only thing he could hope for was that the governor would throw his weight behind getting Smudge a place with Rozzer. Part of him also felt sorry for Andrew, the stronger boy, who would feel the weight of responsibility for looking after his more vulnerable friend. He hoped that he didn't tire of it. Jim would have to make sure that Smudge got all the support that was available to him.

Jim sighed. Sometimes life could be very cruel. He patted

Smudge's hand, even though the lad was away with the fairies. 'See you tomorrow, little buddy,' he said under his breath. 'Hopefully, everything will look better in the morning.'

He checked his watch. Nearly time for him to sign off for the night, but there was one more thing he wanted to do. He left Healthcare and went back up to Starling and along the corridor to see Rozzer.

The lad was sitting alone in his cell, staring blankly at a comic. He looked up expectantly when Jim unlocked the door. His eyes were red-rimmed from crying.

'Is he all right?' Rozzer asked, his face grey with concern.

'Yes. He's going to be fine. He's been given a nice cocktail of drugs and probably won't wake up until the morning.'

A wave of relief washed over Rozzer's features.

'Are *you* all right?'

The lad nodded. 'Yeah.'

'Want to talk about it?'

He shook his head. 'Nah. Not now.'

'Sure?'

'Yeah.'

'I'll leave you then,' Jim said. 'We'll catch up tomorrow.' He turned to go.

'Jim,' Rozzer said. 'Thanks.'

'I wish I'd done more,' Jim said. 'I wish that I could have got you a flat together right away.'

'It's not your fault,' Rozzer said.

'I didn't realise that he was feeling so bad about it.'

'Me neither.'

'We'll watch out for him,' Jim said. 'Both of us.'

He clapped the lad on his shoulder and then, more reluctantly than ever, locked the door behind him.

*

169

Jim jumped into the car and gunned the engine. Never had he needed to get away from the unit more than he had tonight and yet never had he wanted to stay more. All he was looking forward to now was having a good scrub-down and sitting in front of the television for the rest of the night – preferably watching something fluffy and light. One of Cassie's favourite chick flicks would work. Nothing involving blood, gore or death.

He drove down the lanes, more slowly than normal, concentrating as he shifted through the gears, took the corners. Not surprisingly, he felt quite wobbly. Maybe he should have stayed five minutes longer at work, had a cup of tea with a couple of sugars in it, talked to someone about what had happened.

A few more bends and he realised that he'd have to pull over. When he stopped, he noticed that his hands were shaking uncontrollably. Jim gripped the steering wheel to try to steady them. There was a tightness in his chest and he could hardly get his breath. He couldn't get out of his head the picture of Smudge smeared in blood. What if Jim hadn't got there when he had? What if Smudge had been successful, if his cry for help had gone too far? It didn't bear thinking about. There were constant suicide attempts in the unit, but they hadn't lost a lad in years. Jim certainly didn't want it to happen on his watch and definitely not to Smudge.

He sat there taking in deep gulps of air until the feeling had passed and the trembling had stopped. There was still a tight knot in his stomach, but he couldn't sit here any longer. Cassie would be wondering where he was. So, as soon as he felt able, he set off again, concentrating on the road ahead, trying not to think about what might have been.

He was on the home stretch, just travelling up the dual carriageway, well under the speed limit. The flat was in sight and relief flooded into his bones. Then he remembered. It was supposed to be their romantic dinner tonight. Oh God. Jim hit his forehead with his hand. With all that had gone on today, he'd completely forgotten. Cassie had said that they weren't going to exchange presents, just cards, but he hadn't even got her one of those. What a total idiot! There was no way he could go home without one. All she'd asked for was a small thing. How would it look if he couldn't even deliver that?

When he got to the roundabout at the top of their road, he turned the car full circle and headed back towards the Tesco Express, which was always open late. Hopefully, they'd have a decent selection of Christmas cards. Or, at the very least, *any* Christmas cards of *any* kind.

Minutes later he pulled up outside and sprinted in. There was, praise the Lord and all that was holy, a rack of Christmas cards just inside the door. Jim grabbed the prettiest one that he could see. Should he add chocolates? They had some nice ones ready gift-wrapped in classy gold paper. It had been done well. He knew about these things now. Cassie had said no presents. Would it look worse if he took her chocolates when she'd stuck to the plan and had bought him nothing? Best not to risk it.

So he paid for the card, thankful that some divine spark of inspiration had made him remember. Even if it was at the last minute. He'd have hated to go home empty-handed. Then he would have been in deep, deep trouble.

Chapter Thirty-One

'It's freezing out there,' Jim says as he comes through the door, shivering with cold.

Winter has really come on with a vengeance and I wonder if we'll have a white Christmas this year. That would be so wonderful, but it will be the first time in ages if we do.

'Good day?' I ask.

'Not the best,' he admits as he throws down his bag and strips off his coat, his face grey and troubled.

'Want to talk about it?'

'Not right now,' he says. 'I need a shower, a very big glass of wine and a plate of whatever it is that smells so delicious in the oven. I might feel human again then.'

'It's some Spanish chicken dish that I can't remember the name of,' I confess. 'But it tastes as good as it smells.'

'Hmm,' Jim says. 'Then that will do for me.'

'I've put the fire on in the living room and we can snuggle down later.' He does look tired down to his bones.

He looks at me suspiciously. 'No Christmas cards to write? Presents to wrap?'

I laugh. 'No! Well, nothing that can't wait for just one night. I've got stuff that I could be doing for Carter' – Jim lets out a heartfelt groan, which I choose to ignore – 'but I thought that it was time we had an evening off.'

'I need a break tonight,' he says with a deep sigh. 'Believe me.'

'Then you go and get changed and I'll open the bottle.'

'Music to my ears,' Jim says and he disappears into the bedroom.

So I do as I said I would. I open the bottle of red and pour us a couple of hearty glasses. I stir the casserole, which looks dark, rich and scrummy. Good comfort food for a bitterly cold night. I've also put patatas bravas in the oven and I give them a shake. They're golden brown and crisp. Another five minutes and it should all be ready.

It's not long before Jim comes back, all freshly washed and changed. I hand him the glass of wine and he gulps it gratefully.

I go to the oven and lift out the casserole. As I'm standing there, still in my oven gloves, Jim winds his arms around my waist and nuzzles into my neck.

'Hey,' I say, 'what's that for?'

'Just wanted you to know that I love you.' He's saying the right words, but his voice is flat, empty.

I swivel in his arms to face him. 'Are you sure everything's OK?'

'Yes,' he says. 'Everything's fine.'

Why do I get the impression that he's not telling me something? But then Jim quite often keeps to himself the details of his working day. I think he likes to leave it all inside the unit if he can. I hope that's all it is, rather than a problem between us. Despite him agreeing that I should go to Lapland, I can tell that, underneath, he'd rather I didn't go.

'Ready for me to dish out?'

He nods, so I pop the casserole on the table and Jim lays out the warm plates. I fetch the potatoes. Jim refills his glass, knocks

173

it back and tops it up again. Wow. He must have had a really bad day as he's certainly hitting the Rioja hard. Can't think that I've ever seen him do that before. Jim sits down and I take the chair opposite. This all looks lovely, romantic, but I can't shake off a feeling of disquiet. Something's not right and I can't put my finger on it.

I put some music on the iPod – nothing to do with Christmas for once. We eat dinner. The chicken is beautiful and falls off the bone.

'Delicious,' Jim says as he eats, but I can tell that he's not quite here.

'Are you sure you don't want to talk?'

'No.' It's a borderline snap. 'This isn't the right time. I just want some peace and quiet. I don't want to think about the unit. I don't want to think about anything. I want nothing more complicated than a few glasses of wine.'

'Right.' This isn't boding well for our lovey-dovey evening. It's rare to see Jim in a bad mood and it's a long time since I've seen him so scratchy.

I clear away the plates when we've finished. 'Shall we exchange cards now while I wait for the sticky toffee pudding to finish?'

'Mmm,' Jim says, barely registering that I've cooked his favourite dessert.

I sit back at the table and produce my red envelope. 'Perhaps next year we'll do something wonderful,' I suggest.

'Not if you're going to carry on with this Christmas business,' he says.

I'm slightly thrown by this. 'Don't you want me to?'

'Yes,' he says. 'Of course. But you have to admit that it's dominating our lives.'

'That's only because it's taken me by surprise this year. I had no idea that it would be so successful. Next year I'll be better prepared. I only hope that Carter will be a client again.'

'Ah,' Jim says. '*Carter.*'

'What does that mean?'

'Nothing.'

I wonder if this is really about a bad day at work or if it's all down to my trip to Lapland. Jim's said that he's happy for me to go, but I wonder if he is deep down. If the boot was on the other foot, would I be happy for him?

'He's a business client,' I stress. 'An important one.'

'His name is every other word that comes out of your mouth, though,' Jim says.

'I don't think so.'

'I'm just sick of hearing "*Carter this, Carter that*".'

I feel wounded. It's not like Jim to be petty, but I can't help but bite back. 'All you talk about is your young criminals. Do I grumble about that? No. I've actually done my very best to help them out. I've really supported you over the last few weeks, Jim, and have got them both involved in my business. I've welcomed them into our home. I don't hear you complaining then.'

'They've done a great job.'

'They have,' I agree. 'I really like them both. They've helped me out so much and I'm grateful for that. I can see why you want to help them. But I don't complain that they're more important to you than me. Can't you see why I have to pander to Carter Randall? He has spent more money with Calling Mrs Christmas! than all my other clients put together.'

Jim sighs in a disgruntled manner. 'There are more important things than Christmas, Cassie.'

'Because of him we'll have the chance to pay off some of our debts, get our heads above water again.'

'Well, bully for Carter,' he snipes. 'So he's a big, fat cash cow who we must all revere.'

We rarely argue, but I know this could escalate if I let it. I want Jim to be proud of what I've achieved, not try to belittle it. Christmas might not be important to him, but this business – however trivial – has given me life and hope again. It's stopped me from fretting about where our next penny is coming from. It's stopped me from feeling that we're drowning in debt. It's stopped me from sinking into depression between these four walls and I love it. For the first time in nearly a year, I feel like myself again. I have something to get up for every morning. I wish Jim could share that. Perhaps he's happier when I'm sitting at home, trapped here in my own prison, totally dependent on him. Maybe he's so used to locking people up that he'd really rather like me to be locked in here too. If I have my own life, it might be too much of a threat to him. Instead of saying all that, I bite it down.

'Let's not fight,' I offer, but inside I still feel resentful. 'We're supposed to be having a romantic dinner.'

'Sorry,' Jim says, but he doesn't sound sorry either.

'Here.' I hand over my card and wait for him to open it. Perhaps this will soften his mood.

On the front is a teddy, draped with tinsel and holding a heart. The verse reads: 'I love you always, but especially at Christmas.'

'That's great,' Jim says, but somehow his smile doesn't reach his eyes. 'Lovely.'

His reaction is more muted than I hoped for. He hands over his own card.

I rip open the envelope and pull out the card. It's glittery with a picture of a festive cottage on the front, festooned with snow. Across the top of the card in foiled script it says, 'Happy Christmas to you from across the miles.'

I do a double take. Across the miles? I look up at Jim, frowning. 'Is this supposed to be funny?'

'What?' he says.

'Is it some sort of cryptic comment about my trip to Lapland?'

'Eh?'

'Happy Christmas across the miles?' I show him the card.

His face falls.

'Is this about Carter too?' I say. 'Do you not want me to go?'

He's still looking perplexed when he takes the card from me. He stares at the front and then sighs wearily. 'This isn't about Carter. It isn't about your trip to Lapland. In fact, it's not about you at all. It's about me.'

'I have no idea what you're talking about.'

'I forgot about our dinner. I forgot to buy you a card. I ran into the supermarket at the last minute and grabbed the nearest one. I just thought it was pretty. I didn't even stop to read the words.'

'Thanks,' I say. 'I mean that much to you?'

'I've had a really crappy day, Cassie. The crappiest of crap days. I'm sorry. I didn't mean it.'

'I've been running round like a lunatic for the last few weeks, trying to get this business going.' I can hear myself shouting and I don't want to. I want to stop. This is Jim. He hardly ever fucks up. But this was important to me. 'When I could have been doing other things that would actually have earned us some money, I've worked half the day trying to make this meal nice for us. All *you* had to do was buy a bloody card.'

'I suppose the "other things" would have involved Carter Randall,' Jim shouts back. 'Like I said, he's the man who seems to be occupying your every waking moment.'

'And like I said to you, it's business.'

'Is it really, Cassie? Are you sure that's all it is?'

If I'm honest, I'll admit that Carter has expected so much from me that most of my working days and nights *have* been spent sorting out his Christmas for him. I don't want to let him down. If he tells his contacts about me, then my business could really fly. He might be paying handsomely for my services, but he's definitely getting his pound of flesh.

'You're going away with him, Cassie. For four days. And nights. To naffing Lapland.'

'You were the one who said you were happy for me to go with him.'

'If I told you now that I wasn't happy at all, would it change anything? Would you cancel your holiday?'

'It's not a holiday, it's a ...' I run out of words. What is it exactly? I've been running about, so excited about it that I have to remind myself. 'It's a business trip. One that I've organised. It's a holiday for my clients. I'm there in a purely professional capacity.'

Jim raises his eyebrows. 'No one else could take your place?'

In truth, I'm sure Carter could have chosen to take anyone with him that he wanted to. A friend, his assistant, the housekeeper. So why me?

'We talked about this,' I say feebly. My head's spinning. Jim is never unreasonable and I don't know where this has suddenly come from, but it's hit me like a bolt from the blue. Has this been simmering all this time, unspoken? Seems so.

Jim's eyes are bleak. 'Whatever you want to call it, you're jetting off tomorrow night with a divorced millionaire and a handsome bastard to boot. How do you think I feel?'

'You should have said. When I first asked you. You said that you were OK with it. I could have told him no then. At that point, I could have pulled out. Now I'm committed. I can't let him down, Jim. It would look so unprofessional. I simply can't.'

Jim necks his wine. 'But you're happy to let me down?'

Then, for the first time in all the years I've known him, he stomps out of the room.

Chapter Thirty-Two

We wake up still bad friends. My night of passion never happened and we slept back to back, keeping to our own sides of the bed. It's a long, long time since we've done that. I can't even remember when it last happened.

To make it worse, I pretend to be asleep while Jim gets ready for work. He doesn't bring me a cup of tea as he usually does and I hear the door slam firmly behind him when he leaves. I hope he's got a hangover as, apart from one little glass, he polished off all the wine himself and then morosely drained the dregs of a bottle of brandy we'd got lurking at the back of the cupboard. I sat and stared blankly at some rubbish on the television while making bows for Carter's Christmas tree. He knew who they were for – I'm sure he did – and maybe that incensed him even more.

I sigh to myself. I hate falling out with Jim. We hardly ever do it. This business, which has been bringing us together, now threatens to push us apart. I lie in bed, stewing. Should I just ring Carter today and tell him that I can't go to Lapland, that I have to stay at home here and do . . . what? What exactly do I have to stay for? It's true that there's a lot in the diary, but it's all simple stuff. Nothing that Jim couldn't manage with a bit of help from Gaby and the boys. They could easily hold the fort for me. It's only four days, for heaven's sake. It's not as if I'm disappearing for two weeks. And I really don't think that I could bear to let Carter down at such short notice. It would be so amateur. He has been a great supporter and has helped to give me the belief that I can do this.

I worry at my fingernails. Dammit! When it boils down to it, I just want to go on this bloody trip!

I can understand that Jim isn't wildly happy about it and, if I'm honest, I'd love it if he was coming along too. It's going to be mind-blowing, I'm sure. I've organised every aspect to the very best of my ability. That's why I don't want to miss it. I want to make sure that it's every bit as perfect as I've planned. When am I ever going to get to travel in such ostentatious luxury again? I have never even come close to this level of decadence. This is a once-in-a-lifetime experience. Jim knows that. I know that. That may sound selfish, but it's true. I'm sure anyone would feel the same way.

I'm disappointed that he thinks he can't trust me. All these years that we've been together, I've never once looked at another man. This is business. I want Carter as a customer next year so I need to keep him happy. All this festive frivolity is costing him a small fortune and earning me one in the process too. I want Carter to know that I am the best Christmas planner in the whole wide world and wimping out on this trip isn't the way to do it.

I'm going up to Randall Court today. I have so much to do and now I'm kicking myself that I spent hours cooking for our disastrous 'romantic' dinner when I could have been doing so much else.

I have to pack the children's cases and Carter's too. I'm going to make a start on the Christmas decorations, though I'm wondering whether I'm going to get everything done in a day when, in my diary, I'd booked out two. I'd planned to do this earlier in the week, as I'd wanted to clear the decks for him as much as humanly possible, but there's still a bit of a backlog. If I don't get all of the house done today, it will have to wait until I get back. Even Carter must understand that I can't be in two places at once. I also need to check that all is well with the lighting company, which will be back again today to finish dressing the front of the house and to start on the grounds at the back.

Hauling myself out of bed, I make my own tea and get ready to face the day. I'd like to try on all my swizzy ski gear again, but I simply don't have the time. I pack all that I can in a rush. The car is coming for me tonight at five o'clock and the private jet leaves Luton International Airport at six-thirty. Only if Jim comes home as quickly as he possibly can will I get to see him before I leave. I look at my phone. I should call him, leave him a loving message, but I'm not in the right mood yet. Part of me still feels snappy and hurt. *Across the bloody miles*, indeed.

An hour later I'm swinging through the gates of the big house. It's the first time I don't feel intimidated. I don't exactly feel as if I *belong*, but I no longer feel as if I'm here under false pretences. Carter is away in New York, I think, and he's meeting me at the airport tonight with the children. With everyone away, I guess I'll have the place pretty much to myself. He won't see what I've done until after we're back from Lapland and it's such a shame that I won't be able to finish it all in time. What a lovely surprise that would be.

As I park up, I'm grateful to see that the outdoor Christmas tree is still standing in all its glory and I have to say it really is fabulous. I think if Carter wants to have one there permanently, we should think about planting a fir in the spring. It's the perfect spot.

Thankfully, the lighting company are already here and waiting for me. I walk round to the back of the house with the men to discuss the plans. They seem to have come armed with a truck-load of stuff and it's all I can do to stop myself clapping my hands with glee. The trees out here are going to be draped with a multitude of white twinkling lights. I'm having a pergola built, more like a small bandstand really, that will be totally covered in lights too. Inside it there'll be a bench dressed with Christmas foliage. At the edge of the woods there are to be wire reindeer sculptures in a group, all dressed with lights too. I think – I hope – it will look marvellous, magical. Once I've gone through the plan again, I leave the men to it. They're going to be here all day today and most of tomorrow, and seem ultra-efficient. Again, I wish I was here to supervise, but by tonight – if all goes to plan – I'll be up and away beyond the Arctic Circle.

Carter's assistant, Georgina, lets me into the house through the back door and organises Hettie to bring me some tea. The Christmas tree has also been erected in the entrance hall and is equally magnificent. I think that I'll start on that first. I have an extensive layout on the computer at home and I've got a printout with me to double-check everything. I've never done so many spreadsheets in my life and I've certainly never needed one for my own Christmas decorations. The idea is that I'm also going to dress the banisters of the galleried staircase, so that's going to take me a while. Plus the mantelpieces in the rooms downstairs are going to be festooned with swags. Every available nook and cranny is to have its current occupants packed away and replaced by vases brimming with festive flowers. Upstairs, I'm also decorating the children's bedrooms using artificial Christmas trees. More than enough to keep me busy.

I make a dozen trips to the car to bring in my boxes of baubles. I'm just unpacking my first one when Hettie brings my tea.

'Oh, this will look lovely,' she says when she sees my colour scheme.

'I've gone with bright, fun colours for the children,' I explain. 'I just hope Carter approves.'

The boxes are overflowing with baubles and bows in cerise, purple, turquoise and lime green. I've got flowers and garlands in the same shades. There are also key pieces in iridescent glass. I'm aiming for modern but stylish.

'I'm sure he will,' Hettie assures me. 'He's quite an easy man to please. It's nice to see you bring a smile back to his face.'

I do?

'I shouldn't say it,' Hettie lowers her voice, 'but there's not been a lot of happiness in this home for the past year or two.'

'That's sad.'

'So it is,' she agrees. 'It's the children I worry about. They're so delightful. I just hope their parents can sort themselves out. I shouldn't be speaking out of turn, but Tamara has never been much of a mother to them. I think they get in the way of her career.' Then, briskly, 'I'd better let you get on, looks like you've enough to do.'

Perhaps she's thought better of the fact that she's gossiping with me.

'I'm busy trying to fill the freezer so they won't starve while I'm not here over Christmas,' she adds. 'Let me know if you need anything. I can make you a sandwich for lunch.'

She heads back to the kitchen, giving me a friendly wave as she goes. I wonder if Carter has told her that there's a chef coming in for the holidays. Possibly not and I don't think that it's my place to break the news to her. Especially not if I want that sarnie.

I think of my argument with Jim last night, which seemed to come out of nowhere, and I want to call him. I want to tell him that I still love him and that, even though I'm determined to go on this trip, he has absolutely nothing to worry about. He can be jealous of the adventure, but not of the man. I pull out my mobile and go to ring him, but my fingers stall. This isn't really the time. If Jim's having a busy day and is distracted it could all go horribly wrong. I don't want to rush this conversation. So I wonder if I could try to catch him at his lunchtime break. I'm sure he'll pop out to check his messages then – he usually does.

So I put my phone away and, instead, I turn my attention to the tree. I've been watching a lot of American festive decorating videos on YouTube as they seem to be the masters at it, sparing no expense in dressing their homes for Christmas. I only hope that I haven't gone completely over the top. However, a house this size demands something special. You can't just stick up a six-foot artificial tree from Asda and hope for the best. It would be totally lost in here. So I've gone BIG!

I wonder how Tamara used to decorate it. Did she do it herself or get someone in? I think if there had been a regular person, Georgina would surely have got her to do it. Is Tamara really as indifferent a mother as Hettie intimated? My heart goes out to those children as I know exactly how that feels. Doesn't Tamara realise how lucky she is? If I were in her shoes, I'm sure I'd damn well make a better job of it. Then I remind myself that this isn't a competition with Carter's wife. This is me just doing my job to the best of my ability. But, as I look up at the towering tree, I think this year it's going to look better than it ever has before and everyone who gazes upon it will have their socks blown off.

Chapter Thirty-Three

Before I can start on decorating the tree, I have to bring in my stepladders. I totter my way across the gravel with them and set them up in the hall. The tree still looks dauntingly tall even from halfway up it. I'm actually going to have to stretch to even reach the top of the tree.

Finally, I'm ready and I work my way down from the top, feeding the wires of the white lights through the branches. It's a beautiful tree, thick and glossy. I start by twining the lights through the branches – four sets of them. When I've checked that they're working properly, I start on the trimming and add an enormous cerise star to the pinnacle, then work my way down with the bows. I've used wire-edged ribbon – fifty metres of it! – and I carefully tie on the home-made bows. All this I have learned from tutorials on YouTube. I let the tails drape through the tree as artistically as I can manage. So that I can bill Carter accurately, I've kept a record of all the hours I've spent making pretty bows and, believe me, it's a lot. The upside is that you can still watch telly while you're doing them. The key, my internet guru says, is to fill the inside of the tree so that everything's not plonked in a line on the outside. I always thought I was a bit of a dab hand when it came to decorating trees – Gaby usually gets me to do hers too – but I've learned so much.

I add my baubles, starting with the smaller ones on lofty branches and graduating to larger ones around the bottom of the tree, remembering to fill in the middle. I intersperse the baubles with iridescent icicles that, even on a dull winter's day, catch the light spectacularly. This will look totally amazing when I turn the lights back on again.

I've bought some glitzy cerise material to drape around the base to hide the pot and all the wires from the lights. I stand back to admire my handiwork. It looks beautiful, even though I say it myself, and makes this cavernous white hall look warm and welcoming. And oh so very festive!

But it's all taking so much longer than I thought. It's lunchtime before I've finished the tree and I realise that I need to buy some plastic storage boxes for when the time comes to pack everything away. I'm only hoping that I can find somewhere to store it all for the coming months. If I'm going to do this again next year, I want to be able to recycle and reuse.

I get my promised sandwich from Hettie and eat it standing up at the breakfast bar in the kitchen. She's busy so we don't chat much, stopping only to talk about the weather in between mouthfuls for me and stirring or chopping for her. I call Jim, but his phone goes straight to voicemail. There's nothing to do but leave a message.

'Hi,' I say. 'Can you call me?' I don't want to launch into an apology while Hettie is here. I lower my voice and say, 'Love you.'

I hope Jim feels the same, but now I can only wait until he rings back.

After my brief lunch I start on the garland that's going to go up the staircase. There's masses of it. First, I thread on the foliage – fake for ease of handling – winding it in and out of the rails. Then I thread it through with the same ribbons and bows that I've used on the tree. I hook on matching baubles too and little presents wrapped in co-ordinating foil paper. I step back to check it out. Wow. It certainly makes a statement. But I'm never going to get it all done in the next few hours. So I work my way up to the first landing on the stairs on both sides, by which time I've run out of bows. I'll need to make a whole heap more, but I'm not sure when. Perhaps I ought to take some ribbon to Lapland.

I've still got everyone's cases to pack and time is marching on. I guess if I'm late for a private jet it's more likely to wait for me, but I don't want to push my luck. With a slightly panicked glance at my watch, I head upstairs and check out the children's bedrooms. I'll need to do these later in the week when I'm back, but I just wanted to refresh my memory anyway. I click away with the camera on my phone, even though I've already got some photographs. Both rooms are so splendid and I would have loved a bedroom like this as a child. Eve's is a confection in pink while Max's is a typical boy's, all done out in blue. That should go well with my planned colour scheme. I get an unbidden flashback of Gaby and me, squashed into our bunk beds in our cramped, bleak room at home until well into our teens, and I push away the image. These kids have a different life.

Thankfully, they or Hettie or someone has laid out the clothes that the children need to take with them. There's a plethora of ski gear, casual clothing and underwear for both of them and all I really have to do is fold it all into the waiting cases. When I've packed, I heft them out to the top of the stairs.

Now I must do the same for Carter. As I head back towards the main bedroom, I can't resist having a look around. This place really is more magnificent than anything I've seen before. Corridors seem to stretch out in every direction, covered in acres of plush carpet. There are a dozen different doors and I wonder how anyone can need that number of rooms. It really is more like a hotel than a home.

Quietly, feeling like an intruder, I open some doors. They swing in silently and reveal more bedrooms, sitting rooms, what looks as if it could be Carter's office, a well-equipped gym lined with mirrors and a multitude of bathrooms. Then I open the door to what's clearly the master suite and it nearly takes my breath away. It's full-on, no-holds-barred WAG. The bed in the centre of the room is huge, standing on a raised cream-leather platform. There's a modern open fireplace on the wall opposite with a fantastic abstract painting hanging above it. In front of the fire is a cream rug and two ornate chairs. In the corner stands a mirrored mosaic statue of Buddha about two metres high. The wall behind the bed is covered in a bold gold-and-cream flowered design. The bedding is gold, glitzy and looks like pure silk. It's quite the most amazing bedroom that I've ever seen and it makes me dreadfully discontent with my five-year-old Dunelm Mill duvet cover.

There are no clothes laid out here and I can't even see any wardrobes. So I wander round the room, feeling even more as if I'm where I shouldn't be. Does Carter sleep here alone now that Tamara has left, I wonder? It seems such an enormous space for one person. Does it make him feel lonely?

If I can't find a wardrobe soon, I'll have to drag Hettie up here to help me. My search reveals an enormous bathroom off to one side, with a huge modern fireplace and the bath in front of it, in the centre. A flat-screen television is on the other wall with a picture window at the foot of it, showing the garden in its full glory. I guess with nothing but trees to look out onto, you don't have to worry about neighbours peeping in your windows and accidentally seeing you in the nip.

Next to the bathroom, I eventually find the equally huge dressing room. One half of it is empty, the rails standing bare, and I'm assuming that used to be Tamara's half. The other side is filled with Carter's clothes. There's an entire row of identical white shirts and, beneath it, an identical row of black shirts. Surely no one needs that many shirts in one lifetime? Beneath hangs a rainbow array of shirts. I take it all in, daunted. Where on earth am I going to start? Then, with some relief, I see that on an ottoman at the end of the room, again, someone has taken the trouble to lay out Carter's clothes for me. As quickly as I can, I pack them into the waiting suitcase.

What happened in Carter's marriage? I wonder, as I fold his shirts. How can you be dissatisfied when you have the entire world at your feet? What makes people like this so unhappy? Everything that they can possibly want is available to them. All they have to do is just pick up a phone and order it. Surely that takes an awful lot of the everyday stress out of your life? What does Tamara think that she wants in a man if it isn't this?

If Jim and I were so well off I'm sure we'd be happier. We could clear our credit-card debts. We could afford our dream wedding, our own home. We could go on to produce our 2.2 children. If we had this amount of moola we might even go mad and have four or five ankle-biters. As it is, due to a severe lack of cash, we have none. Suddenly heavy of heart, I do up the clasps on Carter's case and tiptoe out of the bedroom, closing the door behind me.

On the opulent landing, I round up all of the cases and, in two trips, take them downstairs to load into my car. Then I pack away all my bits and bobs, putting them in the car too. Another worried glance at my watch. It's getting late and I should be leaving. Still, I haven't managed to speak to Jim. He hasn't returned my call and I haven't tried him again. Hettie comes into the hall and coos over the Christmas tree. I even detect a tear in her eye.

'This looks so beautiful, Cassie.'

'Thanks. It's never been like this before?' I can't help myself.

'No, no. Tamara used to do it herself. It was always very pretty, but this is simply stunning.'

Yay to me!

'I hoped to get more done today,' I confess. 'I'll just have to finish it at the end of the week when we come back.'

'Look after those children for me.' It's clear that she cares for them deeply. 'Don't let them do anything dangerous.'

'I won't.' I don't plan on doing anything too dangerous myself.

Hettie leaves. I quickly take some photos with my phone so that I can show Jim and then realise that I should bring back our decent camera and take some more professional pictures to put together a proper portfolio. By next year, you never know, I might even have a website. The day is sliding away from me and I have so much else left to do, but it will all have to wait now.

The truth of the matter is, I can't wait to get home and see if I can grab some time – even if it's only five minutes – to make up with Jim before I leave.

Chapter Thirty-Four

At home I finish packing my own case and make sure I've got my passport to hand. The weird thing is that when flying on your own private plane there are no tickets, no printing out your boarding pass, no having to book your seat online, no getting to the airport three hours early. No stress. And, with your own chauffeur-driven car, there's no extortionate long-stay parking to pay for, either. This is clearly the way to travel. I feel like Simon Cowell. We're having dinner on the plane too. No menu, no plastic cutlery, no 'chicken or beef?' I just had to order what I wanted. So, out of all the exotic foods in the world that I could have chosen, I plumped for lasagne and salad for us all – simply because I thought the children would like it.

I'm hopping about the flat now, just waiting. I've tried Jim's phone a dozen times more, but it keeps going to voicemail. I can't find the words to leave a more conciliatory message than my earlier one. I just hope he knows how I feel. We've never been apart for any length of time before and I don't want to go away with the mood bad between us.

Having unpacked all the stuff from my car, I take the chance to run through the list of things I still have to do when I get back. There are more presents to wrap, cards to write, and Gaby has a list of companies that need mince pies. She's also going to be making some very cute, individual Christmas cakes this week as corporate gifts, which came in as a request. I make a note to offer these earlier next year. They're a great idea and I'm sure they'll go down well. I've still got the decorations to finish off at Carter's house, but I hope all the outdoor lights will be up and running by the time we get home. I make sure that I've got all the paperwork I need for the activities on our trip. The last thing I want is for there to be any hiccups. I want this all to run as smoothly as possible.

I hear a car pull up outside the flats and peep out of the window. There's a sleek, black limo nearly as long as the communal car park and, with a thrill of excitement, I assume that's my ride. Wow. No beaten-up taxi for me! I just wish that Jim was here.

I think about writing him an apologetic note, but then part of me thinks that he should have called me back by now. It was Jim who bought me a card that he'd barely glanced at. It was Jim who questioned my dedication to my business. It was Jim who sulked all night. He should be holding out the olive branch too. I know that he's busy at work, but so am I. Shouldn't he have found time to respond to my conciliatory phone call? It worries me as he's never been like this before, but there's nothing I can do about it now. I don't want to keep the driver waiting, so I grab my suitcase – wishing it was Louis Vuitton – and dash out of the flat.

When the driver sees me, he jumps out of the limo and holds the door open.

'There are three more cases in my car boot,' I tell him and we walk to my beaten-up old Clio to get them. He eschews any help from me and lifts the cases into the boot of the limo, which are, I have noted, real, actual Louis Vuitton.

Then we're off. I'm cocooned in black leather, shielded from the world and the paparazzi by blacked-out windows as we glide out of the car park and head for the airport. It would be nice to have a doze in this comfy car but, frankly, I'm way too excited. Instead I text Carter. '*On way. Hope all OK?*'

He texts back. '*All fine. Cu soon.*'

Now I can relax a bit. The last thing I wanted was for him to still be in New York or wherever and unable to come.

I text Jim too. '*I love you,*' I type. '*Be back soon.*' And, though I hope for a reply to ping right back, none does.

It's only a short while later that we're pulling into the airport. Our dedicated personal manager, Katie, comes to meet my car.

'Mr Randall is already here,' she says as I emerge and, sure enough, he's sitting in the small but plush waiting room, still in his business attire, tapping away on a laptop. He looks quite dashing in his slim-cut, dark-grey suit and I can see Katie's eyes sliding regularly in his direction when she's talking to me.

As soon as she's finished her briefing, I go over to Carter.

'Hey,' he says, standing up to kiss both my cheeks.

Wow. That's a bit friendlier than his usual greeting, but I guess it doesn't hurt to let the barriers down a bit as we're going to be spending four days together in close proximity.

The small, white ExecLine jet is ready and waiting on the runway just in front of us. I think of all the time I've spent queuing and waiting in airports and my heart wants to weep. Everyone should be able to travel like this. The cases are whisked from the car to the plane without us even touching them.

'I'll change on the plane,' Carter says.

'The temperature at your destination is minus twelve,' Katie says helpfully.

'Wow,' Carter observes. 'That's cold.'

'You've plenty of warm clothing,' I reassure him. 'I packed everything myself.'

'And for the kids?'

I nod.

'Great. Looks as if we're going to need it.'

'Where are the children?'

He looks hastily at his watch. 'They'll be here soon.'

Then, on cue, another car pulls up outside. A moment later, the door to the lounge whooshes open and, along with an icy blast, Tamara wafts in, children in tow. She's wearing a full-length coat in light-grey fur and, for one horrible moment, I think that she might have decided that Lapland is the place to be. She certainly looks dressed for it.

Eve and Max run over to hug Carter.

'Oh.' She's distinctly taken aback when she eventually notices me and turns to Carter. 'Is she going too?'

'Yes,' he says levelly. 'Cassie has organised the trip. It's only right that she comes along.'

Tamara's face says that she doesn't think it's right at all.

'Everyone ready?' Katie sweeps up, breaking into the frostiness. 'Your plane is waiting.' She checks our passports and whisks us out of the door onto the tarmac. Tamara follows.

We're at the steps to the jet now. The night air is cold in this exposed place and the wind whips around us. I stand awkwardly, not knowing quite where to put myself.

'Say goodbye to Mummy,' Carter tells the children.

'Do look after them,' Tamara says snippily. 'Don't do anything stupid. I don't want them both coming back up to the eyeballs in plaster. The school is unhappy enough about their missing lessons in term time.'

'They're in perfectly good hands,' he says patiently.

She bends and hugs Eve and Max to her. Then all her hostility leaves her and I see her eyes fill with tears. 'Be good for Daddy, and come back safely to me.' She squeezes them tightly.

For a fleeting moment, I feel that she might not let them go at all, even call a halt to our Arctic expedition. I can feel my own eyes filling up now and I wonder what she's really thinking.

For a moment her eyes meet mine and although I can see pain in them, they're also saying, 'This should be me, lady, not you.' And, to be honest, she's probably quite right.

Chapter Thirty-Five

The plane is tiny and it's at this point that I'm glad that I don't have a fear of flying. Through the windows, the children wave madly to Tamara. When the airport staff remove the steps to the plane door, she turns away and walks back towards the terminal building. She looks lonely and, even though this isn't my call, I get a pang of guilt as I watch her leave.

The steward welcomes us on board and shows us how to buckle into our seats: four chestnut-leather chairs arranged around a table. Behind this area are two matching sofas with a low coffee table between them. Everything that the steward needs is packed away in walnut cabinets at the back of the cabin. Carter and the children are clearly used to flying like this as they don't gape in awe as I do. I try to keep my mouth closed for fear of looking like an imbecile.

We settle ourselves in and, within minutes, the plane takes off. Suddenly we're on our way. The steward sets the table and dinner is served – not a foil carton in sight – and it's all very delicious. When it's been cleared away, Carter loosens his tie and stretches out to sleep. I entertain the children by showing them how to play Hangman on their iPads.

A few short hours later, the steward comes to tell us that the plane will be landing soon and so our cases are brought to us. We take it in turns to go into the sizeable bathroom and change into our warm clothing. Carter helps Max, then I take Eve in with me and help her to choose what to wear.

'Will it be snowing?' she says as I help to zip her into ski pants.

'I think so. It'll be very cold too.'

'Mummy so wanted to come, but she's busy at work.'

I don't know how much the children understand the current situation between their parents and I don't think it's for me to explain it. 'I'm sure it must be something extremely important.'

'She's busy at work a lot,' Eve says. 'So is Daddy. That's why we have to go away to school.'

'Is it a nice school? Do you like it?'

Eve shrugs. 'I like to be at home better. I have a nice bedroom.'

'I know,' I tell her. 'I saw it today when I packed your clothes.'

'Are you our new nanny?' she asks.

'Not really. I'm just helping Daddy to organise some things for Christmas.'

'Are you a friend?'

'I hope so.' Then, 'We need to get back to our seats as we'll be landing soon.'

'I'm very excited,' Eve says and, I have to admit, so am I.

I didn't realise it, but I feel quite tense about this trip. It is noticeable that the pressure is on me for every detail to be perfect. I'm just hoping that it's all as wonderful as I've planned.

When I've taken Eve back to her seat, I quickly slip into my brand-new ski pants and warm jumper. In the mirror, I look at myself and hardly recognise the person looking back at me. I need to pinch myself a few times to make sure this is really happening to me – even though I'm only the hired help.

A few minutes later, we're approaching our destination. We're flying low and although it's pitch-dark outside I can tell that we're over a desolate landscape of frozen whiteness, broken only by tracts of thick forest. There are very few signs of life. No towns, no houses, no lights at all. This is still somewhere very remote and sparsely populated.

We touch down on a runway covered with snow and ice and I wonder why Heathrow has to close when there are more than three snowflakes on the ground. Kiruna Airport is so tiny that the plane pulls up right next to the terminal building. A blacked-out 4x4 vehicle comes alongside us and I can see our cases being taken to the boot. A moment later we're escorted to the vehicle too. No immigration, no passports. This is Lapland and we're in.

Jan Bergson, a big, blond bear of a man who's going to be our guide for the next few days, is already waiting for us. He clasps our hands warmly and says, 'Welcome to Swedish Lapland.'

The children stare up at him in awe of his size.

I've organised this trip through his company and, as VIP guests, we're going to get his personal attention while we're here. As soon as we're on board, the car sweeps out of the airport and whisks us through the town of Kiruna to our first stop.

We drive for twenty minutes, the pretty wooden houses that line the road gradually thinning out until we're surrounded by nothing but trees. They're heavy with snow and look more like modern sculptures than firs. The sky is clear, bright and filled with a million stars.

The children have their faces pressed up against the windows of the car. 'This is so pretty,' Eve breathes.

'Awesome,' Max agrees. 'Daddy, why do we never have this much snow at home? It's cool.'

'Sure is, buddy.' Carter turns and grins at me. 'Thanks,' he says. 'This was a great idea.'

Moments later, we come to the Mushers' Lodge, which is the headquarters of Jan's business, and we all pile out of the car. Even though it's late, gone nine now, we're heading straight out again tonight to the wilderness lodge that I've booked. But before we leave, there's a little surprise for us all.

The Mushers' Lodge is picturesque, painted mustard-yellow, and next to it is a yard full of fluffy and very bouncy huskies. When they see us they all start barking madly.

Max is first to spot the long, low sledge all ready and waiting. He's wide-eyed with excitement. 'Is that for us?'

'Yes,' I say. 'But first we've got to put on some warmer clothing.'

We're already wrapped up in our ski gear, but the temperature is dropping rapidly. When you breathe in, you can feel even the hairs inside your nostrils freeze. The last thing that I want is the children getting cold. If I take them both back frozen in blocks of ice, I'm sure Tamara will have something to say.

In the warmth of the Lodge, Jan issues us with Arctic clothing. First we get brightly coloured overalls that are so well padded we can hardly move. On top of that we're issued with boots with thick thermal linings, overgloves, balaclavas that make us look like a motley crew of bank robbers, and fur-trapper hats. By the time we're kitted up and go back outside, the huskies have been tied to the sled and they're raring to go. There must be twelve of them or more, jumping at their harnesses and barking so loudly that we can hardly hear ourselves think. It's clear that they don't want to be hanging around. They want to be off and running.

'This is a great idea,' Carter says as he climbs aboard the sled, which is covered with reindeer skins. Max nestles down in front of him. Then I slide in front of Max with Eve tucked between my knees.

'I won't be able to see properly,' Max says. 'Can I go in front of Cassie with Eve?'

It's true that he probably has a great view of my back. Hadn't thought that one through.

'Yes,' Carter says. 'But you must hold on very tightly because we'll be going really fast.'

'*Really* fast?' Max is beaming widely.

So we all shift around while the dogs bark their impatience. By default, I have to be the one to sit in front of Carter so I slot myself in between his legs. He wraps his arms around me and holds on.

'Settle back,' Carter says. 'I don't want you falling off.'

Our bodies mould together and, suddenly, I feel very hot in this Arctic suit. Trying to ignore how close we are, in turn I wrap my arms round Eve and she clings on to Max.

Jan is on the back of the sled, huge fur gloves in place. 'Ready?'

'Ready!' we all shout.

The dogs go into a total frenzy and, with one whispered word from Jan, they shoot off in the style of Usain Bolt out of the starting blocks while we hang on for dear life. The children are shrieking with joy.

The moon is big and low in the sky as we whip through the trees, taking the bends at an alarming rate. But soon the dogs calm down and settle into their stride. The only sound is the whooshing of the sled over the snow. Though it's night-time, the full moon reflecting on the snow makes it seem so bright. The track is narrow through the trees, and overhanging branches shower us with powder snow as we pass. The children giggle with delight. I'm so glad that Jan suggested it when I called him as it really is the most magical way to arrive at our lodge.

Carter squeezes my waist. I turn round to look at him and he's grinning just as much as the kids. If I can make the man who has everything happy, then I must have done something right.

Our speed drops slightly. Now the track is lined with open oil lamps. Their golden flames light our way. Jan slows the dogs further and soon we come to a clearing in the trees. In front of us is our wilderness lodge, home for the next two nights. It's a long, low building made of wood hunkered down in among the firs. The roof is piled high with snow and spectacular, shimmering icicles hang from the eaves halfway down to the ground. A few steps lead up to a wide front porch, which sports a hot tub and a selection of rustic, hand-carved furniture. Bathed in moonlight with the stars twinkling above us, it couldn't look more beautiful and I'm so relieved.

Carter and I help the children to disembark from the sled. The breath of the panting dogs is rising in front of us in a cloud of steam. Some of them stretch out in the snow to cool down. We're miles from anywhere, right in the middle of a forest of fir trees heavy with snow. I can't see any other signs of life. Remote I asked for. Remote I've certainly got.

'You could help me with the dogs,' Jan says to Eve and Max. 'They like a fuss now and they all need to go in their kennels for the night.'

At one side of the clearing, among the trees, there are individual kennels for each of the dogs, their roofs a foot deep in snow.

'Can we, Daddy?' Max asks.

'Of course.'

'If you want to do that with the children, I'll check the lodge,' I suggest.

'Yes, Daddy,' Eve urges. 'Do help us.'

'I'd like that,' he says and he heads off with the children while Jan shows them how to handle the dogs, removing their harnesses and securing them in their kennels.

The dogs, less boisterous after their run, are compliant and affectionate, and the children are in their element. Smiling, I stand

and watch them all petting the dogs. With all the to-ing and fro-ing the kids do between houses and school, I think that it's unlikely that they've ever had a dog before but they've taken to this like ducks to water. Carter is just as enthusiastic and it's nice to see them all having fun together.

So far, so good. I breathe a little sigh of relief. Then I go inside the lodge, keeping my fingers crossed that it's all I hoped for from the pictures in the online brochure.

Chapter Thirty-Six

The wilderness lodge interior doesn't disappoint and a tiny bit more of me relaxes.

It's very rustic, all pine and traditional Swedish furnishings. The whole of the downstairs is open plan, the living, dining and kitchen areas all merging into one. There's a huge log-burning stove in the living area with a roaring fire in it already, making the place cosy and warm. Next to it is an alcove entirely filled with a stock of cut logs, which should keep us going for a while. It's flanked by two brown-leather sofas, furnished with snuggly knitted throws in pale blue and piled high with cushions in blue and white embroidery.

There's no electricity here at all and the room is lit only by the fire and the glow of candlelight. It looks so romantic and, for the first time this evening, I get a pang of longing for Jim. I've been so taken up with the excitement, so worried about getting here and it all being wonderful for Carter and the children, that I haven't given a moment's thought to what's happening at home. Now I miss him desperately. He'd so love it here.

I shrug out of my Arctic suit and kick off my boots – both of which are easier said than done. There's a row of pegs fixed along the wall by the fire where we can dry and warm our clothes, which is where I hang up my suit. Already, I feel as if I've slipped seamlessly into the time-consuming rhythm of dressing to face the extreme cold.

We've just got two nights here before we move on to the famous Icehotel for one night. As well as lighting the fire, someone has been into the kitchen and left us a home-made cake, a jar of hot chocolate, a dish of whipped cream and a bowl brimming with tiny white marshmallows. I know what my first job will be. As there's no electricity and therefore no fridge, there are two ice buckets on the side – one filled with cartons of milk and one holding champagne and white wine, with a good stock of red wine in a rack next to it. A cook is coming in to prepare most of our meals, so we should have everything we need for our stay.

Just off the living area are three spacious bedrooms. The children will share one and Carter and I will take the others. I check them out and find that they're simply furnished too, with warm rugs on the floor and colourful paintings on the walls. The beds have plain white duvets and are piled high with blue-gingham pillows. All very tasteful. Our cases are already here – I have no idea how – and, strangely, they're even in the rooms I would have chosen for each of us. Perhaps my lack of designer luggage has, quite rightly, ensured I get the smallest of the rooms. The children have a larger room with twin beds and Carter has the main suite with its enormous king-size bed all to himself. There may be no electricity but there is, thankfully, plumbing and we have two beautifully furnished wetrooms between us. I'm sure we'll be more than comfortable here and I feel myself breathing more easily. I think I've done a good job in finding this place and I hope that Carter can't fail to fall in love with it.

Then I hear the stamping of boots in the porch and it's time to get the hot chocolate going on the stove. The children barrel inside and I help them to clamber out of their Arctic suits and boots. They leave drifts of powdered snow on the floor, which instantly melt in the heat and turn to puddles.

'That was great fun, wasn't it, kids?' Carter peels off his own suit and I go to give him a hand as he struggles. I tug at his sleeves as he shrugs it off.

'It was brilliant!' they say together. 'Thank you, Cassie.'

'Go and have a look at your bedrooms,' I tell them, 'and then we'll have hot chocolate and cake before bedtime.'

While I hang up their clothes and mop up the puddles, Carter is taking in the lodge. He spots the chilled champagne and wine in the ice bucket. 'I'd rather have a glass of fizz,' he says. 'Will you join me?'

'That sounds nice.'

He opens the champagne, finds glasses and pours it. 'I don't know what I'm celebrating, but I feel I should propose a toast.' He hands me a glass. 'To us,' he says. 'To this trip. Let it be fantastic.' Carter chinks his glass against mine.

The bubbles sparkle in the soft candlelight. 'I'll drink to that.'

We pause to take a welcome sip. Then, while Carter roams around the lodge, I fire up the stove and get a pan of milk going. This is fantastic, just like playing house.

Carter flicks out his phone. 'No signal?'

'That's the only bad news. I hope.' I grimace. 'No phone signal. No wi-fi. Just total wilderness.'

'Really?'

'You'll be unavailable for three whole days,' I tell him. 'But I made sure that I let Georgina know and asked her to warn your office.'

'I'm sure they can manage without me,' he laughs, 'but I'm not so sure I can manage without them!'

'You said that you wanted quality time with your children,' I remind him. 'Now you can focus just on Max and Eve.'

'Sounds like an excellent plan.' He lets out a contented sigh. 'This is more than I could have hoped for. Thank you, Cassie Christmas.'

'All part of the service.' I've suddenly gone shy. He's right, though. I think I have done well.

Carter doesn't take his eyes off me as he drinks. 'I said I'd call Tamara to let her know that we'd arrived safely.'

'No can do.'

He gives a nervous laugh. 'Oh, my word. She'll be furious.'

'Georgina will tell her that we're out of contact, I'm sure.'

I think of Tamara's tear-filled eyes at the airport. Perhaps it will do her good not to have Carter at her beck and call. But that makes me remember that if Carter can't call Tamara, then I can't contact Jim either. We're here in our own little bubble for a few days whether we like it or not. And, I hate to admit this, I think I'm going to like it a lot.

Having bagged their beds, the children come out and I give them hot chocolate laced with cream and marshmallows. We all have a big slice of cake. Perhaps feeding them with sugar before bedtime isn't the best thing to do, but I'm guessing that they're so hyperactive they won't be sleeping much anyway. We all sit in front of the roaring fire, huddled together on the squashy sofa, mesmerised by the shifting flames.

Once we've eaten, they both grow quiet and I catch Eve's eyes struggling to stay open. I'm not sure what my role is here. Is it my place to tell the children when they should go to bed? Instead, I touch Carter's arm and whisper, 'I think the children are tired.'

He glances across at them. 'Come on, guys. Bed.'

'Aw, Daddy,' they yawn in unison. 'Just a bit longer.'

'You don't want to be too tired for tomorrow's activities, do you?' Carter turns back to me. 'What exactly are we doing tomorrow?'

'Just you wait and see,' I say enigmatically. 'We've got a *very* full day.'

'A *very* full day,' Carter echoes, teasing. 'If I were you, I wouldn't waste a minute. I'd go to sleep just as fast as I could!'

They dash off to their bedroom and Carter follows. I top up his glass as I hear him helping them to get undressed and tucking them into bed. How I'd love to be doing that for my own children one day. I listen to him murmuring endearments as he kisses them. Then he calls me. 'Cassie. The children would like you to say goodnight to them too.'

So I go into the bedroom, see them snuggled down in their beds and my heart melts. I kiss their cheeks and tuck Eve's wayward hair behind her ear. They remind me so much of my lovely niece and nephew. 'Goodnight, both of you. See you in the morning.'

'I love you,' Carter tells them. 'Sweet dreams and tomorrow we'll have lots of fun.'

I blow them another kiss and leave their dad to fuss with their duvets again, making sure that they're snuggly warm and covered up to their necks. They're so small, so innocent, and I feel a protective surge towards them. Emotionally, it must be a rough time for them and so horrible to see their parents' marriage torn apart. We like to think that children are immune to the crises of adults, but I know from bitter experience that they're not. And I wonder, was it better not to know my father at all, rather than watch my parents locked in a bitter fight? While I'm here, I know that I'll do my very best to look after these children and make sure that they have a great time.

Seconds later, Carter's back in the living room. 'I'll leave the door open,' he says to Max and Eve over his shoulder, 'so that you can see the fire flickering.'

'Night night, Daddy,' they both shout. 'Night night, Cassie.'

'Goodnight,' I call out and find that there's a lump in my throat.

Chapter Thirty-Seven

The fire casts a warm glow over the room and shadows dance across the ceiling. Outside the lodge, there's no sound at all and even the silence seems deep, muffled by the snow. Carter comes to sit down next to me. I pull the cuddly throw around me.

'Cold?' he asks. 'I could put another log in the burner.'

'No,' I say. 'Just snuggling down.'

'Excellent plan. Room for me?' He slides under the throw himself, then lifts his replenished glass and says, 'Cheers.' He drinks deeply, then lets out a lingering and heartfelt sigh.

I smile at him. 'That bad?' His face looks softer, less careworn in the firelight.

'It seems like months since I've stepped off the work treadmill. Sometimes I wonder why I do it.' He lowers his voice to a whisper so as not to disturb the children and angles his body towards mine. I lean in closer so that I hear him better. 'When I'm with the kids like this, I regret that I'm hardly ever around to see them. That's one thing that Tamara *is* right about. Neither of us dedicates enough time to them and that's all they really want. This is all just top-dressing.' He raises a rueful eyebrow. 'The kids have had it really hard. We like to pretend that they're not affected by our divorce, but I know that underneath they're struggling with it.'

'That's tough,' I agree.

'These few days are so important for me, for us.' He smiles at me and his chocolate-brown eyes look mellow in the firelight. 'We'll have some fun.'

'I hope so.'

'How does your partner feel about you coming away with me?'

'Jim?' I shrug. 'He's fine.'

Carter doesn't need to know that he's not fine about it at all or about his somewhat pointed *across the miles* Christmas card or that we've fallen out over the amount of time I've dedicated to doing Carter's bidding.

'It's work for me, after all.'

He laughs out loud. 'Work. Of course it is.'

'I know,' I agree with a grin. 'I wish all of my jobs were like this. Thank you for asking me to come along. It was very kind of you.'

'You're easy company to be with, Cassie Christmas,' he says and there's a wistful note in his voice. 'The kids have fallen in love with you already.'

My face flushes hot and it's not just the fire.

'Now I'm embarrassing you.' He reaches for the champagne and refills my glass. 'Don't be bashful.' He smiles at my discomfiture. 'Let's talk about work instead. I always find that's much safer ground. How's the business going?'

'Good,' I offer. 'I couldn't have hoped for a better start. Though you are my best client by far and I'm really grateful for that. It means a lot to me.'

'Now we're back onto mutual flattery and not talking about business at all. Perhaps it's this magical place.' He makes a sweeping gesture with his arm. 'Perhaps it won't let us talk about anything too boring.'

'This is my first attempt at it, but I think I enjoy being in business.'

'Me too.'

'I'm hardly on the same scale as you.'

'I started out with very little,' Carter tells me. 'I had quite a privileged upbringing, but when I started my company, I was a penniless student. It was a happy accident, if I'm honest. A friend and I had decided to set up a stall at a local music festival to make a bit of cash and we didn't know what to sell. I hit on the idea of making smoothies laced with booze. I nicked my mother's ancient food processor from the kitchen and we set up a stall with a pile of cheap fruit and some supermarket own-label alcohol. We made a small fortune. I had to rope in extra friends to help go and buy fruit and more booze as we kept selling out. We'd burned out the motor on the food processor by the Sunday evening. It took off from there.'

Carter stands up to stoke the log burner. He opens the door, puts on another hefty lump of wood and then sits down next to me again. A little closer this time, I think. I let my head lean on the back of the sofa while he picks up the story of how he started out in business.

'My friend quickly lost interest. I think he fell in love with a woman from Poland or somewhere and disappeared with her for the summer. I carried on. I took my boozy smoothies to every festival I could. By the end of the summer, I'd decided not to continue with my degree.'

'A brave move.'

'My parents were disappointed. But I was reading history and politics only because I didn't know what else to do. It was never going to enthral me. I found that I loved the cut and thrust of business, Cassie. Making money was more fun than learning about ancient civilisations. I begged a loan from the bank, did a bit of branding and started making Pure Pleasure on a serious basis. Within two years it was a runaway success. I've never looked back. It's taken years of hard work but now I supply clubs and bars all over the world with my drinks.'

'That's amazing. I don't think that Calling Mrs Christmas! will ever reach those dizzy heights.'

'From small acorns,' Carter says. 'In some ways, starting out is the most exciting time. My organisation is vast now. My memory might be deceiving me, but I think I liked it better when it was just me and my mother's food processor.' He laughs. 'I like to think I'm indispensable – don't we all – but I'm sure the company could manage very well without me and not just for a few days while I'm on walkabout in the wilderness.'

'When we're back home, perhaps you could give me some tips on how I can take my business forward.'

'Just trust your instincts, Cassie, and you won't go far wrong.' He smiles at me. 'You already seem to be doing a lot of it right.'

'I think I just got very lucky in meeting you at the beginning,' I confess.

'Throwing a drink over me, if I remember rightly.'

I put my face in my hands, embarrassed at the memory. 'I'm sorry about that. I'm only glad that you don't hold grudges.'

'That's what you *do* call a happy accident,' he jokes. 'For both of us.'

I sip my champagne. My glass is nearly empty again and I'm feeling drowsy. It's probably about time that we both called it a day too. I don't know about Carter but I need my beauty sleep. I want to be fully alert to co-ordinate tomorrow's activities.

'So, tell me, what does Jim do?'

'He's a prison officer.' My heart twists with love for him. 'He works in the Young Offenders' Unit at Bovingdale.'

'Doing a fantastic job for terrible pay?'

'You've got it in one.' My thoughts turn to home. 'I don't know what I would have done without him. I was made redundant earlier in the year and found it really hard to get a job. Jim has been my rock. If I'm honest, Calling Mrs Christmas! was started out of necessity. As no one else would employ me, I thought I'd try to make my own work. This is my dream job. I've always loved organising my own Christmas, though obviously it's very different when you're doing it for clients. Jim has been right behind me. He's even had a couple of his boys from the unit helping me too.'

'Offenders?'

'Yes. Though the boys who've been helping me are getting out very soon.' I don't want him to think that I'm employing hardened criminals. 'They're just about at the end of their sentence.'

'Very noble,' Carter notes.

'Jim's a really great bloke. We've been together for years.' I think of the nights recently that we've spent together just trying to keep up with the rush of orders. I want to call him so much, just hear his voice. 'I'm so lucky to have him.'

Carter meets my eyes and says, 'Actually, Cassie Christmas, I think he's very lucky to have you.'

Chapter Thirty-Eight

I lie in bed with my door open during the night, content to watch the flames of the fire until I doze off. Once or twice I hear Carter get up during the night, put another log on the wood burner and tiptoe in to check on the children before going back to bed. Perhaps he doesn't sleep too well.

You wouldn't be able to tell from the way he is this morning, though. I can hear him moving about the lodge. It's clear that he's bright-eyed, bushy-tailed and raring to go. He's singing softly to himself as he gets up. Unlike Carter, I'm struggling to get out of my bed. I'm quite comfortable under the thick duvet and feel as if I could quite happily lie here until noon. But, of course, I've got my clients to attend to.

I close my door and then pull on my clothes. Hair and make-up will have to wait.

'Sleep well?' Carter asks as I emerge.

'Yes. You?'

He nods.

'I heard you get up and check on the children a couple of times.'

'Oh. I'm not the world's best sleeper. Busy brain. Sorry to disturb you.'

'It's not a problem. Are Max and Eve all right?'

'Fine. I've told them both to have a shower.'

'I'll put breakfast on, then.'

There's a cook coming in to prepare lunch and dinner for us, but I'm on breakfast duty. I didn't look too closely last night, but there's a larder with a plentiful stock of bacon, eggs and a fresh loaf. That ought to keep us going until lunchtime. I set about cooking and, just as I'm about to dish up, the children appear, freshly washed and already in their warm jumpers and ski pants. Along with Carter, they sit on the benches at the long table.

'Cassie, will you tell us now what we're doing today?' Eve asks as she pinches a piece of crispy bacon from the platter I've just put down on the table. 'Please, please! Pretty please!'

'We're going to take out our own dog sleds,' I tell her.

'Cool,' Max says, clearly thrilled by the itinerary. 'Huskies are wicked.'

'Can we help to put the doggies back on their leads?' Eve wants to know.

'Yes, if you want to. Jan should be here very soon.' I'm sure the dogs will let us know when he arrives. 'Then Daddy and I will drive the sleds while you and Max are passengers. Does that sound like fun?'

'I want to drive too,' Max says.

'You can help me,' Carter suggests. 'We can drive together.'

'Double cool!' Max looks as if he wants to bolt his breakfast down and get out there.

I put a dish of buttery scrambled eggs next to the bacon. 'Tuck in, guys.'

While I'm waiting for the toast to brown, I watch Carter helping his children to their food. He strokes Eve's long blonde hair and it's obvious that he adores them both. It must be really hard if he doesn't get to see that much of his kids.

He catches me watching them and smiles up at me. I rescue the toast before I burn it.

'Great breakfast, Cassie,' he says. 'I might have known that you'd be a good cook too.'

'I have a limited repertoire,' I admit. 'But I enjoy it.'

As I suspected, as soon as they hear Jan arrive, the dogs start to bark like mad things. The children, eager to get outside, wolf down the rest of their breakfast. I help them to put on their multiple layers of outdoor clothing and they dash outside into the snow. When I've watched them go, I wash up the breakfast dishes. Moments later, Carter comes to stand next to me and picks up a tea towel.

'You don't need to do that,' I tell him. 'This is your holiday. I'm only making it tidy so that the cook doesn't walk into a complete mess.' I might be able to knock out a nice breakfast but I don't do it in the neatest of fashions.

'This is nice for me,' he insists. 'A pleasant change.'

So we stand and chat, while I wash and Carter wipes. When we've finished and the dishes are stacked, together we gear up and Carter helps me to wriggle into my suit.

I try to take a hands-off approach to helping Carter dress, but it's not that easy. It's virtually impossible to put one of these suits on by yourself and, as the mercury has been steadily dropping since our arrival, you can't risk going outside without one. You'd get hypothermia within minutes. We'll have to watch the children closely.

'All this dressing and undressing is hard work,' I say when it's my turn to wriggle into my suit.

'Here, let me.' Carter grins as slowly, slowly, he slides up the zip of my Arctic suit and I suddenly feel very hot having him this close to me.

'These suits make you very warm, don't they?' I stammer.

'Couldn't agree more,' he teases.

We're both as still as statues. Even the air around us seems to

216

be suspended. His hands are on my arms and it seems as if neither of us can move. Our eyes are locked; both of us are breathing unevenly. And we're close. So close.

Then Eve bursts through the door. 'Daddy!' she says, exasperated. 'Where are you? We're waiting!'

Carter breaks away from me. His hands fall from my arms and I feel almost unsteady on my feet. He smiles at me uncertainly. 'We're summoned.'

I think it's probably a good thing. I'm not sure what happened there, but we definitely shared A Moment.

So, without further ado, we go to join the children outside. Jan, with the help of Eve and Max, has already harnessed the huskies for us. They're barking like crazy, keen to be on the move. There are three sleds today. Carter and Max will take one. I'll take the other one with Eve, and Jan will have his own with all the equipment we need. It seemed like a good idea when I planned it, but now I'm quite nervous of driving my own dogs.

Jan gives us a quick course in sled handling and it all sounds very complicated. The sleds have two brakes and an anchor, but no steering. The only way you can get it to go where you want is to lean your weight over to the left or right to guide the huskies. These dogs, I have to say, look as if they have minds of their own and no amount of leaning is going to influence them. I think I'm just going to hold on tightly for the ride.

'Whatever you do,' Jan says, 'don't let go of the sled if you fall off. The last time that happened I had to chase the dogs for forty kilometres across the snow before I caught up with them.'

I'm not sure who's the most giddy with excitement, the children or the huskies. But soon we're ready for the off. Max climbs into the seat in front of Carter's sled and I settle Eve in with me. Jan leads the way. Hesitantly, I take in my anchor and let off the brake. The dogs shoot forward in the same exuberant way they did last night.

'Hold on tight,' I shout to Eve.

'Wheeeee!' she cries back. Clearly only one of us has any anxiety about this.

We whip through the trees at breakneck speed, being showered with snow as we go. Eve is shrieking with delight and adrenaline is pumping through my veins. Never in a million years did I envisage myself doing something like this. I was content until the beginning of the year to sit in an office day in, day out, never having much ambition beyond that. Now look what I'm doing. If this business can bring me such incredible rushes, then I know in my heart I'm doing the right thing.

It's ten o'clock now and the sun is only just up, peeping tentatively over the fir trees, tingeing the snow on them with a pink blush that makes them look stunning, as if they're dripping with strawberry ice cream.

'The sky's all glittery,' Eve says, holding out her hands to catch it as we whizz along.

The air is so crisp and dry that there are ice crystals in it, sparkling in the sun. It's just amazing. All around us the snow seems to be studded with diamonds.

The huskies trot along happily and, once they've run off their pent-up exuberance, soon settle into their own rhythm. Which means, in turn, that I can ease back on the terror and start to enjoy myself. We follow ready-made tracks through the trees, so the dogs pretty much know what they're doing without my help. Thank goodness.

'Are you OK, Eve?' I shout out, checking on my passenger.

'Yes. It's amazeballs! Go faster, Cassie. Go faster.'

Carter and Max are ahead of us. Perhaps Carter is relaxing too as he turns to wave at us. Eve and I wave back.

We both follow Jan's sled through the trees. The landscape is flat so the terrain's easy to manage for a beginner. The dogs scoop up snow with their mouths as they go to keep themselves cool.

We've been going for a couple of hours when we come to an open clearing near the edge of a frozen river and beside it there's a small log cabin. Taking Jan's lead, we put on the brakes to slow down the dogs. Watching him carefully, I bring the team of huskies to a halt, throw down my anchor and secure the sled with my kick-brake too. The last thing on earth I want is to lose the dogs.

I breathe a sigh of relief. We've arrived safely.

Eve jumps off the sled and bounces in the snow for joy. 'That was *totally* brilliant!'

I can't help but agree. Taking her hands, I join in with her celebration and we dance around. Perhaps I've got some primeval dog-mushing gene because that was more fun than I ever could have imagined. Every fibre of my body is zinging and, at this moment, I don't think I've ever felt quite so alive.

Chapter Thirty-Nine

Jim hadn't heard anything from Cassie in hours. Her last text had come in just before he'd finished his shift. It was only then that he'd seen the string of messages and texts that she'd left. His day had been completely manic – a dozen different fights had kicked off, which had kept him busy, and he hadn't even had time to go out to his locker at lunchtime to check his phone as usual.

He was desperately hoping that he'd be home in time to see Cassie before she left for Lapland, but he'd been delayed at work, filling in a report about Smudge's attempted suicide that had to be done. The paperwork was handed in, but the result was that he had missed her.

Since getting home, he'd texted her but there had been no reply. He'd also tried to call her but a message told him that the caller was not available. Jim could only assume that, wherever Cassie was, there was no phone signal. Were there telephone masts in the Arctic Circle? He wondered if he might not hear from her during the whole time she was away.

He felt miserable about what had gone on the night before. They hardly ever argued and it had been stupid of him not to tell Cassie what had been going on in the unit. She would have wanted to know what had happened to Smudge as she'd grown to like the lads too and would have been worried that he was so troubled. She would have understood why he was feeling so wretched and helpless. Of course she would.

Jim didn't know why he'd clammed up like that. Probably because he didn't want to open the floodgates on his emotions. He cared more about those two lads than he should. Years of being a prison officer had taught him about that. It was best to keep your distance. Hold the prisoners at arm's length. It was the sensible way. Convicts came and went, some of them more often than others. It was best to see them on their way with a cheery wave. Now, here he was, going all soft over two scallies. That was something best kept to himself. Yet, if only he'd explained properly instead of going all moody, Cassie would have appreciated why he was distracted and had picked up that ridiculous card for her. They might even have had a laugh about it. If only he'd confided in her.

But he hardly ever talked about what went on at the unit and it was a hard habit to break. Jim snorted to himself. Look at the price he'd paid for it. Cassie had gone off to the middle of who knows where with a hotshot millionaire and he couldn't even call to say that he loved her. He'd acted like an idiot and now couldn't apologise. He could only hope that Cassie knew how he was feeling.

The truth of the matter was: he was jealous of Carter Randall. Who wouldn't be? The guy only had to click his fingers and people jumped. He wasn't bogged down in credit-card debt. He had mansions coming out of his ears, the kudos of being a well-known entrepreneur. Carter could offer Cassie all that she ever wanted. How could Jim possibly compete with that?

Today Jim was on shift at the unit again. As soon as he'd signed on, he'd gone straight down to the Healthcare wing to see how Smudge was doing.

Smudge lay in his bed looking as white as the sheets that covered him. His wrists were bandaged, his hands, on top of the covers, turned palm up towards the ceiling. He looked so small and all wrong in the cell, as if dwarfed by the big bed, like a child who'd mysteriously landed up in the wrong place.

'Now then,' Jim said. 'How's the patient today?' And, to his surprise, he found his voice sounded choked.

'I'm all right, Jim,' Smudge answered stoically. His eyes were dark, his sockets sunken and blue. 'Doctor said I can go back up on the wing later.'

Jim pulled up the only chair in the bare room and sat next to the bed. 'That's good news,' he said. 'No more nonsense?'

'No,' Smudge agreed. 'That was a twatish thing to do.'

'Rozzer's worried sick about you.'

'Is he?' Smudge's face brightened.

'Yeah. Me too.'

'I feel bad now,' he said. 'I didn't mean to do that. I just panicked.'

'I told you that we're all going to sort it out,' Jim assured him. 'It might take some time, though. I want you to promise me that, whatever happens, you won't do that again.'

The lad shook his head. 'I won't, Jim. Promise.'

'If you feel it all building up, you've got to talk to someone. There's me, Rozzer, the doctors in here, the Listener Scheme. It might not feel like it, but we've all got your back, lad.'

'I'm sorry, Jim.' Tears filled his eyes. 'Tell Rozzer I'm sorry too.'

'You can tell him yourself later when you're back on the wing.' Jim stood up. 'I'll talk to the doctor, see when I can come to collect you.'

'Thanks, Jim.'

'Get some sleep now while you can.' He patted a bony knee beneath the sheet. 'I'll see you later.'

Jim left, locking the door behind him. Rozzer was due out at the weekend and he didn't want to leave Smudge here by himself. He was due to be released in a couple of weeks' time, just before Christmas. Jim wondered if the governor would let Smudge out a few days early if he could find him somewhere to live, especially now that this had happened.

He spoke to the doctor, agreed what time to return to take Smudge to his own cell and walked back to Starling wing.

It might not be long until Christmas, but you wouldn't know it in this place. On the outside, everywhere was draped with festive decorations – shops, supermarkets, pubs. Every other song was a Christmas tune or a carol. In here it could have been any time of the year. The sun could be cracking the pavements, the rain could be pelting down, and the inmates wouldn't know the difference. It was so isolating, another world where the seasons didn't matter.

Christmas was no different. They served the lads a basic Christmas dinner on 25 December – turkey roll in a foil carton, some roast potatoes like bullets, soggy stuffing – but that was as far as it went. There were no decorations, no tree, no presents. Some of the lads tried to store up fruit in their cells to brew illegal alcohol in the run-up to Christmas, but the officers had got wise to that in the last few years. Now they brought in Security to carry out a timely raid in the preceding week, which usually put paid to the prisoners' efforts.

The unit was a miserable enough place to be at the best of times but, during this festive season, it was completely depressing. No doubt there'd be a few more suicide attempts over the coming days. Jim sighed to himself. Something to look forward to.

It was his day off tomorrow, and if he could get both of the lads out on licence, then he would. Normally, it would be a tough call to get them to let Smudge out so soon after getting out of

Healthcare, but he might just swing it. As always, they were tight for places in the unit and he had to talk to the right people.

This morning before he'd left, he'd taken five minutes to flick through Cassie's file. A ton of stuff still needed doing before Christmas. Gaby had her own jobs to do, but there were things that he could be doing to help Cassie out. That would be a nice surprise for her when she got back. God only knows he was missing Cassie like mad. He couldn't even remember when they'd last spent a night apart – if they ever had. The bed was certainly too big without her and he'd chased himself around all night, waking up tired and tangled in the duvet. She was gone for only a few days, but he simply couldn't wait for her to come home.

Chapter Forty

The snow's so soft and dry that we sink up to our thighs in it. Lunch won't be ready for a short while and it gives us an opportunity to play in the drifts. The boys, being boys, amuse themselves by piling the snow as high as they can. I show Eve how to lie back and flap her arms and legs to make snow angels. Carter and Max come over to join us. Carter lies down next to me and takes my hand as we move our arms in co-ordination, laughing all the time.

'How can I have reached the grand old age of forty-two and have never made a snow angel?' He laughs. Then Max and Eve bundle on top of him and they roll about together, giggling.

We chase each other around, scooping up armfuls of snow and cascading it over each other as it's too powdery to make snowballs. And, though it's freezing cold out here, all this exertion is making us hot.

It's good to see Carter spending some quality time with his children and, judging by their delighted squeals, I'm pretty sure they're enjoying it too. He organises Max and Eve to stand together and snaps some photographs. Then I take one of all three of them.

'Let me take one of you and Cassie, Daddy,' Eve says and, before he can either agree or refuse, she takes the camera from him. He slides his arm round me and, self-consciously, we grin at the lens together.

'Lunch is ready,' Jan shouts and we all troop over to the small log cabin.

A woman in the kitchen area has made us thick soup loaded with vegetables. She ladles it into dishes while we pull off our gloves and suits, then we sit at the table while she serves it with warm flatbread. We all tuck in, gratefully.

'I'm hungry,' Max says. 'I just didn't know it.'

'It's all the exercise,' I tell him. 'It works up an appetite.'

'The snow angels were good,' Eve says. 'You make my daddy laugh, Cassie. He's fun when he's with you.'

Carter and I look up from our soup, our eyes meet and his gaze is so searching that it makes me catch my breath.

'I'm sure Daddy's fun a lot of the time,' I counter.

'No,' she says in typical childlike manner. 'Not really. Now that Mummy lives in another house, he's sad a lot of the time.'

'I don't think that Cassie wants to hear about that, darling,' Carter says. 'How's your soup?'

'Nice,' she says and returns her attention to her lunch.

'Sorry,' he mouths to me.

I shrug that it's OK and Carter turns the conversation to more innocuous matters while we finish our meal. We all chatter about the morning's activities and Max and Eve squabble about which of the huskies is their favourite.

'We could each take one home with us,' Eve suggests.

Carter throws up his hands. 'No,' he says with a laugh. 'No doggy souvenirs. No trying to smuggle your favourite husky onto the plane. I'll make sure Jan counts them all before we leave.'

When we've finished eating and my eyes are growing heavy from the delicious food and the warmth, it's back on with our outer clothes and out into the snow again.

The dogs, still harnessed, are lying in the snow, resting. But as soon as they see any activity, they're up and bouncing around, barking their keenness to be on the move again. I only wish I had half of the energy of these huskies. We're going to take a different route now and sled back to the wilderness lodge before darkness falls.

This time I'm going to take Max while Eve travels as passenger with her dad. I feel so sleepy. I don't know if it's all the rushing round that I've been doing beforehand that's made me tired, or whether it's the relief of being here and it all being fabulous that's done it, but I think I could lie down and sleep for a week.

Carter comes up and puts his hand on my arm. 'Everything OK?'

'Yes, fine.'

'Happy to take Max? I think he'd like to drive his own sled,' Carter says. 'We'll have to come back again when he's old enough.'

'Of course. I'll look after him.' I wonder if there's anything I can organise so that Max can have a go by himself.

'Thanks,' Carter says. 'You're really great with them. They adore you.' Then, with one of those full-on gazes again, 'We all do.' He turns away from me, which is just as well as my face feels as if it's glowing like a beacon.

'Load 'em up, kids,' Jan shouts. 'Last one back at the ranch is a sissy!'

I'm so flustered by Carter's comment that, before I know what I'm doing, I stumble backwards into my sled. In doing so, I accidentally knock the anchor out of the snow. Instantly, the dogs sense freedom and leap forwards. I cry out and grab hold of the handles of the sled as I remember Jan's dire warnings about never letting go and losing the dogs. They shoot off, hurtling down the track ahead of them as fast as their little husky legs will carry them.

'Help!' I shout out. 'Help!' I cling on for dear life as I'm dragged along, trees showering me with snow. The anchor bobs along uselessly beside me and I cry out again, 'Help!'

Everything else that I learned in Jan's briefing has gone completely out of my head. I scramble for the brake, but I'm half on the sled, half off. Uselessly, I try to scrape my boot along the ground to stop them. But these dogs have the scent of a novice in their nostrils and are determined to run like the wind.

I risk a look behind and see Carter powering after me, running as fast as he can down the track despite being weighed down by his Arctic gear.

'Brake, Cassie,' he shouts out. 'Put on the brake!' He is just a few steps behind me and is gaining rapidly.

As the sled careens along the track, I try to assemble my scattered thoughts. The brake's here somewhere, I simply have to concentrate. Then, just as I think I'm beginning to regain control, the sled hits a steep bank and the dogs whip round, cutting the corner. The sled and my world tilts sideways.

'Aaargh!' is all I can manage.

I turn to check where Carter is, assuming that he's dropped back, only to see him launching himself at me.

'Aaargh!' I shout again.

Then we both let out an 'Ouf' as he connects with me in a flying rugby tackle, knocking me clean off the sled, and we roll over in the snow. The sled carries on running, but slower now. Instead of charging off into the wide, white yonder, soon the dogs come to a reluctant halt and start up a disappointed whine.

Carter is on top of me and we've created a dune of snow around us. We're both panting heavily. My fur-trapper hat has tipped over my face and covers my eyes. Carter pushes it back with a snowy mitten.

'Are you all right?' he asks, concerned.

I blow snow from my mouth and blink it from my eyes. 'I think so.'

'Why did the dogs suddenly stop?'

'I'm lying on the anchor,' I tell him. Which starts him off laughing. I join in and we lie in the snow, giggling like schoolgirls.

'I don't think you're ready for the Olympic dog-sledding team yet,' Carter says. 'A bit more practice is needed.'

'I thought I was doing quite well.'

He takes off a glove and tenderly brushes my hair from my face with fingers that feel warm against my chilled skin.

'Sure you're OK?'

I nod, quite relieved that my neck still moves.

'You did have me worried for a minute. The way those dogs were running, I thought you might end up back in Hemel Hempstead.'

We collapse into fits of laughter again.

A minute or two later, Jan and the children jog down the track behind us. We're still lying in the snow and neither of us, it appears, is in a rush to get up.

Jan is the first to call out. 'Hey,' he says. 'All well?'

'Fine. We stopped the dogs.' That makes us laugh all over again.

Eve stands with her hands on her hips. 'Now you're just being silly, Daddy.'

'You're right, darling,' Carter agrees and gives me a rueful look. 'We should be heading back now.' He stands and holds out a hand so that I can get up too.

'Make sure the anchor's in place!' Jan shouts.

So I turn over onto my tummy and press the anchor firmly into the snow. That's it, dogs, I think. You ain't going nowhere.

'Are you happy to still take the sled, Cassie?' Jan asks.

'Yes,' I say.

My legs are like jelly but that's nothing to do with being dragged along by a dog sled. I cast a surreptitious glance at Carter who's still grinning at me. Is it me or is there some sort of chemistry building between us?

Perhaps I'm wrong. Maybe it's just because I've never really been in the company of another man for such a long time. I have to be careful to remember my place. Although I'm here at Carter's invitation, I'm hardly his guest. I'm the hired help. If the kids had a nanny, it would be she who would be here in my place. It would serve me well to keep that firmly in my mind.

'I'm fine,' I assure them. 'But does anyone want to come on the sled with me?' I wouldn't blame Max or Eve if they went with Jan instead. In my ears I can hear Tamara's warning not to take the children home with any injuries.

'I'll come with you,' Max says, excitedly.

'Is that all right?' I check with Carter.

'If Max is happy, then I am too.'

The boy clambers straight onto the seat. 'Can we tip it over again, Cassie?' he shouts back at me. 'It looked like brilliant fun.'

I'm not sure that it was fun, but it's something that will stay with me for a very long time.

Chapter Forty-One

We make it back to the wilderness lodge without further incident. Thank heavens. The dogs settled in quickly and we whooshed through the spectacular scenery at a steady but exhilarating pace. All the way back we didn't see another living soul. This place is remote in the extreme.

The days are woefully short at this time of year. Already the sun is sinking quickly and it's twilight when we reach the lodge. We all help Jan to feed and settle the dogs for the night, which the children love doing.

'I will see you all in the morning for another treat,' he says as he waves goodbye to us.

'Yay!' the children cheer.

Tomorrow morning we're going to be trying out snowmobiling – but only I know that. I think of Gaby's kids, my niece and nephew, Molly and George, who would love it here. Carter's children really are very privileged and I wonder if they realise just how fortunate they are. Then I remember that their parents are divorcing and that they seem to spend hardly any time with their mum and dad. Molly and George are surrounded constantly by love and I can no more imagine Gaby and Ryan divorcing than I can imagine being accepted on the Mars astronaut programme. They might not have all the material advantages of Carter's children, but they are lucky in so many other ways.

We all troop inside to find the wood burner roaring away to welcome us. We go through the ritual of removing all our Arctic clothing that we've so quickly become used to. The children sit on the floor while I tug off their boots. I help Carter to shrug off his suit in a businesslike manner, making sure that my hands don't stray where they shouldn't.

The cook has been busy and the delicious smell of our dinner wafts through the lodge. 'Swedish meatballs with potatoes followed by apple cake and cream,' she tells us and, immediately, we're hungry.

I leave Carter with the children and I go for a shower. Standing under the hot water, I think of Jim for the first time today. I wonder if he is missing me and decide, despite our squabble, that he probably is. I've been away from home only for a day, but already it feels like a lifetime away and that worries me more than I can say. Carter's world is so different from mine and so exciting. I wish I could call Jim right now, reconnect, and then I might feel differently.

When I go back into the living room, all the candles have been lit. Carter is sitting at the table, playing ludo with Eve and Max, who have stripped down to their thermal underwear. I make sure that our clothes are hanging up to dry and then set the table for the cook. I nip into the children's bedrooms and put their pyjamas to warm on the radiator. When dinner's ready, I call them over and we all tuck in.

'Daddy is excellent at board games,' Eve says. 'He beat us both.'

He laughs and gives me a sheepish look. 'Can't help it,' he confides. 'Competitive to the last.' Then he claps his hands and turns to the children. 'Ready for another sound thrashing before bedtime?'

'Yay!' they shout and rush towards the board game again.

Smiling, I tut at him and, again, help out with the clearing up. Perhaps if I do as many chores as I can, I'll remember why I'm really here, instead of feeling like I'm part of the family.

I glance over at Carter and the children. Eve is so pretty. She's going to be a heartbreaker just like her mother, I suspect. Max is boisterous, straightforward like most boys. But they are both bright, articulate and unfailingly polite. If I'd raised kids like that, privileged or not, I'd be very proud of myself.

When the cook has finished for the night and leaves, I join them at the table. 'Who's winning now?'

'Daddy,' they both chorus in a disgruntled manner.

'These two sleepyheads are ready for their beds,' Carter says.

'We are *so* not, Daddy.' Eve yawns.

'Say goodnight to Cassie,' he instructs.

'Come and tuck us in again,' Eve begs me. 'It's nice.'

I look to Carter for approval and he nods. So we both go through to their bedroom where I help Eve to get undressed and into her warm pyjamas while Carter sees to Max.

'Can you brush my hair, please?' she says. 'I like Mummy to do it.'

So, feeling very honoured, I take up her Hello Kitty hairbrush and Eve sits perfectly still while I smooth the tangles out of her long, blonde hair. Then she hops into bed and I tuck the duvet round her.

'Night night,' I say. 'See you in the morning. Sleep well.'

Carter has put Max into bed and I kiss him too. Then we leave them to sleep, again leaving the door open to the living room so that they can still enjoy the flickering warmth of the fire and the glow of the candlelight.

'Wine?' Carter says. 'I think we deserve some.'

'Hmm, sounds good. I'm starting to ache now from my extreme dog-sledding.'

He pours me out a glass of red wine and hands it over. 'Then I have an even better idea,' Carter says. 'There's a hot tub on our front porch that would be the perfect antidote to aching muscles.'

'Er . . .' I have, in fact, brought my bikini for this very moment but now that it's here, I feel suddenly shy.

'I think it would be positively rude *not* to use it,' he stresses.

Oh, it does sound good. I can almost feel myself sinking into that relaxing hot water. But do I want to do it while scantily clothed with my far-too-handsome client?

'What about the children?'

'We'll be just a few feet away from them on the porch. They'll be fine. Come on, Cassie,' he cajoles. 'It will be fun.'

But that, I'm afraid, is exactly what I'm worried about.

Chapter Forty-Two

In the bedroom, I change into my bikini. I sit on the edge of the bed and wonder where Jim is now. How I wish that I could ring him, just hear his voice. But it's not to be. The only downside of the wilderness is that it is, indeed, a long way from anywhere, or anyone.

Instead, I wrap myself tightly in the fluffy robe that's hanging on the back of the door, grab a couple of towels and head out to the hot tub. Thank goodness it's only a few steps from the front door as the temperature has plummeted dramatically out here. A quick look at the thermometer tells me that it's a cool minus twenty-five and I don't think I've ever been anywhere so cold before. I'll have to make sure that the children are well wrapped up tomorrow.

Carter is nowhere in sight, so I quickly slip off my robe and climb the steps into the hot tub. This feels like a very intimate thing to do with someone I hardly know and I'm still questioning the wisdom of it. Despite the indecision in my head, I'm already lowering myself into the gently bubbling water when Carter appears. Too late to change my mind now.

Carter has eschewed the fluffy robe and has gone for the towel-low-slung-round-the-hips option. 'Wow,' he says. 'It's cold out here.'

'Jump in quickly,' I tell him. 'The water's lovely and warm.'

He's carrying our wine and he hands my glass to me. I put it on the special tray cut into the side of the hot tub. When he's set down his own glass, he strips off his towel. I can tell that he puts the gym in Randall Court to good use. He has a fine, firm body. Strong legs, broad shoulders and abs that are still well defined. His black swim trunks emphasise his narrow hips. I'm so glad that I got in here first and am now up to my chest in water with no bits of flesh showing. It's not that I'm ashamed of my body. It's a bit on the curvy side for my liking, but in reasonably good shape and has served me well. If it was Jim and me jumping in here, I'd have no qualms. But I haven't been this close to another man in years. So long ago, in fact, that I can't even remember it. I'm acutely aware of my own body and his.

Carter lowers himself into the water, taking the seat next to me. 'Ah, bliss.'

The hot tub faces outwards from the lodge, giving us a fantastic view over the tops of the fir trees. The moon is full and high; the stars are out in abundance. I can feel my stress seeping out of me. My muscles, gently massaged by the water, are slowly unknotting.

We both sit and stare out into the wilderness, not speaking. The silence of the night and the remoteness of the landscape is overwhelming and I think we're both happy just to drink it in. This is more intoxicating than any alcohol.

Eventually, Carter turns to me. 'I'm glad you came with us, Cassie Christmas. Everything so far has been fantastic. The children adore you.'

'They're great kids,' I tell him honestly. 'You must be very proud of them.'

'They're my life,' he says, then laughs without humour. 'Or they should be. It's only when I've spent time with them, as I have today, that I realise how little I engage with them. Even when I'm at home with them, I'm always attached to my phone or iPad. There's always something pressing to deal with from the office. If I'm honest with myself, I never really give them my full attention. Having a great day like today has made me see that.'

'Surely you're at a stage in your business where you could ease off a bit if you wanted to.'

'I could,' he says. 'Theoretically. You never do, though. There's always another challenge to conquer. Once you get gripped by it, Cassie, it never lets you go.'

'The office seems to be managing all right without you while you're here.'

'But we don't know that, do we? One of my manufacturing plants could be burning down as we speak and I wouldn't know.' He laughs and takes a swig of his wine. 'Now I'm making myself panic.'

'Your children are young only for such a small amount of time,' I say. 'Blink and you'll miss it.'

'It wouldn't be quite so bad if it was just me,' he admits with a sigh. 'But Tamara is never around for them either. She's completely embroiled in her company too. When you get so big, a lot of people depend on you for their living. It's hard to let them down.'

'Easier to let down your children?'

'You never think you're doing that, do you?' he says. 'They go to one of the top schools in the country. They have everything money can buy.' Carter looks across at me. 'I thought that I was giving them the best in life. This trip has shown me that what they really want is me to be around. They want me to chase them and play board games with them and tuck them in at night.'

'Kids have very simple desires.'

'You seem to know a lot about them,' Carter notes.

'Only through my sister's children. I adore my niece and nephew and, thankfully, Gaby and I are very close. I see them as much as I can. Virtually every day.'

'Yet you have none of your own.'

'I hope it won't be the case for long,' I confess. 'Jim and I would both love kids. The stark reality, though, is that we were both working in jobs that aren't highly paid. While I was unemployed, we were barely able to pay our rent and our bills.'

'I can't imagine how that must feel.'

'No.' How could he understand? 'There's not much left to spare. Jim and I were saving up to get married and have a family but then – out of the blue – I lost my job. I had no income for the best part of a year and Jim's salary isn't enough for two to live on.' I can't even begin to tell Carter what we owe on our credit cards and that's not been spent on luxuries, it's racked up simply from day-to-day living. 'So we've had to put our plans on hold.'

And I don't know for how long. I'm thirty-five now and well aware that my time is running out. Let's face it, if I'd been with someone as rich as Carter, I'd have half a dozen children by now. The thought makes me flush.

'I realise that I have a very blessed life,' Carter admits.

'You do,' I agree. 'But then you work for it. You've made sacrifices for your wealth.'

It seems ridiculous to admit that Jim and I have put off having children simply because we can't afford them. Can anyone? If all you thought about were the finances involved, then you'd probably never do it. It's just that I want my children to be comfortable, not on the scale of Carter's two, but not to struggle for the basics, the way my mum had to with Gaby and me. My abiding memory of childhood is being cold and there never being quite enough to eat. I couldn't put my own children through that.

'Do you think my marriage has crumbled because we were both too busy chasing money rather than happiness?' Carter asks.

'I don't know, Carter. You and Tamara are the only ones who can unpick what's gone on behind your bedroom door. I think happiness comes from both wanting the same things, having the same goals. When that doesn't suit one person in the relationship, that's when it starts to fall apart.'

'I think Tamara and I always pulled against each other rather than working together.'

'Do you think it's really over?'

'Our divorce lawyers would say so,' he concludes. 'I've tried to make it right with Tamara but, emotionally, she left the marriage some time ago. Now all I can do is try to reach an amicable settlement, but it's taking a long time.' His weary exhalation of breath floats into the air as a little cloud of steam. I manage to stop myself from reaching up to touch it. 'I loved her madly, you know. We always had a very passionate relationship.'

From that I gather they were at it all night, every night.

'But what do you do when the passion dissipates and there's nothing left in its place? Tamara and I can never be friends. We were always either having sex or at war. Not much in between.'

'That's sad.'

I think of Jim and me, who make excellent friends, but have we ever really had passion like that? Is that a better recipe for a relationship? Perhaps the daily grind of our lives has managed to erode any chance of sparks flying every night.

'All I can do now is focus on the children. I want them to suffer as little as possible.' He looks incredibly sad. 'Though I'm beginning to realise that it's probably impossible to protect them completely.'

'You're doing your best,' I reassure him. 'It's clear that they both love you very much.'

'They do,' he says. 'I'm so lucky. I want to do more for them. I want to give them more of me.'

'Well, we've got two more days here for you to enjoy,' I remind him. 'You can't get better quality time than this.'

He puts his arm across the back of the hot tub and leans towards me. 'I could never talk to Tamara like this,' he says. 'Perhaps that's another piece of the puzzle. I hardly know you and yet I can chat to you as if you're an old friend. You're very easy company to be with, Cassie Christmas.'

'You are too, Carter.' There's a tightness in my throat when I say, 'I'm glad that I could be here.'

We're close. So close. The breath from our mouths mingles and caresses in the air. He looks as if he might reach up to touch my face. Then what would I do? His dark eyes are sad, soulful, and I want to see them happy again. If he drew me to him and kissed me now, would I resist?

Instead of touching my face, his hand clasps his glass and he knocks back his wine. 'This is a marvellous place.' His voice sounds shaky.

My throat is almost closed, but I manage to find one word. 'Yes.'

Then we exchange a nervous smile and together we turn to stare out at the all-encompassing sky, both lost in our own thoughts.

Chapter Forty-Three

'Right,' Jim said. 'This is it.' He double-checked the address. This was, sure enough, Randall Court. Bloody hell.

He turned to Rozzer sitting next to him in the car and Smudge who was in the back seat, both with their mouths dropping open. Rozzer was the first to speak. 'We're doing *this* place?'

'Looks like it,' Jim said and, for the first time, realised why Cassie had been so keen to keep Carter Randall on board as a client. Even though he knew Carter was a millionaire, he'd never imagined a gaff as palatial as this.

Jim put the car into gear and coasted up the sweeping drive. He had called ahead to see if it was all right if they came in to finish off some of the decorations in Cassie's absence. Carter Randall's personal assistant had assured him that it would be. Now he was wondering if it was a good idea after all. He'd just wanted to help out, but suddenly he felt hopelessly out of his depth.

Rozzer was holding the pad with Cassie's list of jobs to be done. Jim had checked it thoroughly the previous night and had made sure that they'd got all the right stuff in the boot of the car. However, the jobs that were left to do required a level of artistry that he wasn't sure he had. No, that he was absolutely *certain* he didn't have.

There was still no contact, no news from Cassie. He hoped that wasn't a bad sign, but he was still checking his phone every five minutes – just in case. He was missing her more than he could possibly have imagined and, in some ways, it was a good thing that there was a stack of tasks he could throw himself into while she was gone.

He'd had the lads round to the flat the night before and they'd all huddled round the computer in the spare room to watch tutorial videos on YouTube, just as Cassie did. At the time he'd felt confident that they could pull it off. Now, in the face of it, his self-belief was turning rapidly to nerves. Could they really do it? Women had a natural flair for these things, didn't they? He wasn't sure that a prison officer and two young offenders would make such a marvellous job of the floristry that they'd intended to tackle. Jim was sure that the last thing that any of them had expected to do when they signed up for this was to be making flower arrangements. The lads had come a long way and their capacity for attempting embarrassing things was increasing all the time. They seemed to think that if they could cut it dressed as elves, then they could do anything. It was fair to say that they'd all made a decent stab at some practice pieces – Jim was pleasantly surprised at the quality – but would that translate to the real thing? They'd find out soon enough.

While the lads unloaded the boot of the car, Jim rang the door-bell. Carter's assistant, Georgina, opened the door to let them in.

'Hey,' she said. 'Welcome to Randall Court.'

'Hi,' Jim said and felt too tongue-tied to continue the conversation. Smudge and Rozzer just gaped.

He was glad – so glad – that the lads had been allowed the privilege of wearing their own clothes today. They were both dressed reasonably smartly in jeans, albeit those ridiculous ones with the crotch down by the knees, fairly inoffensive T-shirts and fleece hoodies. They looked as if they had attitude but not necessarily a criminal record. It made Jim think that if they did this again next year, maybe they should have a basic company uniform. Or perhaps he'd just spent too much of his working life in uniform to be able to give it up easily.

Once inside the entrance hall they were all even more overawed. Cassie had described this to him, but he hadn't actually taken in just how opulent everything would be. The tree that she'd already decorated towered above them, looking utterly spectacular. Now he was firmly convinced that their handiwork wouldn't be up to the mark. As far as he was concerned, they might as well just pack up their bags and go home this minute.

'Have you got everything you need?' Georgina asked them.

'I think so.' Leave, leave now, his brain was telling him.

'I'll send you some tea?'

'That would be very nice. Thank you.'

'I'm in the office at the back of the house. Call or text me if you need me.' She left them to get started.

Jim blew out a slightly dazed breath. 'Wow.'

'Fuck,' Rozzer said.

'Language,' Jim reminded him. 'Right, lads, where do we start?'

They all scratched their heads.

'This is one big fuck-off mansion, Jim,' Rozzer noted. 'Sorry, but it is.'

Jim had to agree that there was no better description.

Rozzer picked up an ornament from the nearby side table. It was some piece of modern sculpture that could be a man curled over or a wave. Even though Jim couldn't quite make out what it was, he knew that it was probably hideously expensive.

'Please don't touch anything that looks breakable,' Jim said. 'And please don't steal anything.'

'What do you think we are?' Rozzer said, offended.

Jim lowered his voice. 'I think you're impressionable lads on day release from the local young offenders' unit.'

'Oh,' Rozzer said, putting down the sculpture. 'I suppose you have a point.'

'Look,' Jim said. 'I'm ten years a prison officer and even *I'm* tempted to nick something.'

'We're not thieves.'

'Technically, you are,' Jim countered. 'I know that you're trying very hard to turn it all around and you're doing brilliantly, but old habits die hard. All I'm asking is that you think about me, think about Cassie's business. Don't do anything stupid. Today is the day you prove yourselves to me.'

'We won't let you down, Jim,' Rozzer said. 'You can count on us.'

'We won't touch nothing,' Smudge agreed, having finally found his voice again. 'I swear on my mother's life.'

'Good lads.'

'Do we have to call you Santa today, Jim?'

That made them all laugh. 'Not today, Smudge. Only when I've got the gear on.' Jim looked up at the tree. 'That's what we've got to match up to, lads. Think we've got the ability?'

Rozzer and Smudge shrugged. 'We can give it a go, Santa ... Jim.'

'We'll unpack the boxes, lay out what we'll need. I've got Cassie's rough plan here.' He pulled out a sheaf of papers on which Cassie had sketched out her vision for the garlands that were to twine round the banister and drape over the mantelpiece. There were also a dozen different flower arrangements in vases to do. 'We'll finish that banister first so that we can copy the way Cassie's done it.' Jim had to admit that it looked amazing. A hard task lay ahead of them. 'Let's take our time. Go slowly. Stick closely to Cassie's design. Get it right. Any problems, let's stop and work it through.'

The lads did as they were told without complaint. They all worked together to thread the garland of artificial green foliage through the banister according to Cassie's master plan. Then they added the decorations, lime, cerise and purple baubles, interspersed with bows and little boxes wrapped like presents, as highlights. To think that a few weeks ago he hadn't even known half these words, let alone imagined himself doing festive flower arrangements.

He looked up at the lads. Both were frowning with concentration. Smudge's tongue stuck out to the side as he tried to attach a bow to the garland. Jim smiled to himself.

An elderly lady arrived with a tray of tea and biscuits for them. No mugs here, it was all served on fine bone china. 'That looks pretty,' she said. 'Nice job, boys.'

'Take a breather for five minutes, lads,' he told Rozzer and Smudge.

The lady stood for a moment to admire their handiwork.

'Does it look any different to the rest of the banister?' Jim asked.

She studied it closely and then shook her head. 'No. It looks just the same to me. Very pretty.'

'You've made my day, love,' he said. 'Thanks.'

That gave him the impetus to believe in himself and press on. This was going better than he could possibly have hoped. Cassie would get such a surprise when she came home.

Chapter Forty-Four

We're just finishing up our breakfast when Jan appears. Minutes later and he drives two snowmobiles out of one of the bigger outhouses. The children go crazy as soon as they see them and can't wait to be outside, so there's a mad scramble to climb into their outdoor clothing.

Carter and I help them. We haven't talked much this morning and I wonder if he feels he said too much last night. For my part, I stayed awake into the small hours, my mind whirring. I love Jim, I really do, but there's something about Carter that's very hard to ignore. He seems both powerful and vulnerable at the same time and it's a heady cocktail. On top of that, he's handsome and fun. Our talk made me wonder what I'm doing with my life, where Jim and I are going. I sigh and push these thoughts out of my mind.

'Everything OK?' Carter asks.

I didn't realise he was so close to me. 'Yes;' I say. 'Just a busy brain.'

'Who's holding up the business for you while you're away?'

'Jim.' I hope.

'It's good of you to come away with us, particularly in your key time and with a new business. It was a big ask.'

'I'm just pleased that I could come. I'd love to organise more trips like this and it's given me a great insight.'

It's also given me an insight into how the other half live and I'm not sure *that* is so great. My little two-roomed flat in Hemel Hempstead is going to be something of a let-down after all this.

'You've done a great job,' he says. 'I won't hesitate to recommend you.'

'Thank you. That's nice to know.'

I wonder if Carter is trying to steer us back onto safer ground by talking about business. Perhaps he's regretting our closeness last night. I know that I should be. This holiday is a job and I don't want to let my professionalism slip.

Still, there's plenty to do today. I've already packed our suitcases again as that was our last night in the wilderness lodge and we're moving on. Someone will come to collect the cases and take them to our next destination. Tonight, we're going to be sleeping in the world-famous Icehotel. I can't wait to see it. Every year, the whole thing is built with snow and blocks of ice cut from the river, to open up in time for Christmas. Then, in March, it melts back into the landscape again.

I make sure that the kids have on plenty of clothes. You can get quite hot while running around outside, even in these extreme low temperatures, but for a good few hours this morning we're going to be sitting still on snowmobiles and it's certainly not getting any warmer out there. I start to struggle into my suit and Carter, instantly, is right there.

'Here, let me help.' He moves closer to me and I feel myself flush with warmth.

As much as I'd like to ignore it, I can tell that there's been a distinct shift in the relationship between us. After our long chat last night in the hot tub, we're much more aware of each other. It's as if there's a crackle of electricity around us both and, believe me, it's very disconcerting. Carter's fingers linger a little longer as he helps me into my suit and, although I'm wearing more clothing than I ever have, I can feel every touch as if he's searing me. His hands rest on my shoulders as he appraises my outfit.

'Looking good, Mrs Christmas,' he says, a smile in his eyes. Seems that *he's* not being businesslike at all.

I have to gulp before I can speak. 'Thank you.' Oh, Lord, help me.

Before I melt into a puddle in the lodge, I turn my attention back to the children.

'Ready, guys?'

Max and Eve are bouncing just as much as the huskies were yesterday. They're wide-eyed with excitement when we finally get outside. The sun is high in the sky, making the vast expanses of snow glitter enticingly, but the day is colder than ever before. The mercury in the thermometer is still registering a mind-numbingly cold minus twenty-five degrees. Inhaling is positively painful and we'll all need to wear full-face balaclavas to protect our cheeks from the wind-chill factor. However, the scenery ahead of us is magical and it would be hard to equal the sheer exhilaration of being out here in the cold.

Jan fits us all with our safety helmets and then we're ready to rock. We're heading to the Icehotel on our snowmobiles to spend the last night of our trip there. *The last night.* I can hardly believe that I'm saying that as it feels as if we've only just arrived. Yet, already, we've managed to pack in so much.

I can feel the excitement building inside me and the children can hardly stand still, they're so hyper. Carter and I climb onto our separate snowmobiles. Thankfully, the handlebars and our seats are heated, providing a degree of comfort that is very much appreciated. Eve tucks in behind me, arms clinging tightly around my waist. I look over my shoulder to check that she's all right. 'OK?'

248

She nods. From his own snowmobile Carter looks towards me and gives me the thumbs-up. With a steadying breath, I release the throttle and we're off, slowly at first until we're used to the speed. The steering is vague, like trying to manoeuvre a shopping trolley with wonky wheels. After a few hair-raising minutes I'm soon happily following Jan along the snowy tracks, dodging the low-hanging tree branches, something we've so quickly become accustomed to.

Because we're powered by petrol today, we can climb higher into the hills, the snowmobiles scooting along at a terrific pace. This is fantastic fun. From the way that Carter and Max are whooping ahead of us, I can only assume that they feel the same. Eve is clinging on tightly, arms wrapped round my waist, and I keep looking back to check that she's OK. But I needn't worry as she's loving every minute of it.

We're so high up now that we've left everything behind but beautiful trees almost overwhelmed with snow, their branches weighed down to the ground. It feels as if we're in our own magical little bubble. There's nothing here to touch us, nothing to trouble us.

Jan stops us after a little while, opens the back of his machine and retrieves two thermos flasks that contain hot lingonberry juice – which, if you ask me, tastes exactly like Ribena. We clutch our cups gratefully and enjoy the hot drink. I look out over the vast, empty landscape. All you can see for miles are snow-laden firs and frozen lakes. The sky is so blue, the snow so white, that to take it all in hurts the eyes.

Eve and Max, having finished their drinks, chase each other through the deep drifts. Carter comes to stand next to me and gazes out over the hills. 'This is just beautiful. Awe-inspiring.'

'Yes,' I say. 'It is.'

He turns to me, face serious, and sighs as he says, 'I feel happier than I have in a long time, Cassie Christmas.'

My throat constricts again when I answer, 'Me too.'

I thought this job would be about wrapping presents, writing cards, decorating Christmas trees. That was as far as my ambition took me. But then I hadn't quite banked on meeting Carter Randall.

Chapter Forty-Five

Jim worked all day. It was a full-on shift. There were two gang fights, a dirty protest and a fellow prison officer – a new guy – was caught smuggling in drugs. The latter wasn't uncommon, but when it happened it always left a sour taste in the mouth. He'd seemed like a solid bloke too. All in all a pretty average day in Bovingdale Young Offenders' Unit.

He was exhausted when he left at the end of his shift. Not only did he feel like shit, but he smelled like it too. They always wore full coveralls, masks and gloves to clean down a cell, but the stench stayed with you for hours. He no longer retched constantly when they had to do a scrub, but it was never going to be anyone's favourite job. He always thought that they should make the filthy bastards who pulled this sort of stunt clean it up themselves. Then they might be less likely to smear their own shit up the walls.

The very first thing he needed to do when he got back to the flat was shower and change, get the stink of the unit out of his nostrils. Hopefully, it would liven him up too. He was exhausted. If he was honest, he wasn't sleeping all that well without Cassie in the bed. He found he was chasing himself around, getting tangled in the sheets. Normally, they slept like spoons, hooking their feet together. It seemed strange to spend the night alone. It hadn't helped that he'd been up half the night, watching flipping flower-arranging clips on YouTube. Having made such a great job of the garland on the banister and then the mantelpiece, he didn't want to let himself down by making a complete arse of the vases – which were the last thing left to do downstairs. He'd been on earlies, so had started at seven, but it meant that he was finished by three. It gave him a good few hours to switch hats and get stuck into the Christmas decorations.

Upstairs, all they had to do were the children's bedrooms. It was a tough call to get it all done in one evening, but the lads had proved that they could work well and, as long as he supervised them closely, Jim could see no reason why they couldn't manage to do it all.

The good news from the governor was that both lads were to be released early on licence. Such was the strain on the system that the unit was usually glad to see the back of prisoners to make room for the next wave. It meant that Rozzer and Smudge would both have to wear electronic tags to serve out the rest of their sentence, but they'd be coming out together, which was a result. All he had to do now was find accommodation for Smudge. And quickly.

Jim signed out the lads and escorted them to his car. They were chattery, hyper, a bit punchy, but it was probably due to their having been in lock-down in their cells for most of the day. Or they might just have been happy to be due out of Bovingdale for good. Whichever way, Jim kept quiet and let them burn it out of their systems before they went up to Randall Court.

It had started to snow. A few half-hearted watery flakes splashed onto the car park. The snow probably wouldn't settle but even so it would still send the country into a flat spin. He hoped that Cassie's plane wouldn't be delayed. She was meant to be home tomorrow and, for him, it couldn't come round soon enough. He'd missed her like crazy all the time she'd been away.

'Where is it that Cassie's gone?' Rozzer asked, breaking into his musing.

'Swedish Lapland,' Jim said.

'Oh.' They didn't sound any the wiser. It was only because he'd looked it up on Google Earth last night that he had any idea himself. On the map it seemed a very long way from anywhere. Also, the weather report said that the temperatures were extremely low.

'Is she enjoying herself?'

'I haven't heard from her,' Jim admitted. 'It's very remote up there. And cold. Minus twenty-five last night.'

'Should be called Coldasfuckland,' Rozzer suggested.

'Language,' Jim said.

Cassie was a hothouse flower and she'd be really hating it if it was that cold. 'She probably can't get a phone signal.'

'No phone?' Neither of them looked impressed by that either. It clearly wasn't going to feature highly on their Places to Visit list when they did get out.

At the flat, he made the lads a quick sandwich, then they changed out of their prison tracksuits into their jeans and T-shirts while Jim had a much needed hot shower, resisting the urge to scrub himself down with the nailbrush. Some days he wished he could be anywhere but at the unit.

He loaded up the car with the help of the lads and in the darkness made their way up to Randall Court. The elderly lady let them into the house this time and Jim assumed that Carter's personal assistant had already gone home.

It was stunning, coming back into the house the next day and seeing their handiwork. The lights on the tree were filling the room with a festive glow, and, even to Jim, who was hardly an aficionado of interior design, it looked quite breathtaking. He was sure that the lads actually gasped. Pretty impressive.

'Right,' Jim said. 'Shall I take the vases while you start on the trees in the children's bedrooms?'

'The kids are having their own trees?' Even Rozzer, who'd had a much more middle-class upbringing than Smudge, was amazed by this.

'Trees and a bit of bunting,' Jim said after consulting Cassie's list. Thankfully, she'd done a design for each of the trees too. 'Shouldn't take us long. I'll come up with you and get you started. We need to cover our trainers.' He didn't want anyone leaving a grubby footprint on that pristine cream carpet.

With their feet encased in blue plastic slip-on covers that Cassie had bought, they made their way up the grand staircase, pleased to admire their garland winding its way up alongside them.

'It looks well nice, doesn't it?' Smudge whispered.

'Yes.' Jim beamed at him. 'It does, lad. All credit to you.'

Their chests puffed up with pride. He knew that he'd been right about these two all along. You could feel it in your bones when lads were intrinsically good underneath. They just needed guiding back onto the right path, that was all.

First they went into the little girl's bedroom, a froth of girly pink. Jim felt a lump in his throat. He wondered if, one day, he'd have a daughter sleeping in a room like this. He could only hope so. If Cassie made enough money from this Christmas, then maybe they could start to try for a family. If they got a move on, he could even be a daddy by next Christmas. The thought nearly had him undone.

Jim took in the room again. The only difference with this particular little girl's bedroom was that it was accessorised with all the latest technology. There was an iPod, a flat-screen television and an Apple Mac at a hand-painted desk near the window. And, of course, an Xbox too.

'Wow,' Smudge said. 'Kids have this sort of stuff?'

'Not all of them,' Jim observed. 'Just a lucky few.' He checked Cassie's notes again. 'White tree, pink baubles, lilac bows.' Thankfully, they were artificial trees up here. He wouldn't have liked to try to get real ones up that cream carpet without dropping needles.

'I might have to make a few more bows,' Rozzer said.

Jim smiled to himself, thinking that was probably a sentence that Rozzer had never expected to hear himself utter. Who'd have thought that the lads would have been capable of such delicate work? Who'd have thought that he was capable of it himself?

'Can I leave you to it? The young boy's room needs doing too. That's next door. Want to take one each?'

'We'll work on this together,' Rozzer said. 'Then move on to the other one.'

'I'll do the vases,' Jim said, surprisingly eager to test out his finer flower-arranging skills.

But that would have to wait for a minute. First, he had to return a call from Vincent.

It was gone eight o'clock when they'd all finished. Jim went upstairs to inspect the trees that the lads had decorated. They'd made an astonishingly good job of them.

'Lads, that's fantastic,' Jim said, when he saw the tree they'd created in the little girl's room. He couldn't believe how well they'd done. 'Let me take a picture of it for Cassie's portfolio. She'll be well chuffed.'

Jim snapped the tree for posterity.

'It's the first time I've ever done a Christmas tree,' Smudge said, shyly. 'We never used to have one at home.'

That pulled Jim up short. 'Not ever?'

Smudge shrugged. 'Never.'

255

'Did you celebrate Christmas at all?'

'Not really. Mam and Dad might get even more pissed than usual on Christmas Eve, but that was about it.'

'Your mum didn't cook a Christmas dinner?'

Smudge laughed at that. 'You don't know my mam!'

Jim was probably glad he didn't.

'You've never had Christmas dinner?' Even Rozzer was appalled at that, his family being, by his own account, fairly dysfunctional.

'Nah.' Smudge looked embarrassed now. 'I've seen it, though. On the telly. It looks well good.'

Jim felt an unexpected wave of resentment wash over him. How was it possible that Carter Randall could have so much when there were millions of people out there who had so little? If he thought about it for too long his blood might boil. All this money lavished on just a few bloody weeks of partying. It suddenly seemed ridiculous.

Take this little jaunt that Cassie was on. How much was that lot costing? What was the price of hiring a private jet for a start? It seemed not only ridiculous but downright offensive. If he had that sort of money, he'd want to do some good with it, make sure that others benefited from his wealth. Some people could be so bloody selfish.

He looked around him. Opulence on a scale that he could never have imagined. And for what? It was pretty sickening to even look at.

'We need to go,' Jim said, forcing his voice to be bright. So far the lads didn't seem to be reacting as strongly as he was about the uneven distribution of wealth and he didn't want his blackening mood to affect them. After all, he had some good news for them too. 'I don't know about you, but I'm starving hungry. And we've got somewhere else to pop into before I take you back to the unit.'

256

They all had a look at the boy's room together too. Here the tree was also white but decorated with purple baubles and lime-green bows. It was equally stunning. If it was up to Jim, which it wasn't, he'd give both of the lads a bonus. To do this from a standing start was more than he could have ever expected.

'Rozzer, this is great too.' Suddenly, he felt his professional barrier come crashing down. 'Give us a hug. I'm bloody proud of you both.' Tears welled in the lads' eyes as he grabbed hold of them both. 'Thanks,' he said. 'You're stars. Both of you. Bloody stars.'

Smudge was crying openly now. 'I've never done anything nice before,' he sobbed. 'It looks really pretty.'

Rozzer, himself wiping away a surreptitious tear, mussed up Smudge's hair. 'You soft cu—'

'Language!' Jim said and they all laughed together.

They broke away and took one last lingering look at the tree. Their work here was done and Jim was sure that Cassie would be thrilled.

Chapter Forty-Six

We arrive at Icehotel in unique style, snowmobiling along the frozen Torne river at a giddy speed of thirty miles an hour, shrieking with pleasure. By the time we park up at the hotel's private dock, it's already getting dark. We climb off the snowmobiles and Jan takes our helmets.

I brush away the icicles that have formed on Eve's fringe. 'Did you like that?'

She nods enthusiastically. 'You're fun, Cassie,' she says. 'And Daddy likes you.'

My cheeks redden and it's not just due to the cold.

'I like you too,' she adds.

I hug her to me. 'Well, that's good. Because I like you.'

She slips her small hand in mine and we head off towards the hotel.

Lights guide us to the entrance and give a purple glow to the crisp, deep snow. The Icehotel rises up ahead of us like some sort of fantasy kingdom for a snow queen.

Once more, the children are wide-eyed.

'We're staying *here*?' Eve asks.

'It's pretty, isn't it?'

'And it's really made of ice?'

'Yes,' I laugh. 'It really is.'

Max looks concerned. 'It won't melt while we're asleep, will it?'

'No, it won't.' With the temperature now tipping below minus twenty-five, it seems very unlikely. 'There's nothing to worry about.'

'When I grow up I want to live here and have my own snowmobile,' Max announces. 'Can I do that, Daddy?'

'It sounds like a plan,' Carter agrees affably.

While we're standing still, I can feel my eyelashes starting to freeze and I don't want the children to get chilled. 'Shall we go inside and see if we can find some hot chocolate?'

'Yay!' they both cry.

Normally, I won't leave the flat at home if the mercury hits zero degrees and yet, look at me out here, having fun in the freezing cold. It's as if I've turned into a completely different person in the last few days. I certainly feel a long way from home and all that I know.

We hit the reception area of the hotel, which, thankfully, isn't made of ice. It's busy and welcoming, with a big wood-burning stove as a centrepiece. I order hot chocolate for us all and then go to the main desk to check in our party with Jan's assistance.

I've booked the Royal Deluxe Suite for Carter – the very best room that they have. Of course. The children are in an adjoining suite. I've booked for myself the most basic accommodation, a snow room. Nothing fancy for me, just a very chilly bed for the night. For me, this could well be like sleeping in my own fridge.

The receptionist is taking her time, trawling through her list. She looks up at Jan, worried. 'I have only two rooms reserved,' she says in impeccable English. 'This is difficult?'

I can't have a glitch now, not at this critical moment, when everything's gone so smoothly. 'Please tell me it's not the suites that are a problem.'

'No,' she says. 'I have two suites.'

Thank goodness for that. This is to be one of the highlights of the trip. My stomach unclenches.

'But no snow room. That has been cancelled.'

'It can't have,' I say.

'Yah.' An apologetic shrug. 'Is so.'

I pull out my trusty folder with all the arrangements in it. When I find the confirming email, I put it on the counter. She looks at it, unmoved, and then taps at her computer. 'It was cancelled by telephone yesterday.'

'Who by?'

'Unfortunately, I do not have a name.'

'Damn.' What a cock-up! At least it's only inconveniencing me. 'Have you got anything else?' I ask. 'I'll sleep anywhere.'

She scans her screen again, frowning, before she shakes her head with a finality that clearly can't be argued with. 'I'm sorry. The hotel is very popular. We are fully booked for tonight.'

I turn to Jan. Now what? As my mind is racing, Carter comes to join us. 'Problem?'

'Not with your booking,' I assure him. 'The suites are absolutely fine. It's just that I haven't got a room. Somehow the booking has been cancelled in error. I definitely organised it. I've got the confirmation here.'

'They've nothing else available?'

'You can come back to the wilderness lodge,' Jan suggests.

'Of course,' I say stoically. 'That will be fine.'

It's a convenient solution, no doubt, but my heart sinks. This place looks so magical, so special, that I want to stay here too. I don't think I could bear to climb into Jan's car and drive away from Carter and the children for the night. My eyes fill up at the thought of it.

'Don't worry,' Carter says, gently. 'No need for tears.'

'I don't want to leave the children,' I say, feeling stupid.

'We're all family now.' From the depths of his Arctic suit, he pulls out a handkerchief and dabs at my eyes. 'Max can sleep in with me, and you and Eve can share the other room. If that suits you, Cassie?'

The lump that had blocked my throat eases instantly. 'Are you sure?'

'Of course.' He smiles at the receptionist. 'There's no difficulty with that, is there?'

'No difficulty at all, Mr Randall,' she confirms.

Hmm, she didn't look at me in that nothing-is-too-much-trouble manner. If Carter had been alone in his suite tonight, she looks as if she might well have been offering him bed-warming services.

He turns and grins at me. 'Then that's settled. We couldn't have Mrs Christmas with nowhere to sleep for the night.'

'Thank you, Carter,' I say. 'You're very kind.'

'Nonsense. It was the only solution.'

We're given passes to our cabins, which are in the warm part of the hotel. Jan and I carry our bags through to these areas and leave them there. If you take any luggage into the icy wing, it just freezes up as the rooms are set at a constant minus five degrees. When it's time for bed we'll get our sleeping bags from the equipment desk right next to reception. Then we'll get changed in the warm cabins before going into the icy wing to sleep.

We walk through the complex to have dinner in the rustic homestead restaurant and then, laughing and shrieking, throw snow over each other all the way back to the hotel. The night is clear, the stars sparkling. Surely tonight we'll see the northern lights. Still safely ensconced in our full Arctic kit, we all troop into the Icebar.

It's truly spectacular, with sculptures dotted around. Everything

261

is made of ice. The music rocks out and both of the children's jaws hit the floor.

'Wicked,' Max gasps, mouth gaping as he takes it all in.

'I've never been in a bar before,' Eve says, equally awe-struck. 'It's lovely. I want to stay here for ever.'

'If she's an alcoholic by the time she's twenty, I'll be blaming you,' Carter whispers in my ear.

Oh Lord. I hope they don't tell their mother that I took them into a bar.

All around the dance floor are carved murals of couples doing the tango and, above us, the ice ceiling is decorated with footprints. Next to the dance floor is a small, elevated booth carved from ice with a curved ice bench running along two sides, covered with reindeer skins. I usher the children into it.

'My bottom's cold,' Max says, sitting down gingerly.

'What would you like to drink, kids?'

Eve peruses the menu. 'I'll have a Cheery Chiller. Vodka and cranberry juice.'

'*Without* the vodka,' Carter notes. 'Nice try.'

'I think she's trying to get into the family business early,' I tease him.

He shakes his head, resigned. 'I'm already dreading the day.' He turns to his son. 'For you, Max?'

'Something pink,' he declares.

'I want something pink too, Daddy,' Eve says, not to be left out.

So Carter and I go to the bar. The neon-coloured cocktails, which cost a king's ransom, are served in chunky tumblers carved out of ice, with a sprinkling of salt around the rims to stop your lips sticking to them.

'I could do with getting my Pure Pleasure drinks in here,' he muses. 'And the alcoholic ice lollies would go down a storm.'

'No work today,' I insist and he laughs.

'Old habits die hard.'

We make our choice, a Source of Life cocktail for Carter and one called Frozen Love for me. Plenty of vodka in ours. We pick two non-alcoholic and, as requested, very pink drinks for the children.

Back at our booth, we all clink our ice glasses together and knock back the drinks.

'Wow,' Carter says. 'That freezes your lungs.'

'It tastes nice.' Max sticks his tongue into his ice glass.

Katy Perry's 'California Gurls' blares out.

'This is my very favourite song in the whole world,' Eve says. 'Can we all dance?'

'I'll dance with you,' I tell Eve.

'And Daddy too. I've never seen Daddy dance.'

I raise my eyebrows and look over at Carter. 'Never?'

'It's something that I try very hard to avoid.' Three sets of pleading eyes stare at him. 'Am I really going to have any choice?'

'Doesn't look like it,' I say.

'Come on, Max,' Carter says. 'Let's you and I take one for the boys.' So, together, we hit the ice dance floor.

I can't say that I've ever strutted my stuff in thermal boots and an Arctic suit, but I give it my best shot. The children bounce enthusiastically while I try to rock it out and, although Carter might be dancing rather self-consciously, he's not a bad mover. We all join hands, forming a circle, and dance around, singing at the top of our voices until we're all but drowning out Katy Perry.

We groove it through the next three tunes. I teach the kids how to throw some *Saturday Night Fever*-style poses, which makes them hysterical with laughter. Then, when Carter and I are out of breath and we're getting all hot and bothered in our suits, we head back to the booth.

The children go in front of us and Carter hangs back so I turn to see if he's OK. He puts a hand on my arm. 'Thanks for that,' he says. 'It's sad to say but Tamara never would have let herself go like that. Me neither, if I'm honest.'

I laugh. 'If you can't give it large on the dance floor, when can you?'

'It's a motto that everyone should live by.' Then he looks reflective. 'This trip has really opened my eyes. You're so good with the kids.'

'Thanks.'

'Come to think of it, Cassie Christmas,' he adds, 'you're pretty damn good with me too.'

Chapter Forty-Seven

Jim and the lads stopped off at a kebab van that was always parked by Gadebridge Park. They'd worked so hard that he would have liked to treat them to something more, a decent curry maybe, but time was tight. He had to get them back to the unit by ten o'clock and there was one more stop to be made first.

He ordered them all doner kebabs with extra chilli sauce and no lettuce for Smudge. The lads, grateful for the hot food, wolfed it down in minutes while sitting in the car. Jim left the heater running as the temperature was dropping. They said on the radio that it might fall to freezing that night. He wondered how Cassie was coping in the cold. If she was at home she'd be hogging the gas fire and going to bed in her socks. God, he missed her.

They all swigged from cans of cola. Jim needed a cup of tea and perhaps a small whisky as a pick-me-up, feeling as if he'd earned a treat too. But that would have to wait until he'd dropped off the lads and was safely back home.

'Ready, lads?'

When they'd rolled up their greasy waste papers, Jim took these, along with their empty cans, and jumped out into the cold to toss them into the bin.

'I've got a surprise for you,' he said on his return. 'Before you go back.'

'More presents to wrap?' Rozzer quipped.

'No,' Jim said. 'Something I think that you'll like even more. Buckle up, lads.'

They drove across town to the other side of Hemel Hempstead and, a few minutes later, pulled up outside the Halfway House run by Vincent Benlow. Jim turned round in his seat. 'This is the place I told you about.'

Rozzer and Smudge exchanged a wary glance. 'Looks good.'

'Want to take a closer look?'

Climbing out of the car, they followed Jim down the path and waited, fidgeting anxiously, until Vincent opened the door to them.

'Come on in, my friends,' he boomed, grinning widely. 'Good to see you again. You've come to check out my place?'

Both lads nodded sheepishly. Jim clapped Vincent on the back. 'Thanks again for the call, mate.'

'No worries, man. Cup of tea?'

'No time, Vincent. Got to get the lads back to the unit.'

'Then let's not hang about.'

Vincent loped along the corridor with the others falling into step behind him. He poked his head into the communal television room where two pale youths were slumped in armchairs in front of some reality show. 'All right if I show the lads round, Lenny?'

One of the youths grunted a yes.

At the top of a short flight of stairs, Vincent pulled out a large bunch of keys. 'This is the one,' he said, as he found the right key, unlocked the door and flung it wide open, then stood aside.

Smudge and Rozzer edged nervously into the flat, with Jim following. It was sparsely furnished. Two spindly armchairs flanked the gas fire and a worn sofa hugged the wall opposite. That was it for the living room. The walls were magnolia, but looked dirty and in need of repainting. The brown-and-orange-patterned carpet was the sort of thing you'd have seen in a pub in the 1970s.

A picture window looked out over the garden. The curtains that hung on either side were limp and ragged. Jim peered out, but there was nothing much to see in the dark. At least the lads would have somewhere to sit out in the summer, though.

'There are two bedrooms,' Vincent said.

Smudge and Rozzer looked into both of them, small singles identical in size, each containing a narrow bed, a chipboard bedside cupboard and a slim wardrobe. Tired was the best way to describe the decor. Awfully tired. Only one of the beds was made up.

'You've got your own bathroom too,' Vincent said.

The bath was chipped, the loo cracked and the shower curtain was black with mould around the edges. It wasn't the most hygienic bathroom Jim had ever seen, but a judicious application of bleach would certainly help to improve it. A new shower curtain wouldn't hurt either.

The kitchen was tiny, but big enough to cater for basic needs – with a cooker, a microwave and a small fridge-freezer. It was nice enough. Again, a bloody good clean wouldn't hurt it. They went back to the living room.

'It's a couple of weeks before the lads downstairs leave, but you can be in after that.'

Smudge and Rozzer wheeled around, taken aback.

'This flat is for us?' Rozzer said.

'It can be,' Vincent confirmed. 'If you want it.'

'I thought you couldn't fit Smudge in?'

'It came up unexpectedly,' Jim said. 'I put your names down.'

'Lenny's going back up north to stay with family and Ty's got a new job that provides accommodation,' Vincent explained. 'If you want to live here, it's yours.'

'Both of us?' Smudge reiterated.

'Both of you.' Jim grinned at them. 'The only problem is that you'll be out of Bovingdale before it's vacant, Rozzer. We're going to have to find somewhere temporary to put you until then.'

'It needs a lick of paint, a bit of tarting up,' Vincent said. 'That's all. It's not a bad place.'

Whichever way you looked at it, the flat was certainly a lot better than where they were currently residing.

'We can do that easy enough,' Jim said. Their interior design skills had improved no end in the last week. 'Well, lads, what do you think?'

Both Rozzer and Smudge looked gobsmacked.

'Is this for real?' Rozzer asked.

'Sure, man,' Vincent said. 'We have a strict no-drugs policy though. Mess up and you're out. Instantly. No ifs, no buts.'

'We're both clean,' Rozzer said. 'We want to stay like that. Don't we, Smudge?'

Smudge nodded, seemingly lost for words. Tears filled his eyes and he ran his hand lovingly over the worn sofa. 'It's fantastic,' he said, choked. 'Like a palace.'

It wasn't quite how Jim would describe it, but if you'd previously been living in a wheelie bin, he could see how you'd think that.

'I guess we'll take it then, Vincent,' Jim said.

And, as big and as hard as they might think themselves, Rozzer and Smudge threw their arms around him.

Chapter Forty-Eight

It's eight o'clock and we're just about to order another round of cocktails in the Icebar when the barman holds up his hands and shouts, 'Ladies and gentlemen, the northern lights are here!'

'Let's get out there quickly,' Carter says and, forgetting our drinks, we rush to put on our gloves and balaclavas and dash outside.

Sure enough, he wasn't lying. The sky above us is filled with the most extraordinary coloured lights. Streaks of pink, yellow and green stream down from the heavens, dancing across the horizon as enthusiastically as we just were to the disco music in the Icebar.

'Oh my goodness,' I gasp. 'This is divine.'

'Are they angels?' Eve wants to know.

'They look like them,' I agree. 'Take my hand.'

She puts her hand in mine and we set off, Carter and Max close behind us. Following a throng of people moving away from the glow of the hotel, we head down to the banks of the frozen river Torne where it's pitch black and we can see even more vividly the intensity of the spectacular display.

The colours shift across the sky, mesmerising us as they pulse and throb, changing hue constantly. People gasp out loud the way they do at firework displays as the natural phenomenon thrills us all. We're dazzled and delighted by its beauty. Mesmerised by the miracle of nature we're witnessing. It's freezing out here, colder than it's been up until now, but I hardly notice it. We find our own quiet space and look up, transfixed for so long that our necks start to ache.

Max lies down on the snow, spread out like a star, and looks upwards. 'It's better from down here,' he says.

So we join him on the ground, lying side by side. The whole firmament is ablaze with shifting patterns.

'It's like a spaceship,' Max says. 'Do you think so, Daddy?'

'I don't know. It's incredible, son, isn't it?' Carter shakes his head, mesmerised.

'Yes. Can we see this when we go home?'

'No,' Carter says. 'Only in this special place.'

'Then can we come to live here? I like the snow everywhere and the pretty colours.'

Carter turns to me. 'I never thought that it would be like this. It's beyond belief.'

'We're so lucky to see it.' I know that people come to this part of the world time after time and don't see anything as stunning as this.

We lie in the snow, lost in our own world, just gazing up at the magnificent spectacle until our fingers and toes are totally numb and I seriously begin to worry about the children getting frostbite. When the colours start to ebb, I think we should seize this moment to go back inside, otherwise I'd be tempted to stay outside all night. I check my watch and realise that we've been out here for hours, that time has flown by, unnoticed, while we did nothing but stare at the heavens. How wonderful!

'Should we get the children to bed?' I ask Carter in a whisper.

He notes the lateness of the hour. 'Yes, good idea.' Standing, he says, 'Come on, kids. Let's go and try out these ice rooms. Brr.'

He scoops up Max and throws him over his shoulder. I've noticed that Carter has become a lot more tactile with the children since we've been here, which is nice to see. I take Eve's hand and we head back to the hotel.

In the cosy reception, I get us all hot chocolate and we sit in front of the roaring wood burner, warming ourselves through. When we're all feeling roly-eyed and sleepy, I go to the equipment desk to get our super-insulated sleeping bags for the night and we head off to our cabins to change into our nightwear. We've been told that we need to sleep in thermals, socks, gloves and a hat. As part of the trip, I've ordered for us all soft Wee Willy Winky hats with pompoms on top and snuggly fleeces to get us from the warm part of the Icehotel into the frozen bit.

Carter helps Max to change and I take the other cabin with Eve. We wrestle her out of her Arctic overall and then she stands patiently while I dress her in thermals.

'Do you have a little girl?' she asks as I pull her top over her head.

'Not yet,' I tell her. 'But I hope that I will one day.'

'You're a nice mummy,' she says, smoothing her hair away from her face. 'Like my mummy.'

This is the first time that either of the children has mentioned Tamara and I wonder if they're missing her. To be honest, they've been kept so busy that I thought they wouldn't be worried about her absence. Perhaps that was naive of me. Of course they miss their mum.

'We go home tomorrow night,' I remind her. 'You'll soon be back at home with Mummy.'

'Daddy's taking us straight back to school. I don't think we'll see her until next week.'

271

'Oh.'

'They're both very busy people,' she says. It sounds as if she's been told that once too often.

'I know they are, sweetheart. But they do love you both very much.'

She smiles shyly at that. I pull her into my arms and hold her tight. Her hair smells of woodsmoke from the fire and her body is tiny against mine. She's so easy to love – both of them are – and I wish their mother would appreciate a bit more just how lucky she is. If it were me, I'd be at home with them, looking after them, not dumping them off at boarding school and chasing round the world flogging racy knickers. They are children for such a very short time.

Still, it's none of my business. I'm here to do a job, nothing more. How Carter and Tamara choose to run their private lives isn't something I should get involved with. Yet when I look at Eve my heart turns to mush. She's just so adorable that it's impossible not to care about her, or Max either.

There's a knock on my cabin door. 'What are you ladies doing in there?' Carter asks. 'Are we ready for bed yet?'

'Yes,' I shout out. Then I pop Eve's Wee Willy Winky hat on her head and zip her into her fluffy fleece. She looks incredibly sweet. 'Are you excited?'

She nods, eyes bright.

'Me too.'

So we join Carter and Max, who are also sporting their night-caps and are armed with their sleeping bags.

I laugh at Carter's Wee Willy Winky hat. 'Nice hat.'

'No giggling,' he says with mock severity. 'I take no responsibility for my appearance. You bought them.'

Eve chuckles too. 'You look funny, Daddy.'

But the truth of it is that he's still incredibly handsome even with comedy headgear.

'Right,' Carter says. 'If you've finished laughing at my hat, let's head into our ice rooms.'

My stomach is fluttering nervously as we make our way to our suites. I'm really hoping with all of my heart that this is going to be a unique and special experience. A night that none of us will ever forget.

Chapter Forty-Nine

The Royal Deluxe suite is truly spectacular. Through the arched doorway cut into the ice is a wall beautifully sculpted to look like drifting snow, making the entrance completely private. The anteroom contains two modern armchairs also carved in ice. In front of them is a coffee table in the shape of a snowflake, complete with ice books. Below an ice mantelpiece, flames lick up from an ice fire and next to it are contemporary standard lamps sculpted to look like icicles. We are all agog. Not bad for a room that you can see your breath in.

'Just when you think that things can't get any better,' Carter says in reverential tones. 'This is spectacular.'

And I'm guessing that Carter is used to hotels on a spectacular scale. I feel a little glow of pride.

The children try out the armchairs. 'They're very cold,' is Max's astute verdict as he lowers his bottom gingerly onto the ice.

We go through to the bedroom, whose walls are inlaid with intricate swirls and curls, to find an enormous bed in the centre, set in a carved block of ice and covered with reindeer skins. Its delicate headboard is a veritable snowstorm and the bedside tables are made of ice. Concealed lighting in the walls, in turquoise and the palest of blues, sets off the works of art perfectly. A delicate ice chandelier hangs from the ceiling, sparkling like diamonds. It must have taken hundreds of hours to make it all look so beautiful.

'I thought we'd let the children settle down in the next room,' Carter says. 'It's a bit too early for us to retire yet, don't you think?'

I shrug. 'It's entirely up to you.'

'Good,' he says. 'I've organised a little surprise.'

The children race into the adjoining room, which is connected by a short, arched tunnel and contains two single beds, again both set on blocks of ice.

'A pirate's bed!' Max cries. As we follow them in, he makes a dive for it and rolls around on the reindeer skins, looking as if he's in seventh heaven.

The room divider is a wall in the shape of an open storybook, with one side carved to look like a sailing ship. An octopus waves tentacles set with different coloured lights. At the head of the other bed, shaped like a flower, is an ice sculpture of a fairy princess. 'Oh,' Eve says, momentarily lost for words. She lies down on her bed, rapt.

'Into your sleeping bags,' Carter instructs. 'Snuggle down. Zip yourselves up tightly.'

The children strip off their fleeces and I lay the sleeping bags out for them. They take off their boots to clamber inside.

'Will our boots get icicles in them?' Max asks, regarding them with concern.

'I hope not,' I tease. 'Make sure you put them straight on when you get out of bed though. Don't stand on the snow in your stockinged feet.' I fix their boots so that they're easy for the children to find if they need them in the night.

Carter and I make sure they're zipped in. Snuggled into the Arctic sleeping bags, they look like little bugs in a cocoon.

'It's not cold in bed,' Eve says. 'It's cosy and warm.'

275

'Good. Sleep tight,' Carter says. 'I love you both to the moon and back.'

'I love you too, Daddy,' Eve says.

We both hug and kiss them.

'Night night, Cassie.' Despite his excitement, Max yawns. 'This is the most fun hotel *ever*.'

Carter and I exchange a smile. We go back through to Carter's suite and, as we arrive, someone calls out to us, 'Room service.'

'Come in,' Carter says. A waiter in a thermal poncho and fur-trapper hat brings in an ice bucket – actually made of ice – and sets it down. There's a bottle of Krug champagne in it. He disappears to return with a tray of little ice platters, each holding canapés of smoked salmon, carpaccio of reindeer and caviar.

'Just leave it,' Carter says. 'I'll pour.' The waiter disappears.

'This is fun,' I say, feeling as excited as the children. 'What a treat.'

'This has been a marvellous trip. You couldn't have organised it better, Cassie Christmas.'

He pops the cork and pours champagne for us both. Proper glasses this time.

'It isn't over yet,' I say.

My voice sounds thick in my throat. To be honest with you, at this moment, I never ever want this to end. Being here, in this magical place, has taken me out of my troubles completely. When you have money, you can do what you like, there's no struggle, no living from hand to mouth. You don't have to worry about paying the bills, about the car breaking down, about how to put food on the table. Everything that you want just happens. I sigh to myself.

Carter hands a glass to me and our fingers touch. It might be the cold, it might be the atmosphere, but it's as if they are suddenly set on fire. Our eyes meet and it feels as if Carter drinks

276

me in – even though I'm wearing a fleecy hat with a pompom on top.

'It's cold,' Carter says. 'Shall we slide into the sleeping bag?' A double Arctic sleeping bag is already laid out on the bed. When did that happen? 'It will keep us warm.'

'OK.'

It's a sensible idea as it's more than chilly in here. Even inside the hotel, the temperature never gets higher than minus five degrees. Any warmer and I guess the whole place would simply melt. When Carter's ready to go to sleep, he can lift Max into this bed and I'll go to sleep in the other suite with Eve as we planned.

I slip off my boots and swing my legs round into the sleeping bag. Carter brings over the tray of canapés and the rest of the champagne, then does the same. He tops up my glass and I try a canapé or two. We sit together side by side. He hugs his knees up to his chest, looking younger and more vulnerable than he has so far. I guess that even someone like Carter Randall needs time when he's not being the all-powerful businessman.

'I want to thank you again, Cassie,' he says when we're settled. 'This trip has been more than just a fun break. It's reconnected me with my kids in a way that I haven't done in a long time.'

'It doesn't sound as if you and Tamara have had much fun with them.'

'No,' he admits. 'We probably haven't. Did Eve say something?'

I nod. There's no point beating about the bush.

'I think she's the one who feels it the most.' He shakes his head. 'Poor love. I thought Tamara and I were doing our best for them. Perhaps we're not. We've both been so busy chasing our careers that we seem to have forgotten what really matters in life.' Carter sighs to himself. 'Tamara is very caught up with "image". I don't think she knows how to let herself go any more. I'm not sure I do either. We never would have messed about on the dance floor as you and I did earlier, she'd have been too worried about someone seeing her. She wouldn't have enjoyed rolling in the snow with the children as you've done. For her it's all about image and designer clothes. She wouldn't have risked getting dirty. I don't think I *ever* would have got her on a dog sled or a snowmobile. But it was great. Brilliant fun. The kids loved it.' Carter sounds as if he has the weight of the world on his shoulders. 'I'm going to have to have a serious rethink about how I run the business. Perhaps I need to take on a right-hand man that I can rely on.'

I think of Jim and how much I've been able to lean on him.

'You've shown me that I need to have more fun, find that part of me again,' Carter continues. 'I have to do it for my children's sake.'

I sip my champagne, unsure what to say.

'What am I going to do, Cassie? You seem to be the one with all the answers.'

'I don't think so.'

'Eve and Max think you're wonderful,' he says.

'I've grown very fond of them too.'

'I can buy anything I want in the world, pretty much. The only thing that money can't buy you is time.'

'It can't buy you love either,' I point out.

'You and the Beatles are probably right,' he teases. Then he chinks his glass against mine. 'To love, Cassie Christmas.'

'To love,' I echo.

Carter moves towards me and, in one smooth and unexpected movement, his lips find mine. He hesitates only slightly before he kisses me. He tastes sweet, of champagne and cold air, but his tongue is hot, searching. His hand cups the back of my neck to draw me closer into him. My head swims. I haven't been kissed by another man in years and the sensation is alien and thrilling. Exhilarating. I know that I should pull away, that I should tell him to stop. My brain is trying very hard to make me, but in my heart I can't do it.

Chapter Fifty

Carter and I break away from each other. It's so long since I've done this that I don't really know which of us is supposed to speak first. I know that we should talk about what just happened but, before either of us can say anything, we hear a sleepy voice over my shoulder.

'Daddy.'

It's Eve and we both spin round to face her, probably looking as guilty as hell. I certainly feel it.

'I need a wee,' she says, stifling a yawn. 'I don't know where to go.'

'I'll come with you, darling,' Carter says. 'Sorry,' he mouths to me with an apologetic smile.

'I'll go,' I offer. 'You stay here with Max.'

'Yes, you come, Cassie,' Eve says and grabs my hand.

So our passionate moment has come to an abrupt end but, to be honest, I don't think that's a bad thing as it gives me a chance to gather my scrambled thoughts. To use the facilities, we have to put on our boots and fleeces and go back to the warm part of the hotel. I hug Eve to me. 'Don't get cold.'

'I'm not,' she assures me.

A second later, just as I'm climbing into my thermal boots, Max also trails through. 'I need to go too.'

'Why don't we all go together?' Carter suggests. 'I'd like to see what it looks like when no one else is around.'

So he slips out of bed too and puts on his boots. Quickly, we zip into our fleeces and head off towards the changing area.

In the hotel, all is quiet. The halls are empty and the snow walls deaden the sound. A heavy mist hangs low in the corridors, so that you can see only from waist height upwards. It creates a magical atmosphere and makes us look as if we're floating.

The children run on ahead, trying to scoop up armfuls of the cold air.

Carter hangs back next to me. 'I shouldn't have done that. I'm sorry, Cassie. I didn't mean for it to happen.' Me neither. 'You're with someone else.'

'Jim.'

His name feels wrong, strange in my mouth as if my tongue has thickened. This is too bizarre. It's as if the man that I love has become just a shadow in the background. I've been away from him for only three days, but this place seems so remote from the reality of my life that, physically and emotionally, I might as well be a million miles away.

And now Carter has kissed me and my head is spinning.

In the warmth of the changing rooms, I hug my knees to me while I wait for Eve. What happens now, I wonder? I'm glad that the children interrupted us as it gives me time to think. If only I could get my brain to co-operate. But it seems to be stuck firmly on a loop of nothing more sophisticated than 'What the fuck?' I love Jim. I do. I have always loved him. So why am I feeling like this about another man?

Ablutions over, we all troop back to the fabulous suites. 'I should go and sleep in the other room with Eve,' I quietly say to Carter.

'Have I upset you?' His forehead creases in a frown that I have the urge to smooth away. 'It's the last thing that I wanted.'

'No,' I say. 'Not at all. I just think it's for the best.'

'Max? Do you want to slide in with Daddy and let Cassie have your pirate bed?'

'No thank you,' Max says decisively. 'I want to stay in *my* bed.'

'Eve?'

'But I like being a princess, Daddy. My bed's sooo lovely.'

Carter looks over at me. 'Your call,' he says.

'I can go and sleep in the cabin.' Or curl up in a seat in reception. Anything. I just don't think that getting back into bed with Carter is an option.

'I won't hear of it. We can do this,' he says, as if he's reading my thoughts. 'We can be grown up about it. You'll stay with me. Trust me.' His eyes beseech me and, at this moment, I believe him. 'Come on, kids. Back into bed. This is our one and only night in the Icehotel and there's not much left of it.'

'I want to stay here for ever,' Eve says, dreamily.

'Me too,' Max agrees.

'Maybe we'll come again next year,' Carter says, then kisses them both and zips them up into their sleeping bags. 'This is going to be a hard act to follow,' he whispers to me.

With the children settled once more, we both go through to the main suite. He glances towards the bed. 'Are we cool with this?' Carter asks.

I chew my lip. 'I'm not sure.' In fact, I know in my heart that I've never been less cool.

'You don't have to worry about me,' Carter says. 'I can control myself. You have one half of the sleeping bag and I'll stay firmly in the other.'

'Now you're teasing me.'

282

'No,' he says earnestly. 'Never. We've had such a great few days together, let's not spoil it. We'll snuggle down – separately – go to sleep, forget that kiss ever happened.'

But it's not so easily forgotten, I think. At least not by me.

'I'll feel terrible if you leave,' Carter says. He pulls open the sleeping bag and looks at me endearingly.

I blame it on the sub-zero temperature, but my resistance is very low. Slipping off my boots, I slide into the sleeping bag. There is quite a lot of room for two, so we don't have to touch.

Carter strips off his fleece and snuggles in next to me, pulling the duvet up around our necks. I tug my hat down over my ears.

'Goodnight, Cassie Christmas,' he says, and kissing the tip of his finger he touches it very gently to the end of my nose.

We lie down face to face in the sleeping bag.

'Goodnight,' I say. 'Sleep tight.' I close my eyes, but I know full well that sleep will steadfastly elude me.

Within seconds I hear Carter's breathing change and it's clear that he hasn't been afflicted with the same problem. Opening my eyes, I look at him. His face is inches away from mine. In sleep, the years roll away from him and I can see the boy that he used to be. My heart squeezes and I can't identify the emotion – is it friendship, affection, love? I simply don't know.

So I just lie here next to Carter, wide awake, listening to the sound of his breathing and wondering what Jim's doing now.

Chapter Fifty-One

Jim had taken the lads back to the unit and now he was home alone. Cassie was due back from Lapland the following night and, if he was honest, it couldn't come round soon enough.

He was on a late shift tomorrow so, in theory, he could tidy up the flat in the morning before he went to work. In reality, he was restless. He'd tried relaxing in front of the television with a beer but it just wasn't hitting the spot. So he gave up and, instead, headed to the kitchen to spruce it up. They both liked the flat to look nice and it had been just about impossible for either of them to do any cleaning recently. The place was piled high with boxes of presents, decorations and festive stuff of indeterminate nature. He'd always known that the commercialisation of Christmas had long been accomplished, but he'd never even heard of some of the things that Cassie had bought or been asked to do.

Neither could he get over how much some people were prepared to spend. Take Carter Randall, for instance. The amount he was pouring into his Christmas celebrations was just mind-blowing. It was nice for Cassie's business, but it gave Jim a headache just thinking about it. What he couldn't do for some of the lads at Bovingdale or at Vincent's place if he had that kind of money to splash around. Those sorts of people, with money coming out of their ears, only ever gave to charity if it was some sort of tax dodge. Still, it was Carter's money, supposedly hard-earned, and, at the end of the day, he could do what he jolly well liked with it. If that meant filling his garden with hideously expensive sculptures for a couple of weeks or renting a private plane to jet off in, then that was his call.

He worked off his frustration by scrubbing the sink and the cooker hob. When the kitchen looked less as if a bomb had gone off in it, Jim made a start on the living room. He tidied the boxes into piles, but that didn't really make much of a dent in the chaos. There was so much still to do. Presents had to be wrapped and there were still events coming up. Soon they'd have to start turning jobs down or take on even more staff. There was only so much that he and the lads could do in a few hours and performing miracles wasn't one of them. The cards that needed writing were piling up. He thought it was a good sign that people still wanted to personalise them, even if they had no time to actually write the damn things themselves. On the mantelpiece stood the stupid card that he'd given to Cassie. *Christmas across the Miles*, indeed! No wonder she'd been furious with him. What a plonker. That could go straight into the bin. He tore it in two and threw it away. He'd go and get her another one, a proper one. One that told her how much he really loved her.

He'd run the vacuum cleaner around, but there was so little of the carpet left showing that it hardly seemed worth it. Instead, he made do with a bit of polishing and plumping the cushions on the sofa, then moved on to the bedroom.

What was he going to do with the lads? It was great that he'd managed to get them into Vincent's place and everyone knew that Vince ran a tight ship. He stood no messing from the lads who stayed there and yet was very protective at the same time. Jim knew that he could trust his old friend to give Smudge and Rozzer a good start back on the outside. The only problem was

285

finding them somewhere to stay until the flat became vacant. He wondered if social services would stump up for bed-and-breakfast accommodation for a few days in the interim. Perhaps he'd get onto that tomorrow.

Jim made the bed and hoovered around it. On the bedside table was a photograph of him and Cassie. He couldn't now remember where it had been taken – Cassie was the one who was good at that sort of thing. It must have been somewhere posh as he was wearing a suit and Cassie her one evening dress. They were both grinning into the camera lens and looking the worse for drink, but it was one of his favourite snaps of Cassie and him together. They looked happy, carefree. He ran his finger affectionately over her cheek.

In the spare room you could barely see the small, single futon that was stored against the wall. It contained even more boxes piled high, with a track through the middle of them to allow access to the computer.

He logged on. There were a couple of dozen emails for Cassie, the work still pouring in. Jim scanned them quickly. The only one that might be a problem was a children's party at a school. Whoever did that would have to be checked by the Criminal Records Bureau and neither of the lads would get through that, even if it could be done it in time. He'd have to talk to Cassie about how she'd want to handle that. He sent off a quick reply to each of the jobs that they could fit in the diary without complications.

Then, as he'd nothing else useful to do, he checked Cassie's itinerary. Tonight, it said, they would all be at the Icehotel. He logged onto their site and sat back, quite stunned by the images. Wow. Now he could see why she'd been so very keen to go. There was no way in a million years that he and Cassie could afford to go somewhere like that. He flicked through the posted images of the suites, wondering which one Cassie might be staying in. It might be futile, but he took out his mobile again, punching in her number. Still useless. Obviously, there was still no signal where she was.

He consoled himself that, by this time tomorrow night, she'd be safely home again. The flat was as spick and span as he could make it now. He'd pick up some flowers in the morning. Maybe get a nice bottle of red wine. He might not be able to compete with the Icehotel or Carter Randall, but he could let Cassie know how much she was loved and how glad he was that she was back home.

Chapter Fifty-Two

I'm lying in the sleeping bag, still wide awake – as I have been all night – when Carter opens his eyes. Our noses are inches apart as we face each other.

'Hey,' he says, softly.

'Hey,' I answer back.

He stretches and props himself up on his elbow, but his eyes don't leave my face. 'Did you sleep well?'

'Not too bad,' I lie.

'I was surprisingly comfortable,' Carter says. 'Must sleep in minus five on a bed of ice more regularly.'

That makes me laugh and, I hate to put it like this, but it breaks the ice between us.

'I didn't do anything untoward in my dreams, did I?' he asks. 'Call out your name, try to play octopus arms or footsie with you?'

'No,' I say. 'Nothing like that.'

'I'm very relieved.'

Me too.

In fact Carter slept like a baby whereas I just stayed awake and watched him. If you asked me now I could tell you every curve of his face. I could describe in detail the fine lines at the corners of his eyes. If required, I could pinpoint on a Farrow and Ball paint chart the colour of his lips, the shade of his eyes. I could tell you about every curl of his hair and how hard it was for me not to reach out and touch them.

'You look deep in thought,' Carter says.

Before I have to explain myself, a young girl comes to the room's entrance, singing sweetly. '*Hej, hej*,' she calls as she pops her head around the ice wall.

Seeing that we're awake, she brings us cups of hot lingonberry juice, which is a nice way to start the day. Carter and I sit up together, side by side. I straighten my hat.

'You look very cute,' Carter says. 'And no bed hair.'

What would Carter know about bed hair? Tamara looks like the sort of person who'd go to bed in full make-up and train herself to sleep on her back so that she'd never have a strand of hair out of place.

'Last day,' he continues with a rueful note to his voice.

'Big surprise this morning, though,' I remind him. Carter knows where we're heading to, but the children don't.

We avoid trickier subjects, as said children come through to us and jump onto the bed.

'We're awake!' Max shouts.

'So you are. Don't get cold,' Carter says. 'Snuggle in with us.'

They wriggle into the warmth of the sleeping bag, budging us out of the way with cold feet and sharp elbows. This is so sweet and I have a vision of doing it one day with my own children. Eve curls into me and lays her head on my shoulder. I stroke her hair.

'Did you like your princess bed?'

'Yes. It was lovely, but my nose did get cold.'

'Shall we have a nice hot shower and warm up?' I suggest. She nods her acquiescence.

When we've finished our lingonberry juice, we all slip on our fleeces and say goodbye to our fabulous rooms. I take one last glance around to imprint it on my memory for ever.

Leaving our icy retreat, we head for the changing rooms to shower. I linger under the hot water, still trying to get my head around the turmoil of my emotions. Afterwards, we walk up to the restaurant in the warm part of the hotel and have a delicious breakfast. When we're full of pancakes and bacon, we all climb into our Arctic suits once again and I lead them out of the hotel and down towards the vast swathe of ice that is the frozen river. It's nearly eleven o'clock and the sun is heading towards its zenith. The ice is glistening and all we can hear is the satisfying crunch of snow beneath our feet.

'What are we doing today, Cassie?' the children want to know. They're already bouncing.

'You'll see soon enough,' I say and Carter winks at me.

As we round the corner of the hotel, our transport awaits us. Standing on the frozen river is an old-fashioned wooden sleigh painted in red and white, pulled by four reindeer in multicoloured harnesses.

'Rudolph!' Max cries when he sees them. 'We're going to see Santa!'

Eve is open-mouthed. 'Are we? I thought he was just pretend.'

'Of course he's not,' Max tells her, already clambering into one of the seats.

'Of course not,' Carter agrees.

We all climb in after Max and the driver hands us colourful blankets to cover ourselves with. I sit next to Carter, who pulls the blanket over us both. I notice that his arm is around my shoulders across the back of the sleigh.

We set off and are whisked along the icy river, away from the hotel. The runners swoosh over the snow and the bells on the reindeer's harnesses jingle as we go, which inspires Carter to start up a chorus of 'Jingle Bells'.

Still singing our heads off, we head deep into the forest

following a track marked by flaming lanterns. The reindeer trot ahead of us and the children are rapt as we weave through the snowy trees.

Eventually we come to a clearing surrounded by a range of picture-perfect wooden lodges. The sleigh stops and we climb out again. I've always shied away from the whole mass-market 'Meet Santa' trips and I'm so glad now that I have. This is much more up Carter's street and the children, well, frankly, they look as if they've been put under a spell.

'Is this Santa's house?' Max wants to know, transfixed, his eyes shining with delight.

'Yes,' I tell him. 'But we've got something to do first before we meet him.'

Two young men dressed as elves come out to greet us, looking spectacular. They're not wearing tacky elf outfits like the ones I bought for my elves from a fancy dress shop – these are proper costumes, made of gold and silver brocade, elaborately finished. Each elf has a pale face and tiny pointed ears. If I hadn't booked all this through a tour company, even I could quite easily believe that they are real elves.

They take us into one of the wooden lodges, where we find a roaring log fire, a huge table and two young women dressed as fairies.

'You must write your letters to Santa,' one of the elves says. 'Tell him if you've been naughty or nice and then we will make your toys for you.'

The children's faces are glowing and it's nice to see that, in this hideously cynical age, there is still innocent magic to be found in Christmas.

The elves sit the children down and give them pretty paper and pens.

'What shall I ask for, Daddy?' Eve says.

'Whatever you want, sweetheart,' he advises.

So, while the children write their letters and the elves sing a song, Carter and I sit in the armchairs by the fire.

One of the fairies brings us a tray with two drinks. 'Something for Mummy and Daddy while you wait?'

'Oh, I'm not . . . ' I start and then my voice fades away. I can't bring myself to say the next bit.

'This is mumma,' she says. 'It is a mixture of beer and port wine spiced with cardamom. It is our traditional Christmas drink.'

'Thank you.' I take my glass and swig it down. It smells divine and the warmth and the spices soothe my throat.

We sit in silence together, listening to the Christmas music, while the children – tongues out in intense concentration – compose their letters to Santa.

Soon they're done and our drinks are finished.

'Let us go to see Santa,' the elves say and they lead us from this lodge across the snow and deep into the woods. The children are shaking with excitement and, I have to say, I am too.

My mum never went through the pretence of there being a Santa. With Dad gone, Christmas in our home was a very meagre affair. She never had much interest in celebrating anything and, half the time, even forgot our birthdays. I vow, here and now, that if I do ever have children, I'll bring them here. Every child should experience this at least once in their lifetime.

We reach another of the lodges set among tall snow-covered firs, with lights glowing from its windows. The elves lead us up the stairs. In a small ante-room, we take off our boots and Arctic suits. Then in stockinged feet we're led to a door.

'Ready?' one of the elves asks.

We all let out an involuntary gasp when he throws it open. I could learn a thing or two from this about decorating. The room, warm from the heat of the fire, is filled with candles, flickering beautifully. Above the fireplace is strung a fir garland, hung with presents and stockings. The Christmas tree in the corner is enormous, decked with baubles and tinsel in gold and silver. Sitting in the corner on a majestic white rocking chair is Santa himself. His presence is awe-inspiring. He's wearing wire-rimmed spectacles and his traditional red and white costume. The material shimmers richly in the candlelight. The white trimming is so fluffy that you can't help but want to reach out and touch it. His beard is full, curled and reaches right down to his tummy where his hands nestle on top of it. Santa is smiling benignly.

The children stand and gape at him.

'Come, come,' one of the elves says. 'Santa is so happy to meet you.'

Max and Eve step forward, tentatively, then sit on a bench close to Santa's knees. Carter turns to grin at me, slips his hand in mine and grips it tightly.

'*Hej, hej*. Hello, little ones,' Santa says in a booming voice. 'It is lovely to see you in my forest home.'

The children nod, speechless.

'You have come all the way from England?'

They both nod again.

'On a plane,' Max risks in a whisper. 'A little one.'

'Well, I am very pleased that you are here,' Santa says. 'Now? Have you been good?'

More nodding.

'Santa likes to give presents only to the good children.'

'Yes,' Eve says, breathlessly. 'We've both been very good.'

'Then tell me what you would like me to bring you for Christmas.'

Max nudges Eve in the ribs. Hesitantly, she opens her letter and carefully spreads it out on her knees. Before speaking, she clears her throat.

'Dear Santa.' Her voice is bright and clear. I feel tears spring to my eyes and I glance at Carter who's looking at her adoringly. 'This Christmas I would like my mummy to come home and be in love with my daddy again.' She flicks her gaze anxiously towards Carter and then fixes it back on Santa. 'That's all I want,' Eve stresses. 'No toys. I have lots of toys.'

Santa nods his head thoughtfully and rubs his beard, not missing a beat. 'Well,' he says, eventually, 'I will do my very best, Eve.' He glances over to Carter. 'Sometimes these dreams are the hardest to make come true. There is nothing else that you would like? A doll? A bike?'

'No,' she says firmly and folds up her letter.

My throat closes as I watch her face, earnest and imploring.

'And you, young sir,' Santa says, turning his attention to Max. 'What would you like for Christmas?'

Max looks uncertain. He glances at Eve and then screws up the letter that's in his hand, the one that he took so much care with. 'I was going to ask for a quad bike,' he says softly. 'But all I want is for Mummy to come home too.'

My tears spill over my lashes and onto my cheeks and when I turn to Carter I see that his eyes are wet too. Eve and Max run to him and Carter drops to his knees as they throw their arms around him.

They hug each other and I stand there, not knowing what to do. I look up at Santa who has taken off his glasses and it looks as if he's crying too.

Chapter Fifty-Three

As soon as Jim signed in for his shift, he was called in to see the governor. 'I believe you've been working closely with' – he checked his paperwork – 'Andrew Walton and Kieran Holman.'

It occurred to Jim that Dave Hornshaw was about to tell him he'd been working with them *too* closely. The prison authorities liked you to keep your distance from the lads and most of the time that was easy enough.

'Yes,' Jim said. No point trying to say otherwise.

'The Social Care team feel that they're both ready to leave. If they've got somewhere to go, we can tag them to serve the rest of their sentence.'

'I've organised them a place at Vincent Benlow's Halfway House.'

'Excellent, Jim,' the governor said. 'He'll look after them.'

Everyone knew that the lads had the best chance with Vincent. It was just a shame that so few of them ever got to go somewhere like that. Jim wondered if Rozzer and Smudge knew just how lucky they were.

'Vincent can't take them in for a week or two,' Jim admitted. 'But I'm sure I can find them somewhere to stay in the meantime.'

He could go and speak to social services, see if they could find them temporary bed-and-breakfast accommodation or, at worst, a hostel. It would be tricky as he had no desire for Rozzer and Smudge to mix with the kind of people they were just about to get away from.

'Good.' The governor looked at him over his glasses. 'Then they can leave today.'

Jim rocked back in his seat. Today? That didn't give him a lot of time to organise somewhere for Rozzer and Smudge to stay.

'Is that possible?' the governor asked. 'We can delay their release if it's a problem.'

'No. I'm sure that will be fine.'

It looked as if it would be down to him to sort out their accommodation, but if there was a chance of getting the lads out of here quickly, then why wouldn't he take it?

At home they had one spare bed and a sofa. If it was only for a couple of days, he was sure that Cassie wouldn't mind. She liked the lads, after all. They'd certainly helped her out in her absence. Jim felt that they owed the lads.

The governor peered over his glasses. 'Anything else, Jim?'

'No.' It was clearly time for him to leave.

'Those lads are fortunate that you've looked out for them,' the governor said. 'Make sure they know it.'

'Yes, sir,' Jim said.

But he wouldn't do that. He didn't know why he wanted to help the lads, but he certainly wasn't doing it for the thanks.

Later that afternoon it was confirmed that Mr Andrew Walton and Mr Kieran Holman were to be released from HM Bovingdale Young Offenders' Unit and let back out into the wide world.

Jim went up to the wing and waited outside their cell to escort them downstairs to be processed. All afternoon he'd been contacting various departments of social services and charities he knew, trying to call in favours, and had singularly failed to secure the lads any alternative accommodation for that night. However he wasn't about to go back and tell the governor that, so Jim put down his own address as their intended residence. At the flat, he and Cassie had a single futon in the spare room. One could use that and the other could take the sofa. It would, he prayed, be for only a couple of days. A week or two at the most. He was sure that Cassie wouldn't mind some extra company – albeit some that was a bit smelly and a bit sweary. It was a temporary measure. That was all.

An hour later Rozzer and Smudge were leaving the unit – hopefully for good – under his care. It was fair to say that both looked more anxious than ecstatic to be free again. Smudge glanced constantly over his shoulder as Jim walked them across the car park and let them into the car. Silently, they climbed inside and huddled into their hoodies.

Before Jim drove off, he turned to talk to them. 'You're going to have to crash at my place for the time being. It'll be a tight squeeze.' Then he remembered that previously they had been sharing a cell on a wing with thirty other blokes. The flat would be like a palace in comparison. Even if it was a palace filled with boxes and wrapping paper. 'Feeling all right?'

'Just a bit scared,' Smudge admitted. 'You know where you are inside. Everything's done for you. Out here it's all to play for.'

'You should see that as a good thing. A new start.'

'I don't want to fuck up again,' the lad said. He tore at his fingernails, anxiously.

'It's different this time,' Jim assured him. 'You've got a place to go to. You've got a bit of work experience under your belt. You've got Rozzer and you've got me. We'll see that you're OK.'

Smudge risked a smile. 'When you put it like that, it doesn't sound too bad.'

'You'll do fine, I'm sure.' Jim looked at them both. 'Let's go home.'

The flat was immaculate after his cleaning spree. The lads looked different here in their own gear, even younger if that was possible. Rozzer's clothes were so-so, baggy and garish, but good quality. Smudge's, on the other hand, were threadbare and dirty. They looked exactly as if he'd been sleeping in a wheelie bin in them. The clothes he'd worn going to Randall Court had clearly been borrowed from another lad on the wing. Jim wondered how much it had cost Smudge to secure that deal. Tomorrow they'd have to go into town and buy him something better to wear. Tonight, Jim could give him some sweats and a T-shirt. They'd swamp him, but they'd have to do.

The smell of the prison clung to the lads and he didn't want that to be the first thing that hit Cassie as she came through the door. Both stood awkwardly in the living room, looking around as if they'd never seen it before.

'Don't stand on ceremony,' Jim said, brightly. 'Make yourselves at home. Both put your bags in the spare room. One of you can take the futon in there. The other will have to sleep on the sofa, but it's quite comfy. I've kipped through many a football match on there.' He took Rozzer's holdall from him. Smudge had nothing other than the clothes he stood up in. Not a bar of soap nor a pair of clean pants. 'Why don't you both take a good shower, wash the smell of that place out of your hair?' He hoped that one day Smudge wouldn't look quite as grey as he did now. Get a bit of fresh air on his face, some exercise for his scrawny body and some decent meals down him, and he was sure the lad would blossom.

'You go in first, Rozzer,' Smudge said. 'I'll wait.'

'I'll try not to be too long.'

298

'Lad,' Jim said, 'take all the time you need. There's no rush. No timetable. Enjoy a nice hot shower in privacy. I'll find some clothes for you, Smudge. You can't stay in those.'

They all went through to the spare room and dumped Rozzer's holdall on the futon. Jim found him a towel from the airing cupboard and showed him how to work the shower.

Then, in his own bedroom, shadowed by Smudge, he found the lad some clean clothes, including a pack of new pants from Marks and Sparks. Jim turned to hand them over.

Smudge stood in the middle of the room, arms hanging by his sides, shoulders shaking as he silently sobbed. Tears rolled down his cheeks.

'Hey,' Jim said, sitting on the bed and pulling him down to sit next to him. 'What's all that for?'

'Why are you being so kind?' he asked as he sniffed.

Jim shrugged. 'It's what people do.'

'My own dad used to stub cigarettes out on me,' he said.

Jim slung his arm round the lad's shoulders. 'Those days are over. I generally find if you treat people well, then they do the same to you.' Smudge looked at him ruefully. 'There are always exceptions to the rule, but don't live your life for them.'

'I don't know what I'd do without you, Jim.'

'I'm not planning on going anywhere,' he promised. 'You can rely on that.'

'Is Cassie cool with this too?'

'Yeah,' Jim said. 'She's fine.'

And, as he hadn't been able to call and warn her what he'd done, he could only hope that he was right.

Chapter Fifty-Four

After the visit to Father Christmas, the children are given sleds and play in the woods, sliding down the gentle hills to tumble in a heap at the bottom. Carter and I sit on the porch by a brazier to watch them and have some more of the delicious mumma. He's quieter than he's been the last few days and I don't know if he just needs some space or whether he'd rather talk. After a while, I can't help myself and turn to him. 'Penny for them?'

He continues to stare at the children. 'That hit me like a low ball. It wasn't easy to hear.'

'No,' I agree. 'That must have been tough.'

Carter's laugh is hollow. 'For the first time in my life, I can't give them what they want.'

'They love what you do for them,' I assure him. 'You know what children are like, they say exactly what's on their minds. It's probably because you've spent so much time with them over the last few days. All they really want is more of that.'

'I think it's also because you've been so great with them too. Tamara is never this free and easy with them. She's always so uptight about what they're doing, what they look like. They want the kind of mother they've never actually had. I think that was what their letters were really about.'

I can't comment on that, but Carter is clearly troubled by what he's heard. His dark eyes are sad and I can only try to soothe him. 'You're a wonderful father. This has been a great trip. They've had a marvellous time. One that they'll never forget.'

'I'll never forget it either, Cassie Christmas,' he says. 'It's been perfect. You've made it a lot of fun.'

Add me to the list of people who won't forget too. It's going to be hard going back to the flat, the daily grind, the constant scrimping and saving. To Jim. But that's what we must do. Lunch is booked at the Icehotel and then a car will whisk us to Kiruna Airport where our private jet will spirit us home again.

'Look at us,' Max shouts. 'We're really good at this!'

They both zoom down the hill and, once again, topple off their sleds.

'We should show them how it's done,' I say to Carter.

He tries a smile. 'Think so?'

'Oh yeah.'

I grab his hand and pull him up from his seat. He stands in front of me and, for a moment, we're face to face. Suddenly, the world stops. The children's playful screaming recedes, there's no noise at all. The only thing I can hear is my own blood pounding in my ears and the sound of our unsteady breathing. White clouds of our breath mingle in the air. Carter reaches up and brushes my hair from my cheek. 'Cassie—'

'Daddy,' Max shouts impatiently, 'are you coming to play?'

Carter strokes my skin and his eyes tell me that we have unfinished business. Then he turns away. 'On my way!' He dashes towards the children, towing me in his wake.

Breathless and panting, we reach the top of the small incline and jump onto red plastic sleds to race down the hill, catching up with the children as we go. At the bottom we all pitch into a pile of arms and legs, laughing. I look over at Carter and he's having a rough-and-tumble with Max, joy on both of their faces.

'Come on,' I say to Eve. 'Let's race these boys. Show them that girls are the best.'

'Oh no you don't.' Carter scoops Eve into his arms and dumps her, shrieking, into a snowdrift. 'Boys are the best!'

The children pull Carter to the ground and try to push snow down his Arctic suit. He shouts out in protest and we're all laughing.

For a small moment, my heart is still. I have done this, I think. I have helped this disjointed family to reconnect and I feel proud that I've been a small part of their lives. Soon, too soon, we'll be going our separate ways. But, for now, I want to have as much fun with them as possible before it's all over.

Chapter Fifty-Five

We all pile into the car and wave goodbye to the Icehotel as the car crunches out onto the main road. My heart is heavy as we head to the tiny airport at Kiruna, speeding along despite the roads being thick with snow and ice. The mood in the car is subdued and even the trees, bowed with snow, seem to be sad for us.

'I don't want to go home,' Max says miserably and, quite frankly, I couldn't have put it better myself.

But in minutes, it seems, we're sweeping into the airport. Already I can see the small jet with its ExecLine livery on the tarmac, waiting patiently for us.

We're whisked through the formalities and are welcomed onto the plane by the steward. Soon, too soon, we're belted, buckled and on our way.

Through the window, I watch the stunning, snowy landscape recede as we climb, knowing that I may never be able to afford to come here again. The darkness outside is gathering and I slide the shade down over the glass, turning away. This is it. Our trip is nearly over. The children get their Nintendos out of their backpacks, but they've both got heavy eyes and, as soon as we reach our flying altitude, they've given in to sleep.

'They're exhausted,' Carter says.

'Well, we've all had a very full-on few days.'

Carter takes my hand and holds it tight, speaking in a low voice. 'It's not only the children who don't want it to end.'

'I'm glad you've enjoyed it.' Then, trying to keep the moment light, 'I feel as if my job is done.'

'It's nothing to do with your job,' Carter says. 'We both know that.'

I think it's best if I don't say anything.

'You're a fantastic woman, Cassie,' he continues. 'It's *you* who's made this trip such fun and I don't think that you could have done that if it was simply another job to you.'

There is more truth in that statement than I care to admit.

'I think you have fallen in love with my children and, for that, I am just so very grateful.' His fingers trace over mine and I get a shiver of desire when I really rather wouldn't. 'I'd like to think that you've also fallen a little bit in love with me.'

His eyes search my face. My mouth has gone dry and my cheeks are burning like a furnace.

'I know that I'm falling in love with you.' He laughs as if it's the very last thing in the world he expected. It's certainly the last thing that I expected.

My heart thuds so hard that I think it might burst. Has Carter really just said that he loves me? I believe he did.

It seems as if he's waiting expectantly for me to say something, but my brain doesn't seem to think it needs to comply.

'Cassie?' he says. 'Is it such a shock?'

When I finally find my voice, I say, 'I'm with someone else.'

'Jim.'

Jim. My darling Jim.

'Leave him,' Carter says starkly. 'I want you to be with me. I want you to move into Randall Court. Come and have Christmas with us. The children will be thrilled. *I'll* be thrilled. More than that. I'll be the happiest man on earth.'

'I . . . I . . . I . . .' I have no idea what I want to say. This is like a bolt from the blue.

'You don't have to answer now,' Carter says. 'Of course you don't. I know that you need time to think.'

'What about Tamara?' I manage.

'Our marriage is over,' he insists. 'She's not been a great mother to the children. I can see that now. She's done nothing but put herself first.'

'But she's the only mother they've got.'

'She's never around when they need her. Her business always takes top priority.' Then his face is sad. 'I can't lay all the blame at her feet though. I haven't been a good father either. Well, that's not going to continue. From now on, I'm determined to be the best I can be. I can see that Eve and Max need a woman like you in their lives, Cassie,' he presses on. 'Someone kind, caring. Someone who will love and nurture them unconditionally.'

'I don't know what to say.'

'Promise me that you'll think about it. I'll call you tomorrow. We can go for dinner. Talk about our future.'

Our future?

'I can give you the world on a platter,' Carter says. 'Everything you could ever dream of can be yours for the asking. You're worth it. Even in the short time that we've been acquainted, I know you are.'

I look around at my surroundings. I'm in a gold-plated private jet, and anything I want could be mine. There'd be no need for me to work. I could devote my life to looking after Carter's children. I'm already smitten with Max and Eve, so that would be no hardship at all. I'd have my own ready-made family. Perhaps I could have my own children with Carter, the children I've always dreamed of. I'd never have to worry about money again. No putting it off until I'm old and grey simply because we don't have the funds. There'd be no more economising, no 'value' packs, no own-brand labels. No more crushing credit-card debt. No more hideous overdraft. No more living in a cramped, rented flat. Randall Court could be my permanent residence. My life could be idyllic with Carter. Everything I've ever wanted could be mine.

Then I pull myself up short. Until a few short weeks ago, before I spilled a drink on Carter Randall, all I ever wanted was Jim. He was the only man that I've ever loved. I look at Carter sitting next to me, so handsome that I could gaze at him all day and not grow tired of the view. It's not just his looks, or even his money, he's a good and kind person too. Do I love him? I hadn't even dared to consider it a possibility until he declared his feelings for me.

But what about Jim? I love him too. He's kind and caring, and I have loved him for a long time. Can my head really have been turned so quickly? I have no idea what to do.

The steward comes to tell us that we'll soon be landing. Even the idea of it is painful.

'Say that you'll think about it,' Carter asks earnestly.

'Yes. Of course, I will.' In all honesty, I'm not sure that I'll be able to think about anything else.

Chapter Fifty-Six

'Right,' Jim said. 'Now that you both smell divine' – the lads laughed at that – 'you can help me to prepare dinner.'

In the end he'd given both of them some of his own clothes. Even the stuff that Rozzer had put on, which had been kept in storage, smelled strongly of Bovingdale and he didn't want that distinctive aroma permeating the flat. All their kit would need washing – that which didn't need binning – so the first thing he'd done was show them how to sort their laundry and use the washing machine. There was a load already running. Rozzer filled out Jim's old jeans and T-shirt without any trouble, but everything hung off Smudge. He looked like a child in grown-up clothing. Like Tom Hanks in that film *Big*.

'Now. Can either of you cook?'

They both shook their heads.

'OK. We're going to start easy. Spaghetti bolognese tonight. That suit you?'

Both lads grinned.

'I want you on chopping onions, Rozzer. You can fry the mince, Smudge.'

'I don't know what to do,' the lad admitted.

'I'll show you.' Jim poured some olive oil into the pan. 'A little bit of that. Wait until it gets hot.' He tipped in the meat. 'Now all you do is stir it until it goes nice and brown, but don't burn it. Keep it moving.'

Smudge took the wooden spoon from Jim and cack-handedly stirred the mince.

'You need to learn a few basic dishes,' Jim said. 'You want to eat good, nutritious food. You've got a nice little kitchen in your new place and there's no need to exist on ready meals or live on takeaways. It's cheaper and better for you to make your own food from scratch.'

'I always liked the idea of being a chef,' Rozzer admitted. 'Sometimes I used to help my mum to cook.'

'Will you ring her now that you're out?' Jim asked.

'Dunno,' he said with a shrug that was supposed to indicate that he didn't care. 'I'll see how it goes.'

There was no point pushing it. Perhaps when the lads were established in their own place, Rozzer would feel more inclined to get in touch with his parents. Though how you could leave your own lad to struggle in prison and never even come to visit was beyond Jim. Perhaps they didn't deserve Rozzer's compassion as they had shown none to him. Still, it was easy to judge when you didn't know the whole situation. Maybe there was more to it than met the eye. The only role Jim had now was to try to get them back on their own feet and help them to become self-sufficient. The rest of it was up to the lads themselves.

'Onions in. Fry those off,' he instructed Smudge, who did as he was told without question. 'Ever prepared garlic?'

More head shaking.

'Come closer.' Jim motioned for them both to stand either side of him, then started his demonstration. 'Garlic bulb. Garlic clove. Chop off both ends. Peel away the skin. Into the crusher.' He showed them said kitchen implement. 'Bish, bash, bosh.' The garlic oozed out of the other end. 'Into the mince and onions.'

The lads looked as if he'd showed them the secrets of alchemy. 'If you haven't got one already, we'll get one for your kitchen.'

They both exchanged a glance at that and grinned.

'*Our* kitchen,' Smudge said with a disbelieving beam.

'Yeah.' Rozzer punched him playfully. '*Our* kitchen.'

Jim suddenly choked up. These lads had nothing and they were so thrilled that they'd now have a place to call home. He'd do all he could to help them settle in. 'Bloody onions,' he said as he cuffed away a tear.

'Yeah.' Smudge wiped his eyes too.

'Tomatoes,' Jim said, getting back to the business in hand. 'Tin of. They go in next. Chop them up.' He whizzed the knife about in the pan. 'And some dried herbs.' Jim handed the jar to Rozzer. 'Just a pinch.'

'When is Cassie back from Coldasfuckland?' Smudge asked as he stirred.

'Tonight. But not until late.'

'Shall we save her some of this?'

'Yeah. I'll put some in a bowl so that I can microwave it for her later if she hasn't eaten.' He'd meant to pick up a bottle of red wine and flowers but, with all that had happened, it had gone completely out of his mind. He'd do it tomorrow, for sure. On his way home from work. He glanced at the clock. Cassie's itinerary said that she'd be home at about eleven o'clock.

It wouldn't be ideal for her to arrive at the flat to find both of the lads. That was a surprise that she could probably do without. But what else could he have done? He had to bring them home with him. There was no way that he could have left them in the unit a minute longer than they needed to be there. As there was no other accommodation available at such short notice, he couldn't stand by and let them be spat out onto the street to fend for themselves. Anyone would have done the same thing.

'Is this ready now?' Smudge asked.

'We need to let it simmer for a while, so that the meat cooks through and all the flavours develop.'

The lads looked impressed. 'It smells well nice.'

'This is the first thing I've ever cooked,' Smudge said proudly.

'Well, let's hope that it tastes as good as it smells.'

'I think I'm going to like cooking,' Smudge added. 'Can we do something else tomorrow?'

'That's the plan,' Jim said.

'We can wrap some presents for Cassie later,' Rozzer suggested. 'Or do something. As a thank-you.'

'That's kind,' Jim said. 'She'd like that. We'll have a look at her list and see what else we could do.'

'This is just the same as being in a proper family,' Smudge said. 'I always wondered what it would be like. Why have you not got kids, Jim?'

'Oh, you know,' he said, evasively. 'It's not happened yet.'

'You should crack on. You'd be a great dad.'

'Yeah,' Jim said. 'One day. Until then I'll have to make do with you two.'

They all laughed at that, but there was a truth in the words that made his chest tighten.

Chapter Fifty-Seven

When the plane lands at Luton Airport we taxi to the small terminal building reserved for the famous and the fabulously rich. This beautiful dream is coming to an end. Already a car is parked up waiting to whisk us home.

Coming to a standstill, the engines are cut. We all fuss about, gathering our belongings as the steps are put into place. I make sure that the children have everything with them and there are no Nintendos or iPads lurking down the sides of the seats. As we move out into the night, a cold, cruel wind whips across the runway. I help the children down the steps of the plane.

'Got everything?' Carter asks.

'I think so.' He squeezes my hand and the tears that never seem to be far away spring up again.

'No crying,' he says and brushes a tear away with his thumb.

'This has just been such a brilliant trip.'

'It has,' he agrees. 'But we have a lot to look forward to as well. Remember that.'

Taking Eve and Max by the hand, we go to cross the tarmac. As we do, another fancy limousine sweeps towards us.

'Oh no,' Carter whispers in my ear.

It's only seconds before I realise why he's so disappointed. The limo pulls up next to us and, from the back, Tamara emerges.

'Mummy!' Eve shouts.

The children both drop my hands and run towards her as she sashays to meet us. Tamara crouches down and scoops them into her arms. 'My babies,' I hear her say. 'Mummy's missed you so much.'

'We've missed you too,' Eve says.

I glance across at Carter who's trying to be stoic, but looks so forlorn. All I want to do is hug him but, given the circumstances, I daren't even risk it.

Eventually, while Carter and I stand there like lemons, Tamara untangles herself from the children and comes over to us.

'Hello, Carter,' she says. 'I missed the children so much that I couldn't wait to see them. I got your flight time from Georgina. Hope you don't mind.'

'No, of course not. It's lovely to see you,' he says cheerfully, but I can tell that his brightness is forced. 'The children have missed you too.'

'I thought we could all travel home together,' she says. 'You, me and the children,' she stresses with a barbed look at me. 'To Randall Court.'

'I . . . er . . .' Carter looks racked with indecision.

'Can we go together, Daddy?' Eve asks. 'Please?'

I can tell that Carter is torn. I'm sure that the last thing on earth he wants to do is get into a car with Tamara.

To help him along, I say, 'That sounds like a marvellous idea.' My expression says that he must do this for the sake of Eve and Max, for the sake of domestic harmony. 'Can I take the other car home?'

'Of course, of course,' Carter agrees, eyes troubled.

'We'll speak tomorrow. Sort things out.'

'Yes. We will.' He looks as if he wants to say more but, obviously, he can't. Instead, he says, 'Eve, Max, come and say goodbye to Cassie. Thank her for arranging such a marvellous trip.'

'Cassie can come with us too,' Eve says. 'There's lots of room in Mummy's car.'

'I've got things to do,' I tell her. 'But we'll catch up soon.'

I bend to hug them both tightly. At this moment I feel as if I don't want to let either of them go, so I know how hard it must have been for Tamara to see them swan off with their dad and another woman. Little does she know how our relationship has changed in the last few days. I'm not even sure that I can get my head around it myself. A few weeks ago Carter was nothing more than a client. I'd have been glad to even have classed him as a friend by the end of our trip to Lapland, but now it seems that he wants more from me. And I can't even begin to decide whether I have more to give him in return.

My head is whirling. I'm so flattered by Carter's attention. Who wouldn't be? He's holding the full deck. He's handsome. He's charming. He's great company. And let's not forget, he's ferociously rich. I thought that my head would never be turned by material things, but it has been. Is it so awful of me to admit that? I can't help but think that a relationship with Carter would transform my life in an instant. All my current financial strain would be lifted in a flash, just disappearing into thin air. I'd no longer be bogged down by bank charges and phone calls from credit-card companies. I'd be free to live without this gnawing worry. There's a feeling of utter relief about the idea that I can't even begin to describe.

But what about my lovely Jim who's waiting for me at home? My Jim whom I've loved for years without faltering? Until now.

'Thank you, Cassie,' Eve says. 'It's been really lovely. I liked the huskies and the Father Christmas parts best.'

'Good.' I want to smooth her hair, but now it seems far too intimate a gesture with her mother standing watching my every move.

'Thank you,' Max says. 'You're very good at playing.'

'Thank you, sweetheart.'

'It's cold,' Tamara says with a dramatic shiver. 'We should go.'

Does she not realise that we have just returned from minus twenty-five degrees in Lapland? We are people who laugh in the face of this measly version of cold!

'Come on, children.' She gathers Eve and Max to her again.

My heart twists to watch them go.

'Goodbye,' Carter says. He risks a peck on both of my cheeks. Suddenly, the urge to feel his warm lips on mine is overwhelming. I want to kiss him. I want to kiss him so much.

'Goodbye,' I say. 'What time shall I ring you?'

'I'll call you,' he says and, with a wave over his shoulder, he walks to the limousine with Tamara and the children.

I wait until they all climb into the car, the doors thunk closed and it executes a leisurely turn before speeding away.

So. Now I'm the one standing alone on the tarmac feeling forlorn. I sigh to myself and head to the car that's waiting for me.

'Good evening, miss,' the driver says as he opens the door for me.

'Thank you.'

I sink into the plush leather but, this time, its luxury holds no joy for me. It's simply a vehicle that's taking me away from Carter, from Eve, from Max.

I try to control my breathing. I try not to cry. I have about half an hour, less, to get my head right.

I am going home. Home to my flat. Home to my worries. Home to Jim. And the sooner I can stop this longing, this keening feeling inside of me, the better.

Chapter Fifty-Eight

The limousine pulls up outside my flat. When previously I'd always be excited to be home, I now feel sick and somehow lost.

It's been raining since we left Luton Airport and, as the driver lifts my suitcase from the boot of the car, I realise that it's pouring down. That just about puts the tin hat on it really. Even though I've just met the real Father Christmas, all my Christmassy feelings have flown right out of the window. There's nothing but a damp ache in my bones.

Having come straight down the M1, we've not passed a single thing that suggests that Christmas is looming large, just mile after mile of blackness and gloom. It's wrong, so wrong, to have Christmas without crisp, white snow.

In seconds, my hair is plastered flat to my head, but I don't care.

'Shall I carry your case into your apartment for you, miss?'

'No,' I say. 'I can take it from here, thank you.'

I don't know whether I should tip him or not and now I feel embarrassed. Thankfully, as it's raining, he doesn't linger. As soon as is politely possible, he's back in the limo and pulling away, leaving me standing in our car park with my case.

With a sigh, I look up to see a few meagre Christmas trees in the windows of the flats, but they seem a half-hearted attempt at festivity. Then I notice that the light is on in our flat and that, at least, gives me a slight lift. It means that Jim is home. As I haven't been able to contact him, I wasn't sure whether he'd be at work or not. I think it's better that he's at home and waiting for me.

I push open the main front door and climb the stairs, dragging my case behind me. All I can do for the moment is put Carter and this trip firmly out of my mind. There's lots of work to do now that I'm back. I have to get on with life and throw myself into it wholeheartedly.

Putting my key in the lock, I suddenly get a feeling of panic. In such a few days, this place now seems completely alien to me. Behind this door is my home, my loved one. So why do I feel so strange, so disconnected? I take a deep breath and turn the key.

As the door swings open, Jim dashes out from the living room. His face lights up when he sees me and I want to lie down on the floor and cry with relief. Nothing has changed at all. When I look at him, I still love him. He comes to me, wraps me in his great big, bear-hug arms and rocks me against him. Neither of us speaks. We just hold each other tightly and I can feel Jim's heart thudding happily.

'Hey,' he says. 'I've missed you so bloody much.'

'I've missed you too,' I tell him and, at this moment, it doesn't feel like a lie.

'Have you had a good time?'

'Brilliant,' I admit.

'You saw the northern lights?'

'I did.'

'Were they as fabulous as you'd hoped?'

'More than that.'

Everything about the trip seems to have made me into a different person. The things I've seen, the things I've experienced, how can I ever forget them, the way they made me feel? How will I fit back into my own rather mundane life?

'I'm pleased for you.' Jim lets me go and then picks up my case. Before he turns to head back into the living room, his face darkens slightly and he lowers his voice. 'I should warn you that we've got visitors.'

'Visitors? Now?'

'I haven't been able to call you,' Jim continues. 'Things have been happening here.' He pulls me into the kitchen and closes the door.

I'm worried now. 'Like what?'

'The lads were released today. Smudge and Rozzer.' He glances anxiously over his shoulder. 'I didn't know what else to do with them, so I've brought them here.'

'To stay?'

'For a few days. A week. Well, a couple of weeks at the most.'

Weeks? I can't even say that out loud.

'They've got a flat in Vincent's place, but it's not ready for them yet. This is only a temporary thing.'

'Where are they going to sleep?'

'Rozzer's on the futon in the spare room and Smudge is going to have to take the sofa.'

I don't know what to say.

He frowns at me. 'Tell me what you're thinking. Are you OK with this?'

'What if I'm not?'

He looks taken aback by that. 'I thought you would be. If you want them out, then I'll try to find them bed-and-breakfast accommodation.'

'It's not that I don't want them here,' I say. 'It's just that it's a shock. You know them, you see the boys every day, but I hardly know them. They've done a bit of work for me, but that's all.'

317

'They're great kids,' Jim stresses. 'They just need a break.'

'I'm not disputing that.' Our conversation seems to be turning into a whispered row. 'But how will we manage? This flat is barely big enough for two of us. We can hardly make ends meet ourselves and now we've got two extra mouths to feed?'

'It won't be for long.'

'I don't want to feel uncomfortable in my own home with two lads from Bovingdale here under my feet.'

Jim looks wounded. 'I didn't know you'd feel like that.'

All the fight goes out of me. 'To be honest, I didn't know it myself until it came out of my mouth.'

'I'll look for somewhere else for them tomorrow,' he says, the expression on his face showing that he's really disappointed in my reaction. And, truthfully, I'm disappointed in it too.

I put my hand on his arm. 'Don't, Jim. They can stay here. Of course they can. We'll manage. I'm tired. That's all. It's been a very—'

My voice fails me. What can I say to Jim? How can he know that I'm not myself, that I have one foot out of the door on this life, that he needs to fight for our relationship, not expend his energy on two ragamuffins that he's brought home because no one else is interested in them? How can a few words explain the emotional rollercoaster that I've been on? I swallow down the emotion and find my voice again.

I settle on, 'It's been a tiring few days.'

'Tiring?' He laughs. 'You've been swanning around Lapland on a dogsled. You left the itinerary behind, remember?'

'It might seem like that to you.' I try not to bristle. 'But, in one way and another, it's taken it out of me. I've worked very hard to make sure everything was perfect.'

'So that two spoiled little rich kids could see Santa?'

'Jim, I have just walked through the door only for you to tell me that there are two ex-cons living in our flat. I'm not the one in the wrong here.' I decide not to tell him about the dark thoughts in my heart.

He caves in, instantly. 'Of course,' he says. 'I'm being stupid.'

'Carter's children are actually really nice,' I tell him.

'So are Rozzer and Smudge,' he pleads. 'No one else gives a toss. All I want to do is help.'

I take him in my arms again. 'They can stay. Of course they can. We'll work it out.' I smile, but I realise that it's weary and doesn't touch my soul.

'The lads made their first spag bol,' he says. 'I showed them how. They were really proud of it. Didn't taste half bad. They've left you some in a bowl in case you were hungry.'

'Oh,' I say. 'I ate on the plane.'

Grilled chicken with couscous followed by chocolate mousse. All of which was worthy of a Michelin-starred restaurant. But now I really wish that I had room to eat the leftovers of the meal that the boys have made.

'I'll keep it till tomorrow,' Jim says. 'It'll still be tasty reheated for lunch. I'm on earlies, though.' He pulls a face. 'It would have been nice to go out for breakfast or something.'

A walk down to McDonald's for an Egg McMuffin. I feel awful that, suddenly, this holds no thrill for me when once – a few days ago – I would have seen it as an indulgent treat. 'That would have been great.'

'I'll get the lads to cook, so that there's no extra work for you. They need to learn how to do it for when they're out on their own. I don't want them to starve.'

I can see how much these boys mean to Jim and I reach out to stroke his face. 'You are a very kind man.'

He makes a dismissive noise.

'I can show them some dishes too,' I offer. 'It's no trouble.'

'I'm sure they'd like that.'

'Just put the kettle on and I'll go and say hello.'

'They can stay?'

I nod. 'Of course.'

'Do I tell you enough how bloody fantastic you are?' Jim says.

But I'm not fantastic. The truth of the matter is that in my mind's eye there's a picture of Carter on the steps of Randall Court, his arms open, and I'm looking at my tiny little flat, filled with young offenders, and finding it wanting.

Chapter Fifty-Nine

I find enough bedding for the boys. Just about. Rozzer has an old duvet and a pillow, which Jim had to go into the tiny loft space to retrieve. Smudge didn't fare as well and has a couple of well-loved picnic blankets from the back of the car and a cushion for his head. Neither of them looked perturbed by the lack of a co-ordinated duvet set and seemed grateful to have anywhere to lay their heads at all.

Both Jim and I tuck them in like children and I get a flashback to doing the same for Eve and Max at night in Lapland. I wonder where they all are now. Did Carter and Tamara have an argument when they got home or are they playing nice for the children's sake? I do hope they've managed to keep things civil. The kids have had a fabulous few days and don't need it spoiled by rowing parents. I realise that I'm worrying for them, but what can I do? My hands are tied.

When the boys are both settled and the queue for the bathroom has subsided, Jim and I go to bed. Normally, I'd walk from the bathroom to the bedroom in just my nightwear of T-shirt and tatty old shorts. But, with Kieran and Andrew around, I have to dig out my dressing gown for a bit of modesty.

Jim is already in bed, reading with the light on. He seems really excited that the lads are here and I wish I could be the same. I think I must be still be running on adrenaline or jet lag or something as I feel weird and disconnected. I thought that everything was the same, but it simply isn't. The bedroom looks like somewhere I've never slept before. Now that we're alone, I'm awkward with Jim. Even more so as I slide into bed beside him.

'Come here,' he says and pulls me into his arms.

His body is warm, solid and should feel so familiar, but it doesn't. We usually spoon together so easily but, this time, we don't seem to fit together right.

'Can't get comfy?' Jim asks.

'I think I'm overtired. Just need a good night's sleep.'

'You were in the Icehotel, weren't you?'

I nod. 'Didn't sleep a wink.'

'Can't imagine it's that comfortable.'

'No.'

How can I tell Jim that it's perfectly comfortable, that it wasn't the cold or sleeping on reindeer skins that kept me awake? How can I tell him that it was a magical experience and that my own bedroom in a block of flats in Hemel Hempstead simply can't compete? When I think of the snow and ice sparkling, glittering, everything here seems flat and grey.

Also, this time last night I was in bed with another man and I can't get that out of my mind. Something else Jim doesn't need to know. I think about calling Carter tomorrow and my stomach flips with nerves. What shall I say? What am I going to do? It's a conversation that could shape my whole future and take me in a direction that I never even imagined a few days ago. It could take me away from Jim. The thought makes me feel nauseous.

'Let's have a welcome home cuddle,' he says. 'I've missed you so much.'

I feel like a corpse, my body stiff and unresponsive. Jim twines his arms round me and starts to nuzzle my neck. One of our

322

'making love' signals. All couples have them, don't they? Jim nuzzles my neck. Sometimes he has a shave before bedtime – a sure sign that he's in the mood for love. If I'm feeling sexy, I twine my foot around Jim's and caress it gently. Tonight, the neck nuzzling is failing miserably. In fact, it's making me really uncomfortable.

Jim goes to move above me, but I stop him from kissing me. He looks at me, puzzled. 'Everything OK?'

I shrug and lower my voice to a whisper before speaking. 'I feel a bit weird doing this with the boys right next door. What if they hear us?'

Jim grins. 'We'll be really, really quiet. You'll have to promise not to cry out my name in ecstasy.'

That makes me smile too. Oh God, I love this man. How can I be thinking of leaving him? Yet, deep in my heart, I am. What would he think if he knew that I was lying here with another man on my mind? Only a few hours have gone by since I left Carter and this somehow seems too soon. I need time to adjust to my circumstances again. Perhaps even to change them. I can't make love to Jim. I just can't.

He props himself up on his elbow and gazes at me quizzically. 'Is this going to last *all* the time the lads are here?'

'I don't know,' I admit. 'We've always had the place to ourselves. This seems odd.' Again, if I lived at Randall Court, I could find a whole selection of extra bedrooms for the boys to occupy.

'We'll have to get a hotel room,' Jim teases.

'Perhaps we should get *them* a hotel room.' It sounds more snappy than I mean. 'How long do you think they'll be here?'

'I don't know,' he confesses. 'They'll be gone as soon as Vincent can take them. You can see why I had to help.'

'Of course I do.' And I *do*. 'But it's not going to be a walk in the park. You're at work first thing tomorrow. What am I going

323

to do with them?' I hope that they'll be up early too as I've got a lot to do – although I've no idea what – and the computer is in the spare room.

'Give them some jobs. Something that will keep them occupied in the flat. As soon as I'm home I'll take Smudge into town to get him some proper clothes. After that I'll take them round the agencies that they need to be in contact with. Smudge is going to need a lot of extra support, maybe some counselling.' Jim sighs heavily. 'One thing I didn't tell you . . .' His voice falters and it's clear he's struggling to carry on.

My heart starts to pound. Does Jim have a secret too?

'The night we had a row. Before you went away?' He rubs a hand over his face. 'Smudge had attempted suicide that day. I was all over the place.'

'That was barely a few days ago,' I say. 'How come they've let him out?'

'End of his sentence,' Jim says. 'They can't keep him in for that. He's someone else's problem now.'

Ours, it seems.

'Poor Kieran.' My heart goes out to the boy, it really does. 'What happened?'

'He tried to slash his wrists. Not in a serious way. It was nothing more than a cry for help.'

He must have felt pretty desperate, nevertheless. That helps me to understand Jim's behaviour a bit better now, even though I'm worried that he felt he couldn't talk to me about it. 'You should have told me.'

'I know,' he says. 'It was too raw.'

But, now that he has told me, I have to confess that I'm even more worried about what we've taken on. What if he tries it again and we're not quick enough to respond? Shouldn't someone properly trained be caring for him? These are damaged boys and I simply don't know if I can manage. Jim's used to this, but I'm not.

'He's going to need professional help,' Jim adds. 'I'll see what I can get him signed up for. Plus they've got to check in with their probation officers too.'

Jim really has taken on a lot. I love it that he cares so much, but I can also understand why people would be more keen to turn their backs, face the other way.

'It won't be for long. I swear,' he promises.

'Let's settle down,' I say. My brain is so exhausted that I can't think straight. 'I'm really tired now.'

'OK.' Jim kisses me tenderly. His fingers stroke my face. 'I love you.'

'I love you too,' I say. And I do, but my tongue feels thick in my mouth.

We lie down and Jim turns off the light. Within seconds, as usual, his breathing has deepened into sleep. I, on the other hand, lie awake, my mind in turmoil.

My thoughts, of course, run to what Carter said to me. Do I want to stay here or do I want to go? It's as simple as that. There might not be much to hold me here in material terms, but can I turn my back on all that Jim and I have built up? Could I walk away when there's still so much love between us? I'm not in this dilemma because I've fallen out of love with Jim. It's just that I might be in love with someone else too.

I've glanced at the clock for the millionth time and note that it's gone three o'clock, when I hear a muffled shout coming from the living room. It's clear that Smudge is having a bad dream. He starts to cry out, getting louder and louder. It hits me that I'm afraid of getting up and going into my own living room in case, in his half-sleep, he might not know where he is and attacks me or something.

'Jim!' I shake Jim's shoulder. 'Jim. Wake up.'

He grunts and stirs.

'I think Kieran's having a bad dream. I'm worried about going to him on my own.'

Now Jim's awake. He's rubbing his eyes and climbing out of bed in one movement. I follow him.

'Stay here,' he says, but I stick with him.

In the living room, Jim turns on the lamp. 'What's up, lad?'

Kieran is awake, wild-eyed and still shouting. Jim crouches down beside the sofa and holds him by the arms. 'You're all right,' he says, soothingly. 'We've got you, Smudge. We've got you.'

The shouts turn to racking sobs and Jim cradles the boy in his arms while he cries.

Rozzer comes through from the spare room in nothing but his boxers. He's scratching his head, yawning sleepily and dragging his duvet behind him. 'I've got it, Jim,' he says. 'He does this most nights.'

The boy is much calmer now, so Jim moves away and Rozzer takes over. 'Mate,' he says. 'It's me. Go back to sleep now. We're cool.'

'I'm frightened, Rozzer.'

Rozzer yawns. 'You're always frightened, bro. But I'm here now. And Jim. We've got your back. Shut up and go to sleep.'

'OK.' Kieran lies down again and slides a thumb into his mouth.

He looks so vulnerable and terrified that I want to cry for him. But I'm so scared for myself that tears won't come. I should have known that these boys were troubled, but you can never be sure just how much. I want to be kind and nurturing like Jim, but I'm also a bit frightened of them both. What if they revert to their old ways now that they're out of the unit? Will Jim be able to help keep them on the straight and narrow?

Rozzer lays out his duvet on the floor. 'Probably best if I stay here,' he says. 'Then we can all get some kip.'

'Shout if you need me,' Jim says. 'We're only in the next room.'

'Will do,' Rozzer says. 'He'll be all right now, though.'

Jim puts his arm around me and I realise that I'm shivering. 'Cold?' he asks.

'I'm not sure.'

'Let's go back to bed.' He turns me towards the bedroom and, compliant, I walk ahead of him. 'There's nothing to worry about now.'

But there is, I want to tell Jim. There's lots to worry about. It's just that he doesn't know the half of it.

Chapter Sixty

It's two weeks until Christmas. Fourteen days. The final count-down. The first thing I need to do is check the computer. The snow, the cold and the fun in Lapland has clearly wiped all my work responsibilities from my brain as I can't remember at all what was in the diary before I left. Having a handsome million-aire tell you that he loves you and wants you to move in with him and his children also tends to scramble the grey matter, I've now found.

Jim was up early and brought me and the boys a cup of tea. Jim was first in the shower, then Kieran and, finally, Andrew. I lay there, listening to the sound of the water, the sound of strangers in my home, and wondered what I'd do if I needed to use the loo urgently. Cross my legs, I guess. Carter's house has more bath-rooms than we have any type of room.

When the coast is clear and I finally get up, both of the boys are dressed and watching breakfast television. The room is fuggy and smells slightly stale. I want to open the window and air it, but they might think it's because of them and I don't want to insult them.

They jump up when they see me.

'Can we get you some tea?' Kieran says, eager to please.

'That would be nice. Thank you.'

'Sorry about last night,' he says. 'Rozzer told me. I don't know I do it.'

'It's OK. Did you sleep after that?'

'I think so,' he says with a shrug. 'Your sofa's a lot more comfortable than my bunk was.'

'Good. I'm glad to hear it.'

'Is there anything we can do today? We want to earn our keep. We're not just going to sit around and get under your feet, Cassie.'

'I'll check the computer, see what's on for this week. I'm sure there'll be something.' If I'm honest, I can't even believe we're so close to Christmas, let alone think what's coming up in the diary. 'The only thing for definite is that I have to go and finish the decorations at Randall Court.'

'It's all done,' Kieran says.

I spin round. 'What?'

He shrugs. 'We went up there with Jim while you were away. We did the kids' bedrooms, the garland thingy and Jim did the flower arrangements.'

'You did?' My heart is beating erratically. I have to get up there today. What if they've made a terrible hash of them? I'm charging Carter an absolute fortune and I don't want the lads messing it up. That place has to look immaculate. Even more so now that Carter and I, well ... I can't even finish that sentence myself.

'It looks great,' Kieran adds as if reading my thoughts. Then a chink appears in his confidence. 'Well, we thought so.'

'Great.' But I hear myself gulp uneasily.

I go into my emails and check what's come in. There's lots more wrapping and present buying to be done. Some people certainly like to cut it fine. I think today I'll get the boys to try to make a real dent on the outstanding list as the flat still looks like a warehouse with all the cardboard boxes stacked in it. If we can get some of those shifted today, it will give the four of us some much needed breathing room.

Kieran brings in my tea. 'I made you some toast too,' he says. 'Hope that's all right.'

My heart softens. 'That's very kind.'

'No,' he says, his face anxious. 'You're the kind one, Cassie. Taking us two on. Not a lot of women would do that.'

'You can stay as long as you need to,' I tell him, honestly. 'Hopefully, you'll both have your own place soon.'

'I can't believe it. That would be just fucking awesome.'

I raise my eyebrows.

'Sorry, sorry. Awesome, I mean. Without the "fucking" bit.'

We both laugh.

'I want to do it right this time,' he says, shuffling uncomfortably. 'I feel I can with Jim behind me.'

'He thinks a lot of both of you.'

'He's a great bloke. The best. You're a great couple.'

'Thank you.'

'Best let you get on.' Kieran nods at the computer. 'Just tell us what to do when you know.'

'I will.'

When he's gone, I sit and stare blankly at the screen. I chew my toast, not tasting it, simply because I don't want to offend Kieran. Checking my watch, I see that it's not yet seven o'clock. I feel bleary-eyed after my disturbed night and still can't assemble my thoughts coherently. Perhaps I should phone Carter right now. Catch him before he starts work. But what would I say to him? Maybe I should wait until he calls me. Buy myself some thinking time. After chewing at my lip and my fingernails, I decide that's just what I'll do. I need to check that the decorations are perfect, so I'll have to bite the bullet at some point.

330

In the meantime, I must get down to business. Calling Mrs Christmas! isn't going to organise itself.

I've had a couple of emails in, asking for someone to erect outside lights, so I'll call the customers and find out what it is that they want. Let's see if the boys can do that with me tomorrow. That would keep them out of mischief. There are several more people who want tree-dressing, which is lovely because that's my favourite thing to do. Someone asks me to organise a festive deep-clean of their house, which is a new one on me and doesn't sound very festive. However, within minutes, I've fixed it up with an agency for a 10 per cent cut of the fee. Then I have half a dozen requests from people asking me to do their Christmas food shopping. That may not be glamorous, but I'm charging quite heartily for it and not everyone has time to do it themselves or wants to risk leaving it to the pickers and packers of Tesco online. I could get Gaby to help me with those. Someone wants a singer to go to their house for an hour on Christmas Eve for a drinks party. I have only a couple of people on my hastily assembled contacts list, so I hope that one of them is still free or that they know someone who is.

My last request is from someone asking me to hire china and crockery for their Christmas celebrations and to go along and decorate their dining room. They also want to know if I can organise a chef for them, so I'll ring the company who is going to provide the chef for Carter and the children and check if they can do it. It's nice to see that Carter isn't my only client with money to burn. I'm going to set the boys off with their wrapping chores and then I'll come back and organise the rest.

Now that I'm back at my desk in my poky flat, I'm beginning to feel as if Lapland was just a beautiful dream. Last night, Lapland was the reality and being back at home felt totally surreal; now it seems like the other way round. Did it really happen at all? Did I imagine what Carter said to me? Perhaps I did.

I check my watch. Nearly nine o'clock and Carter still hasn't called. I stare at my mobile, willing it to ring, but it's immune to my silent pleas.

I should just ring him, get this over with. My stomach swirls with panic at the very thought of it. I feel as if I'm bothering him. But then I remember all the things he said last night and know that he'll want me to contact him as soon as possible.

So, with trembling fingers, I pick up the phone.

Chapter Sixty-One

By noon, the boys have wrapped and labelled dozens of presents. They kept the television on all morning as they cut, wrapped and ribboned, but that's fine. There's been the sound of laughter too, so it seems as if they're quite relaxed in their work and I hope that the horrors of Bovingdale will soon be long behind them. They've also kept the tea and coffee flowing my way too, so, despite my misgivings about having them here, they do appear to be happy to slip into a normal domestic routine.

I've been steadily working my way through my list of Things To Do and, in between each task, have been calling Carter. So far I've phoned him ten times. He's yet to reply. I haven't left a message as, frankly, I don't even know what I want to say to him.

Being once again sent straight to his voicemail, I hang up. Now I'm worried that when he sees his list of 'missed calls' he'll think that I'm not simply keen to talk to him but have turned into a stalker. I might not be able to speak to Carter himself, but I can't put off going up to the house to see what Jim and the boys have done in terms of decoration. Pulling out the plan, I glance over it to refresh my memory. There's a lot of work here and I can't believe they'll have done it all to my exacting standards.

Taking a deep breath, I phone Carter's office at Randall Court. Georgina answers.

'Hi, Georgina. Is Carter around today?'

'No,' she tells me. 'He left long before I got here as he had to take the children back to school this morning. Then he's in London all day.'

'I'd like to come up and check the decorations.'

'Sure,' she says. 'Any time. They're looking fantastic.'

That's a relief to hear. 'Can I come up at four?'

'Yes, certainly. I'll see you then.'

So I hang up, glad that there's a plan in place. Jim will be home by then to keep the boys occupied and I'll be free to go without worrying about leaving them alone in the flat.

I make Kieran and Andrew a sandwich and some soup for lunch, remembering that boys who are growing into men have hollow legs. It would be nice to see the gaunt, grey look go from Kieran's face while he's here. That boy needs some good home-made dinners inside him to fill him out. He keeps the sleeves of his sweatshirt pulled well down, but I still catch a glimpse of the fine, healing cuts on his wrists.

I take five minutes to sit with them. 'You've got through a lot this morning.'

'We're glad to be busy,' Andrew says.

'Why don't you write out a card for your parents while you're at it?' I suggest, nodding to the growing pile. 'Tell them you're out and where you're living.'

He shrugs.

'It's Christmas, Andrew. I'm sure they'd be pleased to hear from you.'

'Dunno.'

'Think about it.' I turn to Kieran. 'Do you have anyone you'd like to send a card to?'

'No,' he says. 'I need to stay well away from my old life. I don't want anyone knowing where I am.'

That's sad, I think, but from what Jim has said he might well be right.

When they've eaten and have both gushed over my skills in the sandwich-making department, they carry some of the wrapped gifts down to my car for delivery to a couple of addresses on my way to Randall Court.

At three o'clock Jim comes home. He breezes through the door of the flat and kisses me straight away.

'Had a good day?'

'Just trying to get back up to speed,' I tell him. 'I'm going up to Randall Court this afternoon.'

'Checking up on our handiwork?'

'Thanks for doing that. I'm amazed. I hadn't expected you to.'

'Thought it would be a nice surprise,' Jim says. 'The lads did a really good job.' He glows when he says it.

'Georgina told me. I just want to make sure that absolutely everything is done so that I can tick it off the list.'

'There's still a lot of work coming in.'

'Not long now and Christmas will soon be all over.' Then what happens, I wonder? Where will I be in January? What will I do with myself? Will I even still be here at Christmas?

Jim lowers his voice and jerks his head towards the living room where the boys are sitting. 'Are you OK after last night?'

I nod. I still feel shaky when I think of Kieran crying out. 'It's just taking a bit of getting used to, but they've been great this morning.'

'Glad to hear it.'

'We had lunch together and I've made you a sandwich,' I tell Jim as he follows me into the kitchen. 'It's on the side covered with clingfilm. There's some soup in the pan. I'm just going to do burger and chips for us all tonight so it's quick.'

'I'm sure the lads will like that.' Then Jim wells up and surreptitiously brushes a tear from his eye.

'What's wrong?'

'For a minute it almost felt like having our own family here. I feel quite protective of them both. It's nice to see them blossoming.'

'Being out of that place must be a huge relief.'

'Yeah. I'm sure it is.' Jim checks the pan, giving it a stir. 'I'll take them into town when I've had this. There are a few errands they need to do.'

I kiss his cheek. 'I won't be long.'

Jim catches my arm as I go to leave. 'We are all right, aren't we?'

'Yes. Of course.' I can't meet his eyes.

'I thought things were a bit … I don't know … strange … last night.'

'It did seem a bit peculiar,' I admit.

'Is it just having the lads here? Nothing more?'

Shaking my head, I say, 'Nothing more.'

He laughs, but I can tell it's forced. 'I wouldn't like to think that you'd had *too* good a time with Carter Randall.'

And, of course, that's exactly what happened. Jim's not stupid. What can I say? How can I tell him how I feel when I don't even know myself?

'I'd better go.'

He pulls me into his arms and holds me tight, whispering into my hair, 'Make sure you come back to me, Cassie.'

'I will.'

But my heart is troubled as I walk out of the door.

Chapter Sixty-Two

Having delivered the beautifully wrapped gifts to their intended homes, I wend my way out of Hemel Hempstead and up towards Little Gaddesden. Even though I'm doing all these Christmassy things, I still can't believe that Christmas itself is just around the corner. I haven't even begun to think about what we'll do ourselves. I haven't thought about one bit of festive food or gifts or decorations for our own home even though it's usually all I think about at this time of the year. Then I pull myself up short. Will I even be at the flat with Jim by Christmas? The very thought of it makes me feel sick. But can I really walk away from Carter, his beautiful children – who I've also grown so very fond of – and the life of ease that he can offer me?

My car grunts and grinds its way up through the forest. Everything has been thoroughly grey and miserable today. The sky, now edging towards darkness, is sullen, brooding. Even the trees look weary. No fabulously brilliant, snow-rich forests here. Just damp, heaviness and gloom. I haven't spoken to my sister since I've been back. Perhaps if I do she'll furnish me with some useful sisterly advice and guidance as my head is still spinning. I can't hold onto one single thought and make sense of it.

A few minutes later, when I pull into the drive of Randall Court, my mind is still in a jumble. I sweep up the drive, seeing it with new eyes, but still feeling as much in awe of it as when I first came here. Could this place one day be my own home? It seems impossible even as it crosses my mind.

I drive past the towering Christmas tree and park outside the row of garages, then jump out of my car and crunch across the gravel to the house. Even though I know that Carter isn't around, just being here is giving my spirits a lift. Who wouldn't want to live in a palatial home like this? Is it superficial to be drawn to it? Wouldn't anyone be? I sigh to myself and ring the bell.

While I wait for the door to be opened, I admire the vast Christmas tree. It's beautifully illuminated and, as it's dark now, I can appreciate the full impact.

A few minutes later, Georgina opens the door and lets me into the entrance hall. It's all I can do not to gasp out loud. In the corner the other Christmas tree twinkles for all it's worth and looks absolutely stunning. The decorated garland that I started off now winds all the way up the banister of the galleried staircase and it too looks amazing. I can't believe that Jim and the boys have managed this.

'This is incredible.'

'I know,' Georgina says. 'You've done a great job. The house has never looked so beautiful at Christmas.'

I wonder what Carter thought of it. And, more importantly, how Tamara reacted. I really want to ask Georgina what happened last night when Carter got home with the children. Were *they* all right? Was *he* all right? Did Tamara stay or did she go? A cold feeling settles on my chest when I even think of that. However, I realise that Georgina's probably no wiser than I am as they got back so late and I don't want to show undue interest.

'I'd like to look at the other rooms we've decorated.'

'Help yourself. There's no one else here today,' she says.

'Not even Hettie?'

'Day off. She's popped into Berkhamsted for a while.' Georgina checks her watch. 'She should be back before too long.'

I feel as if I'd like to see Hettie, chat to her. If she gave the children their breakfast this morning, she'd know if everything was as it should be.

'Mind if I go back to the office while you look around? Carter has left me a flurry of things to do.'

'No. Go ahead.'

'Call me if you need me.' She means on her phone. You could probably shout for ever in this house and no one would hear you. Then I remember that the first time I came here and met Carter, he and Tamara were having a right old shouting match and I heard that all right. It seems so long ago and yet it's a matter of weeks.

Georgina leaves me to attend to her duties and I go into the living room. There's another garland over the mantelpiece and Jim, or whoever did this, has followed my plan perfectly but have also added their own flair. It looks sensational. If you didn't feel Christmassy before, you would do if you spent a few minutes looking at this.

In all of the vases there are lovely festive flower arrangements. I take a moment to sit on the sofa, sink into the plush cushions and drink it all in. It's just wonderful. How would I feel if this was, in part, mine? This room alone is probably bigger than our entire flat. I can't imagine Carter and the children in it by themselves. It's too vast and needs to be filled by a huge, robust family with lots of noise and animals. Gulping, I realise that it's way too easy for me to picture it.

Did Tamara like it, I wonder? Then I realise that this is no longer her home and what she thinks doesn't really matter. It's Carter and the children who are important.

Before I get too comfortable, I drag myself up from the sofa and climb the stairs, stopping on the way to check Jim's handiwork as he knew I would. I have to say that they've all done a great job. Who knew that Jim even had it in him? And he's done all this to take the pressure off me. As happy as I am, I also feel like sitting on the stairs and crying.

I go into Eve's bedroom first, which looks so girly and pretty, exactly as it should. Switching on the Christmas-tree lights, they sparkle brightly, making the room look like a palace fit for a little princess. Sitting on Eve's bed, I stroke the duvet where she would lie. An array of soft toys are piled on her pillow. I pick one up and cuddle it to me. I wish the children were here now so I could see how excited they were about their bedroom decorations. I know for sure that Eve will have loved this. I wish I could have been with her last night when she saw them for the first time. I would have given anything to see her reaction.

Reluctantly, I put down the teddy, first giving it a kiss on its nose. Then I go through to Max's room. It smells of him and my heart keens as I breathe in the musky scent of schoolboy's socks and abandoned trainers. Equal care has been lavished on his tree, which fits perfectly with the boyish theme of his room. I can hardly believe that I had the skill to design this and that it has been executed so well by Jim and the boys without any supervision from me. Jim has always had a creative streak, but I'd no idea that he was capable of such intricate work. I wonder if he's actually made a better job of it than I could have. Max will have absolutely adored it and, again, I regret that I wasn't here to witness its effect on him. How I wish that I could have come straight back to Randall Court with them last night, to see their smiles light up their faces when they saw the house and their rooms in all their glory. But it wasn't to be.

No matter what Carter has said, no matter that I might, at some point, be here in a different capacity, at the moment I'm still the hired help. When Tamara swept in, I had no choice but to take a back seat.

Before I get too melancholy, I look out at the vast expanse of garden. It's pitch black now and no one has turned on the lights. I should go back downstairs and find the switch, check that everything's up to scratch out there too.

The feeling that I'm an intruder starts to loom up on me again. As I can find no excuse to linger up here any longer, I decide that I'd better make myself scarce. After drinking in the view one last time, with a heavy heart I turn away from the window and force myself to leave.

Chapter Sixty-Three

I make my way back down the main staircase and, just as I'm about to call Georgina to tell her that I'm leaving, I hear a car on the gravel as it swishes up to one of the garages and parks. My stomach starts an involuntary flutter. I hope to God that this is Hettie returning from her trip to Berkhamsted and not Tamara.

Heart in mouth, I hurry to the window in the hall and look out. When I see that it's Carter's car, my emotions are sent into a flat spin once more. Carter climbs out and I stand, frozen to the spot, as he marches briskly towards the front door. I can feel myself trembling all over, so I listen to his key in the lock when he lets himself in.

He looks up as he comes into the hall. 'I hoped that was your car,' he says. 'I was sure it was.'

Before I can speak or move, he comes towards me and takes me into his arms. His mouth is on mine, hot, searching. I want to pull away. I really do. My brain is quite happy to tell me that this is wrong, so wrong. But my body is convinced that it's absolutely right, so right. I give in to the passion that has gripped my entire being and sink into Carter's embrace, realising that resistance is futile. He kisses me long and hard and all sense of reason goes from my mind. If I'm honest with you, I feel so overwhelmed that my knees threaten to buckle and I don't know how I even manage to remain upright.

When he eventually pulls away, leaving me weak and wanting more, he looks at me tenderly. 'I didn't think you'd come,' he says. 'I thought that you'd go home to Jim and never want to see me again. Have you brought your things with you?'

'No,' I say. 'I ... I ... I've only come to see what the decorations look like.'

At that he checks himself. 'The decorations?'

'Yes.'

Carter laughs. 'Who cares about the decorations? I want *you* here for Christmas. That's all that matters to me.'

'I've been trying to call you all morning.'

'I know. I've been manic. First day back.' He throws his laptop bag onto the nearest chair. 'Then I spoke to Georgina when I was on my way back from London and she told me you were here.' He grins and my insides turn to liquid. 'My driver broke every speed limit going so that I could get back to see you.'

'I didn't know if you'd still want me.'

He looks deep into my eyes. 'Of course I do. Why would you think that?'

'I wasn't sure if it was just because we were away in such lovely surroundings, in our little bubble. Then, when we got back to find Tamara waiting for you, I thought the situation might have changed.'

'It hasn't,' he says. 'Tamara stayed overnight – in the spare room – for the children's sake.' He sighs. 'There's no doubt that she misses them desperately.'

'They miss her too.' Eve's letter to Father Christmas couldn't have stated that more emphatically.

'I know. That tears me up inside,' he admits. 'But too much has gone on between me and Tamara for us to ever go back. This

343

isn't the life that she wants. She's never happier than when she's embroiled in her business or jetting off to the States. Tamara doesn't want to be stuck at home with the kids. Or with me. She'd go insane.' He glances forlornly round the hall of their mansion. 'I've realised that I want someone to be here for the children, to make a proper home for them. You were so great with them on our trip that it really opened my eyes. I want you, Cassie. I want you here for the children. I want you in my life permanently.'

'I can't make such a big decision so quickly.'

'In every business decision I've ever made, I've gone on nothing more than gut feeling. It's the best way.'

'This is an emotional decision about my entire future. It's not business.'

'It's the same thing,' he insists. 'You know in your heart what's right.'

'I still love Jim,' I tell him. 'This has come like a bolt out of the blue, Carter. I can't simply turn off my feelings for him.'

'I still have feelings for Tamara too. Whatever our differences, she's the mother of my children. We'll always be connected.'

I don't have that permanent link connecting me to Jim. If I walk away, I walk away for good. There's no reason for us ever to see each other again. The thought makes my stomach go cold.

'I can offer you all this,' he says, gesturing around the house. 'We don't know each other that well, but I can tell already that we could have a great relationship.'

And that's the rub, really, isn't it? I hardly know Carter. I know that I like what I've seen so far, but Jim and I have a history. We've a love that's built on a strong foundation. Our life together hasn't always been easy – especially not the last year – but we've stuck together and have a bond that I'd always thought was completely unbreakable.

344

'I need time to think,' I tell Carter. 'I can't rush into this.'

He twines me in his embrace again and his hot, firm lips find mine. In his arms I lose myself once more. I feel like a different woman, not myself at all.

'Take all the time you need, Cassie Christmas,' he murmurs. 'But you will be mine.'

Chapter Sixty-Four

I leave Carter and Randall Court, dazed. I'm not even sure how I drive home, but somehow I'm pulling up outside the flat. I park and then sit in the car for endless minutes, unable to move.

For the first time in my life I don't want to go back into my own home. It's a horrible feeling. Jim's car is here, so I know he and the boys are in the flat. They're also more than likely working on Christmas stuff for me and I'm so very grateful for that. But still I stay stuck in my seat.

Staring out of the window, I see nothing. I try to think what I want to do, but no obvious solution comes. All I have is a maelstrom in my head that's paralysing me. Eventually, my phone rings and I manage to motivate myself to pick it up. Jim's name is on the display.

'Hi,' I say softly.

'You've been sitting in the car for ages,' Jim says. 'Everything all right?'

I look up and see that he's standing at the living room window, looking down at me. He must have heard me pull up. He waves at me. I rouse myself to wave back. 'Yes. Everything's fine. I was just thinking.'

'Why don't you come and think inside?' he suggests. 'The kettle's on. The lads and I have got something to show you.'

'OK.'

My limbs are heavy, reluctant, but I make myself move and climb out of the car. The stairs make me feel as if I'm hauling myself up Everest, not just a couple of measly flights to the top floor of our block.

The door is already open when I reach the landing and, taking a deep and steadying breath before I do, I go inside. There's clearly been a new delivery as boxes fill our tiny hallway.

'What's all this lot?' I ask.

'One of the companies – Evans – have dropped off their corporate gifts for wrapping,' he says.

'Wow. I didn't think there'd be this many.'

'It's a big order,' Jim says. 'I can get the lads to make a start on it, if you want.'

'Yes. Good idea.' Both Jim and I can tell that I'm not the slightest bit interested in Evans' corporate gifts.

'Tea.' He hands a mug to me.

'Thanks.'

'You seem distracted. Want to tell me what's wrong?'

'Nothing,' I lie. 'I'm fine.'

'Come and look at this,' he urges. 'Close your eyes.'

'I might spill my tea.'

'Give it back to me then.' Obediently, I hand it back and he puts down both of the mugs. 'Close, close.'

I close my eyes. Jim takes me by the shoulders and steers me into the living room. I stub my toe on a box.

'Oh, sorry about that,' he says. 'Open now!'

Opening my eyes, I see that, straight ahead of me, in the corner of the room a Christmas tree has been put up.

'Oh.' The tree is tiny, as befits the scale of our room, and is standing on a side table. Next to it Kieran and Andrew beam shyly.

'The lads and I did it for you,' Jim says. 'To welcome you home.'

The meagre strings of lights draped around it blink hopefully. The decorations are pretty, if minute in size, clearly applied with the same meticulous care that Jim and the boys lavished on the resplendent trees at Randall Court. But its modest stature, its inadequate attempt to warm my troubled soul, to turn our rented flat into a haven of festive delight, pierces my heart with pain. My eyes fill with tears.

Jim is grinning at me too. My head spins. I open my mouth but nothing comes out. Now his face bears an anxious look.

'I know it's not much,' he says. 'We knew that you wouldn't have much time to do it yourself and we thought the place needed a bit of Christmas cheer.' The boys are also looking worried now. They glance nervously at Jim as I continue to stand and stare. 'Do you like it?'

'I ...' But before I can speak, my knees weaken and Jim catches me as I sink to the floor.

'Hey,' he says as he carries me to the sofa. 'What on earth's the matter?'

I'm crying now. Not silent tears, but noisy, distraught ones. They stream from my eyes and pour down my cheeks untram-melled. I can't seem to stop them flowing.

Jim turns to the boys. 'Can you give us five minutes on our own, lads? Maybe take a stroll down to the shop.' He finds some cash from his pocket and hands it to them. 'Get us all some nice biscuits.'

They look so confused and hurt, but I can do nothing to stem the flood. It feels as if every emotion I've ever experienced wants to howl its way out of me.

Jim takes me in his arms. 'Hush, hush,' he says. 'Tell me what's wrong.'

I sob against his chest.

'Nothing can be that bad.'

Still crying, I look up at him. His kind eyes crinkle and that sets me off again.

'You know you can tell me anything. I'll understand.'

The thing that's tearing me up inside is that he will. Jim will understand why I'm feeling like this. He always does.

He holds me tight and the feel of his chest is solid, comforting. Jim says nothing, but he rocks me gently like a child. Eventually, my tears subside until I'm sniffling pathetically.

'Now can you tell me what's wrong?' He looks into my face. I don't want him to see the deceit written there.

'Carter . . .' I say, forlornly.

His forehead creases into a frown.

I can hardly force the words out of my throat, my heart. 'He wants me to leave and be with him.'

Jim takes a deep and steadying breath. When he speaks his voice is calm, level. 'Is that what *you* want?'

'I don't know.' Tears stream down my face.

His arms drop away from me and I sit back on the sofa, still snivelling.

'Do you love him?' Jim asks.

I put my head in his hands. 'I don't know that either.'

'Are you . . .' Jim's shuddering exhalation shakes his body. 'Are you having an affair?'

'No,' I say. 'A kiss. Nothing more.'

I think of lying with Carter on our bed of reindeer skins at the Icehotel, him stroking my face, so innocent and yet so guilty. But when he kissed me just now at Randall Court, I wanted him to. I wanted him to so much.

'I could give you a speech about staying with me, urging you to look at all that you'll be giving up, but how can I?' Jim holds out his hands to take in the flat. 'Compared to him, what have I got to offer you?'

'Don't say that,' I sniff.

'You must have thought it too, Cassie,' he says sadly.

'I don't know what to do,' I cry. 'Tell me.'

'Stay,' he says sadly. 'That's what *I* want you to do.'

If only it were so simple, we wouldn't be having this conversation at all. I know that and Jim knows that.

'Maybe I should go to Gaby for a few days,' I suggest. 'It'll give me time to think.'

'Don't,' Jim says. 'If you leave, then I'm frightened that you won't ever come back.'

'My head feels as if it's about to explode.'

'You've had a wonderful time with him,' Jim says, crouching down in front of me and putting his hands on mine. 'I understand that. He's a handsome bastard and a bloody millionaire.' He runs his fingers through his hair, exasperated. 'But think of all that we've got between us. We want to get married, start a family. That's just around the corner, Cassie. Truly it is. Now that you've made such a success of your business, we can do it. If not next year, then soon. We're so close. Don't be in a rush to turn your back on that.'

Yet we're not close. Not close at all. I want a wedding, a child, a home of my own. I want to be free from debt. I want a cupboard that's not filled with Tesco Value products. We might be able to stretch to one of those things but we are a long way from achieving our dreams. Despite what Jim says, it could be next year, it could be the year after, it could be never. That's the reality of the situation.

If I don't get away to think about this, I know I will stay here. Part of me can't bear to turn my back on Jim and all that we have together. He's right about that. But I also know how different my life would be with Carter and if that sounds totally heartless and selfish, it also sounds very appealing. I wouldn't have to work. I'd walk into a ready-made family. I could have children of my own, straight away, without having to worry where every single penny would come from. I could pay off my credit cards. I could have great, big, fuck-off, fancy Christmas trees. I could have everything that I could possibly want in my life. Apart from Jim.

'Say something?' Jim pleads.

'I'm going to stay with Gaby,' I say softly. 'For a few days.'

'Stay and talk.'

'I can't. It's difficult with the boys here.'

'Is that what this is really about?'

'No, no,' I insist. 'They should stay. They need you.'

'But *I* need *you*.'

'It'll just be for a short while,' I promise. 'I need to get my head clear.'

'What can I say? What can I do to make you change your mind?'

I shake my head. 'I'm going to get a few things.'

'The lads will be devastated too,' he says. 'They think you're great. They need you too, Cassie. This is a critical time for them.'

But I feel that it's a critical time for me too.

It would be so easy to stay. To stay in my life as I know it. Not to cause all this hurt. But would I come to regret it? Not now, not next year, but one day? When times are hard, when Jim and I are struggling to make ends meet? What if we need to find money to pay for IVF treatment? How would we do that? At what point would I look back and think, I should have left him for Carter? I don't know.

What I do know is that Carter's waiting for me at Randall Court with open arms. I could go straight to him. Now. I could

351

throw a bag in my clapped-out car and drive to his door. But I couldn't do that to Jim. I love him too much. And that's the difficult bit, isn't it? Do I love him too much to walk away?

'I have to go.'

In the bedroom I pack a few things. I don't even know what. Yet, somehow, I fill a bag. Jim comes to watch me while I do it. His face, all of a sudden, looks lined and weary.

When my bag is packed, he takes me into his arms again. 'Don't,' he breathes against my neck.

'I have to,' I tell him. 'I have to be sure.'

'I'll be here, Cassie,' he says. 'When you're ready, come back to me.'

I nod. My throat is closed and, anyway, what words could I say to make this right?

'What about your work?' he says. 'There's all kinds of stuff in the diary.'

'I'll sort it out,' I tell him.

'The lads and I will still help,' Jim says. 'This is your busiest period. Don't try to do it all by yourself. You'll make yourself ill.'

'Thanks.' I head towards the bedroom door. 'You're so lovely.' I break down again.

'Don't get in the car while you're upset like this.' His voice is laced with worry. 'Let me drive you to Gaby's.'

'I'm fine. Really.'

Jim's face is bleak. 'You're not going to him?'

'No.'

More sobbing. Jim takes me in his arms and holds me so tight that I can hardly catch my breath. This is the hardest, cruellest thing that I've ever done. It takes all my strength not to unpack my bag and stay. But is that the right thing to do? Is Jim's happiness more important than my own? How can I decide that when I don't even know what would make me happy any more?

Eventually, I have no tears left. I look up and see that Jim is crying too. I kiss his lips, tenderly, then pull away from him. And when I walk out of the door, I don't look back.

Chapter Sixty-Five

I get as far as the end of the road before I have to pull over to the kerb and sob. I was crying so much that I couldn't see a bloody thing and was likely to crash into something or someone. I don't care for myself, to be honest, but I don't want to hurt anyone else.

Should I phone Carter to tell him that I've left Jim to give myself time to think? I stare at my phone through my tears but I just can't make the call. Instead, when I've managed to pull myself together, I limp my way to Gaby's house, sticking to twenty miles an hour and ignoring the honking horns in my wake.

Ten minutes later I'm ringing Gaby's doorbell. Her face falls when she sees the state of me and the bag in my hand. 'What on earth's the matter?' she says, hugging me.

'I've left Jim,' I sob.

'Don't be stupid,' she says.

'I have.'

She leads me into her kitchen where her husband, Ryan, is sitting at the table.

'Hello, sis,' he says. 'What's up?'

'She's left Jim,' Gaby fills in.

He laughs at that.

'No. I have.'

'Have you had a row?' my sister presses me. 'I know that it doesn't often happen in your house, but it is quite normal for couples to fall out. It doesn't mean that you have to leave.'

'We haven't had a row,' I sniff. The tears aren't far away again. 'I've met someone else.'

Ryan splutters his tea out all over the table. He really does.

'What?' My sister is goggle-eyed.

'Carter,' I say, flatly. 'The man I've been away with to Lapland.'

'I know who he is,' Gaby says. 'Carter the red-hot millionaire.'

'Yes.'

'Oh, Cassie.' She looks at me with despair. 'How could you?'

'I haven't done anything,' I say. Not yet. 'But he wants me to be with him and I just can't think straight any more. What shall I do?'

'Drink wine,' Gaby advises and proceeds to shoo Ryan out of the kitchen so that we can talk by ourselves.

I put my bag on the floor and flop down in the warm seat that he's vacated. Gaby eyes my bag. 'I guess you're planning on staying?'

'For a few days. Until I've sorted my head out. Is that OK?'

'Of course, you idiot.' She pours us wine. Red. Big glasses. Then sits opposite me. 'So?'

I knock back the wine. It tastes bitter and too cold, but I'm not in the mood to be fussy. All it has to do is hit the spot and bring me some oblivion. I'm halfway down the glass before I can find my voice. 'We just had the most fantastic trip to Lapland. Everything was perfect. We flew on a private jet, Gaby.'

'You're leaving Jim so that you can upgrade your style of travel to Boyfriend Air?'

That stings, but I hate to admit that there is a kernel of truth to my sister's question. 'It's not just that. It's everything, Gaby. I have strong feelings for Carter, there's no doubt about that.'

'Would you leave Jim for him if he lived in a cramped flat and drove a ten-year-old Vauxhall?'

As always, Gaby has cut right to the chase.

'I don't know. That's why I wanted a few days away to think.' More wine. 'The fact is, though, that Carter doesn't live in a cramped flat, he lives in a great, big, shiny mansion. He drives a great, big, shiny Mercedes. If I went to live with him, I would get all that too.'

'So it's the whole package that's attractive? The life of luxury? The chance to become a WAG?'

I nod even though it pains me to admit my shallowness. 'Who wouldn't want that?'

Gaby sighs. 'Knowing how hard it is for us to make ends meet, I can't argue with that, Cassie.' Her eyes are bleak when she looks at me. 'But Jim? How could you do this to Jim? It'll destroy him.'

'Don't you think I know that?' I put my head in my hands.

'Does Carter love you?'

'He says that he does,' I tell her. 'I've spent only a few days with him, Gaby. I can't tell if his love is for real. It's the same for me. I can't stop thinking about him, that much I know. I adore his children too and I miss them terribly. But is that love?'

'I think love is different things at different times. Love to me now is Ryan and me, working away at the daily grind to provide a better life for our kids. What we want from our own relationship has, largely, been put to one side. For you, it's different. You don't have the glue of children to keep you together.'

'Carter's wife left even though they've got two fantastic kids and, on paper, he's everything a woman could ever ask for.'

'Then you have to ask yourself why.'

'I so want a family, Gaby.' Tears prick my eyes. 'I want to be like you and Ryan, but we've never had the money to be able to start. There's always something else that needs to be paid for.'

Gaby's laugh is bitter. 'That never changes. If people thought about what a couple of kids would cost in a lifetime, no one would *ever* have them.'

'All those problems would be solved with Carter. I'd never have to worry about money again. He wants someone to be at home to look after his children, be a proper mother to them.'

Gaby bristles at that. 'I have to work, Cassie. It doesn't make me less of a mother.'

'You know what I mean,' I say placatingly. 'You're still always here for your kids. Tamara is flying all over the world. She's never at home. Neither is Carter. The kids are both stuck in boarding schools being looked after by strangers and he wants them to come home. He's realised that he was putting his business first and he wants to change.'

'Are you sure that he loves you or does he just see you as the ideal solution to his current domestic problems?'

'I don't know.' I pour us more wine and then start to cry again.

'Oh, Cassie.' Gaby slips onto the seat next to me and takes me in her arms, rocking me as she used to do as a child when I was upset.

'I still love Jim. What am I to do?'

'Sleep on it,' Gaby advises. 'You're exhausted. Perhaps it will all look different in the morning. You'll have to kip down on the sofa.'

'I know. I'll be fine.' She hands me a tissue. I wipe away my tears and blow my nose. 'Thanks. I know I'm a stupid fool.'

'Think carefully before you jump,' Gaby warns. 'You might have a long way to fall.'

Chapter Sixty-Six

Jim was still sitting on the bed, head in hands, when he heard the front door open. For a moment, his heart lifted. Then he heard the voices of Smudge and Rozzer and knew that it wasn't Cassie coming back, full of remorse and realising that she was making a terrible mistake. He wiped the tears from his eyes with his sleeve and tried to pull himself together.

'Jim,' Rozzer shouted out. 'Are you here?'

His limbs like lead, Jim made himself stand up and go into the living room. He tried to paste a smile onto his face, but knew that he was making a bad job of it. 'Hi.'

'Bloody hell.' Rozzer threw down the carrier bag he was holding. 'You look like shit.'

'Thanks.' Jim accepted the comment with a wry glance.

'What's happened? Did you and Cassie have a row?' Rozzer flicked a thumb back towards the door. 'We didn't see her Clio in the car park.'

'Yes,' Jim said. 'We've had a row.' The first big one in living memory. Perhaps if they'd had *more* rows, he might have known how to handle this one.

'Has she flounced off in a huff?' Rozzer asked him. 'My mum used to do that all the time.'

'No,' Jim said. Cassie wasn't a flouncer. She wasn't much of a crier either. But this time it was clear from her demeanour that the situation was breaking her heart as much as it was his. 'She's gone to stay with her sister for a few days.'

'Shit, Jim,' Rozzer said. 'That doesn't sound good.'

'No.' Jim sighed. 'It's not, lad.'

'Is it because of us?' Smudge asked quietly. 'We've not made Cassie fall out with you, have we?'

'No, Smudge.' Jim shook his head sadly. 'It's much more complicated than that.'

'We don't want to be any trouble. You're both the best thing that's ever happened to me.' Now Smudge had welled up too.

'It's not you. Believe me, it would be a lot easier if it was.'

Both lads stood there looking forlorn. Jim was sad for them because he'd so wanted this to be a time for celebration for them. They were out of prison and should both be as happy as Larry. Whoever Larry was.

'She's met someone else,' Jim said baldly. It was better if he just came clean. He didn't want them worrying that they weren't wanted here. The last thing he needed was them going out on the streets or something. He'd rather they were under his roof where he could keep an eye on them. 'The bloke that she went to Lapland with.'

'But you're great,' Smudge rushed in. 'How could she meet someone better than you?'

'I guess I'm not the right person to ask that question.'

The sad thing was that he couldn't blame Cassie. How could he begin to compete with someone like Carter Randall? What could he offer when Randall could give her all she could ever want and gold-plate it at that? All Jim could do was stay here, be as solid as ever and hope that Cassie would eventually see that as a good thing. It didn't seem like her to turn her back on everything that they'd done together, all their hopes and dreams. She was a loyal, devoted woman who'd never given him a moment's pain. He had to hold onto that thought.

He'd loved Cassie since the first time he'd laid eyes on her. Whether she came back or not, he was sure that he'd never stop loving her until the day he died.

'Is there anything we can do?' Rozzer said, interrupting his thoughts. 'You've always been there for us. Now we can be here for you.'

Jim risked a smile, but it threatened to set off his tears again. 'Thanks.'

'Do you want a cup of tea or something?'

'Yeah,' Jim said. It was hard to keep the emotion out of his voice. Cassie was gone and it was possible that she was never coming back. He wondered if he would ever get used to that. 'Tea would be champion.'

'I'll put the kettle on then,' Smudge said. He went to leave the room and then turned back. 'I don't suppose that you'd want a hug or something too?'

'Yeah,' Jim said. 'Why not?'

They both came and wrapped their arms around him. In the middle of the living room, they stood together in a bear-hug. He inhaled the scent of their clothes, their hair – they smelled of washed skin and hair gel – and he felt pleased that the stench of Bovingdale was leaving them. They could be his own boys; he was old enough to be their dad – just about. It was all that he wanted for himself and for Cassie. Now Carter Randall, with a click of his fingers, could give it to her.

The tears flowed again and he wasn't ashamed of crying in front of the boys. Sometimes life dealt you low blows and they were worth crying over. And when the lads both started crying too, he pulled them to him tightly.

Chapter Sixty-Seven

When Gaby and I have finished the bottle of wine, she furnishes me with tea. In the kitchen, I sit and text both Jim and Carter. I let Jim know that I got to Gaby's safely and that I'm not going to contact him for a week to give myself time to think.

He texts back, '*I love u.*' And a line of kisses. Which has me undone again.

When I've stopped crying, I text Carter and tell him that I've left my flat and am staying with my sister. I also tell him that I won't contact him for a week while I get my head clear. He rings me instantly.

'Come to me,' he says without preamble. 'Bring your stuff straight up to the house.'

'I can't,' I say. 'I need some time to get my head round this. I'm not sure what I'm doing, Carter.'

'But you love me,' he says. 'You love the kids.'

I don't think that's in question.

'Think of the life you could have.'

'That's what I am doing, Carter. However, I need to do it by myself.'

I don't need to tell him that when I'm with him all sense of who I really am goes out of the window. I need to make this life-changing decision in the cold, clear light of day. Not in Carter's arms, Carter's house, Carter's bed.

'I want to be with you, Cassie,' he says plainly. 'I'll do whatever it takes.'

'Just give me some space, some time. That's all I ask. You shouldn't ring me for a few days.'

'I love you,' Carter says.

There's a space where I should answer but I can't make myself say the words.

'I'll leave it at that for tonight. Sleep tight, Cassie.'

'And you,' I say. 'Give my love to the children.'

'They miss you.'

'I miss them,' I tell him honestly. 'Goodnight, Carter.' I hang up.

In the living room, Gaby is making up my bed on the sofa. 'You should go home,' she says. 'You have a fantastic man waiting there for you.'

'I know.' I plonk myself down on the corner while she plumps pillows in a disapproving manner. 'This isn't about Jim not being fantastic.'

She sits next to me. 'What is it about then, Cassie?'

'Life has just been so hard, Gabs. I've had a nightmare year. Being made redundant, struggling to get out of bed in the morning to face the day, the constant battle just to pay our bills. I'm tired of it. Tired of it all. Then I start up Calling Mrs Christmas! and I'm finally good at something. On top of that Carter comes along – he's warm, handsome—'

'Loaded.'

'Loaded,' I concede. 'He makes me feel like a princess.'

'Perhaps that's because it's a fairy tale rather than being real.'

'But it *is* real. Carter's for real.' At least I think he is. 'No one has made me feel like this before. He could take me away from the rat race and give me a life that I could only ever have dreamed of. Can I really reject that outright without, at least, thinking about it carefully?'

'Bloody hell,' Gaby says. 'You make me want to fight you for him.'

'He's a very special man.'

'He's a ruthless business entrepreneur,' she counters. 'Someone who goes all out for what he wants. He's also in the throws of a messy divorce. Do you want to be stuck in the middle of that?' My sister sighs. 'Just make sure that he doesn't railroad your feelings. Take time to decide what *you* want. You'd better get some sleep. You look completely exhausted.'

I feel emotionally drained.

'Go up and use the bathroom. Both of the kids are already in bed. They should be asleep, but I expect at least one of them isn't. I'm sure they'd like a goodnight kiss from their favourite auntie.'

Taking the hastily packed overnight bag that I've brought, I head upstairs. In the bathroom, I wash and change into my pyjamas. Then I go through to George's room. He's already asleep, arm thrown above his head, tangled in his duvet. His Moshi Monster's pyjamas have ridden up. I pull the top down to cover his tummy and rearrange the duvet around him. He'll wake up cold in the night otherwise. I smooth his hair from his face and tenderly kiss his forehead. I love these kids more than life itself and wonder for the hundredth, millionth time what it would feel like to have children of my own. How powerful must that love be? How can people like my own mother, like Tamara, take their own children so much for granted? I would bleed for Molly and George and I'm just their auntie. They are both so like Max and Eve, that I wonder if that's why I've become attached to them so quickly.

In Molly's room, I find her still awake and playing with her favourite doll. They're having an animated conversation about biscuits.

'Hey,' I say. 'It's probably time that you were asleep now. School in the morning.'

She hands over her doll and I put it on her shelf for safe keeping. 'Teddy?' When I hand him over, she snuggles down into her bed.

'Love you,' I say. My thoughts go to Carter's children and I wonder if I will ever be able to tuck them into their beds again.

'Love you, Auntie Cassie,' Molly says. She takes in my pyjamas. 'Are you living here now?'

She must've somehow overheard snippets of our conversation. 'Just for a few days.'

'What about Uncle Jim? Where's he living?'

'He's still at the flat,' I tell her.

'Oh.' Clearly this is beyond her comprehension and, to be honest, I'm glad about that.

'I'll see you in the morning.'

'Night night,' she says and her eyes grow heavy instantly.

I tiptoe out and go back downstairs. Gaby and Ryan are watching telly.

'There's nothing on,' Gaby says. 'But we're watching it anyway. We'll have an early night so that you can get some sleep.'

'I don't want to kick you out of your own living room,' I tell her. 'Besides, I don't think that I'm going to be doing much sleeping tonight.'

'Don't dissuade my missus from an early night,' Ryan says to me. 'I was hoping I might have my wicked way with her.'

'No chance,' Gaby says. 'We've got visitors.'

'It's your sister. She'll put her fingers in her ears.'

'I will,' I confirm.

'Who asked you?' Gaby teases.

'By the way,' Ryan says, 'you're totally mad, woman. That's all I'll say on the subject.'

'Thanks.' I know that Ryan is one of Jim's biggest fans. They're as much like brothers as Gaby and I are actual sisters.

Gaby and I snuggle up on the sofa under the duvet. I have no idea what programme we're watching, as the pictures pass in a blur in front of me but don't reach my brain. It takes a huge amount of effort to keep still and not rock backwards and forwards in anguish, or to answer when Gaby or Ryan ask me a question. All the time my mind is whirring and my inner voice chants to me, what I am going to do? What am I going to do? What *am* I going to do?

Chapter Sixty-Eight

Jim was drunk. He could tell. The bar in front of him was swaying about and his glass appeared to be tap-dancing. Even in this state, he knew that wasn't right. The lads, also, were eyeing him with grave concern.

'I'm fine,' he slurred. 'Aslutely fine.'

Rozzer looked around him, worried. 'I think we should take you home, Jim.'

'Jush one more for the road.'

'I think the road has also had enough. Come on, mate. Time to climb the wooden hill to Bedfordshire. We'll treat you to a kebab on the way home.'

A kebab on the way home from the pub with two ex-cons? How had his life come to this? Ah, yes. Now he remembered. Cassie had left him. For a fucking millionaire. That's how. Jim downed the dregs of his pint, just as his legs decided to give way beneath him.

'Right, that's it,' Rozzer said. 'We're going home. Smudge, you take one shoulder, I'll take the other.'

Though Jim could hear himself complaining loudly, they heaved him out of the pub. The cold, fresh air hit him like a slap. He would have liked to say that it sobered him up instantly. But, with hindsight, it didn't.

'Easy does it,' Rozzer said. 'You weigh a ton, matey.'

They made their way down Marlowes, the main street in the town, passing similarly inebriated groups of drinkers. The Christmas party season was full on now and there were clearly gangs of office workers out on the lash for the night. Scantily clad women with tinsel and the remnants of party-poppers round their necks threw up in the gutters or were snogged against the windows of W. H. Smith's. It was such a depressing tableau that suddenly Jim wished he'd drunk even more to be able to cope with it.

If Cassie was gone for good, he'd be back on the dating scene and he could just about remember how very hideous that was. Now he felt miserable. Were these people unaware of what was going on in his life? How could they just carry on partying, loving, living as if nothing had happened when his world had been turned upside down? Could they not feel the pain that he was in? He felt as if it pulsed out of him like a radar. Surely it was so strong that they could touch it, sense it pressing against them? Yet they all seemed oblivious to his suffering.

The Christmas lights, all beautifully strung out along the main shopping street, twinkled in the cold darkness. He didn't want it to be Christmas. It was a season he had come to hate with a vengeance. If it hadn't been for bloody Christmas, then Cassie would still be here with him now.

The lights looked offensive in their garishness. Their overt cheerfulness made him want to lie on the pavement and weep. If it hadn't been covered in so much blood and vomit he might have done just that.

'Come on, Jim,' a voice said to him. 'Give us a hand. Move your legs. We're not far from the taxi rank. Soon be home.'

'What?' Jim said.

'We'll soon be home.'

'You promised me kebab.'

People were always promising him things and not delivering. Cassie had promised him for ever when, in reality, it had meant a few short years until she found someone better.

'I think we're past the point of a kebab,' the voice said. 'Maybe home and straight to bed. You're going to have one hell of a head in the morning.'

'Jim,' someone else said. 'We're worried about you. Help us out here.'

But he didn't want to. A smiley angel grinned down at him from the top of a lamp-post. Her wings fluttered red, yellow, red, yellow. He hated them. An overwhelming rage raced through his body and, out of nowhere, he wanted to smash the angel's silly face in but someone was holding him back. Jim struggled, pushing away from his captors. He lurched across the pavement and started to run towards the angel. Seconds later he was scaling the lamp-post while voices shouted out behind him.

'Oh fuck,' one said. 'Let's get him down before he does any harm or kills himself.'

Either prospect, Jim thought vaguely, held no fear for him. He shinned further up the lamp-post. Seconds later, his hand was on the light-bulb skirt of the angel. He knew that it should be hot, but Jim couldn't feel it burning his hand. He couldn't feel much at all.

'Oh no.' He heard the voice way below him. 'Jim, get down.' Now two of them were pleading with him. He didn't know who they were and it was none of their business anyway. 'Jim. Come down. Now.'

But Jim didn't want to come down. He wanted to stop this stupid, rotten angel from smiling at him. He gripped it firmly and pulled. The angel came away from its mountings surprisingly easily, leaving him holding it in his hand. It was heavier than it looked and, suddenly, he felt unbalanced.

'Oh Christ,' one of the voices said. 'He's going to fall.'

Bugger, Jim thought. He's probably right. And, with that, his grip slipped and, without meaning to, he let go of the lamp-post and toppled through the air. The ground rushed up towards him. It was then that he heard the sound of the siren and saw the blue flashing light.

Chapter Sixty-Nine

When the world stopped spinning, Jim was sitting in the back of a police riot van and, if the cold air had failed to sober him up, then this had certainly done the trick.

He was handcuffed, looking sheepish, with Rozzer and Smudge sitting next to him. 'Why are you two in here?'

'We asked if we could sit with you,' Rozzer said.

'Oh.'

'Fuck, Jim,' Rozzer continued, in a low voice. 'We're in a right mess.'

'What did I do?' he asked.

'Shinned up a lamp-post and pulled a frigging angel down. They're talking about doing you for criminal damage.'

'Oh.'

'Oh? Is that all you've got to say?'

Jim couldn't really think of much more. His head hurt and his mouth felt as if he'd swallowed a small hearthrug. 'I'm sorry.'

'You could lose your job,' Rozzer reminded him, somewhat unnecessarily. 'You can't be a screw with a criminal record.'

Jim was only too well aware of that. Ten years of impeccable service in the prison and it could all end in one moment of madness. Well, it served him right. He shouldn't have been so stupid.

'It doesn't have to be like that,' Smudge whispered to Rozzer.

'We could take the rap for Jim. Tell them it was us what did it and not him.'

'You're on licence,' Jim reminded the lad. Clarity was returning to him rapidly now. 'You'd be straight back in Bovingdale before your feet could touch the ground. That's not going to happen.'

'I wouldn't mind,' Smudge continued. 'You've done so much for me, Jim. I don't want you to lose your job. That would be pointless and you can really help people inside. I'd never have got through my time in there but for you and Rozzer.'

Jim noted the fine lines of scabs down the inside of Smudge's wrists, evidence that he hadn't quite made it through his sentence at Bovingdale unscathed. Even when the external healing was complete, the scars underneath would stay with him for the rest of his life.

'He's right, Jim,' Rozzer murmured. 'We should carry the can for this. You've got so much more to lose.'

'No,' Jim said. 'I'm not even listening. This is my bad. I'll deal with it.'

God, what would Cassie think? If this stupid prank didn't push her into the arms of Carter Randall, then nothing would. Could you see Carter Randall doing something so mindless? No. Neither could he.

'Talk some sense into him, Rozzer,' Smudge said.

'Smudge is right. This could end your career. Let us carry it for you, Jim.'

That almost had him undone. 'You'd do that? For me?'

'You're the best,' Smudge said. 'Those lads at Bovingdale need you.'

And he hadn't given anyone a second thought while he was acting like a prat. He'd been blind drunk and crazy with grief. The price he might have to pay would be high.

The van doors were open and he could see the clean-up operation going on down the street. Drunks were being ushered away. Pissed women too far gone to stand unaided were being escorted to taxis. It was like the Wild West out there and, for a brief moment, he'd been Billy the Kid. Jim hung his head in his hands.

'You tried to fight the copper,' Rozzer said. 'You were well out of your tree.'

'I don't know what came over me.'

'Strong lager rage,' Rozzer said. 'I can't touch the stuff.'

'Right.' A voice boomed out and a policeman stuck his head round the van door. 'Where's my next customer?'

As Jim looked up, the burly policeman did a double take.

'What are you doing in here, Jim?'

It was Graham Banber, another lad he'd gone through school with. The benefits and the pitfalls of being born and bred in the same town were that you knew everyone.

'Had a head-off job,' Jim admitted. 'Drank too much, shinned up a lamp-post and pulled an angel down.'

'We did it,' Smudge piped up. 'It wasn't him.'

Graham looked at the lads sceptically.

'It was me,' Jim assured him.

'I suppose this is the offending angel?' The policeman held up a large object made of plastic, tinsel and light bulbs.

'Yes,' Jim admitted. 'That's the one.' It looked quite pretty after all and he could find no reason now why he'd meant it such harm.

The policeman straightened her tinsel. 'She doesn't look too much the worse for her ordeal.'

'It fell on top of him,' Smudge offered. 'So it didn't hit the ground.'

'I thought it was you up the lamp-post?' Graham said to Smudge.

Even in the darkness, you could tell that Smudge was blushing. Not much of a liar really.

'It was definitely me,' Jim said. 'Moment of madness.'

'These two look a likely pair,' Graham said.

'Lads from Bovingdale,' Jim said. 'I've taken them under my wing.'

'Showing them bad habits?'

'That wasn't my intention.' He gave Rozzer and Smudge an apologetic smile. 'They're good lads.'

'Must be if they were going to take the hit for you.' The policeman raised an eyebrow at Rozzer and Smudge, leaned in and undid Jim's handcuffs. 'Are you fit to stand?'

'Yeah,' Jim said. 'You'd be surprised how sober I am now.'

'On your way then. Don't do it again. Take this as a verbal caution. You just got a get out of jail card, Jim. Literally. Do something like this again and there won't be another one.'

'No.' The cuffs were taken off and Jim rubbed his wrists. 'There won't be any need. I've learned my lesson.'

'Good to hear,' Graham said, helping Jim out of the van. Great, fat flakes of snow had started to drift down from the sky. He and Graham watched them fall to the pavement and remain there for a second before melting away. 'White Christmas,' said Graham.

'Yeah.' Jim thought that he might never want to celebrate Christmas again.

Graham held up the angel. 'I'll deliver your friend back to the council so that they can put her back up.'

'Thanks, Graham. I really appreciate this.'

'No worries, mate. Just don't be a prat again or I might not be able to look the other way.' He clapped Jim on the back. 'Better get yourself home or Cassie will be worried about you.'

'Yeah.'

'How is that lovely lady of yours?'

'She left me,' Jim said.

Chapter Seventy

I don't sleep. Of course I don't. I lie awake and stare at Gaby's living room ceiling, trying to get some sense into my addled brain. When that doesn't work, I put their television on again and watch countless episodes of *Come Dine with Me* with the sound turned down as low as it will go until daylight starts to creep round the edges of the curtains.

When Gaby comes into the room in her dressing gown and with bed hair at seven o'clock, I'm wide awake. 'Coffee?' she asks.

'Please.'

'Sleep?'

'No.'

Her expression says that she's not surprised. When she goes through to the kitchen, I fold up the duvet and stow it with my pillows behind the sofa. I'm obviously planning on staying here again tonight. I follow Gaby into the kitchen where she's clanking about, making breakfast.

'Can I log onto your laptop to check what I'm supposed to be doing today?'

'Sure. I know that I've got three dozen Christmas cupcakes and the same quantity of mince pies to bake later and you're delivering them somewhere.'

I wander over to the worktop where the computer is kept. Jim had the sensible idea of storing everything on Dropbox so that Gaby could access it too and check what she was supposed to be doing. I log in and, not that I doubted it, Gaby's bakery order pops up. Most of what I have to do today is based in the flat and I check my iPhone to see what Jim's shifts are. According to the calendar, he's on an afternoon shift, which means that he should be in work for eleven o'clock. If I get to the flat after that, it's safe to assume that our paths won't cross. While I'm doing my 'thinking', I suspect it's best if we don't meet.

The doorbell rings and Gaby, busy doling out Weetabix, says over her shoulder, 'Can you get that, love? I'm waiting for some last-minute Christmas prezzies from Amazon.'

I pad towards the front door. This *is* last minute for my sister who normally has all her presents bought by July. When I open the door, a man is standing there with an enormous bouquet of red roses all wrapped with festive red ribbon.

'Wow,' I say. 'Are you sure you've got the right house?'

'For Mrs Cassie Christmas?'

I laugh. 'That's me.'

'Happy Christmas,' he says. Then he hands over the flowers and hotfoots it back to his van, eager to get out of the cold.

Overnight a sprinkling of snow has fallen. It's pretty, but it's hardly Lapland. I shut the front door and lean against it while I pull the card out of the bouquet.

'*I love you. Carter XX,*' is all it says.

I take the flowers into the kitchen.

'Was it my prezzies?' Gaby asks.

'Roses,' I say, stunned. 'For me.'

Gaby spins round. 'My goodness. That's huge. There must be two dozen there.'

'Easily,' I agree.

'I take it they're from one of the men in your life?'

'Don't make it sound like that,' I say. Then I sigh. 'But yes. They're from Carter.'

'Are you going to ring him?'

'No. I said that I'd try to stay away from both of them while I sort my head out. I should stick to that.'

'Good luck,' Gaby says. 'Carter seems to be one determined man.'

I look at the roses. They're absolutely beautiful. I think my sister might well be right.

Chapter Seventy-One

When I get to the flat, there's no sign of Jim, which is exactly what I wanted. The boys are in the living room and are already busy at work, boxing up presents.

'Hi,' I say as I throw down my bag. 'Everything OK?'

'Fine,' Andrew mutters. He and Kieran exchange a glance. I feel my lips purse. They both look as shifty as hell.

'What's wrong?'

'Nothing.' Another glance. 'Everything's cool.'

'Okey-dokey.' If that's the way they want to play it.

'Jim's given us the list of what needs doing,' Andrew says, clearly happy to be on safer ground. 'We thought we'd crack on.'

That's so typical of Jim to still think about the business and keeping the lads busy. 'Is Jim all right?'

They both shuffle uncomfortably and look at their feet. Eventually, Andrew says, 'Yeah. He's cool.'

'Good. I'm glad to hear it.'

'Is it really over between you and Jim?' Kieran asks tentatively. There are tears in his eyes and, if I'm not careful, he'll start me off again too. And I've already cried a river.

'I don't know,' I say honestly. 'We're just having some time apart.'

'He's dead miserable without you.'

'I'm miserable without him.'

'Then come back,' Kieran says as if it's the simplest thing in the world.

'It's not that easy.'

Andrew shoots him a look and they both fall silent.

In truth, in such a short time, this doesn't feel like my home any more. I feel the way I do when I'm at Carter's, that I'm an intruder, an interloper.

'You look as if you're doing a good job,' I say more brightly than I feel. 'Can I leave you both to it?'

I've got some bookings to check up on, paperware and balloons to order for a party, a couple of last-minute chefs to book and invoices to send. Which means I can hide myself away on the computer for what's left of this morning. This afternoon I've got deliveries to make and some presents to collect for wrapping. Where once I was all bouncy and sparkly, looking forward to Christmas, now I haul myself wearily, step by painful step towards it. All I'd like to do is lie down on our bed, pull the duvet over my head and never get up again.

Instead, I leave the boys to their tasks and go through to the spare room. I close the door and immerse myself in work, bashing through my to-do list like a woman possessed. The more I work, the less I can think about other things. My phone pings all morning with texts from Carter.

'*I hope you like the roses.*'

'*Call me, I want to hear your voice.*'

'*What are you doing for lunch?*'

I ignore them all. From Jim, there's nothing.

At four o'clock, I pack up my stuff and make sure that the lads have got plenty to do for tomorrow. They help me load up the car with all that I need for the next few jobs. Back in the flat, I collect my bag and coat, ready to leave, but before I go I say,

'You can call me if you've any problems, you know that. Don't hesitate.'

They both stand there looking like lost souls and all I want to do is take them in my arms and cuddle them.

'What are you having for dinner tonight? Did Jim leave instructions?'

Again that glance that tells me something is amiss, but they're not willing to share.

'No,' Andrew says. 'I don't know what we're supposed to do.'

I check in the kitchen and they both trail behind me. 'There's a bag of pasta here.' In the fridge, there's bacon, which I put on the work surface. 'If you fry some onions and the bacon together, then stir in a tin of tomatoes and let it simmer, that will be quick. Grate some cheese and sprinkle it on top. There are some dried herbs in the cupboard too.'

'Right.'

Neither of them moves.

'This isn't about you,' I assure them. 'Really it isn't. It isn't even about Jim.'

'It's about this other bloke,' Andrew supplies.

So Jim has told them what's been going on between us. I suppose they have a right to know.

'Yes.' That seems to sum it up in one uncomfortable nutshell. 'I suppose it is.'

Now none of us knows what to say. They're not my kids, not my responsibility at all. Yet I feel as if I'm letting them both down. Kieran looks like a kicked puppy. The timing of all this is so terribly, terribly wrong and unfair. I want to be here for them as a mentor, a friend, as Jim is, but I seem to be making a total hash of it all.

'I'm sorry. I'm really sorry.'

They both fidget and stare at their feet.

'I'd better go. I'll see you tomorrow.'

Then I let myself out of the flat and my heart hurts just that little bit more.

I do the deliveries of presents, collect some more and then head back to Gaby's house where, hopefully, she will have baked all the required cupcakes and mince pies for tonight's event.

Chapter Seventy-Two

When I pull up outside my sister's house, there's a big, red Mercedes parked on the drive. It looks brand new. I feel like wolf-whistling it as I squeeze past, trying not to touch the gleaming paintwork. It's the exact same colour as my roses.

I open the door to her house, expecting her to have a visitor, but she's alone and is just finishing a twirl of buttercream on a cupcake.

'Top car,' I say. 'Whose is it?'

Gaby licks buttercream from her fingers then grabs a bunch of keys from the counter and tosses them to me.

I catch them on the fly. 'You're kidding me?'

'I took delivery of it an hour ago for you.'

'Why did you do that?' I ask. 'I can't keep it.'

'Then I suggest you ring Carter and tell him that.'

'Oh God.'

'How does he know where you are?'

'I've no idea.' Obviously Carter has ways of finding out.

'He's going all out for you,' Gaby says. 'I'll give him that.'

'This is not what I wanted.'

'Can *I* have it then?' My sister grins at me.

'No.' I smile back. 'Take this seriously.'

George comes into the kitchen. 'That's a *nice* car.'

'It's Auntie Cassie's.'

'No, it's not.' I glare at my sister.

'Someone bought it for her.'

'Not Uncle Jim?'

I glare at Gaby again as if to say, 'Now look what you've started.'

'Is it the same person who bought the flowers?' George wrinkles his nose at that.

'Yes.'

'Could you ask him if he'll buy you a puppy too and I'll look after it?'

'Nice try,' Gaby says to her son. To me, 'No puppy.'

'I have to ring Carter,' I say. Molly is watching cartoons in the living room and, as I have no space of my own, I clutch the keys and march out to the car.

The inside of the Mercedes smells of newness and there's a satisfying clunk when I close the door. It's all black leather and pristine chrome, seductive. Just as Carter intended, I imagine.

I punch his number on speed dial.

'Hi,' he says after a couple of rings. 'How are you?'

'I'm . . . *weird*,' I manage. I wanted to be mad with him, trying to buy me with roses and a car, but now that he's here on the end of the line, I can't be cross.

'Where are you?'

'I'm sitting in the very shiny car that's just been delivered.'

I can hear the smile in his voice when he asks, 'Do you like it?'

'Of course I like it. Who wouldn't? It's beautiful.'

'Good. I'm pleased.'

'But I can't keep it, Carter.'

'Why not?'

'I can't run something like this. I couldn't even afford to fill it with petrol. And I don't want to think that you can buy me.'

'I'm not trying to "buy" you, Cassie. I wouldn't be that crass. It's just that I would like you to have a car that's new and reliable. Something smart and sexy, just like you.'

'It's worth a fortune.'

'That's relative.'

'I'd feel like an idiot swanning around in this.'

'Then I'll get you something else. What would you like?'

'I can't accept it.' I sound firm even though I don't feel it. 'You must take it back.'

'Keep it for a few days. Try it,' he cajoles. 'Then see how you feel.'

I *feel* as if I can't think straight. This car gives Carter an unfair advantage over Jim, which pulls me up short. This is exactly what it's all about when it comes down to it. The proof of Carter's advantage is sitting here in my sister's drive, all shiny and new. I don't have to drive a knackered old Clio with a clunky gearbox any more. This is my future. It's here right now. The roses. The car. My head spins.

'Thank you.'

'You'll keep it?'

'For now.'

'I love you,' he says.

I hang up. But I don't go into the house. I sit in the car, the scent of expensive, new leather filling my senses, and I stare out at the falling snow.

Chapter Seventy-Three

I go through the rest of the week in a daze. Somehow I manage to work my way through all of my commissions, but I couldn't have done it without the help of Kieran, Andrew and Jim.

Yes, Jim.

I haven't seen or spoken to him, but he's been quietly toiling behind the scenes to keep Calling Mrs Christmas! moving along. I can't thank him enough for that and I certainly couldn't have managed without him. I would have had to cancel some of the things I've taken on and I'd have hated to let people down.

Still, it's all nearly at an end. Christmas is looming large and nothing can stop it now. One more week to go and then my work here is done. All the jobs lined up in the diary tail off on 25 December. After a few Boxing Day parties, a scattering of events for New Year's Eve and some taking down of lights and trees, everything ends. January lies ahead like a vast, empty wilderness. The thought makes me go cold.

I haven't spoken to Carter either, though he has constantly called and texted, asking me to contact him urgently. Nor have I driven the shiny Mercedes. The snow is quite thick on the ground now and, strangely, I feel much safer slithering about in my old Clio, clunks and all, than I would in that.

On Saturday, I turn up at the flat, which still looks like a packing warehouse. I can barely see the boys, buried amid piles of paper and ribbons and boxes. They have some Christmas lights to put up on a house this afternoon – the first of several over the next few days – and I'm going to drive them over there and supervise.

When they see me, they both look up, worried.

'What's the matter?'

'Jim,' Andrew says and my heart tightens with fear. 'He's Santa today down at the cricket club and he's forgotten the presents.'

Their eyes stray to six large sacks of presents that are waiting patiently in the corner. I relax. I thought it was going to be something much worse. Presents I can deal with. What I couldn't cope with is if anything had happened to Jim.

'Damn,' I say, relieved and anxious at the same time. 'Has he realised yet?'

'He's just phoned. Can you run them down there?'

'Yes,' I say. 'Text him back. Tell him we're on our way. I'll drop you at the house to fix up the lights on the way back, if that's OK. Let's go.'

So they both abandon what they're doing, jump up, grab the forgotten sacks of presents and we rush down to my car. The Christmas lights and toolbox go in the boot. The boys sit in the back with sacks of presents on their knees. There's another sack of presents on the front seat and one more in the footwell. We speed down to the cricket club in Boxmoor as fast as my little car can go.

Ten minutes later I'm pulling into the car park. We all pile out of the car, load up with the sacks and rush them inside. When I open the door, we're knocked backwards by the noise. It sounds as if a thousand parrots are being strangled. The Christmas party is already in full flow, with dozens of hyperactive children racing around the bar area that looks out over the cricket pitch. The sound level is quite startling and the look on the boys' faces says that they are only happy that they're not required to be elves today.

In the corner, I see a flash of red and look over to see Jim. Amid the hubbub, he's sitting on a large wooden chair in the far corner. I nod to the boys to indicate where he is and we make our way towards him. Thankfully, the children are too busy working themselves into a frenzy to notice the arrival of their gifts.

'Hi,' I say as we reach him. It feels unreal to be meeting up in these circumstances when we haven't spoken for days.

'Sorry,' Jim says. 'I don't know what I was thinking. It was only when I sat down that I realised I'd forgotten them.'

'It's not a problem.'

'I know you've got a lot on,' Jim says. 'I didn't want to put you out.'

'Oh Jim,' I say. Everything in my heart tells me to throw my arms round him and hold him, but my body refuses to comply. I can tell how distressed he is, but he's trying to put a brave face on it. I feel wretched.

'Let's step outside for a minute,' he suggests.

'Boys, guard those presents with your life,' I tell them and they stand by the sacks like nightclub bouncers.

Jim slides open the patio door to the side of us and we step out into the freezing air. I pull my coat more tightly around me. We move out of view from the window and Jim pulls off his red hood and his beard with a weary sigh.

'I don't much feel like being Santa today,' he admits.

I'm shocked by his appearance. His face is grey and looks drawn. It's obvious that he's not eating as, even in this short time, he's lost weight from his cheeks.

'Are you OK?'

Jim shrugs and tries a smile. 'I'd like to say yes,' he tells me. 'But the truth is, I have been better.'

'I'm sorry.' This is my fault. All my fault.

'How are you?'

'Not much better than you,' I admit.

'We're a pair of idiots,' he says.

The wind whips around us, picking up the snow on the ground and in the trees and swirling it into a frenzy, showering us with damp powder.

'Where do we go from here?' Jim wants to know.

'I'm not sure yet.'

'Are you with him?'

'No,' I say. 'No. I'm still sleeping on Gaby's sofa.'

'You shouldn't be doing that,' Jim says. 'You should be at the flat. It's where your work is. This is your busiest time. I'll move out.'

'You've got the boys there,' I point out. 'It's not a good idea to disrupt them again.'

'You're more important to me. Their flat is likely to be ready soon. I spoke to Vincent yesterday and I'm hoping they'll move in before Christmas.'

'That would be nice.'

He looks down at his Santa outfit. 'Despite all this, I can't say that I'm looking forward to Christmas this year.'

'Me neither,' I admit.

'You've still got a lot to do,' Jim says. 'And I've got a couple of dozen crazy kids waiting for me, so we'd better get on.'

He puts his hood back on, then slips his beard onto his chin and jiggles it into place. I think of the night we made love beneath the Christmas tree at the Hemel Hempstead Means Business event with Jim still in his Santa outfit. The night that I first met Carter Randall. How much has changed since then.

Jim slides the door open. 'Keep well, Cassie.'

I put my hand on his arm. My throat is dry and tears sting my eyes. 'I miss you.'

He lets out a weary breath. 'God knows I miss you too.'

I should kiss him. I want to kiss him. Instead, I stand there frozen solid.

The moment passes and we go back inside. I check my watch. 'Come on, boys. We've got lights to put up.'

'I'll speak to you soon,' Jim says.

'Yes.' Now we're awkward with each other again.

'You have to do what's right for you. I understand that.'

I can't speak at all. If I do I might beg Jim to take me back and that would be the wrong thing to do while I'm wired up with emotion.

The boys walk ahead of me and I wave as we leave. Jim sits back down on his chair and pastes a big smile on his face. My heart feels as if it's breaking. This is even worse than when I left the flat.

As we near the door, there's a tug on my sleeve and I turn to see who it is. At my elbow there's a small girl, angelic-looking, about five years old. 'Hello,' I say. 'Who are you?'

'I'm Amy,' she says.

Crouching down, I smile at her and ask, 'What can I do for you, Amy?'

'What did you say to make Santa cry?' she wants to know.

My head snaps up. I look back towards Jim and see that he is, as Amy said, crying.

Chapter Seventy-Four

It's the day before Christmas Eve and I honestly don't know where the time has gone. I've been so flat-out busy that I've almost – *almost* – not had time to think about my current predicament. I've been deluged by a last-minute flurry of present buying, card writing, event planning and goodness knows what else that has had me running full pelt towards Christmas. I haven't had a minute to myself. So much for me having time to 'think'. I've done anything but. In fact, if I'm honest with myself, I've tried to push my decision firmly to the back of my mind.

Of Jim, I've seen nothing. Every day I've wanted to wait for him at the flat and, every day, I've bottled it. I just hope that he's coping all right. The boys have been doing a sterling job and, with a final push tomorrow, we'll have cleared everything in the diary in the nickiest nick of time.

I've been out all day today, so I haven't seen the boys yet, but I've just spoken to Andrew on the phone and he's got everything in hand. I can't believe how much the pair of them have blossomed in the past few weeks. No wonder Jim is so proud of them. He placed all of his faith in them and they've come good for him.

I pull up outside Gaby's house, in my cronky car, and park behind the shiny and still untouched Mercedes. Exhausted, I sit in the car for a few minutes, just breathing. These few days off over Christmas will be very welcome indeed.

Carter, unlike Jim, has phoned me a dozen times a day. It's only because I have no idea what to say to him that I'm not taking his calls. When I talk to him all reason goes out of my head and I find myself agreeing to everything he says. So it's best that I don't talk to him at all. On cue, a text pings in. I stare at my phone and then bury it in the depths of my handbag. I can't deal with Carter now.

Once out of the car, I swing into Gaby's house. She's now given me my own key, which is possibly a bad thing. She's in the kitchen, baking.

'I never want to see another bloody mince pie,' she says by way of welcome.

'My sentiments exactly.' I throw down my handbag.

'Don't get me wrong,' she says. 'The money has been more than welcome in the run-up to Christmas, but can we move on to something else in the new year? Can I do some birthday cakes or something?'

The truth of the matter is that I still haven't had the time or the inclination to consider my future beyond Christmas.

Gaby slides two trays into the oven, wipes her hands down her apron and then turns to me. 'Wow,' she says. 'You look terrible.'

'Thanks.'

'Sit down.' She moves newspapers and magazines from the kitchen chairs. I do as I'm told, suddenly feeling very weary. 'I'll put the kettle on. Will you have a mince pie?'

I shake my head. 'I'm not hungry, sis.'

She slides into the seat opposite me. 'You can't go on like this, Cassie,' she says softly. 'Look at you. You're not eating. You're not sleeping.'

Guilty as accused.

'Much as we love having you here, you can't spend the rest of your life in limbo on my sofa.'

'No.' I start to cry.

'Oh, don't cry.' Her arm goes round me. 'I didn't mean to upset you. I'm just worried for you. We all are.' She reaches out and smoothes my hair from my face, still mothering me after all these years. 'What about Christmas Day? Are you planning to spend it here? Is Jim coming? You'll have to let him know. You can't let him be on his own.'

'He has the boys.'

'Who will feed them? Can't they all come here?'

I think of the fun we've had at Gaby's house at previous Christmases. It's normally my favourite day of the year. I love being here surrounded by my family, the ones I love. How bleak it could be this time. Will it seem even worse as I've spent the past few months helping to create the perfect Christmas for so many of my clients? I can't bear the thought of Jim being alone with the boys. Then again, I can't bear the thought of Carter rattling around in that big house with just him and the children.

'You're running out of time, Cassie. You have to make your decision. It's unfair on Jim to keep him hanging on. If you don't love him any more, you have to let him go.' She fixes me with her eyes. 'He might hurt for a time – you both will – but Jim's a great bloke. He's resilient, Cassie. Give him credit for that. He's handled this like a gentleman.'

'He has, hasn't he?' That doesn't make me feel any better. Worse, if anything. If he'd ranted, raved, threatened, it might have made it easier for me to leave. But he has been stoic, understanding, kind. As always.

Gaby nods. 'It won't take him long to find someone else and move on. Believe me.'

I look up at her, anguished. 'You really think that?'

'I do,' Gaby says. 'You shouldn't beat yourself up too much if you choose Carter. If you can't get him out of your mind, perhaps he is the man for you. Jim won't be alone for ever. You've had a great relationship. One of the best. But, in time, he'll find someone new to love.'

He will, I think. His capacity to love is enormous. Jim will be fine without me.

Then it comes to me in a rare moment of clarity. It's so clear to me that it hurts. I know who I want. And, though there's still pain in my heart at what I'm about to do, I'm absolutely sure that I've made my decision.

Chapter Seventy-Five

I get into the shiny red Mercedes. The engine purrs into life and I blip the throttle. The whole thing exudes luxury.

Light snow is falling when I pull out of Gaby's drive. It's dark, late, and I probably shouldn't be driving at this time of night. I should be curling up on the sofa with Gaby and Ryan to watch television or I should be round at the flat doing some last-minute work. But I'm not. Instead, I'm driving out to Little Gaddesden, to Randall Court, to Carter. I want him to be the first to know about the decision I've come to and it doesn't seem right to say something so monumental, so life-changing over the phone.

It's the night of Carter's big Christmas party and I need to go out and check that everything is all right. I've made all of the final arrangements with Georgina and even had to draft in Andrew and Kieran to help with any unforeseen details as there was so much to do. I wonder if Carter has been calling to ask me to be there by his side tonight as his new partner, but I could never have coped with that.

I head out of Hemel Hempstead, keeping to the tracks in the main road already made in the settling snow, and then turn off to wind up through the country lanes. The flakes splatter against the windows and are swooshed away by the silent wipers. I'm more comfortable in the opulence of this car than I thought I would be.

The seat feels as if it's contoured especially for me and I'm cocooned against the elements. There's been little traffic up here, but the car feels sure-footed even in the snow.

I turn up the iPod to drown out my mounting anxiety. The soothing sounds of George Michael's 'December Song' fill the car. As I climb higher, I have this stretch of the road to myself. It seems as if there's no one else out on a night like this. Quite sensibly. I hope the snow hasn't stopped people from coming out to Randall Court, not after all the work that has gone into putting on the perfect festive party. The trees hang heavily over the lanes, reminding me of the trip that Carter and I took to Lapland. How long ago that seems!

I wonder if the children will be there tonight and whether I'll get to see them. I do hope so.

Before I know it, the gates of Randall Court come into view and, without even a moment's hesitation, I swing into the drive.

What I hadn't anticipated is the queue of cars that's in front of me. Vehicles are also parked all along the verge leading up to the house. Most of them must have come in the other direction from the main road. It seems that the weather hasn't put the guests off in the least. My nerves decide to notch up a gear. I feel like turning round and going home. I try to calm myself by thinking that, with all the arrangements I've so meticulously put in place, nothing should go wrong.

I realise that this perhaps isn't the ideal time to slap Carter with my decision, but when is? I want to tell him as soon as possible. Christmas is right upon us and, if I don't tell him now, then when exactly do I tell him? We'll both have plans to make. All I need is to steal him away for a few minutes.

While this is going through my mind, I'm inching further and further towards the house. The lights are all on in force, making it look absolutely stunning. Icicles of light cascade down the front, making it look like something out of wonderland. The huge Christmas tree by the drive, sparkling for all it's worth, is magnificent.

I come to a halt behind a stream of Mercs, Aston Martins and goodness only knows what else. I wish I was in my Clio purely for novelty value. Yet in this car, I blend in perfectly. A security guard raps on my window. I remember organising this too.

'Do you have your invitation, ma'am?' he asks.

'I'm the event planner,' I tell him. 'From Calling Mrs Christmas! The hired help.'

He smiles at that.

'I've just come to check on how everything's going.'

'Park at the far side of the garages,' he says, pointing out the way. 'I expect you'll want to use the back door.'

'Yes,' I say. 'I do.'

Sneaking in sounds like a much better plan than rocking up at the front door in my jeans and Primark jumper.

So I drive the Merc past the bank of garages and park up. When I turn off the engine, I see that my hands are trembling.

As the security guard suggested, I walk round to the back of the house, my boots crunching in the snow. The sound of party music drifts out across the lawns. That'll be the band I arranged that came so highly recommended. They certainly seem to be getting the party going. I can also hear the animated voices of the guests, bathed in a glow of festive warmth. I stand and watch them through the window, all togged out in their designer gear and dripping with jewels, chatting, laughing, champagne glasses brimming. It looks as if I've organised a good do.

I turn to take in Carter's garden, which is truly spectacular. I stop for a moment as it actually takes my breath away. The plethora of white lights draping the trees twinkle in the darkness. The pergola that has been created looks magical. Cloaked in fresh snow it's simply incredible. All in all this is a job well done and I should be proud of myself. Instead, I have a sinking feeling of dread in my stomach.

The back door is open and, taking a deep breath, I let myself in. The kitchen bustles with caterers who look as if they're doing sterling work. Plates of canapés whizz in and out. I wonder if I should stay here to supervise this, but they seem to be doing marvellously without me. For a moment, I assume there's no one in the kitchen who can help me and then a woman turns towards me. Out of her usual cashmere and jeans, I hardly recognise Carter's assistant, Georgina.

'Wow,' I say. 'You look gorgeous.' She's wearing a silver evening gown and looks stunning. Like a catwalk model.

'Cassie,' she says, 'Carter's been trying to get hold of you for days.'

'I'm sorry,' I say. 'I should have returned his calls. Is everything OK?'

'It's fabulous. I popped in to send someone for more champagne from the cellar.'

'I should be here to make sure everything is running smoothly.'

'Everything's fine,' she says. 'Really. No need to worry. I spoke to Andrew and Kieran earlier and sorted out the few queries I had.'

'You did?'

'They're great, aren't they? So helpful.'

'Yes,' I echo. 'Great.'

I didn't even know that she'd spoken to them and I feel proud that they've been able to assist her without me breathing down their necks.

Georgina takes in my outfit. It's clear that I'm not dressed to party. I look down at myself and suddenly feel scruffy and out of place. 'I just want a quick word with Carter,' I offer. 'That's all.'

'All his guests are here.' She gestures towards the hall, a concerned frown on her face. Her voice is anxious when she says, 'It may be difficult for him to get away. I'm not sure . . .'

'It's important,' I tell her. 'Very important.' It's about my future. 'He'll understand.'

I wonder if Georgina has any idea that the relationship between Carter and me has moved beyond the realms of business. If she does, she gives nothing away.

She relents. 'Of course. I'll go and get him.'

'I'll wait outside,' I say. 'If that's OK. In the pergola.'

'I think that may be a good idea,' she says, then kisses me on both cheeks. 'Happy Christmas, Cassie.' She disappears to find Carter.

I go outside again into the crisp night and wander down the garden. Marvelling at its beauty momentarily distracts me from the task ahead.

In the pergola, I sit on the bench, which is draped with foliage, just as I'd planned, and pull my coat tightly around me. I'm hidden from the house, secreted away in a magical world. It's a clear night, freezing out here, and the moon is high and full. My breath hangs in the air like a cloud. The snow is falling more thickly now, fat, lacy flakes fluttering to the ground. The weathermen have promised us a white Christmas and it looks as if we're going to get one. But I'm not dreaming of a white Christmas, I'm dreaming of something entirely different.

This is the biggest decision I've ever had to make. It will shape the rest of my future. The thought makes me shiver inside. I can only hope that I'm making the right choice.

Chapter Seventy-Six

Before long, I hear the crunch of footsteps approaching and my stomach goes into knots of apprehension. Seconds later Carter pops his head round the foliage. He's turned up the collar of his dinner jacket against the cold. My heart melts when I see him.

If I stand up, I know that he'll take me into his arms and I don't think that I could cope with that right now, so I stay seated. Instead, he comes to sit down next to me.

'This feels very clandestine.' He takes in the pergola. 'It's a romantic and beautiful refuge. I'm sorely tempted to leave it here all year round.'

'I could arrange that for you, if it's what you really want. I'm glad you like it.'

'Oh, Cassie.' He looks at me and sighs. 'What are we going to do?'

I feel tongue-tied, but I have to tell him how I feel. 'I didn't want to come into the house tonight. I looked through the window and saw everyone enjoying themselves and I realised that it's not my world.'

'I'm not sure that it's my world either,' Carter admits. 'There are hundreds of guests in there, eating my food, drinking my champagne, and I hardly know any of them. I'm a stranger at my own party. What's that about?' He reaches out to take my hand and holds it tightly. 'You're cold.'

I feel numb more than cold and shrug his concern away. 'I'm OK.'

He looks as if he doesn't believe it.

'Really,' I add.

'Good.' He toys with my fingers absently. 'The garden looks fantastic. Max and Eve adore it.'

'How are the children?' The question hurts my throat. I long to see them both again.

'Home from school,' he says. 'They keep asking about you.'

'I miss them so much,' I tell him honestly.

'I knew you would.' Carter sighs. It looks as if he's weighing his words carefully before he speaks again. 'I have been calling you *all week*, Cassie.'

'I know. I just had to have time alone to think.' I take a deep breath. 'I've made my decision, Carter.' I turn to him and tears are shining in his eyes.

He holds up a hand. 'Before you say anything more, I have something important that I want to say to you first.' He presses on before I can object, his gaze not meeting mine. 'Tamara has come back. She wants us to give our marriage another try. For the sake of the children.'

He sits there looking forlorn, his face drawn in anguish. I want to reach out and stroke his cheek, but I don't. I want to speak but I don't trust my voice, so we sit in silence, cocooned in the twinkling pergola, cut off from the rest of the world.

'Please say something,' he urges when the silence has gone on for too long.

'I'm glad,' I manage, as tears squeeze out of my eyes and roll onto my cheeks. Carter tenderly brushes them away with his thumb. 'Honestly I am.'

'I love you,' he says. 'You know that. I *do* love you. If the circumstances were different, if the timing were different—' He runs out of words.

'It's the right thing to do.' I can't, however, stop myself from sobbing.

'I owe it to Max and Eve.' His voice sounds bleak as he continues. 'Tamara might be flawed, she might be a pain in the bloody arse, but she's their mother.'

And I, of all people, know all about that. However inadequate your mother might be, whatever her faults, she's the only one that you'll ever have. No one can take her place.

'I desperately wanted to tell you,' Carter said. 'How could I text that to you? I was trying to see you, believe me.'

'I do.'

'Tell me that you understand.'

'Yes.' My body is shaking and only part of it is due to the cold. 'Of course.'

'My heart is telling me to call a halt to this now. To tell Tamara that we'll never manage to patch things up. But my head says that I have to try to make a go of our relationship.' I can feel the pain coming from him. This is not an easy thing for him to do. 'I can't deny Max and Eve that chance. I think of the letter that Eve wrote to Santa and it breaks my heart.'

In Carter's shoes I'm sure that I would feel exactly the same.

'God, I feel wretched doing this to you. Will you be all right, Cassie?'

I nod. The tears still flow, but I turn to say, 'You may not believe this, but I actually came to tell you that I'm staying with Jim.'

'Oh.'

That obviously takes him by surprise. Perhaps a man who is used to getting what he wants would automatically assume that

I would choose him. For a moment, I think that it was a close-run thing. However, I know where my heart truly lies. I know who I want my future to be with, who I want to marry, who I want to raise children with.

We both manage a teary laugh. Carter pulls me to him and wraps his arms around me. Even as I rest my head on his shoulder I feel my resolve waver.

'I'm sorry,' he whispers in my hair. 'This has been so difficult for us both. I never meant it to be.'

'And I never meant to fall in love with someone else.' But it was so very easy to love Carter and his children. So very easy. 'It's always been Jim and that's how I want it to stay.'

'He's an extremely lucky man.'

'I'm not sure he sees it that way right now.'

The snow starts to fall even more heavily now. Flakes whirl slowly to the ground. I hold out my hand, beyond the pergola, and catch one. It melts instantly, gone as soon as it is there. I look up at the sky. 'This reminds me of Lapland.'

'Our trip was a very special time for me, Cassie Christmas. You're so natural and full of warmth, you showed me what I want from my life, for my children. I'll be forever grateful to you for that. How I wish we could have all stayed in that blissfully happy bubble.'

'Me too.' It's a time in my life that I'll always hold in my heart.

'You have a gift for making people's Christmas wishes come true,' he says. 'All the children wanted for Christmas was to be a family again with Tamara and me. Thank you for helping me to see that.'

'The future has to be about what's important for them.'

'I know.' He sighs as if he wishes it could be different. 'I do hope that you'll carry on with your business.'

'I plan to. It's been hard work, but I've loved every minute.'

Some of it more than I should have. 'I couldn't have done it without Jim,' I confess. 'He's held it together for me.' While I've been falling apart. 'Jim and two of the boys from the Young Offenders' Unit where he works. He's given them a chance to turn their lives around and they've really grasped it with both hands.'

'He sounds very noble.'

'No,' I say. 'He's just a nice, ordinary man who tries to do his best for everyone.'

'I'm sure the boys will really benefit from having someone like that in their lives.'

'I hope so. They've done me proud in the business too. It was a risk taking them on but Georgina says they've been wonderful at co-ordinating the party with her. I can't ask for better feedback than that.'

'She told me so. I didn't realise the full extent of their background, though. Sometimes it makes me feel guilty that my children have so very much.'

'That's just life, isn't it? The way the cookie crumbles. The boys just need a break. Basically, they're good kids who have taken a wrong turn. If we can help, I want to get them back on track. I'm going to try to continue the business throughout the year in some capacity so that I can give them work for as long as they want it.'

'If you put your mind to it, then I'm sure you can do it.'

'I hope so. Jim has already arranged for accommodation in Halfway House, a supervised flat in Hemel Hempstead. So they'll soon have their own place to live. It's just a matter of keeping the work coming in now so that they stay out of trouble.'

I look out at Carter's resplendent mansion and think of Kieran having to live in a wheelie bin and wonder why life is sometimes so unfair. My heart surges with pride, with love, for Jim and the boys. They are good people. Really good people.

'It's just like you. Always thinking of others.'

'You're also putting other people's needs ahead of what you want,' I remind him. If it weren't for the children, there's no way that Carter would be trying to patch up his relationship with Tamara. 'Sometimes it's simply what has to be done. It will come right.'

His head rests again on top of mine and he strokes my hair. 'Will we be able to remain friends?'

'I don't think so,' I tell him. 'A clean break is probably for the best.'

'The children will be devastated. *I'm* devastated.'

'There are no winners in this, Carter. But they'll forget me. Children are remarkably resilient. It's their mum who's important now.' I reach into my pocket. 'I've brought gifts for them. Just silly little things.'

There's a pretty, pink bracelet for Eve – not a designer label, but one that I know she'll love. And there's a SpyPen for Max that has a compass, a secret compartment and it writes in invisible ink.

'That's very kind of you.' Carter takes them from me and slips them inside his jacket. 'I'd better get back inside before I'm missed,' he says sadly. 'Or Tamara and I will be having our first row sooner than I'd like.'

'I really hope it works out with her. For everyone's sake.'

'At the moment, she's promising the moon. She says she's going to cut back on her workload, not travel so much. She wants to do more things together as a family. It all sounds like good news, doesn't it?'

I nod but the forced hopefulness in his voice makes me want to cry again.

'I've started to look for a new CEO to take some of the pressure off me. I can't expect it all to come from Tamara. I have to meet her halfway. If we're both going to be at home more, we've even talked of moving the children to a local school. Perhaps if we both try hard enough, it really could work.' He risks a wary smile. 'We'll see.'

He turns me towards him and cups my face in his hands. 'Oh, Cassie Christmas,' he sighs, 'how will I live without you?'

And that's what finally confirmed my decision for me. I could imagine a life with Carter so, so easily, but it was impossible to imagine a life without Jim.

Chapter Seventy-Seven

I ease myself away from Carter. 'I should leave now.'

'I love you,' he repeats, his voice thick with emotion. 'Don't ever forget that. If you ever need me – for anything – you know where I am. You only have to call.'

'Thank you,' I say.

But I know that if I'm going to make my own relationship work with Jim, I can never call Carter again. I can only hope that Jim will forgive me and we can get back to where we were. I have a lot of work to do to regain his trust.

I reach in my pocket and take out the keys to the shiny red Mercedes. 'I can't accept this,' I tell him.

Carter folds my fingers around them. 'Please do. It would make me very happy. Think of it as a small Christmas gift. Something to remember me by.'

That's exactly why I can't accept it. Nevertheless, I put the keys back in my pocket. I haven't the strength to argue about it.

'Goodbye, Carter.'

He grips me in a final tight embrace. 'I'm finding it hard to let you go.'

I close my eyes and breathe in his scent. There will always be a secret piece of my heart reserved for Carter Randall, but that's all it must ever be. Now I want to go to Jim. I want to go to him and love only him once again.

'Goodbye, Cassie Christmas,' Carter says.

We pull away from our embrace. Carter buttons his dinner jacket and flicks up the collar. He's shivering now.

'I'm just going to sit here for a minute longer,' I say. 'Gather my thoughts.'

'How can I walk away?'

'Your guests, your children, your wife are waiting for you. Just leave me here.' I smile at him though my eyes are glistening with tears. 'I'll be fine.'

So Carter stands up, pulls his jacket more tightly around him and says, 'If you ever see the northern lights again, think of me.'

'I will.' Of course I will. How could I not?

He blows me a loving kiss and, with a shake of his head, turns abruptly and strides away across the garden, back to the house.

I watch him go, with a lump in my throat and a tear in my eye, but I feel peace settling in my heart.

I wait for five minutes, unmoving. Then, as I start to lose the feeling in my fingers and my toes, I think that I'd better shift myself before hypothermia sets in. Making myself stand up, I rub my arms to get some warmth back into them.

I cross the garden, leaving behind the special, secret place and skirting the hubbub of the party. At the front of the house, guests are arriving all the time and the drive is filling up with more and more swanky cars. As I pass the security guard, I hand him the keys to the shiny red Mercedes that brought me here. 'Can you please make sure that Mr Randall gets these at the end of the evening?'

'Sure,' he says and pockets the keys.

I check my phone, but there's no signal at the moment. Maybe

406

the weather is affecting it. Perhaps it will be better if I walk to the end of the drive and try again. I can call a cab or, if that fails, walk to the local pub and ring one from there.

The snow is heavy now, settling on my hair. My coat will soon be soaked. I always knew that I would leave the car behind, but I hadn't made any other plans for my getaway. A warmer and more waterproof jacket, at the very least, would have been more appropriate. Better still, I could have asked Gaby to come and collect me. But I didn't think of that. For someone who's supposed to be a professional planner, it seems I didn't think of much at all.

Halfway along the drive, I turn and look back at the house, at the party in full swing. I think of Carter inside with his wife, his children. At an upstairs window, I see a figure. I'm sure it's Tamara, hair piled high on her head. And I'm sure she's staring directly down at me. Then she swishes the curtains closed and disappears from view, shutting me out of her life. That's as it must be.

Turning away from the house, I plod on.

My feet are getting wet too. Snow seeps in through inadequate seams in my 'fashion' boots. Wellingtons would have been an idea. I try my phone again, but still no joy. When I reach the end of the drive and my spirits are dragging on the floor of rock bottom, I look up. Opposite the gates, I see a familiar sight.

Jim's car is parked there and, if I'm not very much mistaken, Jim is sitting inside.

Chapter Seventy-Eight

'Cassie!' Jim is out of the car as soon as he catches sight of me. My heart skips a beat and I could cry with relief when I see his strong, sturdy presence in the snow.

He rushes across the road to where I stand. 'Where's your car?' His face is dark with anguish. 'Why are you out here by yourself?'

In my surprise, I say, 'I could ask you the same.'

'I called Gaby to see if you wanted me to bring you up here to check on the party. I didn't want you driving in this snow. She told me that you'd already gone.' He looks awkward now. 'I was just worried. I wanted to make sure you'd got here all right.'

'Oh, Jim.' Now I can't hold back my tears and I start to cry. He takes me in his arms.

'Hush now,' he says as he comforts me. 'Nothing's that bad that it can't be fixed.'

'I hope you're right,' I sob.

'Is the party going off OK?'

'It's fine,' I tell him. Though, to be honest, it's the last thing on my mind.

'The lads will be pleased. They've been on tenterhooks.'

'They've done a great job. *You've* done a great job. Georgina is full of praise for them both.'

'They've really enjoyed it, Cassie. I've seen them grow in stature over the last few weeks and it's fantastic.'

'I'm pleased for them.'

'Yeah, well . . .' Then he doesn't seem to know what to say. 'I thought you were still at Gaby's because your car was outside. She told me that you've got a brand-new Mercedes now.'

'Did have,' I say. 'Briefly.' I glance back at the house. 'I've just given the keys back.'

'I was frightened I'd see it upside down in a ditch on the way up here. No one should be out driving in this.'

'It hasn't stopped the party-goers,' I note. A steady stream of cars are still turning into Carter's driveway. 'Or you.'

'Well,' Jim says, shuffling uncomfortably. 'I wanted to make sure that you were OK. I didn't like to think of you out in this by yourself.' Then I think it registers with him what I've said and he frowns. 'Why did you give the keys back?'

'Because it's all over,' I tell Jim. 'I came up here to tell Carter. I thought I owed him that much.'

'It's over?' Jim looks as if he can't believe his ears.

I nod.

'*Really* over? You've said no to all this?' He waves a hand towards the house and grounds.

I nod again, unable to find my voice.

'You're coming back to me?'

'If you'll have me.'

His eyes fill with tears. 'You're kidding me?'

'Can I come home?'

'Cassie, that is my only Christmas wish come true.' I fall into Jim's arms and he picks me up and twirls me round.

A BMW turning into Carter's drive toot-toots at us, but neither of us cares. Jim lowers me to the ground but keeps me in a bear-hug, then kisses me deeply. His lips feel so good, so familiar on mine. The snow swirls around us, getting deeper and deeper.

When he lets me go, I say, 'I've been stupid. So stupid. Please forgive me.'

'No more of that.' He puts a finger to my lips. 'I don't care what's happened as long as you've come back. Let's get you out of this cold and go home now.'

I don't think that I've ever heard a better idea.

Chapter Seventy-Nine

This time, as I walk up the stairs towards my own front door, I feel as if I belong here. This is my home and it suits me just fine. I called my sister from the car to tell her that I'm staying at the flat tonight. In my own bed, with my own lovely Jim.

I can hear the television as Jim opens the door and we both turn and smile at each other. Sure enough, sprawled out on the sofa in front of *The Transporter* are Andrew and Kieran.

'Hey,' Jim says. 'Look who I've brought home.'

They sit up straight and spin round.

I feel a bit sheepish now, hand in hand with Jim. 'Hi.'

'You've come back to us,' Kieran says.

I shrug. 'Yes.'

They both instantly abandon the television and come to hug me.

'It's been rubbish without you,' Kieran says.

'Well, I'm back for good now.'

Jim and I exchange a warm smile. And I mean it. Every word. Whatever the future holds, I'm going nowhere without this man by my side.

'You know, we should clear off and let you have the place to yourselves,' Andrew says. 'You don't need us two hanging around.'

411

'Funny you should say that,' Jim grinned. 'I had a call from Vincent while I was sitting in the car at Little Gaddesden. Your flat's ready.'

They both stare at Jim, wide-eyed.

'You can move in tomorrow.'

'Christmas Eve?'

'Yep.'

The lads turn and high-five each other and then it's another round of hugs.

'Our own place, bro. In time for Christmas,' Andrew says. 'Can you believe it?'

'No.' Kieran is close to tears. 'I can't.'

'We'll have a last-night celebration here,' Jim says. 'Crack open some beers and phone for a pizza. Then, tomorrow, Cassie and I can take you down there.'

'Thanks, Jim,' Andrew says. 'You've done so much for us.'

'All I ask is that you stay on the straight and narrow from now on. Don't give Vincent a reason to throw you out.'

'We won't,' they promise in unison.

'Right.' Jim claps his hands. 'Let's find that pizza menu.'

Half an hour later the food has arrived and we're all squashed up on the sofa together, under a blanket, tucking into pizza. The fire is on, the lights are low. *The Transporter* is replaced by *The Muppet Christmas Carol* – a true sign that Christmas is upon us. I can't believe that the boys have never seen it before. Perhaps they thought that they were too cool, but no one is too cool for the Muppets.

We have a few beers together and the boys toast my homecoming. I look around as they're all laughing at the antics of Miss Piggy and realise that we've grown into a family, as unlikely as that is. The thought brings a lump to my throat. Tomorrow I'm going to decorate the flat. Properly. The small tree that Jim and the boys put up can go into the hallway outside the flat to brighten it up, but I'm going to go big in here. Full-on festive. I shouldn't forget that, despite the ups and downs, this year I have a lot to celebrate. There are only a few bits left to do in the diary, so I'll have plenty of time. If people haven't got their Christmas planned now, then it's too bad. We can take some decorations down to the boys' new home too and spruce that up. I don't want it to be bare for them over the festive holiday.

I look around at our small, cramped living room and feel more content than I've ever done. I realise that I could never have lived in Carter's world. It is too glamorous, too superficial. I'd rather be here with Jim and the boys, watching a film on telly and eating takeaway pizza than at a champagne-fuelled party with people I don't know. This is what's real and I'm glad that I came to my senses before it was too late.

Silent tears course down my cheeks.

Jim turns to me, concerned, and whispers, 'OK?'

'Never been happier,' I assure him and he squeezes my hand beneath the blanket.

Eventually, all this emotion starts to take its toll and, as the credits are rolling, my eyes roll too.

'Let's go to bed,' Jim says. As the boys settle down for the night – one on the sofa, one on the floor next to it – he takes me by the hand and leads me to our room.

He undresses me slowly and carefully as if he still can't quite believe that I'm here. Then we make love, tenderly, silently. Afterwards we lie in the dark, wrapped in each other's arms. This is where I belong. I sigh to myself, happily, and settle against Jim's warm body.

I'm home, I think. I've finally come home.

Chapter Eighty

Vincent gives each of the boys a key and we walk up the stairs behind them to their flat, carrying boxes. Not that they have all that much to move in.

I was up very early and slithered down to the supermarket in my trusty old car. With all that's been going on I've barely given a thought to our own Christmas and I realised that I had no food, no nothing, in the cupboards. I also desperately needed to buy the boys a few bits. How could they move in here without some basic provisions? All they have is what they stand up in.

I've filled a box with groceries and store-cupboard staples to get them going. In another box there's a small, starter dinner service and some mugs. I also got them a cheap kettle and a toaster too. After Christmas, we'll see what else they need and buy it in the sales. Due to the success of Calling Mrs Christmas! there's plenty of money in our bank account – for once – and we can afford to help them out. Which is really nice. After all, a lot of what I've been able to take on has been due to the boys stepping up to the plate and throwing themselves into speed-learning skills they never knew they could master. I do, however, recognise that the success of my business very nearly cost me everything and vow that I won't make that mistake again.

Kieran slips his key into the lock. I notice that his hand is shaking as he says, 'This is the first time I've ever had my own key.'

He's grinning from ear to ear and Kieran isn't a boy who smiles easily. His cheeks are pink with excitement. It's nice to see that his grey pallor has finally started to leave him. Due to a diet of regular home-cooked meals, he's also started to fill out a little and doesn't look quite so gaunt either. Jim and I will have to make sure that the lads are still eating well when they're on their own, but I suspect that they'll still have more than the occasional meal with me and Jim at the flat. Wait until I've got time to cook a Sunday roast again. They won't be able to stay away. I hope so, anyway.

The door swings open and we all troop inside. The living room is stark, bare, but I know that with a bit of effort we can make this into a home for the boys. I've brought with me a pretty artificial Christmas tree and some decorations. While Kieran and Andrew are settling in, I can get started with that.

I've also bought them each another little gift this morning, which I've wrapped up and am itching to give them. For now, I just enjoy watching them as they wander through the flat, speechless.

'This is ours,' Kieran says eventually. He looks around in wonder, as if it's Buckingham Palace. 'This is really ours.'

He sits on a bed in one of the tiny bedrooms.

'A little present.' I hand over one of my packages. 'There's one for you too, Andrew.' Andrew takes it, suddenly bashful.

Kieran enthusiastically rips off the Christmas paper. 'I can't remember the last time anyone bought me a present,' he says shyly.

'I thought he could keep you company if you're having a bad night.'

Inside is a teddy bear. It's a traditional bear, furry and brown with a kind face.

Kieran crumples up, hugging the bear tightly. 'I've never had a teddy bear. Not ever.' He sobs as if his heart is going to break.

Jim and I sit down next to him on the bed and cuddle him while he weeps.

'This is the start of a great future for you, lad,' Jim says softly. 'If you want us to, we'll be with you every step of the way.'

'I can't manage without you.'

'You've got me too,' Andrew says, choked. 'We'll be all right, mate.'

When Kieran's tears abate, he thanks us again.

'Come on,' I say, chivvying him up. 'We've got a lot to do. Shall we crack on?'

The boys nod. I also ran into TK Maxx this morning and bought some cheap bedding. The duvets are thin and we'll probably have to replace them with something a bit more substantial, but they'll do for a week or two. I find the right box and give them a bundle of bedding each.

While the boys are making up their beds, Jim assembles the Christmas tree and stands it by the window. It's about five feet tall and is fashioned to look like a fir with snow on it. Already the cheerless room looks better. Cushions, I think. The boys need some cushions and a few more homely touches to help make this rather dreary flat into a home.

I'm just lifting the Christmas decorations out of the box when Kieran and Andrew come through from the bedrooms.

'Wow,' Andrew says when he sees the tree. I think it might set Kieran off crying again.

'Want to decorate it?' I ask. 'You're the experts now. I'll make a start on the kitchen.'

So I hand over my duties and leave them with the overflowing box of baubles and tinsel.

Jim is already cleaning out the kitchen cupboards with some Cif when I join him. He's wearing yellow rubber gloves.

'Did I ever tell you that I find the sight of a man cleaning in rubber gloves a real turn on?'

'No, you didn't,' Jim says. 'But I'll keep that in mind for future reference.'

I wind my arms round his waist and lean my cheek against his back. 'I left the boys decorating the Christmas tree.'

'I think they'll be all right here,' Jim says. 'Vince will look after them.'

'So will we.'

'I'm a bit worried about what they will do for work come January. I don't want them to have to sign on for benefits. I'd like to see them both in gainful employment.'

'We've got a few bits and bobs in for January, but I'm hoping that I can carry on the business throughout the year. I thought I'd see if there was a market for a birthday planning service and I've become a dab hand at organising events. Even in a short time, I've made some great contacts.' I don't dwell on the fact that my best contact will have to be strictly off the radar from now on.

'One thing I've discovered, Cassie, is that if you set your mind to it, then it will happen.'

'Thanks, Jim. That means a lot.'

He turns and pulls me to his chest. I rest my head against him. How could I have even thought about walking away from this man?

'I know the past few months haven't been easy but I feel that I've learned so much. I've found out a lot about who I am as a person and what I can achieve. I've also realised what's important to me and I won't forget that in a hurry.'

417

'It's Christmas, Cassie. Let's not think about what's gone wrong or what might have happened. We should simply count our blessings and have some fun.'

I smile up at him. 'Sounds like a plan.'

'Shall we go and see how those lads are getting on with the tree?'

'Yes. Let me make us all some tea.'

I also bought mince pies at the supermarket for us, but I'm never ever going to tell my sister that Mr Kipling has temporarily taken precedence over her home-made ones.

So I find the new kettle in one of the boxes and plug it in. I search out the mugs too and I put the tea bags, coffee and sugar in the cupboard that Jim has just wiped.

When the tea's ready, we carry it through to the living room. Jim balances the box of mince pies on top of one of the mugs. Trays, I think. They need a couple of those too.

In the living room, I'm pleased to see that the boys have just about finished. Andrew is draping the last bit of tinsel and Kieran has a large silver star in his hand. They're bouncing around like overexcited children and Jim and I exchange a relieved glance. It's going to work out for them here, I'm sure. It's amazing to see how far they've come in the short time since I've known them. All the swagger and surliness, the prison attitude, has gone from them and they're just two boys in need of love, affection and direction.

'We should have a topping-out ceremony,' Jim says.

Kieran glances at Andrew and, when he nods, he hands the star to me. 'You should do it, Cassie. After all you're Mrs Christmas.'

'So I am.' I beam at them. 'Someone get ready to turn on the lights.'

'Jim,' Andrew says. 'You should perform the switching on of the lights.'

418

'Makes me feel like a celebrity.' Jim gets into place. 'Ready!'

Taking the star, I stand next to the tree. My throat is tight when I say, 'I place the star on this tree, to shine love and laughter on this home. May you both be very happy here.'

I slot the star into place and Jim flicks the switch on the lights. They twinkle out hopefully.

'A toast,' I say. 'We need a toast.'

Jim hands round the tea and we break out the mince pies.

I lift my mug high. 'Happy Christmas, boys,' I say. 'Happy Christmas to us all.'

When Jim, Andrew and Kieran lift their mugs and I hear them echo 'Happy Christmas!' I feel my heart wants to burst with joy.

Chapter Eighty-One

We stand at the door of the boys' flat. 'If anything goes wrong, ring me,' Jim instructs. '*Anything*. Please. Whatever time of day or night. I've always got my mobile on. So has Cassie. Don't struggle on your own.'

'We'll pick you up at about eleven o'clock in the morning to take you to my sister's house for Christmas lunch,' I add. 'Is that all right?'

Both of the boys nod, but they look terrified by the prospect.

'Are you sure you'll be OK?' I think it's the third time he's asked them, but I can tell that Jim is anxious about leaving them on their own. 'If you're going to have a beer, make it one or two. No more. I've told Vince that you're reformed characters. I don't want you drunk on your first night here.'

Andrew grins. 'I don't think you need to lecture us about drinking, Jim.'

Jim flushes. 'Yeah, very funny.'

I look at them, perplexed, but no one lets me in on the joke.

'We'll just have a couple,' Kieran promises. 'We've got to have a little celebration.'

'No pot,' Jim warns. 'Not even one small spliff. If Vincent catches even a whiff of it, you'll be out on your ear quicker than you can say "high".'

'We won't, Jim,' they swear.

'Just relax. Watch some telly. Go down to the communal lounge and meet the other lads. Enjoy the place,' Jim says. 'See you in the morning.'

I hug them both. 'Sleep well. Enjoy your new home.'

I slip my hand into Jim's as we walk away, aware that they're both at the door watching us. We turn and wave, then disappear down the stairs.

Back in the car Jim lets out a shaky breath. 'Didn't think this would be so hard,' he says. 'If we had the room, I'd want them with us.'

'You can't watch them every five minutes,' I point out. 'You have to let them fly. I'm sure they won't let you down.'

'I hope you're right, Cassie. I couldn't bear to see either of them back in Bovingdale.' Then his voice catches and I squeeze his hand. With that, he breaks down and cries. He puts his head on the steering wheel and sobs while I hold him.

I think this is the past few weeks catching up with him. Jim is always so stoic, so strong, but there's only so much a person can take and I bitterly regret my part in this. 'I'm sorry,' I whisper into his hair. 'I'm so sorry.'

When he's finished crying, we hug each other and I wipe his face with the tail of my blouse.

Jim settles back in the driving seat and gives me a watery smile. 'Now, Mrs Christmas, do you want to go and get that big Christmas tree you talked about? I can't have you with the least-decorated home in the land.'

'Make haste to the nursery,' I tell him. 'But, first, there's just one more stop that I need to make.'

A few minutes later we pull up outside Mrs Ledbury's home. I leave Jim in the car while I run across the road and ring her doorbell.

'Hello, dearie,' she says when she comes to answer it. 'How lovely to see you. Have you come for a cup of tea?'

'No,' I say. 'I can't stay. I've got masses to do. I just wanted to ask you what your plans are for tomorrow.'

She looks at me, puzzled. 'Why, nothing.'

'No visitors?'

Mrs Ledbury shakes her head. 'No.'

'You can't have Christmas dinner alone,' I tell her. 'I'll send Jim for you in the morning. You're coming to my sister's house with us.'

'I couldn't possibly,' she says. 'I've got food in. I'll be absolutely fine here.' But she can't fool me, I saw her eyes light up at the suggestion.

'I won't take no for an answer,' I insist. 'You can eat what you've bought on Boxing Day. You're coming and that's that. Have your glad rags on and he'll be here just before midday.'

'If you're sure,' the old lady says. 'I don't like to impose.'

'We'd love to have you.'

I haven't actually told Gaby that there'll be an extra guest yet, but knowing my sister she won't mind at all. Like me, she wouldn't want to see anyone at home alone on Christmas Day. Besides, the tiny Mrs Ledbury hardly looks as if she's going to eat Gaby out of house and home.

'Oh, my dear,' she says, 'how kind. I had to admit that I was dreading it just a little bit. The cottage can be very quiet at the best of times.'

'We'll make sure you have a nice time and Jim will bring you home afterwards too.'

'You're a lovely girl, Cassie.' She rests a papery hand on my arm. 'Thank you for thinking of me.'

I kiss her soft cheek and skip back to the car.

'All done?'

'To the nursery,' I say and we head off to choose our Christmas tree. I've got boxes and boxes of decorations going spare and I want to make the flat look lovely.

'I feel terrible, I haven't even bought you a present,' I say to Jim as he drives.

'You're home.' He takes my hand in his and says, 'That's the only gift I need.'

I hear the happiness in his voice and that's the only gift I need too.

Chapter Eighty-Two

Together Jim and I carry the tree up the stairs to the flat and wrestle it round the angle of the stairwell. It looked quite small in the field behind the nursery, but now that we've brought it indoors, it seems a lot bigger.

'Are you sure this is going to fit?' Jim voices my thoughts. 'I think you've got used to doing things on a bigger scale.'

'It'll be fine,' I assure him whilst panicking inside. The smaller tree that the boys decorated is already brightening up the landing and this is to replace it, but I'm dreading the moment when we liberate the big one from its tight net sleeve.

We manhandle it through the door of the flat and into the corner of the living room, which, even in its current state, it fills handsomely.

'Here?' Jim asks, puffing heavily.

I nod and Jim sets the tree into the new stand we've bought, while I go to find the scissors. With a second of trepidation, I cut open the net sleeve. A multitude of branches spring free from their confinement. Not only is it much taller than it looked, but it's also much thicker. The intoxicating scent of pine is almost overwhelming. It's a beautiful specimen and, because of the number of trees I've ordered from the nursery in the last few weeks, I was given a great price. It dominates our small room, making us both laugh out loud.

'Well,' Jim says, 'I think it makes a statement.'

'It's enormous,' I agree.

'I could chop some off it,' he suggests.

'That would be a shame. Can't we just leave it as it is? It's fun.'

'I'm worried that it might come alive in the night and kill us as we sleep in our bed.'

I laugh. 'Get the decorations and we'll make a start. I only hope we've got enough.'

'Shall I phone the lads?' he says as he heads towards the stash of decorations in the spare room.

'If you want to.'

So while I wind two sets of white lights round the monster Christmas tree, Jim phones Andrew. As we left less than two hours ago, he assures Jim that they're both absolutely fine. Relieved, Jim joins me to help with the decorations.

Even though my tree-dressing skills are now finely honed, it takes an age for us to finish. But when I stand back to admire my handiwork, I get a lump in my throat as it looks so good. Jim twines his arms round my waist and I lean back against him.

'That looks fantastic.'

He's right. It might take up half the room, but it seems to embody the spirit of Christmas perfectly. It's big, it's brash and its totally OTT, but it warms the flat completely. The lights twinkle in the gathering darkness.

'Look at the time.' We've spent the latter part of the afternoon on the tree and now the evening is looming. My stomach rumbles. 'We've had nothing to eat since that mince pie this morning. I bet you're starving. What shall we have for dinner?'

'I'll whip something up,' Jim says. 'You tidy away the boxes.'

I agree to the deal because the last thing on earth I want to do is cook. Jim heads to the kitchen, while I gather up any remaining decorations and take the boxes into the spare room to stash away. For the final time before Christmas, I check the diary. I make a few calls and leave voicemails for the chefs who are going to provide sumptuous Christmas lunches for my well-heeled clients, just to remind them where and when they're due.

Carter, of course, is on the list and I run my finger over his name as I dial the number of the chef I've booked for him. I get a pang of longing that I push down. I hope that he and the children have a great Christmas, I truly do. I can't help but wonder what I'd be doing now if I'd made a different decision and had chosen Carter, if Tamara hadn't gone back to her family. Who knows? I guess a part of me will always wonder what might have been. It's only human. But it's now up to me to make the very best of what I do have.

I leave a message for the chef, telling him that Carter Randall is a very special client and he should make them the best Christmas lunch he's ever created. Then, that's it. I hang up. Close the diary. Calling Mrs Christmas! is finished for the season. All I have to do now is relax and enjoy my own Christmas.

When I go back through to the living room there are two champagne flutes sitting on the coffee table. Not proper ones like Carter would have, but plastic ones that we use for picnics. Jim pops the cork of the bottle he's holding.

'Wow! Champagne. We're pushing the boat out.'

'That's because we can,' Jim says. 'You've made quite a lot of money in the last couple of months, Cassie. I thought we should at least celebrate your success.'

'I'm all for that.' We clink our glasses together. Well, as they're plastic it's more of a clonk. 'To us.'

'Yes. To us,' Jim echoes. We swig our champagne. 'To go with it I've prepared a fabulous dinner.'

He disappears into the kitchen and comes back with two trays bearing beans on toast. 'No expense spared.'

'It looks perfect,' I tell him. And it does.

We sit on the sofa in front of the television, eating our beans on toast and watching *The Polar Express* through the branches of the voluminous and twinkly tree.

When the film finishes, we push the trays aside and cuddle up together.

'Let's make next year a good one,' Jim says softly. 'Whatever you want to do, we'll do. We can get married, start a family. We'll find the money somehow. Why wait?'

'I'd like that.'

'Then let's do it.' He takes me in his arms and kisses me deeply. My body yearns for him.

'I love you,' I say.

'We could make a Christmas baby,' he whispers against my neck.

Moments later we're on the rug and, when we make love beneath the Christmas tree, I know that everything is going to turn out fine.

Chapter Eighty-Three

On Christmas morning, we arrive at my sister's house at nine o'clock, still a bit bleary-eyed due to our champagne extravaganza last night, but there's no doubt that we're also feeling loved up. Even in the short distance from the car to the front door, Jim wraps his arms around me.

'Merry Christmas!' Gaby grabs us both in a warm embrace the minute we walk in. 'They've been up for hours,' she says, with a nod of her head towards the living room. The sounds of two boisterous children bellow out. 'My seasonal goodwill has been sorely tested. I was screaming at them to get back in their own beds at four this morning.' She rolls her eyes. 'You can entertain them now while I get cracking with lunch. I've made them save some presents. Good luck.'

My own Christmas shopping hasn't been done in my usual leisurely manner this year. It's been fitted in while I've been browsing the internet for perfect gifts for my clients. I have, however, found some great presents for my family too. George and Molly will get the latest must-have toys, which will guarantee me my place as Favourite Auntie for another year.

We're hardly through the door when the children barrel into us. 'Auntie Cassie,' Molly says. 'You must come. Look what Father Christmas brought me.'

As she pulls me by the hand towards the living room, I say over my shoulder, 'There's one extra guest for lunch, sis. Mrs Ledbury.'

'Your client?'

'Is that OK? She was going to be on her own and I couldn't bear it. I said that Jim would pick her up after the boys.'

'That's fine. I've got an emergency present tucked away and there's enough here to feed the five thousand.'

'Want me to give you a hand?'

'I think you're going to be busy on present-opening duty for a while, but when you've got a minute that would be nice.' Jim has already disappeared with George. 'Your gifts are under the tree. I'll come in when you get to those. Give me a shout.'

So, towed by her daughter, I leave Gaby in the kitchen and go through to the living room. My sister's home, always immaculate, looks as if a bomb has gone off in it. Wrapping paper is strewn everywhere and we might easily be in an overstocked branch of Toys Я Us. Ryan is sitting in the middle of it all, shell-shocked.

'Is Christmas over yet?' he says, stunned.

'Nearly,' I tell him. 'Hang on in there for a few more days.'

'Days?' He groans. 'Is it too early to start drinking?'

'No,' I assure him. 'It's Christmas.'

I sit on the floor with Jim amid the multitude of toys, feeling overwhelmed already. Molly and George sit with us and attack the remaining pile of gifts with gusto at the same time as showing us what they've already got. I can only wonder when they'll get time to play with it all.

For a moment my mind strays to Carter and the children. I wonder what they're doing now. Is their Christmas more subdued than this? I hope that they're having a great time, surrounded by love, and they're all happy. Then I force my mind away from them before I start to feel sad.

Jim glances over at me. 'OK?'

I brighten the smile on my face. 'Great.'

'These are for you,' Molly says and proudly hands us two prettily wrapped parcels. 'I did that.' She points at the bow on mine. 'With Mummy's help. A very little bit of help.'

'Well, it looks lovely.'

Gaby comes in with a tray of Buck's Fizz for the adults and orange juice in posh glasses for the children. Jim has just a small glass of the fizz as he'll be driving again later. 'The turkey's coming along nicely,' she says. 'I can relax for five minutes now.'

We raise our glasses and make a toast together, shouting, 'Merry Christmas!'

I open my present from Gaby and Ryan. It's a jewellery tree made out of crystal. 'How beautiful. Thanks, Gaby.'

'I'm hoping that you might have a little extra something to put on it this year.' She winks theatrically at Jim.

'You might be lucky, sis,' he replies.

Gaby's eyebrows shoot up. 'Really?' She spins to look at me.

'No announcements today,' I say, 'but watch this space.'

'That deserves another toast,' she says. 'To watching this space!'

We all laugh and join in. Jim and I exchange a secretive glance. When the dust settles, I need to sit back and take stock of how much money Calling Mrs Christmas! brought in and then we can make plans for next year. I'm sincerely hoping that one of them will involve the sound of wedding bells.

Gaby swigs her champagne. Clearly all this toasting is giving her a taste for it. 'We should all go out together and have a knees-up when the madness of Christmas is over, have a proper catch-up.'

'Sounds good,' I say. What Gaby means is that she wants the lowdown on any hint of wedding plans.

Turning back to our presents, Jim gets a Dennis the Menace

mug and a kit to make a chocolate pizza, which he's delighted with.

We listen to Christmas songs and drink more Buck's Fizz and play with the children's toys. Uncle Jim is soundly thrashed at Operation.

'I'd better think about going for the boys soon,' Jim says, checking his watch.

We didn't call them when we got up in case they were still asleep, but, hopefully, they're up and about now. It sounds stupid, but even though we settled them in their own place only yesterday, I can't wait to see them.

'I want that paper cleared away,' Gaby says to the children. 'We've got guests coming. Shall we go and see what's happening in the kitchen, Cassie?'

Jim and I trail after her. It looks to me as if Gaby has got everything in hand and the turkey is starting to smell delicious already.

'I'll be off then,' Jim says, kissing my cheek.

'Can you pick up Mum too, Jim?' Gaby asks.

'Of course,' he says and disappears out of the door.

I take a piece of peeled carrot out of the pan and eat it. 'She *is* coming then?'

'Yes,' Gaby says. 'As far as I'm aware. No cancellation phone call as yet.' She smiles at me. 'You know what she's like. Be nice to her.'

I sigh. 'I will. Something made me realise the other day that no matter what her faults, she's the only mum we've got.'

'She might not have been there for us when we needed her,' Gaby says, 'but we turned out all right, didn't we?'

'Thanks to you.'

'One day we'll want to phone her and she won't be there.' My sister busies herself taking packets out of the fridge and freezer. 'Let's make the best of her while we can. She does try.'

'No she doesn't.'

We both laugh at that.

'You're right,' Gaby agrees. 'She doesn't. But it's Christmas, so let's put all that behind us and have a good day.' She hands me a packet of ready-made pigs in blankets, which I slice open and arrange on a baking tray. 'Is everything all right between you and Jim now?'

'Yes,' I say. 'I hope so.'

'No regrets?'

'Only that I caused such a mess in the first place.'

'Are you sure that you're where you want to be now?'

'Yes.'

'I'm glad. I couldn't have stood for you to leave Jim.'

'As it happens, me neither.'

'And Carter was all right about it?'

I shrug. 'He's going to try to work things out with his wife. I hope he does. I don't think that I'll be hearing from him again.'

'Just as well. Make this Christmas a new start.'

I go and hug my lovely sister. 'Thanks for putting up with me. I don't know what I'd do without you. It was something you said that made me see sense.'

'Thank goodness for that!' she says. 'I just want you to be happy.'

'I am.' I sigh contentedly. I'm here with Jim, with my family. What more could I ask for?

Chapter Eighty-Four

Jim's car pulls into the drive. 'They're here,' I say to Gaby who's currently tasting the gravy.

'Aprons off!'

I finish peeling the parsnip in my hand and do as I'm told.

'More fizz at the ready.' Gaby grabs the glasses.

I don't point out that our boys are, quite probably, more WKD than Moët & Chandon.

Jim rings the doorbell and I go to answer. Behind him, Kieran and Andrew are gently helping Mrs Ledbury up the path.

'Your mum wasn't ready,' he says, raising an eyebrow. 'I've to go back for her in half an hour.'

That is so typical of her.

'What lovely boys,' Mrs Ledbury says. They pause while she tackles the doorstep. 'They're so kind.'

I kiss her on both cheeks. 'Merry Christmas, Mrs Ledbury. You look really lovely.'

It's clear that she's taken care with her hair and has put on a little bit of make-up. She's wearing a very festive red twinset with her pearls and a long black velvet skirt. Very stylish.

'Thank you, dearie.'

'This is my sister, Gaby.'

'It's so very sweet of you to have me in your home.'

'You're more than welcome,' Gaby says, taking Mrs Ledbury's arm and leading her into the living room.

Then Jim stands aside. 'You might not recognise these two.'

The boys stand in the hall, bashful. Jim's right. I hardly know them at all. 'Blimey,' I say. 'You two scrub up well.'

Kieran blushes furiously. 'We went shopping yesterday,' he says. 'Rozzer ... Andrew ... thought we should.'

They're both kitted out in new shirts and smart trousers. Their trainers have been scrubbed clean. Both have washed and combed their hair. They're freshly shaved and their faces shine. It's clear that they've dressed to impress.

'Well, you both look great.'

'We bought them and everything,' Kieran says earnestly. 'No nicking.'

'I'm pleased to hear it,' Jim answers wryly.

Kieran looks down, admiring his own shirt, stroking the front of it. 'Rozzer helped me to pick it out.'

'He has excellent taste,' I assure him.

'We bought some presents too,' Andrew says, lifting the carrier bag in his hand to show me.

'With the money we got for working for you and Jim.' Kieran's eyes shine with excitement.

'It seemed only right,' Andrew adds.

'We didn't expect anything,' I tell them. 'But it's very thoughtful of you. How did your first night in your own flat go?'

'Cool,' they say in unison.

'Vince had organised a quiz in the lounge, so we met a few of the other lads, had a beer together. Just one, Jim. Honest. It was well sick.'

'And Kieran slept right through the night.'

'I did,' Kieran says proudly.

I don't ask him if the teddy helped, but I hope it did. I hug them both to me tightly. 'Come and meet the rest of the family. Don't be shy.'

So I take them through and introduce them to Gaby and Ryan. They hand out gifts to everyone – perfectly wrapped packages due to all their practice over the last few weeks. I feel so very proud of them. Gaby and I have both got goodies from Lush, Jim and Ryan have some special Christmas beers, and there's a Moshi Monster gift pack for George, which I know he'll adore. For Molly, there's a perfume-making kit. I wonder how they can have chosen such terrific presents. I kiss them both and they flush furiously.

Although the teddy bears we gave to both of them and the bits and pieces were the main presents from me and Jim to the boys, I hand them T-shirts. They're just white, printed with the word FREEDOM, but it makes us all laugh.

'I never want to be buying you one that says BANGED UP on the front,' Jim says. 'Don't make me do it.'

'No, Jim,' they both promise.

Then I pick an envelope out of my handbag. 'An extra present for you, Andrew.'

He takes it from me, puzzled. I hope it's what I think it is. When he opens it, his face brightens. 'It's from my mum.'

So he did take the chance to write her a Christmas card when I suggested it. I wasn't sure that he had, but I'm so glad that he felt able to. Tears threaten to well up. 'That's nice.'

'Yeah.' He passes the card to Kieran. 'She says she was pleased to hear from me.'

'Nice one, bro,' Kieran says.

Andrew takes it back and tucks the card carefully into the back pocket of his jeans.

It's a small step but, perhaps in the new year, they can start to mend their relationship. I do hope so.

Minutes later, any shyness has already been forgotten, and both of the boys are on the floor playing with George and Molly – also getting a pasting at Operation. Jim slips away to get Mum and I add the final touches to the table for Gaby.

The roast potatoes are just coming out of the oven when Mum finally arrives. Gaby says, 'She's here. Jim's car's back.'

I tip the parsnips into a dish, dot some butter onto the carrots and toss them. Gaby takes out the tray of pigs in blankets and the dish of stuffing and we rush them to the table.

Mum comes into the kitchen as Gaby is plating up the turkey. 'I'm sorry I'm late,' she says. 'I hope I've not delayed you.'

'Perfect timing, Mum,' Gaby says and winks at me. 'Merry Christmas.'

'Merry Christmas, darling.'

Mum's hair is dyed bright red and she's wearing an emerald-green, low-cut top and a black skirt. Whereas Mrs Ledbury's is velvet, my mother has plumped for the leather option. To be honest, it could have been longer too. It doesn't even reach her knees. Her heels have got to be five inches high and the shoes are covered in studs. She always dresses way too young for her age, but at this moment my heart goes out to her. She's the only mum we've got and we're all that she's got.

My eyes fill with tears and I go to hug her. Mum looks surprised and her face settles into a smile. She feels small, vulnerable in my arms. In a few years she'll be just like Mrs Ledbury but with more inappropriate clothing. I suddenly feel a surge of overwhelming love for her. She's my mum – the one and only – and I should care for her more.

Tears splash onto her shoulder.

'Hey,' she says. 'What's all this?' She smoothes them from my cheeks with her thumb.

'Nothing. I love you, Mum. I don't tell you enough.'

'I love you too, silly billy,' she says. 'We're family, of course we love each other.'

That makes me want to cry even more.

Mum softly strokes my hair. 'We don't get together often enough. Just me, you and Gaby. We never have time for a proper catch-up. I miss both of my girls.'

'We'll do better next year,' I promise. 'We'll have a girly day out. Soon.'

'I'd like that.' Perhaps my mum is mellowing too, coming to realise what's important and what's not. 'What do you say, Gaby?'

My sister joins the group hug. 'I say, that sounds like a marvellous idea.' She smiles over Mum's head at me and I know that things will be better from now on. 'Come on, grab yourself some fizz, Mother. I'm just about to serve lunch.'

It's going to be a bit of a squash round Gaby's dining room table, but we'll manage somehow. The room is done out in traditional red and gold and she's brought out all of her best crockery. Everything sparkles.

'The table looks really nice,' I tell her. 'Very festive.'

'Up to Calling Mrs Christmas! standards?'

'Definitely. You might find yourself with another job added to your list next year.'

'I'm up for it if you are,' she says. Gaby's been such a great help to me too and I'd like to do something special for her in the new year.

Despite everything that's gone on, I would love to carry on this business. It's just a shame that it's not Christmas all year round. I hope I can fill the gap but, if I can't, at least I've got the next six months to plan something bigger and better for next year.

Everyone else comes through and Gaby allocates places.

'Mrs Ledbury, this is my mother, Angela,' I say.

'Oh my, Angela. I thought you were another sister,' she says. Which, not surprisingly, ensures that my mother adores her instantly.

'Come and sit together,' I say and usher the two ladies into comfy chairs rather than the hard ones that have been drafted in from the outer reaches of the house.

Kieran and Andrew are talking football with Ryan and it's clear that the children are besotted with them both already. It's nice to see how easily they've slotted into our lives.

Jim slips his arm round my waist. 'They're doing good.'

'They're doing *great*.'

So we all sit down to lunch and, credit to my sister, the food is excellent. The wine and the laughter flows. This is one day that I don't count the calories but I do, however, take the time to count my blessings.

After lunch we all muck in to clear up and I make coffee for everyone. Gaby has bought SingStar for the PlayStation especially for Christmas and we fire it up. We all have a go, even Mrs Ledbury who surprises us with moving renditions of Dolly Parton hits in a lovely clear voice. I give it my best shot with Shania Twain and Jim sticks to the Kaiser Chief's 'Ruby', which he belts out at full volume. The children – with help from us all – sing Paul McCartney's frog song, 'We All Stand Together'.

The boys are in the throes of a raucous and rather tuneless version of the Proclaimers' song, '500 miles'. They're holding nothing back either and it's wonderful to see. Tears of laughter are streaming down my cheeks when the doorbell rings.

'I'll get it,' I say to Gaby. It's the least I can do as she's been up and down all day. I dance and sing my way into the hall and to the door. Out of the window, I can see that it's snowing again. So this is Christmas, I think with a smile on my face. We've made it.

When I fling open the door, Carter is standing there.

Chapter Eighty-Five

My heart leaps to my mouth and prevents any words from getting out.

'Hi.' His face is incredibly sad and he shuffles uncomfortably in the falling snow. 'I know that I shouldn't really be here, but I couldn't stay away.' He turns back towards his car. 'Max and Eve are with me. They wanted to wish you a Merry Christmas and they've got a gift for you.'

'Oh, Carter.'

'Tamara's got a migraine and has gone to lie down. I thought we'd slip out for an hour.'

Jim appears in the hall. 'What's the matter?'

'Nothing,' I assure him. 'Carter's brought the children to wish me a Happy Christmas. They're in the car.'

'I'm not here to cause trouble.' Carter holds up his hands. 'The kids wanted to see Cassie. And I had something I wanted to talk to you about. Both of you. I just—' He shrugs. 'This is very awkward. I should go.'

'You'd better come in,' Jim says gruffly. 'It's Christmas. I'll close the door to no one on Christmas Day.'

'If you're sure.' Carter looks to me for confirmation.

'You'd better be prepared to do a turn on SingStar,' I say and, somehow, that relaxes the mood.

So Carter goes to get Max and Eve and, as soon as they're out of the car, they run into my arms and I hug them to me tightly.

'We've brought you a present,' Eve says and hands me a beautifully wrapped package.

'Take off your coats and boots and let's go inside.'

In the hall, the children take off their outdoor clothes and Carter strips off his jacket. I get a flashback to all the dressing and undressing of thermal gear that we did in Lapland and push it to the back of my mind. They all follow me through to the living room.

This should be interesting. I take a deep breath before I say, 'This is Carter.'

It's fair to say that Gaby looks shocked. She looks from me, to Jim, to Carter and back again. I can offer no explanation at this point. Jim shrugs his acceptance.

'These are his children, Max and Eve.'

'You'd better sit down,' my sister finally manages. 'I'm Gaby. This is my husband, Ryan.' Carter shakes his hand. 'Our mother, Angela. Mrs Ledbury. Andrew and Kieran.'

'Ah, the gentlemen who've been making such a good job of my Christmas decorations.'

The boys flush with pride.

'These are my two,' Gaby adds. 'George and Molly.'

'Nice to meet you all,' Carter says politely.

'If you're staying,' again she shoots a look at me, 'would you like a drink?'

Carter takes in the mess of cups and edges onto the corner of the sofa next to Mrs Ledbury. 'Tea would be fine.'

Gaby heads towards the kitchen, indicating with her eyes that I should follow, but I don't. I stay rooted where I am. I can't face an inquisition right now.

Eve has gone shy and she clings to Carter's side when she says, 'Open your present now, Cassie.'

I do as I'm told and fumble with the paper. I don't know how I'm feeling. My heart is pounding in my chest, that's for sure. Inside there's a fabulous knitted scarf in dove-grey cashmere. 'Thank you. It's gorgeous.'

They both grin at me. 'Daddy gave us your presents. They were lovely too. Weren't they, Max?' She digs her brother in the ribs.

'Yes, thank you,' he pipes up.

'I would have saved them,' I say. 'But I didn't expect to see you.' Even saying that brings tears to my eyes.

'You can share our toys.' Molly steps in boldly. 'We've got lots. More than we need. Would you like to sing a song with us?'

Eve looks to Carter for approval and he nods.

So we turn SingStar back on and they settle on One Direction's 'What Makes You Beautiful', which is, not surprisingly, one of Eve's favourites. We all join in – even Carter. The living room is filled with music and laughter and if there's such a thing as Christmas spirit, then, surely, this must be it.

If you'd asked me what was the last thing on earth I'd expect to be doing on Christmas Day, it would be this.

Chapter Eighty-Six

'Come on, young man.' Mum tugs at Carter's hand. 'Let's do a duet.'

He looks more than horrified but, gamely, he gets up with her. They sing 'Islands in the Stream' – Carter mumbling through the lyrics while my mother, flirting for England and wobbling on her teetering heels, trills up and down the scales. Soon we're all in hysterics. The boys sing together again and then Jim and I take the microphone. Avoiding anything too emotive, or anything with the word 'love' in the title, we crank up the volume on 'Eye of the Tiger'.

Carter and the children sing Jessie J's 'Price Tag' and my heart swells to see them. The lyrics may be a bit too close to home but I know that a few months ago that he wouldn't even have contemplated doing this. Whatever problems he might have with Tamara, I know that he is trying to be a better father to the kids now and that can only be a good thing.

I help Gaby to make more tea while everyone sits down for a break. The children play with the mountain of toys while Carter talks to Andrew and Kieran. Let's hope that he's imbibing them with a bit of entrepreneurial spirit for the future.

'Are you OK with this?' Gaby whispers to me while she clatters about with cups.

'I think so.'

'What about Jim?'

'He was the one who asked them to come in.'

No doubt we'll talk about it later. But, like Jim, no matter what has or hasn't happened, I simply couldn't have faced turning Carter and the children away.

'Weird,' Gaby says. 'It's a damn good job that Mum doesn't know what's been going on.'

'You haven't told her?'

'No,' Gaby says. 'I've hardly seen her over the last few weeks. The less she knows about that the better.' Then she lays her hand on my arm. 'It *is* all over with him, isn't it?'

I nod. 'Absolutely.'

'I just wanted to be sure.'

We take the tea back through. Jim has joined Carter and the boys while it's Ryan's turn to take a pounding at Operation with the children. The time flies by and soon the evening is drawing in.

'We should go,' Carter says. 'I've called on your hospitality for too long now.'

'It's been a pleasure having you,' Gaby says and there's a surprising warmth in her voice. 'Eve and Max are welcome here to play any time.'

Hopefully, she's now seen why I've become so attached to them. They're great kids.

'Thank you. I'm sure they'd like that,' he says. Then he looks uncomfortable again. 'Could I have a word with you, Cassie?'

Glancing anxiously at Jim, I follow him out into the hall. Eve and Max fuss with putting on their shoes and coats.

'You've all been very kind,' he says. 'The children have had a wonderful time.'

'And you?'

444

'Me too,' he admits. 'Christmas would have been very quiet otherwise.'

'It was slightly strange having you here.' I lower my voice so that Max and Eve can't hear. 'But I've enjoyed it as well. I was worried about the children.'

'Tamara and I have had our first row already,' he whispers back. 'I don't know how long we'll be able to play happy families together. The truth is that I don't love her any more.' He looks totally defeated. 'The children might be better off if we're apart.'

'I hope it works out.'

Carter shrugs. 'Only time will tell.' He blips his key fob so that the car doors open. 'Go and wait in the car, guys. Say goodbye to Cassie.'

I bend down so that they can both kiss me. 'Merry Christmas,' I murmur to them both as I hug them tightly. 'I'll see you soon.'

I hope that's true and that, at least in some small way, I can still stay in their lives.

When they're gone, Carter pulls an envelope out of his jacket pocket. 'This is a cheque in payment for your business services.'

'I haven't even sent a final invoice yet.'

'I hope this will more than cover what you've billed me for.' He presses it into my palm and still my fingers tingle at his touch. I wonder if this feeling will ever entirely go away. 'You've got a real winner with Calling Mrs Christmas!, Cassie. Don't let it go.'

'I won't.' I have plans for my business. I'm just not sure what they are yet.

'There's another cheque in there too,' he says. 'I wanted to do something for those two boys.' He nods back towards the living room. 'I hope you're going to bring them up to the house when you dismantle everything after Christmas.'

To be honest, I hadn't even thought that far ahead. I'm sure I will though, as they'll both be keen to go up there too.

'There's enough money for you to help them out in whatever way you see fit. You can use it to keep them employed or for their accommodation costs. It's entirely up to you.'

'I can't accept this.'

'I hope you will,' Carter says.

Jim comes out into the hall. Perhaps he thinks that Carter and I have been alone for too long and I realise that it might be some time before I get his trust back. 'Carter wants to give me money to help the boys.'

'That's very generous,' Jim says, 'but we don't need your assistance.'

'I think you do,' Carter insists. 'I know how much you've done for them both already. They've just been filling me in on the details. This would make it so much easier. Money is something I'm not short of. I can help.'

Jim still looks uncertain.

'I'd like to set up a foundation or something too,' Carter continues. 'An organisation that will help disadvantaged kids to get into work. I'd like you to be involved. Both of you.'

Jim and I exchange a glance.

'It's something we'd have to talk about,' Jim says, his voice thick with emotion. 'I'd need to know more, but I wouldn't rule it out entirely.'

Carter looks relieved. 'I'm really sorry about what went on, Jim. I hope we can put that behind us.'

I'm not sure that these men will ever be the best of friends, but they seem to have reached an uneasy truce. That's more than I could really hope for.

'I'd better get going. Tamara will be awake soon and wondering where we are.' He slips on his jacket. 'I'll say goodbye.'

He shakes Jim's hand and kisses me in a brief and businesslike manner on the cheek.

446

'I'll walk you to your car,' Jim says.

'Goodbye, Carter. I'm glad you dropped by.'

'Me too,' he says.

Carter might have everything that money can buy, but I can quite truthfully say that I've never seen a man look so terribly lonely.

Chapter Eighty-Seven

Jim followed Carter to his car door.

'Thank you again,' Carter said. 'I realise that this can't have been easy for you, but I very much appreciate you inviting me to join your Christmas. You have a fantastic family.'

'You have great kids,' Jim said. 'It was for their sake. And for Cassie's. I know that this has been hard for her.'

'Yes.'

'I love her,' Jim said evenly. 'I always will. If you ever make a move on her again, I'll rip your bloody head off.'

'And if you ever let her down,' Carter countered, 'I'll be right there to pick up the pieces.'

They grinned at each other and Jim held out his hand. 'A gentleman's agreement.' They shook on it. 'Merry Christmas, Carter.'

'Merry Christmas, Jim.'

Carter got into his car. Jim stood and watched him drive away, disappearing into the snowy landscape, before he turned and went back into the house.

He went back to his family, to the lads and to someone who loved him enough to walk away from all that Carter could offer. Jim considered himself to be a very lucky man this Christmas.

Chapter Eighty-Eight

We spend the rest of the evening in a turkey coma and watch seasonal rubbish on the television. I snooze with my head on Jim's shoulder. Then we force down more food and soon it's time to go home.

Mrs Ledbury's eyes are heavy and even my perennially youthful mother is flagging. I yawn as I nudge Jim. 'I think it's time to hit the road.'

'I'll take your mum and Mrs Ledbury first and come back for you and the lads,' Jim says. 'Come on, posse. Let's load up.'

So Mum and Mrs Ledbury get their coats and handbags and presents. Gaby makes up little parcels of turkey in tinfoil for them to take home for Boxing Day.

'Take them in and make sure their lights and heating are on, Jim.'

'Of course,' he says.

'It's been lovely,' Mrs Ledbury says. 'Thank you so much.'

'I'll phone you,' Mum says. For once, I believe that she will.

My sister and I kiss them both, then stand in the cold on the doorstep and wave as they leave.

'You haven't forgotten that we're doing all this again tomorrow?' she says to me as she closes the door.

'No.' I yawn. It really has been an exhausting few days, both physically and emotionally. Tonight, I really need my bed. 'I'm looking forward to it already.'

'Don't bring anything,' Gaby instructs. 'There's still mountains of food.'

'Why don't we take the children to Ivinghoe Beacon with their sledges? They'd like that.'

I know that Max and Eve would love to come with us too, but I have to stop thinking like that. It would bring me into too much contact with Carter and I have to make sure that doesn't happen.

'Great idea. I'll call you in the morning.' Gaby joins in the Mexican-wave-like yawn I started. 'Not too early. I need a lie-in. Christmas is hard work, isn't it?'

'Yes. You've done a marvellous job.'

'I think everyone enjoyed it.' She raises an eyebrow at me.

'I think so too.'

'We *will* have that talk, Cassie,' she says to me and I smile as I remember that my sister misses nothing.

Soon Jim is back from his first taxi run, so the boys and I put on our shoes and coats. I hug Gaby tightly. 'Did anyone ever tell you that you're the best sister anyone could ever have?'

'You,' she says. 'Frequently.'

'Well, you are. And you're the best brother-in-law,' I say to Ryan as I hug him too.

The boys express their thanks and there are more hugs all round. It seems as if our family has claimed two extra members today and I'm so pleased for them. Then we all bundle into the car and wave furiously as we drive away.

A few minutes later we pull up outside the boys' flat at the Halfway House.

'We'll see you tomorrow, lads,' Jim said. 'Do you want to come sledging?'

'Yeah!' they're both quick to answer.

'I'll send you a wake-up text.'

'Thanks for a great day,' Andrew says.

'This is the best Christmas I've ever had,' Kieran adds. 'In fact, it's the *only* Christmas I've ever had.'

'Go on, you two,' I say. 'You'll make me cry.' I kiss them both goodbye.

In their thin shirts they hunch up against the cold. We watch them go into the flat before we pull away. 'We must get them thick coats,' I say to Jim. 'They can borrow some for tomorrow, but I'll need to take them to the sales.'

'We can use Carter's money if you want to.'

That surprises me. 'You're happy with that?'

'I guess so. If we can use it to help the lads, then I shouldn't be too proud to accept it.'

I lean over and kiss his cheek. 'Did I ever tell you that you're the best bloke in the world?'

He grins at me. 'Yes. But don't ever stop telling me.'

'I won't. I promise.'

We see the light go on in the boys' flat and take that as our cue to pull away.

It's snowing again now, fat splashes against the windscreen. Jim has to drop his speed and we crawl along, so it takes us a lot longer to get home than it normally would. When we turn into the car park outside the flat, the surface is all slithery. I'm weary when we finally climb the stairs. The little tree up here shines out brightly, lighting up the landing, and it feels good to be home.

'It's been a very long day.' Tired out, I stretch. 'But it's been fabulous.'

'One more cup of tea before we go to bed?'

I nod and, as soon as we're inside, Jim goes to put the kettle on.

I'm sitting on our wide windowsill in the living room with the curtains open when he comes through with our tea. This is one of my favourite spots in the flat, but it's been piled up with boxes for the last few weeks and I haven't been able to get to it. Now it's free of clutter once more. For the time being. The room is in darkness apart from the twinkling of the Christmas lights on our monster tree.

The snow is thickening quickly. Even though our car hasn't been parked out there for very long, it's already got a generous covering. Snow blankets the cars, the trees and the houses, bringing a gentle hush with it. Tomorrow will be a perfect day for sledging, providing, of course, that the roads are clear enough to get up to the beacon. It will be great to meet up with Gaby, Ryan, the children and the boys and have some fun. But, for now, it's just me and Jim.

I press my cheek against the cold glass. Jim sits next to me and I snuggle into his chest, his strong, unwavering warmth, and he wraps his arms around me. And I know that this is exactly where I belong. We sit and look out of our window, gazing out over the winter wonderland in our own little corner of the town, watching the falling snow, enjoying the silence. I turn and my lips find his.

If anyone should try to call Mrs Christmas now, I'm afraid that they'll find her otherwise engaged.

Acknowledgements

Thank you so much to Jean for all the help with the information on young offenders and their care. Very much appreciated. Also to all our lovely companions who shared our trip to Lapland and made it so much fun. Thank you to Lovely Kev for not minding going to bed with a woman wearing more clothes than she went out in and for getting me off a snowmobile when my knees had frozen solid. But then it was minus thirty-five degrees.

Research in Lapland

Minus thirty-five degrees, and what to do when you want to take eighty huskies home with you

When I decided that I wanted to write a book about those who have a lot and those who have very little at Christmas, I wondered what you'd do if you were a millionaire who wanted to reconnect with your kids. If money was no object, what would you do with them? A visit to Lapland seemed like the obvious answer.

I know that 'research trips' always sound like one big jolly – and I can't lie, there is sometimes an element of that – but I also feel that it's really important to go to the place that you're writing about. It's not only helpful in getting your facts right, but something about soaking up the atmosphere, of actually being there, seems to throw up plot ideas that you hadn't previously thought of.

So, idea formed, a trip was duly booked to Lapland. I'd just like to say at this point, that I'm the world's chilliest mortal. I don't part with my cardigan until the thermometer pops past eighty degrees minimum. Obviously, in the UK, I spend a lot of time wearing a cardigan. I hate the cold. With a passion. My ideal research trip would be, say, to the Bahamas!

Our first stop was the 'outdoor shop' where Lovely Kev and I stocked up on anything that said the words Arctic Strength on the label. I was very concerned that the world weather forecast said it was minus twelve degrees in Kiruna and that's exactly where we were heading.

We'd booked a week in a musher's lodge with two nights in a wilderness cabin. I don't think I'd quite grasped how 'wilderness' the wilderness could be. Activities included building an igloo, dog sledding, snow-mobiling and cross country skiing. I had the gear – lots of it – I could do this!

I think the first startling thing about going way above the Arctic Circle into Swedish Lapland is that it isn't very far at all. A few short hours from Heathrow with a quick change at Oslo and we were there. Three flakes of snow at Heathrow had caused major disruption on our departure and yet we landed at Kiruna Airport on a runway that was entirely made of sheet ice and snow! The temperature was minus fifteen, but because the air is so dry, rather than the dampness of England, it didn't feel too horrendously cold at all.

The landscape is just staggering; miles of nothing but snow except for fir trees that are so laden with snow that they look like sculptures. Even before we got to the real, proper wilderness, it looked fairly remote to me.

The mushers' lodge was warm and comfortable – thankfully. We were kitted out with even more Arctic gear – thermal overalls, sturdy boots and huge mittens. This is where we met our team of huskies for our first taste of dog-sledding and they were just wonderful. Much leaner and smaller than I'd imagined. These huskies are working dogs – all muscle and not an ounce of fat on them. They have eighty of them at this lodge, all of them stunning. We loved them even when all eighty of them spent most of the night baying at the moon! For our dog-sledding excursion, we started by helping to get them from their kennels to harness to the sleds and even the tiniest one could have dragged me halfway round Lapland! There were incredibly powerful.

Once they're harnessed to the sleds, they just go crazy, eager to be off. We had a basic introduction to the joys of driving a sled – the brake being the most important bit – and off we went. As soon as you timidly release said brake the huskies shoot off at a break-neck pace, completely disregarding any ideas you might have of steering the sled. They just want to run – and fast!

I think it was the best fun that I've ever had while wearing six layers of thermal clothing. You just hang onto the back for dear life while they race through the most spectacular scenery. Our ultimate destination was the wilderness lodge and, with a brief stop for a barbecue in a snow dug-out, we arrived mid-afternoon, just as darkness was falling. In February, there's a limited amount of daylight in Lapland as the sun lays in bed until ten and retires again about three o'clock. But with a full moon and so much snow about it never did feel that dark.

The wilderness lodge was amazing, beautifully equipped with cosy sofas and bunks, but there was no electricity, no running water and just a long-drop toilet in a wooden hut in the woods. There was, however, a lot of red wine, candles and, thankfully, a very efficient wood-burning stove that Lovely Kev got up and fed like a hungry infant all through the night! (Thank you, Kev!)

We were slightly worried that the temperature was dropping steadily. At the lodge, miles from anywhere, the thermometer recorded a rather chilly minus 29. Going outside to the loo in the night was definitely a challenge!

We learned the art of building an igloo – the right type of snow is crucial – and some brave souls spent the next night huddled into them. I was far too much of a wuss for that and opted for the warmth of the cosy log-burning fire again. The next day we cross-country skied back to the musher's lodge and as we crossed the frozen river Torne, the temperature dropped even further. Icicles formed on the peak of my hat and the hair in your nostrils froze. The air was so dry that crystals of ice were falling like glitter. It felt just like being in a snow globe.

We also took a snow-mobiling trip, which took us up into the hills on powerful motorbikes that plough through the snow. We ended the journey by speeding along the frozen River Torne at fifty miles an hour, at which point my eyelashes froze together. When we came to a halt, Lovely Kev had to help me off the bike as my knees where frozen in place. It took me about half an hour of clinging to a radiator in the lodge before I was able to stand up straight again. And to think that when I wrote *The Chocolate Lovers' Club*, all I did was eat chocolate for a year!

The culmination of our trip was to spend the last night in the spectacular Icehotel; an ice palace carved out of blocks of the River Torne every year in December, which melts away again in March. We had a tour of the fabulous art suites, all individually carved and were allocated to us for the night where we'd sleep on reindeer skins in a cool minus five degrees. The suites are different every year and ours was called Café Mudra and featured a four metre high female 'buddha' sculpture with a giant coffee cup as a bedside table. The place is stunning with ice-carved chandeliers and an Icebar, which sells the world's most expensive vodka shots. There's also an ice chapel where brave couples regularly get married – with the brides wearing thermals beneath their wedding dresses.

By the time, we'd settled for the night it was minus 36 degrees. Our guide was delighted. It meant that we had an excellent chance of seeing the Northern Lights.

It happened sooner than we expected. During our excellent dinner – which always features a lot of reindeer-based products – the maître d' came into the middle of the restaurant and announced, 'Ladies and gentlemen, the Northern Lights have arrived!'

Cue mass exodus into the garden! Having hastily grabbed our Arctic gear, we stood and watched a spectacular display of pink and yellow lights radiating down from the sky. A truly wonderful sight. We were thrilled. Another box ticked on our Arctic experience. The lights faded and we returned to our dinner, happy.

What we didn't realise was that the best was yet to come. Later that evening, we went down to the frozen banks of the River Torne, away from the lights of the hotel and into pitch darkness where we were treated to the most mind-blowing display of the Northern Lights we could ever have hoped to witness. For hours, in minus 36 degrees, we gazed at the sky and gasped. Lights in every hue – red, green, yellow – shifted across the sky. It was like a natural firework show. When our necks became too stiff, we lay on our backs on the snow and stared upwards, transfixed.

At two o'clock in the morning, we sadly had to abandon this beautiful exhibition and head for the warmth of the Icehotel's reception. Lovely Kev's camera had frozen up and, with no feeling left in our fingers or toes, we were quite worried that we would be next.

After some warming hot chocolate, we collected our double thermal sleeping bag and, as advised, we changed into thermal underwear. The word thermal crops up a lot in this part of the world! Suited and booted, we headed off to our icesuite in the frozen part of the hotel.

Spending a night in the Icehotel is surprisingly comfortable and cosy. The sleeping bags are made of some space-age material that gets hotter and hotter from your own body heat. It was just like having an electric blanket on. I didn't want to turn the lights off as I wanted to be able to see our lovely statue and enjoy the room all night – well, what was left of it!

At seven o'clock you're woken up by someone bringing you a cup of lingonberry juice, which is exactly like Ribena. Then you head off to the changing rooms for a gloriously hot shower. While I was there, I got chatting to a lady who said that she was on her tenth visit to the Icehotel and had never seen the Northern Lights before. It made me realise just how very, very lucky we'd been with our timing.

Too soon our lovely trip to Swedish Lapland was over. We had to say goodbye to those gorgeous huskies – with a tear in my eye as I wanted to take them on the plane with me – and head back to London. It had been a week of fantastic experiences, each one better than the previous and I'd got some fantastic material for my book. If you've already read it – and haven't just skipped to the back – then you'll know how I worked those in to give Cassie, Carter and his children a trip to remember. It's one that I'll never forget too. And if you ever need an igloo built, don't forget to give me a call.

If you enjoyed *Calling Mrs Christmas*,
you only have to wait until the spring
for Carole's next bestseller,

A Place to Call Home

Uplifting, heart-breaking and emotional, this is a novel of
new beginnings, of discovering love and of finding
A Place to Call Home.

EXCLUSIVE!
Read on to enjoy the first three chapters!

Chapter One

I stare anxiously at the clock. It's nearly two in the morning and my eyes are gritty from lack of sleep. In the bed next to me Suresh snores heavily, and I'm grateful that the sleeping tablet I slipped into his drink a few hours earlier still seems to be working well.

Even so, when I go to get out of the bed, I take care to lift the duvet cautiously and lower my feet quietly to the floor. I tiptoe across the room to collect my clothes from the chair in the corner. It's a bright night, the moonlight filling the room and illuminating me more than I would like.

For a moment I stand with my shalwar kameez gripped in my arms, watching the sleeping form of my husband of ten years. My heart's pounding in my chest and there's a sick feeling in my stomach, but I know that I have to do this. Whatever happens, I can no longer stay. It will be the last time I will ever be in this bedroom, in this house, with this man.

As soundlessly as possible, I make my way to the bathroom along the hall. Suresh's mother and father sleep at the back of the house, in the biggest room, which overlooks the garden. Thankfully, Sabina's room is at the other end of the hall to them. In the dead of the night, the only sound I can hear is my own nervous breathing.

I change my clothes in the bathroom, stripping off my nightdress and putting on the same shalwar kameez that I wore yesterday. I fold my nightdress carefully. That will come with me too. And my toothbrush. I'd like to freshen my mouth, but I don't dare risk running the tap. The walls are as thin as paper and I cannot risk doing anything that might wake anyone else.

The face that stares back at me in the mirror is thin and tired. This woman looks afraid. Afraid but determined.

Along the landing and I ease the handle on the door into Sabina's room. My child's pink nightlight fills the small space with a warm glow and I go straight to her bed, crouching down beside it.

I stroke my daughter's silky hair which is long and dark like my own. Sabina's hair, however, is tangled with sleep whereas my own hangs down my back in a heavy plait.

'Sabina,' I whisper in her ear. 'Sabina, my daughter.'

The child opens her eyes and gazes at me. The trust I see there is heartbreaking. For so long I've failed her, but not any more.

'Mummy is taking you on an adventure,' I murmur. 'We must be quiet though. As quiet as little mice. Can you do that for me?'

With sleep-filled eyes, she nods at me and I help to lift her out of bed. I put my finger to my lips. It's a needless gesture. Sabina doesn't speak. Not ever.

Quickly, quietly, I change her from her nightwear into her shalwar kameez. It's spring, but the nights are still cold, so while Sabina tiredly buckles her shoes, I get her coat from the wardrobe. My heart is in my mouth for fear of the door squeaking, but thankfully it's silent. I've done my best to furnish this room nicely. She has a pretty duvet cover, curtains and a lampshade that looks like a ballerina's skirt. But it's not enough, is it? The important things are love, affection, joy, and in this I've been so lacking.

Sabina, all buttoned up, sways sleepily on her feet, and I sit her down for a brief moment. Under her bed, tucked far into the corner, I have a bag already prepared for this event. It's taken me weeks to get to this point. Months even. We have a holdall that I bought cheaply from the market. It's very small, so that I could hide it adequately, and is filled with only enough clothes to last us until tomorrow. After that, I don't know what we'll do.

'We must go,' I say. My finger goes to my lips. 'Remember. Very quiet.'

I take Sabina's tiny, warm hand in mine and I hope the contact comforts her as much as it comforts me. Leading her out of the room, we inch along the landing. Still I can hear Suresh's snores, and that calms me a little.

I don't know what my husband does for work, but I do know that it's not good. Sometimes he brings home men to our house and they laugh together until the small hours. Sometimes he doesn't come home at night at all. I never know which it will be, so I've had to wait a long time for this, the perfect moment.

On the stairs, I count our way down. The seventh stair creaks and I'm worried that it will sound out in the dead of the night, so I make sure that we step over it watchfully. Sabina is very slight for her eight years and, though I too am small, I lift her over it with ease. Her face is solemn, concerned. She trembles in my arms and I hold her tightly.

We make our way along the hall and to the front door. Lifting my coat from the peg, I slip it on and then pull my scarf over my hair. What will I do now if Suresh suddenly appears on the landing? Will I still be brave enough to bolt for my freedom? Or will I return meekly to his side despite vowing that I would never do so? If he sees us he'll know, instantly, that we are fleeing. Fleeing from him, from his fists. When he attacks me, as he surely will, can I fight him off? Or will he decide that, this time, he must kill me once and for all? The thought makes me shake. What then would happen to my darling Sabina?

Looking down at my daughter's anxious face, I know that I have to do this. If not for me, then for her. I have to be a good role model. I have to be the best mother that I can possibly be so that my child will grow into a strong, happy and independent woman. All of the things that I'm not.

Staring at the holdall in my hand, I realise that I'm leaving with the same material possessions I arrived with from Sri Lanka all those years ago, to be, for the very first time, with my new husband. How full of hope I was then! I should reach deep inside myself and try to find that feeling again now.

I ease the lock on the front door, the lock that I secretly sprayed with oil last week so that it wouldn't make a noise and give us away.

'Ready?' I whisper to Sabina.

She nods and we both step out into the darkness.

Chapter Two

I stand with Sabina by my side and stare back at the house. It's featureless, identical to the dozen or more that are the same in our terrace. There's nothing to make it a home. No name, no pretty flowers in the garden. It's as cold and blank as the people who live in it.

I take Sabina's hand and we hurry away from the house. 'We must walk quickly,' I say to her. 'Can you manage that?'

She nods her acquiescence.

Normally I wouldn't use the underpasses in the city, especially not after dark, as they're a haven for muggers and drug addicts. But, as I haven't been allowed out at night for many years, there's a strange giddiness in having the freedom to put myself and my daughter at risk. The Redways are the quickest and straightest route to the

Coachway and our escape, and I don't want to risk getting lost.

We don't live in a very nice area in Milton Keynes. Our house is right in the heart of the city, on an estate that has seen much better days. However, I'm grateful for that now as it isn't a long walk – about an hour, I'm thinking – to the Coachway and our ticket out of here. The train station is far away, at the other side of the city, and I'd have needed to call a taxi, which I couldn't risk. Too many of Suresh's friends drive cabs and he'd instantly hear of my departure. I'm better to rely on my own devices.

'Are you all right, my child?' I ask Sabina. I can see my breath in the night air, a little puff of steam.

She nods again, but nothing more.

I'd give anything to hear her complaining. If only she would whine about us walking too fast, or it being too cold, or demand to know about our destination. If only.

For months, I've stolen money from my husband's wallet as often as I was able. Just a little, as much as I could manage without him noticing – £5 here, £10 there. I've kept it in an old Quality Street tin at the back of my wardrobe, underneath a pile of towels that we don't often use. Now I have £800 and my way out of here. It's in the bottom of my holdall, rolled and secured with elastic bands, £100 in each precious one.

We make our way in the darkness. Due to council cutbacks the streetlights are switched off, and it takes longer than I anticipated as I'm uncertain of the way. Sabina and I take a wrong turn and we walk for nearly quarter of an hour before I realise from the signposts that we're heading in the opposite direction to where we want to be. So we have to retrace our steps. Then, as I'm beginning to despair and the sky is beginning to lighten, I see the building of the Coachway ahead of us in the distance. I can hear the gentle thrum of traffic from the M1 behind it and it sounds like music to my ears.

'Not long now, Sabina,' I urge. 'We're nearly there.'

The building is modern, recently built, and the lights shine out harshly in the darkness. Hand in hand, we cross the final road to reach it – two conspicuous figures standing out in the emptiness of the night. I hope that Suresh hasn't woken and found us gone. I pray that he doesn't think to come looking for us in his car when we are so, so close to escape. My hand tightens on Sabina's fingers and, picking up our pace, we walk faster.

The first coach to London isn't until half-past four and we have a little while to kill until then as, I'm relieved to say, we have made good time. With trembling fingers and my back to the waiting room, I slip some money from one of the rolls in my bag and buy our tickets from the machine, feeding in the crisp notes that I have stolen from my husband. At this hour, there are very few people here. A man in uniform carrying a clipboard lets his gaze fall on me as we pass. When I feel it linger, we go to sit in the corner furthest away from him, where a big plant in a pot obscures his view. The café is shuttered for the night and I've nothing to give my child but a carton of juice that's in the holdall.

'Do you want a drink, Sabina?'

She nods and I get out the carton of orange and fix the straw for her.

I check that my rolls of money are safely secreted once again in the bottom of the holdall and relish the comfort that they bring. Then I get the tickets out and clutch them to me. Two travelling to London Victoria. One adult. One child. One way.

As we sit on the cold wooden benches, I huddle my daughter to me and relief washes over me. We're not free yet, I think, but we've made it this far.

Chapter Three

The sky begins to lighten and the coach arrives. Sabina and I board as quickly as we can. The driver wants to take my holdall and put it in the luggage compartment under the coach, but I cling to it. This is my lifeline, my future.

I find us seats and put the holdall by my feet, then settle Sabina next to me. Within minutes all the passengers are on board and we speed out of the coach station and turn on to the motorway. The amber lights of the road blur past my eyes and the anxious breath that I've been holding is finally released. We're on our way. Already Sabina's eyes are heavy with sleep and I cuddle her in to me. 'Are you comfortable?'

She nods at me and snuggles in to my side.

'Rest now,' I tell her. 'When you awake, we'll be there.'

Soon she sleeps beside me and, as I nurse her, my mind goes over what has led me to the point where I feel the need to flee for our safety in the middle of the night.

I've lived in this city for ten years, since I came here from Sri Lanka to meet and marry my husband, Suresh Rasheed, but I know so little of it now. It's changed so much and, for some time, I've gone only where my husband has taken me. Some weeks I wouldn't go out of the house at all. I wouldn't dare. If Suresh came home and found that I wasn't there, he'd fly into a rage. Yet I never knew when he was coming home, as he'd never tell me where he was going. Soon it was simpler not to leave the house at all. If there was shopping to be done or errands to be run, his mother would go, and take Sabina with her. I'd be left behind, anxious and fretting, to clean the house or to cook the meal. A prisoner in my own home.

I had no friends that I could turn to as, eventually, Suresh wouldn't allow me to see anyone other than his relatives. So the few women that I'd become close to had fallen away over the years as they couldn't bear to see the evidence of my controlling marriage. Now there's no one I can call on who isn't connected to my husband's family. I couldn't trust one of them to help me in case they should tell Suresh of my whereabouts and he'd find me and drag me back. I can't allow that to happen.

Yet it wasn't always like this. The first year when I came to England was a happy one. My husband and I took pleasure in each other's company. Suresh was never open or overtly affectionate towards me. He didn't like to hold my hand or kiss me, but he was considerate and a steady man. I thought that, in time, we could make a good marriage.

We rented our own house near to his parents, who had been settled in England for many years, since Suresh was a child himself. Our place was small but comfortable and I kept it clean and pretty. I did my utmost to make it a loving home. When, very soon, I became pregnant, he was so pleased to find that I was with child.

Then Suresh changed. Almost overnight. I'm still not sure why. It was many small hurts, I believe, that harmed his personality.

When my dear Sabina was born, he was delighted to become a father. Soon after, though, he became withdrawn, difficult. I feel that he was jealous of the attention I gave to my tiny, mewling daughter, but is that not what new mothers do? I knew from the moment I saw her that she was my life and that I would never love another human being more than this helpless bundle who clung to me for her every need. The whole of my heart was suddenly filled with her, and perhaps Suresh felt that there was no room left for him.

Within weeks, he was made redundant from his job, and that

severely hurt his pride. Try as he might, he couldn't easily find work despite walking the streets and seeing all his contacts. Eventually we fell into financial difficulties; our bills weren't paid and we hid when men knocked at the door. We were forced to give up even our modest home and move in with his parents.

To start with my mother- and father-in-law were kind people, fun-loving, smiling. They tried their best with us all crammed together in their home and they loved their new granddaughter very much. But soon that changed too as their son became increasingly difficult to live with.

Before too long Suresh stopped looking for work at all and stayed in bed until late in the morning. He'd never been a man of great faith but he no longer prayed at all. My husband started to drink heavily, and he fell in with the men who now keep him out at night.

It saddens me to say that my own faith is long gone too. At home we liked to embrace all faiths – sometimes we'd worship at the Buddhist temple, sometimes at the Hindu one. My mummy also liked to take us to the Catholic church sometimes, if there was a festival for the saints. 'It is better,' she always said, 'to keep one's options open.' Perhaps she felt one god would, eventually, turn out to be better than another. Now I'm not sure there's a god at all. My only instinct is survival. My parents would be disappointed in their daughter.

Sabina is close to her paternal grandmother – the only one she's known. They would cook together in the cramped kitchen and she'd show my daughter the family recipes, as she did for me when I first arrived.

But she too is a woman who's now scared to speak. One day, as we prepared the evening meal together, I looked at my mother-in-law and saw my future self. That vision of my life began to make me anxious. She's a woman who clings to the shadows, who is intimidated by her own son. My husband's father, too, is frightened by what his eldest child has become and they've both retreated into their shell. They don't speak up for fear of his wrath. They would stand by, powerless, while he hurt me. It's very sad and I'll miss the people they once were, but I must think of myself now and my child.

At first they tried to protect us, but soon they became frightened for their own safety. I'm frightened for them too. His mother would cry bitter tears for our pain, but that didn't stop the bruises. I came to realise that keeping Sabina and myself from harm was entirely down to me. I didn't dare tell them that I was leaving as I couldn't risk them knowing my plan. The less they were aware of, the better.

My daughter shifts in her restless sleep and I stroke her hair to soothe her. 'Hush, hush,' I murmur.

The bus is quite busy, but everyone is sleeping or in their own world, listening to music on earphones. No one pays us any attention, which is more than I could have hoped for.

A year ago, my husband beat me so badly in front of my daughter that she stopped speaking. I was curled into the corner of the living room while he rained blows on me and, as I looked up, my eyes met Sabina's. She'd come down from her bedroom when she heard the noise. It wasn't the first time that she'd seen her mother slapped or punched by her father, but this was much worse.

Sometimes she cried out and tried to intervene, and it tore my heart in two that she should witness such things. As Suresh's fist made my head rock back, I saw her eyes wide with terror, her mouth frozen as if to scream, but no sound came out. The sight of her was so pitiful that it even stopped my husband in his tracks and I was able to hurry her from the room to soothe her, my own agony forgotten.

My injuries healed, my bruises faded, my broken bones mended, but my daughter's pain goes on. From that day to this, she's never uttered a single word. She hasn't laughed with joy or cried out with fright. Before that she was bright, articulate, clever for her age – and she was funny, so funny. It was a delight to listen to her childish chatter. Now she makes no sound at all. Not even when we're alone and there's no one else to hear. It's as if she can't forgive me, and I don't blame her. I can't forgive myself.

When it happened, that was the very moment I realised that I had to get far away. I had to put a stop to this and I vowed to leave. How long would it be before I was unable to recover from the beatings? Would there come a point when the slaps and punches were aimed at Sabina too? There was no way I intended to let that happen. Already, she'd been hurt enough by this. I'd never wanted to harm a hair on her beautiful head and yet I'd allowed this terror to take her tongue.

The only way to right this wrong is to protect her now above all else.

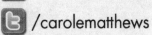